Publishing Co.

Oaklands, East Grinstead

United Kingdom

© Simon-Paul Ridgeway

All rights reserved. No part of this book may be reproduced or transmitted in any form or means, electronic or mechanical, including photocopying, recording or by any information storage and retrieval system, without permission in writing from the publisher.
The characters in this book are entirely fictional.

ISBN 9781724129079

Kafkaesque, Kalashnikov & Kaput

Kafkaesque, Kalashnikov and Kaput

Forward

An irreverent look at Urban Legends, in the Diaspora that is modern day South Africa.

The stories usually have their origins in some fact, but as a result of innate human fear, they are partially fabricated to sound more entertaining. The idea of Kafka's writing is central to these myths. Our innate fear is borne by the anxiety of a changing society, in which the political power shift has given most South Africans a sense of purpose, but where doubt still lingers in the minds of those who question the credibility and wisdom of a 'one man, one vote' system in a society where impressionable minds can be easily swayed. The reader is given the option to decide to what degree that might be prevalent in their minds. By reading into these stories their sense of isolation from a rapidly changing political and social system, the reader can determine their own degree of that isolation. But to the reader who recognises their reality, there is a certainty in the manner in which we view each conclusion. The reader is taken on a journey with each story, intended to give them an opportunity to reflect on their own beliefs. Where the conclusion to each story leaves the reader is as subjective as all those dinner table conversations that evoked these written short stories. Social circumstances will dictate what their reaction will be. The intention is to challenge our current understanding of where the white man fits into this 'Brave New World'.

Our cultural differentiations will often provoke our understanding of these myths. But to what extent our social circumstances dictate where the story will end, can and will be determined by each and every one of our individual experiences. I try to lead the reader in a specific direction and then with a twist in each tale, develop an unexpected conclusion. This is intended to challenge what we accept as normal, but the conclusion each reader draws from the story is dependent on where the fit into our evolving society.

Every myth and story, that constitutes the basis for 'Urban Legends', has its origins in reality. The idea is to provoke a reaction so as to entertain and expose those myths. But, as with all good myths, the truth often will lay outside the realm of reality, dependant on the misgivings of the story teller. As is usually the case, when a story is told by someone with a specific agenda, that story can be relayed to provide conclusive evidence of the 'story-tellers' own thoughts and feelings. I am no different, but I hope to do justice to some of the most wonderful dinner table fables I have had the pleasure of listening to!

The twist in each story is deliberate, so as to jolt the reader out of their preconceived worldly experiences and provide an unexpected ideal, which the reader can chose to assimilate or ignore. Often the reader may wish to change their perception, but more often than not it is my intention to draw attention to those different perceptions without intending to convince anyone otherwise. Moreover, it is a book a short stories intended to highlight this wonderful society, which we all have a common interest in, and where our life paths will often intersect, unexpectedly.

Index

1. Bundu bashing
2. Aids Education
3. Casinos and catering
4. The snake and the bottle
5. The Insurance Scam
6. The Weekend
7. The Property Guru
8. Nancy's Necessity
9. An Explosive character
10. Peter the Pumpkin eater
11. Craving for mud
12. The Muti Murderer
13. The 'Importance' of being Margaret
14. Traffic Violations
15. The Medicine Man
16. Golden Treasures and forgotten fables
17. The Nightingale Robberies
18. Retribution from the grave
19. The Tanzanite Scam
20. The Flower Lady
21. Gangster's Paradise
22. Fat-bellied Cops
23. Genuine Bling
24. The Valindaba Tragedy

Bundu bashing

"Thank you for letting me know!" She would need to be fresh for the morning's meeting. "Good night." The phone clicked and he was gone, but the bumpy ride through the bush would haunt her that night. She was alone in the early hours of the morning, with her fear and a guilt which she could not explain.

"After all," she considered. "It had not been fair to think she might have been the one lying dead in the bush right this minute." She may well have been the one lying prostrate, having been raped and discarded like an unwanted rag-doll in ditch on some lonely stretch of African road!

But life was not fair as only Sue would attest to. She was a loner through circumstance, but now the events of the evening flooded back to her as the tears rolled down her sunken cheeks. How would she cope with her guilt? Was she the victim or the victor? Had her sense of survival offered her an escape from the depravity of an uncaring world, or was it pure luck? So many others may have instinctively pulled over to help. But she had not! Did that make her selfish or was it pure instinct that drove her?

Sue had been at the office late, and despite her obvious need to get home to the shoebox she lived in somewhere in northern Johannesburg, she had to get that sales report prepared for the sales meeting Friday morning.

Sue was a dedicated team player and had done the obvious. She had stayed late, and finally switched off her PC at about ten that evening, and set off home after switching the office lights out, and triggering the alarm with her remote control gizmo. The journey home was twenty minutes from Sandton at this time of night, and Sue was famished. She had a slice of quiche waiting for her, and it would settle the hunger pangs, and she would lift her spirits with a glass of merlot saved from Dave's visit the evening before.

Yes, she lived alone, but, 'hey' didn't everyone these days. At twenty-seven, her maternal instincts were non-existent, and she could care less for the pitter-patter of little feet. That was a culmination of twenty years of abuse, not physically, but more poignantly it was mentally, by a rather less than emotional father. He had always wanted a boy; someone who he could take to practice, and to the game on Saturday. A boy he could cheer on when he crossed the line with rugby ball held aloft and cherish the oddly shaped ball as he had done so often as a young nipper, on the golden sands of Umhlanga's beaches. He had never returned to the place, never taken Susan, his only child and the 'apple of his eye', he had told everyone at the Christening. Reality was a stark reminder, and an insidious re-claimer of truths. He had never taken her to Durban, where he had grown up with all the friends he adored as a child, and whom he had spent ceaseless hours sparring with on beach and lush green kikuyu grass. Sue was the inheritor of all his failed dreams, and now Sue was driven. Driven and alert to all the possibilities growing up in Johannesburg's northern suburbs would hold in store for her. But cognoscente of its dangers!

Walking out of that single-storey office park, earmarked for redevelopment, she had headed straight to her car. It was a car, "but had off-road capabilities"; so the salesman at the neatly tiled showroom had convinced her. It was everything a young attractive, single woman would need in a dangerous city like Johannesburg. Fraught with its dangers, "you would need to be alert at traffic lights; don't stop at traffic lights after ten in the evening", those words had warned, and only too aware of high-jacking, he had sold her on this compact, but feisty looking little suburban utility vehicle. It was her pride and joy. She had traded up from the old reliable hatchback and never looked twice in 'Betsy's" direction, as she had slipped effortlessly into the driver's seat, and her destiny with sales executive. From the marketing of her cold soulless Italian brand-name bathroom fittings, she could only look forward to better things. This car would give her the edge, and taken with the leather upholstery, it screamed success.

The colour even had the garish hue of silver flecked into the metallic black, which in this yellow lit car park, had reminded her of the egg-plant fruits her mother had kept on the kitchen counter in a shallow dish to ripen in the afternoon sun. That sunlight had filtered through the half mast, lace curtains that had sufficed for décor in their urban squalor that was Parkhurst. It was a suburb that on their first visit had seemed devoid of life. People had warned her father, that to buy in that suburb would bring nothing but heartache. It was 'in-for-a-dig' to live in that community of misfits, and ex-pat war veterans, returned from war with scars of fortitude written on their haunted faces. The suburb had been built by the English government of the time, to house lower income families, and unlike its plush neighbourhood dwellers to the north, these properties had been built on an eighth of an acre, and like her shoebox home now, had been adequate. But it was all he could afford at the time, on his meagre wages at the security company where he drove the vans that distributed the banks much needed cash.

Now Sue had fond memories of that west-facing kitchen with its old linoleum counter tops, and cold floors. She reminded herself to pop in and see her folks that weekend out of a sense of duty. Mom had a bridge game and needed a fourth, whilst Dad, she said, was up the local with his mates at the Moth club. That was where he had always strayed, even in the days she had wished he would be there to cheer her on at the athletics day. He had not and she had turned her focus inwardly, blaming herself that she was not worthy of his love!

Sue had pressed the button on the remote control for the car. Nothing. She pressed it again. From behind her, she heard a loud beeping noise that took her off-guard. She swung around expectantly looking over her shoulder for the source of the noise that had alarmed her. She had fully expected some brazen attack, and she had stiffed fearing the worst. She had seen the little red light above the shatterproof glass doors flicker, and then turn green.

"Damn!" She had pressed the wrong confounded button. The remote was clenched together with keys and her remote for the car, and one for the house, and a myriad of other keys. Some obsolete, and others superfluous.

"Hell!" She thought. "Mental note to self"! "Get rid of some of these keys. Get another key ring for the house keys and keep them in the car instead. There was one of those fancy glove compartments on the dash, that if the car was stolen she would not have to worry about car thieves finding them. The little cubby hole was hidden from the un-trained eye." Her thoughts now keeping her tossing frame from the much vaunted slumber she desired.

"Shit!" This triggered her thoughts. "Have to get that damn debit order sorted! The bank had been ringing her cell phone from an undisclosed number incessantly. She knew it was them, she had not had time to change the banking details for the debit collection on her new account."

She had walked dutifully back to the office door. Clicked the little man button with a chap striding out like the Johnnie Walker man. Everywhere you looked; there were those massive billboards, cryptic and enticing! She didn't drink the stuff, "so who cares!"

The beeping once turned off, had then left the parking area eerily quiet. With one concerted effort, she had clicked again. "Beep, beep" it went and after an interminably long second, the little green light turned red, and Sue had turned on her heels. That glass of merlot beckoning.

Looking over her shoulder once more for comfort, she had seen the red eye twinkling at her. "Why would it have switched itself off she thought? It is a machine? Who knows? It might have a faulty button! She might have pressed it too hard". Anxiety raised itself in the pit of her stomach. She was alone in that car park. "What the hell was she doing? That report could have waited to the morning." Suddenly she had felt the trepidation that many a solitary individual may have felt in the darkened confines of that parking lot. She was either foolhardy or just plainly ignorant of her circumstances!

Sue had remonstrated with herself. "Have to set a good example for the sales team. Sales Executive was a slippery mud soaked Catfish away from her, and no letting up in her strategy would do!"

Sue remembered walking back to the car a little more briskly. This time she looked down in the light that was afforded her by the yellow, haze filled car park lighting. The bunch of keys screamed at her. "Sort me out." Life was too complicated.

"Oh for that momentary lapse into nothingness. Feet on the coffee table and a comforting glass of Stellenbosch's finest to while away the midnight hour until slumber embraced her."

The plastic remote had found its way into her left hand, sales file in right. She caressed the button. Was it the correct one? Yes! The car erupted into action. Door clumped open. Hazard lights for good measure flicked, so as to guarantee safe passage to the drivers' seat.

Sue had slipped seamlessly into her pride and joy. The ride home to her six hundred thousand Rand townhouse was a mere five tracks of Mariah Carey, and a heartbeat away from utopia. She was content. As content as any young South African single woman could be in this Calvinistic, chauvinist society. That sales manager had tried his luck again earlier while Sue was constructing her sales report. He was dimming the lights in the office whilst the cleaning staff had been finishing up for the night, before heading out to the mini-bus that collected them after six.

Sue had learned, if not all the tricks in the book, then most, but had not expected him to stay behind, because he said, "his wife was having dinner out with her friends and the lads were heading down to the sports bar for a beer and some nachos." He would "stay behind a little longer and help her with her report"!

Sue's mobile phone came to hand as he had turned back, having closed the self-locking glass doors, and headed for Sue's desk.

"It was Dave trying to get hold of her again." She commented. "Dang! The mobile phone reception was up to shit again. Those cell phone service providers should be taken to court in a mass class action", Dave had said. "Sue them for all they are worth. Make an example of them and their profiteering! They deserved nothing less!" Dave was a Puritan. An idealist. He would take them on one day he had told Sue.

Phone to her ear, she had rung his number. There was no reply. It would go to voice mail like every other time she had called to chat. "Confounded phone." She had thought to herself. Then without looking up at the approaching sales manager, she had started a fictional conversation.

"Oh Hi Dave. Were you trying to get hold of me? Yes. No. Still at work, finishing off my report. Uhha, ya that sounds nice. Emmhhhh no. I don't think so. What you want to come and fetch me from work?"

Humphrey, the sales manager had lurked. He tottered on the edge of the desk. This had not gone to plan.

"Okay sweetie. I will wait for you here!" Sue looked up to acknowledge Humphrey for the first time during her intently awaited call. He was not there.

He had breezed past her into his office cubicle with its wooden panel walls, and chrome coloured window frame. A vantage point from which to look out on his sales force, from the comfort of his plush leatherette office chair, with three modes of attitude. One for, 'Get to work and bring me the sales', two for 'Did you say the deal is closed?' and three, the most reclined of the lot, 'Hey! I told you, you would close it.'

Sue had half turned, relieved. Humphrey was making his way out, locking his office door on the way.

That was an unpleasant memory, but now, Sue recalled making her way down Rivonia Road. She could have turned right into Graystone and done the Sandton Drive shuffle, but Rivonia took her past the old haunts she had frequented as a student, and they brought back fond memories. As she hit the bottom of Rivonia, and under the highway, she had cautiously edged forward over the solid white line; there was no other traffic, but road works had rendered the street lights out of order and the place was ominously dark. As the light had turned green, she was already on the move, second gear engaged and the engine revving above three thousand. If she kept to sixty, she would nail the robots at the bottom of the hill, and not have to slow for the oncoming slope. Sue could taste the delicate peach of Stellenbosch and the aftertaste of tannin.

As the road wound its way through the suburbs of the north, she had already been onto the third track and with a lilt in her straining voice, she had sung along to her favourite. The mood had lifted, and she could almost hear her kitten's meows, in greeting to her late arrival, and smell the faint hint of cat box manure. She had raised the kitten on pronutro and milk, having discovered its near lifeless body outside the local SPAR, and not given a moment's hesitation before whisking it up, and carrying its limp, but still warm skeletonal body to her car. This had been her redemption for all the mean things she had said of her best friend Jill. They had had a falling out of sorts over the latest man in Jill's life, and Sue, who would not suffer fools gladly, had seen right through his ruse. Russell was his name and broken hearts was his game. Sue had known the inevitable break up would reunite them, but that was three months ago? Was the sex that good?

Sue was now recalling how she had swooped through the dip past playing fields and how she was at the corner before she had time to consider the plight of all those thousands of dejected animals at the SPCA. It was disgraceful! Why allow animals to breed in the first place, when with just a simple operation, family pets could be neutered and rendered to a pitiless existence, devoid of the young they all yearned for. A bit like herself, she surmised, but nonetheless a merciful commitment to this earthly discontent. Somehow, she knew it was inevitable. With clever pharmacology, and a Government with real intent, this country would be better off without all the thousands of unwanted kids, destitute and dependant on hand outs.

The Clay Oven or what it used to be in her day, where she would party there with friends, was up ahead to her right. Now it was a disco she had been warned to stay away from. "Drugs" They had told her. It was a den of iniquity in this modern, thriving Johannesburg, which Government neglect, had allowed to be held to ransom by drug lords and corrupt customs officials. The drugs flowed in through the border posts, and Airfreight terminals, unchecked and untaxed. All the while, the average Joe paid huge taxes and then more for private security against the rampant crime those drugs proliferated. Those in the know, bought houses in leafy suburbs, and bought the apartheid that previous Governments had yearned for. It was all about money! Sue was going to buy her way up the food chain and if her raw talent as a salesperson was truly recognized, she would be swishing along in her BMW SUV before long, and living in the walled communities that this money bought.

She remembered passing the casino, where she had spent evenings, dining with friends in that cloistered, surreal world, under its own painted sky, and quaint utopian Tuscany village. "How peculiar" she thought, "that a system dependant on after tax income, could illicit such huge profits in turn, from people who could least afford it. Casinos were a corrupt form of money lending! Jesus would have turned their tables over and chased the croupiers away. Those insidious profiteers had been banned from the previous South Africa, but the system that had been in place had allowed them to descend on supposedly free, black run Governments in the old Homelands. Much like the Americans had done with the Indian reservations! Some corrupt official would always allow those moneylenders in. Two thousand years of biblical tutorage had only served to educate those who dismissed the words of Jesus as garbage. The new government turned a blind eye on these proceedings, because the huge profits attracted huge taxes, and the merry-go-round persisted.

Those thoughts transcended the lateness of the evening, and Sue had merely been intent on getting home. Home was where the heart is, and where her two-day old merlot waited. The simple pleasures of this life, could garner such emotive responses. She could almost taste that smooth red liquid; in Pavlovian exuberance, she had licked her lips.

Suddenly she remembered being alone. Completely alone! There was no traffic careering towards her to keep her alert. No extraneous activity to break her thought patterns. Just a lonely single carriage road, heading down into a dip. Suddenly and inadvertently, Sue could feel a sense of the foreboding she had felt then. She sometimes felt this way, when alone and happy in her thoughts, and a demon; or was it an angel would come and sit on her left shoulder? There would be this nagging sense of imminent danger. She had been in sticky situations before! Once, when taking a short cut from Krugersdorp, she had missed her off-ramp and ended up in the middle of Diepsloot, whilst fires raged around her. Unbeknown to her it was the winter furnaces, the taxi drivers used to warm themselves, but had she been in any other mood, she may well have turned tail and run. She didn't! She drove through the melee, intent on getting home and putting her gas heater on. This had been just such, one of those moments.

As Sue remembered hitting the dip, the road had narrowed further, and all of a sudden in front, and as clear as day in her brand new ellipsoidal headlights, "guaranteed to illuminate any dangerous traffic", she saw what looked like a body lying in the middle of the road. Sue had never seen anything like this. Was that blood gushing from a wound on his head? Sue swerved, but instead of slowing and passing on the empty right hand side of the prostrate form, she instinctively heard the salesman say.

"With this baby, you can bundu-bash through any situation if need be."

Sue careered off the road, and whilst there was a shallow dip on the left, it was no match for her little two-door off-roader. She bumped irreverently, straining the seat belt against her torso, one, two three, over and up through the dip again and onto the gratefully smooth tarmac on the other side. Without a pause to consider the plight of that poor man, she had accelerated, and headed straight for the local police station. "This was awful. The poor chap must have been a victim of a hit and run?" She found her abandoned cell phone in the drinks tray on the dash. She would call that number! "What was it again? 1011...No, 10101? No. How stupid. Why not just a simple '999' like they had in any other civilized country in the world? Was this an emergency? Yes", she thought. "He may still be alive. There was hope that if an ambulance was called now, he might be saved. Hell, there seemed to be an awful lot of blood on the road." It turned her stomach. Yuck! It was like that time her friend Nick had an epileptic fit in her bathroom, and had collapsed head first onto the tiled floor. She had spent hours cleaning up the sickeningly red blood that had coated the floor in a smooth lava-like flow, like those paint adverts on TV. Sue needed to get to the police station. It was somewhere up on the left, and if she hurried, she would get there in time to call an ambulance.

Sue remembered looking at the orange display lit digital clock, just before hitting the dip. It was around ten-thirty. She would probably find a night shift, ready for bed, and no real urgency to react! Should she call Dave? He could get on the phone and get the emergency services there quicker. No! He would not answer the phone, and besides; he would probably think she was stalking him! No. She would wait to get to the police station and then report a hit and run. She swept through suburbs, left then right. Over a bridge, under a highway, chasing time, adrenalin coursing. Sue was on a mission.

At the police station, Sue had zipped up to the old clinker-brick seventies style building, two steps at a time, and was in the cold, concrete floored interior in three or four bounds of a precarious high-heeled prance. There was a Constable, seated at his raised stool, behind a wooden counter, chiselled by etched scratches and circular stained coffee mug symbols all along its length. The constable had been filling out a report. Any one of numerous reports, he would probably, but dutifully complete that night. Completed in a hand writing style proudly South African, and symptomatic of an education system dragged through countless classrooms, in numerous townships, spread out all across this bounteous country. An endearing symbol, of an attempt, in between looted and burned school classrooms, to make a statement about South Africa's history. Education, even in the basic standard six, cursive, writing patterns of some of its learners, was a badge to be worn proudly. It differentiated this Constable from the millions of less fortunate, who would not find a pension-funded, medical aid gifted employment opportunity in this melting pot of cultures.

15

Sue eagerly relayed her story. She waited. The Constable had not looked up once during her entire recounting of her story.

"Had he ignored her purposely?" Sue stood, perched on the end of her toes, ankle straining over fake Gucci inspired strapless slip on, heeled work shoes.

The Constable finally looked up after signing off on the report, destined for a claim which some Insurance company fraud investigator would peruse for inconsistencies. The Constable, now about to give his full attention to Sue, had greeted her.

"Good evanning." Syllables pronounced in inimitable good manners.

Sue had greeted him on her arrival! She was sure she had! "Had he been so intent on his report that he had not heard her?" In her urgency, Sue was sure she had slipped in the "Good evening Constable" guaranteed to get his attention. No! It appeared she hadn't. He awaited her response. Sue was gutted. She knew she would have to repeat the whole saga again. She did!

Without a hint of recognition on his face, he turned, pulled another form from a wooden in-tray perfectly positioned beside him. He would have made a perfect Government official! She remembered he was!

Without any comment, he began to fill out the form one perfectly scripted letter at a time. Sue was distraught! "What about that poor man lying in the middle of the road, bleeding to death? The Constable was impervious to his plight!" As he began, he looked up. "Your name?"

Sue had stood, motionless, jaw dropping to her suitably curvaceous bosom. Just as he had applied the pen to paper, a young, what looked like Reservist chap, appeared through a glass door at the back. Sue smiled intently trying to attract his attention. It worked. He stopped.

"Hello" she flirted almost unabashedly. He greeted her.

"Great thanks. How are you?" She had his attention.

"I would be fine, but I just witnessed the most awful accident on Witkoppen." She had directed her desperate comment. He was all ears.

"Whereabouts? We have not received any call out." This was not kosher. Usually, he would get the call to hop in his unmarked Golf, and speed off to assist. Any drama was his privilege. There had been no call.

"No, I am only reporting it now." Sue was sure to get his reaction.

"Whereabouts on Witkoppen? We'll send a squad car immediately!" He was now her knight in shining armour. Smiles abounded. He slipped back into the office behind and re-emerged with an equally energetic, but somewhat more rotund fellow Reservist.

Sue had explained where she had seen the accident. He grabbed his walkie-talkie radio in one hand, his car keys in the other, and bravado, only years of Clint Eastwood movies could hone, he set off. As he eased past her, Sue had slipped him her card from its pride of place in her wallet. He had paused, looked at the proffered card, smiled and said, "thank you Susan, I will let you know." And he was gone, rotund man in pursuit.

Sue thankfully escaped the constable and his forms, just as she heard the squeal of tires, and the faint whiff of burnt rubber invaded her peaked senses. She made her way home, a sense of community spiritedness alive within her still palpitating heart. She had felt re-invigorated. A thought of blue clad uniforms filled her senses. It had been a rush.

At home, Sue had taken her glass of merlot from the fridge and dimming the lights just adequately enough, settled into her favourite sofa, plush cushions enveloping her aroused senses, and slightly chilled Stellenbosch aromas filling her brightened outlook. She did not make a habit of flirting with younger men, but there was something about him that caught her attention. Was it the uniform, or was it the whole heightened sense of expectation. She smiled inwardly, knowing he would call.

Whilst the evening had grown quiet, Sue heard the far-off rasp of a motor bike. "Some other late night reveller on his way home, destined to become another statistic." The room was still, apart from the gentle purring of her kitten, Whiskers devoured, and now cradled in the crook of her arm and contentedly sharing a moment of life's wonderment. The peace and tranquillity stretched beyond the midnight hour, only to be rudely, but wilfully interrupted when Sue's mobile phone had rung.

"Hello?" she answered, not recognizing the number. She had been anticipating this.

"Hi, I'm sorry to be calling you at this time of night." The voice seemed less assured now. Not the brazen action man she expected. "It's Tyrone from the police station!" Who else could it have been? Her heart skipped a beat.

Sue responded a little too enigmatically. "No. I was up. Could not sleep after seeing that awful accident!" Sue would have to invite Tyrone over for coffee to thank him.

"Yes, I know awful." He repeated. The silence was a reminder of the life's subtle twists and turns.

Sue had broken the silence, their respect conveyed to the departed. "You did not manage to save him?"

Silence again. "No! But we will be able to get the other two to hospital and perhaps a critical care unit."

"The other two?" Sue was confused. She had only seen one body in the road!

"Yes. They seem to be suffering multiple lacerations to the legs and buttocks, but the other guy's head was squashed." He had suddenly stopped himself, as he realized too much detail was not going to help his cause.

"Oh!" Sue was confused. "Was that the man who was lying in the road?" Sue had seen the blood.

"In the road?" Tyrone was tired after a double shift, but he was not totally confused. "There had been no one in the road!"

Sue was now flummoxed. She had definitely seen the body in the road.

"No, all three were lying in the ditch on the side of the road. Very peculiar, as there was no sign of skid marks where they must have been thrown out of the back of a bakkie. No bakkie even?" Tyrone's voice trailed off.

"Oh!" Sue had gasped. Suddenly she was anxious. The idea of thinking about this a second longer, had no appeal to her.

She was now alone again with her thoughts having abruptly ended their conversation. This whole saga had seemed to play itself out in surreal reality. Sue was almost certain that had she stopped, she may now be a statistic. She would use that as her excuse to shut out that vague but horrendous experience. The thought that she had possibly run through the bush over those poor men was too gruesome to contemplate.

"There I go again", she remonstrated to herself. "They were lying in the grass with the intention of high-jacking her, and possibly God knows what?" No this was fully understandable. She had reacted as any young woman might, fearing the darkened road and the risk of the unknown; she had done the right thing. No one would know what had happened, beside her and she was the one who would now live with the sickly feeling. She suddenly thought to herself. "I better get the car washed in the morning!" Yuk what a thought? Where had the man with the blood soaked head gone? She could not be sure, but he probably had gapped it after her foray through the bush. He had abandoned his accomplices, she surmised. This allowed Sue to fall into a fitful slumber.

Aids Education

Michael was a funny little man. No one who knew him well could quite put their finger on it. He looked Jewish, but had an English name, sounded effeminate but had a wife and kids. No he was a typical modern day man-about-town, intent on eking out his destiny in a world gone crazy, with social norms and societal concerns.

Michael had started his current furniture manufacturing business in an old Apartheid era Bantu state to the north, where tax incentives had proven deliciously appealing, and factories had been built to accommodate like-minded entrepreneurs with the skills and desire to kick-start these Bantustan economies. It was a vain attempt by a supercilious society intent on creating a division for themselves between the haves, and the have-nots. Michael was quick to see the opportunity those tax rebates would provide, and had subsequently kept the factory there to ensure the families he supported were given an opportunity to survive off of the meagre minimum wage earnings the factory workers earned.

That and the fact that the timber used to create the furniture came from the sprawling forests that had emerged from the cooler climes around the rolling hills of the North Province. The proximity to good timber, rendered the operation even more profitable, but now those factories had been put under enormous pressure by the less than sympathetic ANC government, with whom these Provinces now bargained for funding and political favours. Michael could have moved the factory back to Gauteng, and a mere twenty-minute drive from his plush suburban office, on an acre of walled supremacy in Bryanston. He had not, favouring the two-hour trip once a week to check up on the management of his furniture business, to the relative ease of a local factory, at ten times the rental. This was his retirement nest egg, he had defended himself from eager Insurance company salesmen, who, including his brother, had tried to sell him on the benefits of a retirement annuity, and the limitless returns of the stock market. He had resisted, preferring to keep his nest egg churning out the profits in cash, rather less substantial than before, but none-the-less, adequate. "Cash was king" he believed, and no amount of bullying and cajoling would change his opinion.

Besides the cash deals he generated, kept him from the scrutiny of overzealous SARS officials, who would need to have little incentive to audit his now quite substantial property portfolio. One day he would list a property company, put the proceeds into a Blue Chip portfolio, and walk away into the sunshine of an Indian Ocean island retreat. For now, he was content to earn tax-free benefits afforded him by the rentals of numerous office parks, dotted around Johannesburg's bourgeoning north. Content even though his work force was being decimated by a scourge of unmistakable proportions, which if left unattended, would bring sheer misery upon his workers, and deny hundreds of children an opportunity as he had had, growing up in the relative calm of a small holding outside Harrismith in the Free State.

Having come from nothing, Michael was all too aware of how poverty could reduce the human spirit to its lowest common denominator. He had lived a less than salubrious lifestyle as a young man, entering the fray that was early seventies Johannesburg, with its still famous pass laws, and riots that had merely provoked an even more energetic endeavour, from the Apartheid Nationalists, to spread the work force of South Africa, as far and wide as possible. Never expecting their fate, the work force of this pristine, idealistic society had been open to this migratory engineering assault. Choosing to find employment, as all those strapping young Zulus had done in the earlier part of Johannesburg's history, they now migrated to areas where jobs were plentiful, and relatively well paid. History was about to repeat itself, and those workers who had children twenty years ago, now had to contend with their children migrating back to the cities, and the passionate vibe that was 'Jozi'.

When the older partner too whom he had become a protégée in the late seventies, had then died, Michael had inherited the factory and a piece of Bryanston big enough to sub-divide. Michael had then set about marrying his school sweetheart, who had followed him from Harrismith, and waited ten long confused years, whilst he cleaved a place for himself in the sanctity that was a relatively extravagant lifestyle. Michael married, to conform to the peer pressure of his family heritage, and when his father passed on years later, having doted on his grandchildren for just long enough to leave Michael the farm outside that quaint but rapidly expanding transportation hub, which was now worth something in land value. The circle had come full circle. Michael had learned well from his 'centre of influence', and was now able to put these valuable lessons to good use.

When he had sold his first office development in Rivonia, a very suitably named Chiselhurst Office Park, Michael had made some very important contacts at local Government level. This was to be an opening too many more deals he would strike up with his ANC contacts, and who would offer him advice on future tenders he might find attractive. It was 1999, and the Millennium Bug had not yet devastated the financial records of thousands of parastatal departments, who had not kept up to date with changes to computer software that the sinister bug was destined to destroy in the infant democracy of South Africa. Trepidation hung in the air like a fog bank on the Natal Midlands, and detractors of the new Thabo Mbeki Government, having resigned themselves to the success of the past five years of Madiba euphoria, were now circling like vultures. This bug would wipe out the entire Governmental financial system, and the Broederbond would be waiting in the wings to pick up the pieces left by an ill-advised and fundamentally lazy ANC Government. The process had only taken five years to unravel, and now Mbeki, who had little help from those who had not wanted his tenure as President to succeed, were plotting. However, it was not the Millennium Bug that was lurking, that they needed to concern themselves with. The hype of its devastating effects on the world's financial systems was a smoke screen, for would-be experts to earn hundreds of millions of Rand in commissions and huge bonuses, for the sale of new systems that the Government needed to put in place. No! It was not the Millennium Bug they needed to worry about!

Thabo Mbeki, an intellectual, who had been effective in garnering the support of International Financial Institutions, with his learned repose, and his aloof exterior, had shown that the intelligentsia of the New ANC Government were not necessarily the right people to be running an infant democracy, fraught with problems of service delivery. After all, how was an effective Government to run itself, when high-ranking Ministers were spending the bulk of their days in learned discussions over late breakfasts, early lunches, and lavish dinners. No! Somebody needed to be at work, putting highly idealistic plans into place; these plans which were concocted over volumes of good Cape wines, and even more elaborate cocktails, were highly unrealistic. This was a recipe for disaster as the vast majority of hard working South Africans saw their inheritance being splurged on very visible luxuries. One hundred and eighty million Rand airplanes did not help their cause, but like most insidious rumours that start, it is always the least obvious, and plainly scurrilous that holds the imagination of the proletariat. In Mbeki's case, it was a bug that had captured the imagination of the general population, but not the Millennium Bug. The bug, which was actually a virus, was in fact the Human-immunodeficiency virus, or better-known HIV. This was to be Mbeki's Achilles heel during his lengthy, lethargic tenure. Thabo Mbeki, very early on in his term as State President of South Africa, had placed on record his objections to the science behind the cause of AIDS, which was becoming a serious factor among lower income black working populations. Whilst Mbeki debated the merits of the science, people were actually starting to die! Was it the cause of poverty? Or were there some real issues that the Government was overlooking?

Well it was precisely this debate that had raised its ugly head on more than one occasion during a dinner party hosted by Michael at his very significant villa he had now built for himself in an exclusive, very secure cul-de-sac on the river overlooking a golf course in the Northern suburbs. When his dinner guests had accepted his invitation, Michael had been at pains to ensure, all the right people had been invited, as the ANC grape vine was as effective as a modern day Twitter blog. There was no one who should be left off the list, for fear that, they might feel deprived and this slap-in-the-face would result in them all cancelling. It was a who's who of local MEC's Health ministry officials, and Government doctors. They were all there. Michael was going to make a pitch over coffee's served in his finest Davididov china, with Macchiato inspired coffee aromas wafting through his drawing room, in which hung in central focus, a Thomas Baines landscape, and juxtaposed in Mamelodian splendour, in pride of place above the fireplace, a Chimayo relief.

The dinner guests arrived in typical African time keeping fashion and dinner was served half an hour later than expected. This had been anticipated and the guests, who were weaned off their Blackberry and given a very tasteful and full-bodied sherry, were left to mingle, while the catering company made plans. The soufflés had sunk and they would not be able to resurrect them, despite the plethora of medical attendees. Michael would ensure that the outside caterers never worked again in his events, when they served up a fruit sorbet that was not 'fresh'. This was his way of ensuring the food chain was dealt with expeditiously, whilst in point of fact the sickenly-sweetened fruit was devoured with an alacrity that only hard working humans with substantial appetites could justify. The evening would not be an entire failure it seemed.

As the after dinner conversation flowed and before the nine o'clock cell phone calls would prompt a mass exodus to waiting children, eager for parents to collect them from their private school functions, the stage was set. Michael began a foray into the much-vaunted ideals of sex-education among the general population, as devised by Doctors, and the multitude of advocates of HIV denialists. "HIV could be contained" even as medical evidence seemed to denounce, "If the people were educated to understand the benefits of family planning and the use of condoms."

Everyone was in agreement. There were no detractors amongst the loyal royal. The Government's commitment to HIV was to advise people in rural areas on how to grow their African potatoes, beetroot and garlic. The official stance was against ARV's or ineloquently pronounced anti-retroviral, which was a dirty word amongst the gathered. They could barely stomach to mention the abbreviated ARV in its shortened version, much less the full version! Protagonists like the AAC who had embarked on a smear campaign against Thabo, would feel the full wrath of Governments official policy on rabble-rousers, and they would meet their own fate through the liberal application of force against them. No one knew who would implement this force, "But it would happen."

When the gathered conspirators were ready to send out a lynching mob to deal with the troublesome Indian chap, Michael mentioned an interesting discussion he had had with a well-respected American HIV denialism on his recent trip to South Africa. He had all their attention. Michael began.

"Well it has to be said, he has a point." What that point was the other eavesdroppers were now to become a party to. "Education was the key to stemming any efforts of anti-government action that detractors in the AAC would be able to muster. If the Government was seen to be educating people on the ravages of a potential fatal virus, then they would be the champions of its benefits, and the AAC would have their spirited reign cut short. It was a conspiracy, you see." This was what he wanted them to believe. They were all happy to be inspired by this talk.

"The pharmaceutical industry is hankering to get your hard earned budgets spent on ARV's." There was no doubting it. The departments had been swamped by tenders to provide ARV's to the population, especially here in Gauteng, where the largest budgets existed, but the lowest HIV infection rates occurred. Michael was Lording it up over his dinner guests, but in a nice way. They would eat from the hand that offered them solutions. They were under attack in this infant democracy that they had fought so gallantly to win. Manning the burning tire barriers in the townships for the benefit of foreign journalists, and a momentary place on the front pages, they had cut their teeth on liberation politics. All had been well rewarded for their dedication to the cause. Brightly coloured outfits and Armani suits now draped those robust exteriors, where once the sackcloth of victims had hung.

Michael continued. "If education is the key, I have been told, that the only effective way to demonstrate the use of condoms, is by offering all Health departments, an opportunity to distribute some form of demonstration kit. Without being too delicate, the clinics that provide the education are going to need fake phalluses." There was a quiet moment as English was translated to Xhosa, Venda and a few Afrikaans guests. "Yes, penises. They need a phallic symbol, so as they can demonstrate the use of the condom, and how it can be applied."

There was a titillated guffaw from a few of the ladies, and a hand covered cough from the male guests. Each knew exactly where Michael was going with this.

"Sure. If the clinics each had their own demonstration kit, they would be able to explain sex education in the most basic of forms, and as Peter explained it to me, 'de-stigmatise the use of condoms'."

He had mentioned Peter Rawlings by first name. He was their God. Their salvation from the onslaught of aggressive Pharmaceutical Company's intent on wrestling huge amounts of funding from the State coffers. Any chance they had to counter their detractors was a chance worth pursuing. They listened intently.

"Now I don't know the first thing about HIV and AIDS, but I do know it is a sexually transmitted death sentence, if left unattended." They all nodded earnestly. They knew this too. Even Peter had acknowledged that what was known about the virus was that it was spread through sexual contact.

"In South Africa, the biggest concern is the ignorance of the working population in regard to what constitutes AIDS. Some think it is all a ploy by the Afrikaners to reduce the black population by forcing them to wear condoms. Others believe it is just a disease that affects homosexuals and prostitutes, but the worst scenario is the millions of men in this country who think that the possibility of contracting the virus is only a woman's problem, because the thought of having to abstain from sex, in any form, goes against every fibre of their ancestral beliefs. Men are the procreators, and a woman is merely the vestibule through which procreation takes place. If one looks at the fertility iconography of African tribes, it is possible to see the female symbol is always secondary to the male potency symbol. It would take decades, if not a hundred years of education to change these pre-conceived ideas, and unfortunately, the people do not have that amount of time. In a generation, the number of infant mortalities and abandoned AIDS babies is going to swamp the countries health system." Peter would have been the first to acknowledge this.

The stage was set for his pitch. Michael had a learned and intently keen audience. Somehow, he being divorced from ANC politics made the whole subject more palatable. The conspiracy theorists had already determined that if this rejection of HIV and the science behind it was intended to be a way of the Xhosa dominated Government eradicating large swathes of the Zulu nation from the democratic process, it was not working! HIV affected, and infected everyone, not just the less educated and more rural heartland of Kwazulu Natal. No! The process of stemming the tide of political implosion amongst the ANC was going to be dependent on a co-ordinated education process.

"I have been discussing this idea with Peter." The listened avidly, nodding agreement. "He has mooted an idea which might have its origins in the Favelas of Brazil, but it is none-the-less as important to the South African Diaspora. If every clinic in South Africa was equipped to give sex education to woman, and ultimately these ideas filter through to the younger population, there is a good chance that the tide of infections could be stemmed. This was Peter's idea." He left them hanging on his last sentence, which they all hunkered around him to hear what it was.

"My factory in Venda is geared to produce table legs for the furniture we produce into the lower income markets of Gauteng. Those machines are tooled to turn thousands of table legs every day."

They waited expectantly. The idea was formulating itself in their minds.

"We simply tool the machines to turn out wooden phallus symbols by the thousands, so that they can be distributed to every clinic in South Africa. That would provide the opportunity for nurses and counsellors to demonstrate the use of condoms and begin their sex education process in earnest."

The formulated idea was standing like a beacon of hope in their minds. Like the great phallic symbol of the Hillbrow Tower, it was etched in their minds as some grand deliverance from this ghastly pandemic. If only they could rid themselves of the responsibility of having to sit in one meeting after the next, being told the statistics of infant mortality in Gauteng's hospitals, and being reminded every day they had to attend meetings in the inner city of Johannesburg, by the hordes of street children begging at the window of their black SUV's which even with tinted windows, could not shut out the very obvious scourge. No! This was a solution, which could begin the process of reclaiming lost ground to their detractors, and partially satiating their guilty consciences.

Mpho was the first to speak. "Michael, you are a genius." He offered with a hint of the condescending disdain that only ex-doctors could. Having given up the pursuit of immortality through his devotion to the 'Hippocratic Oath'; he had then pursued Academia, so as to ensure the grace of his wisdom be handed down in perpetuity. "That is a brilliant idea!"

They all smiled. It had been given the thumbs up. All that was needed now was for the potentially tricky ideals of the tendering process to be sidestepped, and they would have a solution of workable proportions. This was their cue.

Mpho shook Michaels hand, a double grip, with left hand over right clasped for good measure, an endearing commitment to the cause. "Good night Michael. We will talk in the morning. I will have my office call you, and the contracts drawn up."

The others all stood in line to shake his hand. He was the messianic symbol of their redemption. A portal to their continued governance and a testament to the fortitude of thinking outside the box. Michael had solved their all-consuming problem in one simple phallic solution, and now he was their God. This would be like printing money. The wooden penises would cost him very little; the machines although tooled to turn them would need to be adjusted to fit the eight inch parameters required, and then there was the smoothing and sanding process. Easy as a lion shoot in a Northern Province game park. They would need to ensure no splinters, or that would obviate any potential benefits of showing the use of the condoms.

The following day, being a Friday, was a breeze. Administration day in most Governmental offices, which precluded the obvious twelve o'clock Friday lunch meetings, but which gave ample time for the various intricacies to be ironed out, and then the fast track of the ordering process. Government departments could work very quickly when needs be. And this was a potential 'needs be' situation.

Michael was in business with that month, the first orders being place, and the machining operation in full swing. The wooden demonstration units were turned out in their thousands, and with no limit to the number required, the process was a lengthy one. Michaels 'woodies' were being delivered to every clinic in the country before long, and the cash was rolling in. With any luck, he could sell the factory as a going concern, and have the proceeds in his pocket before the tender was completed. Some brash entrepreneurial empowerment partner would see this opportunity, and Michael would be out, and happily ensconced on his Indian Ocean resort before too long.

April came and went and the education of South Africa's needy continued. The winter set in with a vengeance in those rural villages, high up in the escarpment, and in the cooler climes of the Cape flats. Winter came and went, and the population of the country emerged from their virtual hibernation. Clinics that had operated with their demonstration kits, ordered in quantity were now gearing up to roll out the new education process with renewed vigour and the scene was set for the MEC's to visit their much vaunted clinic facilities and hold aloft their phallic symbols in a vain attempt to ward off the evil scourge and claim victory.

Unfortunately for them, after a period of relative inaction and one peculiarly South African symptom of genetic heritage, they had arrived at the pre-designated clinics, with press core in tow, only to find that the condoms that had been delivered with the demonstration kits, had been manufactured in China, for a population that was to say the least, not quite as well-endowed as their South African counterparts. The condoms could not fit over the demonstration kits, tearing at every attempt, so with that the solution was to find another use for them. Needless to say, by the time the MEC's arrived, the wooden phalluses were burnt embers, already discarded to the late August winds, and along with their charred remains, so was the much hyped education system.

Michael was now a faint but irritating memory, having taken his nest egg and retired to the sanctuary of his island.

Casinos and catering

Tony had been head hunted by the top landscapers in the country. His was a worldly experience that only a lifetime of fleeing one African dictatorship for another could etch into the memories of those near and dear to him. If ever there had been a man destined for greatness, but hamstrung by his own arrogance, it was Tony. Having been through the continent of Africa from the Moa Moa uprisings of 1950's Kenya, to the Copper Belt of Zambia, with its visible wealth, but unenviable leadership vacuum, Tony had tried his hand at most skills. With an unbridled passion for work, which saw him rise at 5 o'clock every morning, and which would see him physically active for most of those working hours, Tony would have won any employee of the year award, if his pride had allowed him to stay in one job, or dedicated to one business for long enough to qualify. His real passion had been animals, and having been brought up on a small-holding in the quaint port town of Dartmouth, Tony had been educated in animal husbandry. So, with a contract in hand, and the early sixties still wrought with Colonial enthusiasm, Tony had exported wild animals to the 'pre-quarantine' extravagance of Harrods' basement animal pens, and there was no end to the desirability of the exotic breeds. Tony continued this business until the obvious concerns of imported diseases had rendered the Government of the day to act. The opportunity gone, Tony maintained his interests by acquiring the Blantyre Zoo.

What drove Tony was his unswerving desire to make something of his life. He was to forge the sword that King Arthur had inspired among all Englishmen with a penchant for travel and conquest, into the landscape that was Africa. He was no apologist for Colonialism, having experienced everything the bleeding hearts liberals had thrown at him. Suffering their unconscionable rhetoric, but knowing in his own heart, that Africa did not have a place for them. Africa was a continent that would be cleaved out of the rock of granite formations that its billion-year history had exposed through the elements, and its unchallenged savagery, that had been exposed despite the attentions of the American 'Peace Corp' and other liberal groups. To a man like Tony, they espoused a foreign belief system, and exposed their own weaknesses. No! Tony was no 'apologist', but an advocate of brutal physical discipline if those in his employ, or under his management stepped out of line. If he was to be stabbed in the back, it would be by several of his own European ilk, and not by some disgruntled labourer, with a chip on his shoulder and a grudge for having been dealt the low cards, in a high stakes game that required the application of intelligence.

No! In point of fact, it was this unswerving dedication to his own peculiar moral code that had seen him survive the ravages of this savage continent. He had been a military man. His father before him had served, although having had to suffer the ignominious fate of many wireless operators in the Royal Navy during the Second World War. His father had gone completely mad from the constant Morse code, and the constant bombardment of torpedoes in the escorts that ploughed the North Atlantic. Tony had suffered at the hands of his father's own discipline, when home on shore leave during the early years of his life. This was to be his introduction to a life that literally needed to be man-handled by himself, if anything was to be made of it. Having become only too aware at an early age that there were no free lunches, unless you had the privilege of a birthright of Aristocratic proportion, Tony had realised his passions would require him to embark on a quest. This fact, and his desire to escape that system of repression, was what had driven him into the African hinterland, and his destiny with fate.

Tony had been head hunted undoubtedly, because his reputation as a man who got things done, had been his own undoing. Whoa, betide the man who stepped into his path, with no good reason to be there, and heaven help, despite his own atheistic views, the man who double-crossed him. So when he was offered the project of creating the landscape for the 'King's' latest Casino complex, Tony had ruefully accepted. Their paths had crossed, and unbeknown to the 'King', they had had previous business interests in common. This was the setting for the beginning of what would become the costliest landscaping contract in the company's history.

When the project had been shown him, Tony could immediately appreciate the scope and size of the endeavour. This was to be an African theme park, but on a grand scale that would have even grabbed the fictional character, Allan Quartermain's attention. The grandiose gardens to rival any African Babylonian creation, involved the building of dams, water features and flowing gardens that would equal the greatest creations on the African continent, stemming four thousand years of pre-history and re-creating the epics of that Semitic era of 'Josephanic' self-aggrandizement. Had Joseph really become Pharaoh? And what could a similarly diminutive man, with the grand vision of his ancestors, bring to the fragile land of Southern Africa?

So on their first meeting, they had sized each other up. The two men had very similar attributes, but one was hindered by circumstance and opportunity. They would have been good sparring partners were it not for the fact that Tony stood a considerable head and shoulders above the 'King'. Yes! Had they been equals on any other field, then Tony would have been more than a match for him. But this self-absorbed 'pharaoh', had the prestige formulated by the accumulation of wealth, a very African symptom. Here the wealth of a man was gauged by the size of his herd of cattle. Prestige was dependent on how many maidens one accumulated as wives. It was a truly African symptom, and Tony was unfortunately no match for the 'King' in that regard. But to say he had not been given fair opportunity was misleading. He was hamstrung by an inability to make unemotional decisions. Tony's life was systematically wrought by chaos, which was self-imposed. Decisions in the past may well have gone his way, had he been able to divorce passion from shrewd financial gain. Like his relationship with his glamorous wife Valerie, Tony suffered the dramatic fluctuations of a life similarly passionate. Whether he had learned anything in his previous forty years of work, was only to be ascertained in the months to come. Life and the Cosmos, had an intriguing way of fulfilling destiny. They had crossed each other's paths many years before, and unbeknownst to the 'King', whose memory had faded with each successive deal, Tony had been double-crossed! This was to be the beginnings of an interesting partnership, for which Tony would have given his left leg, to have put his size twelve boot right up the 'King's' posterior. There was smiles, acknowledgements and conscious attempts by both to cooperate, but the 'King' knew that once the project was finished, Tony would be discarded like all the other contractors he had used, and Tony knew that this project would cost a lot more than what they had budgeted.

When the first sods had been wrenched from the African soil, and the bulldozers had erased a billion years of sub-soil, the project truly started to take shape. Never before had the forces of human enterprise been thrown with such alacrity at the Southern African landscape. Even the grand imposing tower of the Great Zimbabwe would not match the greatness of this project. Those millions of stones had been carved to create that magnificent free-standing structure, hewn from the surrounding granite in a show of early human dexterity. This would be different however. Modern tools, would leave the rudimentary applications of those Iron Age craftsmen, looking more than antiquated. The time scale was tight. The project was to be in place for the opening of the casino as quickly as was humanly possible, because the 'King' had his investors to please, and an eager population to fleece. So in a turn of events, with the project being managed with savage intent, the casino and hotel were wrestled from the earth, and a concrete structure to rival any before was created.

The landscaping had continued throughout the building process, with hanging gardens emerging from the dusty African ground, and a marvellous feature that would have the tourists flocking, literally to see this wonder of modern man. The gardens were created with lawns, huge fountains and in pride of place the bird park. Thousands of water fowl and every conceivable bird had been purchased by Tony from as far afield as the Makgadikgadi Pans in Botswana. Taking these beautiful birds, and relocating them required one important feature that should not be overlooked. Most birds are migratory, and birds that fly would naturally return to their original habitats. There was nothing natural about this project, but Tony did have a masterful plan. When the caged birds were brought in, just as the project was being completed, the birds' wings were pinioned, so as to ensure they would not fly anywhere. This was a grand solution, and on the opening day of the casino, thousands of the Western suburban residents flocked from the city to visit the new casino.

Some walked the stately grounds with children in tow. Most just headed for the slot machines. Two things were clearly evident from the hoards that had gathered. The first was that the casino was too small and the 'King' had severely underestimated the numbers of ardent gambling fans who would frequent the casino; the other more poignantly for Tony, was that the vast number of visitors had no interest in his garden of Eden, resplendent with Peacock and Flamingo. This was not lost on the 'King' who despite his royal welcome was already seeing the queues of gamblers waiting to use machines. It was to him like watching customers arriving at a concession stand, with money in hand, and being told they would have to get their candyfloss somewhere else. He was livid, and the design team would be fired immediately. He needed people with vision, like himself, who could respond to initiatives, and think boldly outside the box. "Who was responsible for this lack of fore-sight?"

"Those bedrooms could easily be turned into a series of private gambling rooms. A club Privet with a difference. The rest of the existing facility including the kitchens and office, could be gutted and expanded for the main casino."

The architect was fired, the project manager lost his bonus, and Tony was rehired.

The next six months was spent with workers already happily ensconced in their rudimentary living quarters on site, and the building on of a magnificent new casino complex next to the already functioning, but inadequate original. Building contractors were promised bonuses for each day saved on the new, bigger and improved 'Babylon'. They would finish their work ahead of schedule and be rewarded handsomely. Every day that the new refurbished casino stood empty, the investors were hankering for the 'King's' head. He did not disappoint, and taking a personal reinvigorated view of his empire, he returned regularly to ensure his subjects laboured dutifully. On the last week that he deemed it necessary to take a visit to the resurrected palace, the tour through the splendid improved gardens gave him pause for thought.

"Where are all the birds that we bought for the water park?"

Tony was in attendance. He had seen this coming.

"Well, they are wild fowl. They spend the majority of the day wading through the shallow water of the dam, or feeding in the deeper water."

"Yes, but I don't see 'them'." Replied the 'King' with a not so subtle sarcastic tone to his voice, which heightened his not so endearing manner.

"Well that's what I am telling you." Tony was quite flippant. His grudge for all those hours he had laboured over Cape Maclear, and the manner in which it had been wrestled from him all those years ago had not lessened his contempt for this man.

"You see, when the birds rest at night, they find nesting areas on the beach and inland, so they are safe from predators!"

"What predators? There aren't any in this dam."

"Yes the river system that feeds the dam has brought crocodile into the dam from upstream."

"What! You're telling me that a million Rand's worth of birds have all been eaten by crocodiles?"

"No," Tony was enjoying this moment. "Not those predators!" He paused before explaining.

"Because the birds could not fly to safety, and because they nest away from the water at night, the workers have been catching them, and have eaten them all. A flamingo is about the size of big turkey when it is put in a pot!"

The snake and the bottle

It was Dave's pride and joy. A brand new Mercedes sports, which had a flip top roof and an array of gadgets that would satisfy his 'motor head' desires for just long enough, that he would only start getting bored once the five-year noose around his neck had been settled. The banks were the financial equivalents of the mafia, and Dave knew it first-hand. He had previously bought a BMW, which his friends had warned him, 'The moment you drive that off the show room floor, you'll lose thirty percent of its value!"

He could have cared less, as his company travel and subsistence allowance had paid for it, and like the millions of other motorists Dave passed on the roads every day of his everyday sales job, he was only loaning this car for the time being. In a system where cars cost more than the houses people lived in, the stakes had been skewed somewhat disproportionately in favour of motor manufacturing companies, where huge profits were to be made. "Was it any wonder", he had told the salesman in Sandton, that the large luxury German brands had not left South Africa during the years leading up to 1990 and the un-banning of the ANC.

Apartheid, like its counterpart in Israel, was a system that could be countenanced because the profits, outweighed the negative publicity of having factories pumping out luxury sedans for rich white people. After all, the beneficiaries of those hard-earned wages were the black people in the poorest area of the Eastern Cape, and they needed to earn a living, so the Government would give them good reason to stay. Plying them with incentives, and lucrative tax breaks in order to keep them here. The loser as always was the man in the street. He paid top dollar for these products, and would be the victim of the crime, which owning a luxury vehicle in a society divided by a chasm of economic prosperity, the size and depth of the Great African Rift Valley, was bound to invoke.

Dave was no different. He could choose to be a member of the 'Black Sash' and wear his heart on his sleeve, or get on with the business of living, in a system he did not design, but for which, he was the grateful recipient of its racial laws. "Apartheid, he had argued was not, in his opinion, such a horrendous ill. It was merely a system, whereupon like-minded people had made their way into an area, where they lived together in community, brought on by their natural affinity for one another. For all their grand ideals, he had not noticed any of his church congregation, with whom he had served as a Choir boy and then later as a sacristan, choosing to opt out of the leafy suburban cloistered life of Westcliffe, and live in the squalid conditions of the townships. The Government had merely, he suggested, coerced these people to live together, just as the Greeks lived in their communities, the Portuguese refugees from Mozambique lived in La Rochelle, and the ex-Zimbos' had descended on Natal, and the last 'British Outpost.'

"What was so wrong with that?" He argued over his bridge games at the local Golf Club." If he could afford to live in Lower Houghton, and he was earning enough to pay those exorbitant premiums on his BMW, why shouldn't he be entitled to have one." His playing partner of ten years, had just shaken his head. He had always driven the car his father had offered him on his twenty-first birthday, and had never been interested in replacing it. This was adequate, and got him to his job in the city, without the risk of high-jacking or worse. This was a life of privilege which had been handed down in a generation from the heady days of the sixties. A classic education in good Anglican tradition, and a sense of expectation.

This had all changed during the Soweto Uprisings, and suddenly, a society secure in its own moral place in this severely challenged society, had been forced to look inwardly at their entitled lifestyles, and begin to appreciate how badly the blacks in the townships had it. Growing up in that environment many had chosen to take action by providing their own varying degrees of objection to the system that failed the vast majority, and others chose to pray to change it. All the while Dave got on with his education, and began his ascent on those lofty idealistic stone built homes on the Ridge, intent on proving his disapproving father wrong. To say there was bad blood would be an understatement, as Dave had always desired the keys to the Roller, and the inheritance he would never claim. His father, having forced his own way through the fray, and bought himself a place on the Ridge, would never countenance his two children having an easy ride. So Dave and his sister were given a good education, a pat on the bum, and told to go and seek their fortunes.

Sara had done the clever thing. She had left South Africa after her University education and headed for London, and the freedom to do as she pleased. Dave felt his place was here, with his mates, where a scratch handicap golf score bought one an easy entry to the club, and his not so shabby surname entitled him to free drinks after the local four-balls. He was somewhat of a local celebrity, and his desire to be acknowledged ensured he would always be a big fish, in a small pond. It was not so much that Dave had an ego, as the manner in which he seemed to remind everyone around him, all the time that he would one day succeed. He was driven by this passion to claim a place for himself, in a society which was evolving constantly. So when the club committee, agreed to allow the first black members to join, it was somewhat of a slap in the face to Dave, whose earnest belief, was that you earned the right to become a member through either playing a good game of golf, or waiting in the queue like everyone else. That they had deemed to give a membership to a black, and worse still a practicing member of the ANC, was a slight on those who had waited patiently for their turn. Dave was not impressed, and for the first time since his formative years as a proud member of this club, he began to doubt the system.

So having taken umbrage over this, Dave began to do what any self-righteous single white male would do. He bought himself an expensive BMW, and began trawling the plethora of single moms who were divorced and had a ready-made family. So for the first time in his twenty years as a member, and a confirmed bachelor, Dave embarked on a plan to get himself another life. He did not want his own children, secretly harbouring thoughts of spiting his father, whom he knew would have killed for a grandson, and someone worthy of inheriting his fortune. Dave just put it down to laziness. He did not feel like having to contend with dirty nappies and four in the morning bottle-feeds. Dave's life of entitlement had effectively immunized him from any hardship, and he would settle for the road less travelled, thereby effectively ensuring his father's dying wishes would be ignored. So Dave got married to the older more, worldly Carla, who had been divorced through a need to prove her own ego right! She fancied a younger man, secretly having had a penchant for one of her son's school friends, but knowing that particular endeavour was out-of-bounds. But Dave, fifteen years her junior was fair game!

Dave was a typical white South African male, but his world was all the more, richer for his peculiar slant on societal norms. He was a classic anarchist with a penchant for screwing up his traffic fines and telling traffic police, "to go to hell". This was his take on the very socialistic society South Africa was becoming, and he wanted no part of it! Dave just wanted to play golf, like any other intelligent man his age. He had been only too aware of the club's desire to have a full time professional, now that the clubs' membership fees were sufficient enough to cover that expense. He would be first on the list of those earmarked for the position, and with that he could bow out of the commercial world, and with his father being on the ailing side of health, he would inherit the house on the Ridge, the summer retreat at St Francis Bay where he would have somewhere to entertain his mates, and spend the rest of his life playing golf. However, plans made, were a contorted mirror image away from reality, and Dave would once again be disappointed.

So getting back to the BMW! When Dave had bought this expensive sedan, with chrome mag wheels and a hefty price tag to boot, he had never considered the possibility that his dream of a fast lifestyle of golf, cars and women, and not necessarily in that order, would be so far from reality. What could possibly go wrong. He lived an uninspiring spiritual life, now that he had left the church, choosing his Sunday morning round of golf over the seven thirty service, and the fellowship of Anglicans. This was a problem that plagued the church, and he had witnessed the fall off of numbers in the congregation since the days he was at College. His father, intently aware of this, having been the Chairman of the Finance Committee, had put it down to the changing demographics of the area. What was happening, was that the older generation were retiring to Retirement Villages in other areas, and this ensured that the numbers dwindled with the passing of many of the wonderful people he had served as a sacristan. His world was changing around him, but he had no way of preventing it. The younger Anglicans could not afford the homes that their parents had lived in, and besides, they had all moved to new jobs in different cities and other countries. The society he had grown up in was changing forever, and he could only sit back and watch it dissipate. This was natural demographics, not imposed by statute, but this was lost on Dave.

When the BMW, which we need to focus on, was stolen, a part of Dave's world went out the gate with it. He had parked at the golf club, in the member's enclosure, but a late night revelry of sorts, after a great tournament, had seen his expensive BMW, stolen from inside the club parking area, and not a single security guard had witnessed anything! When the police had eventually arrived at the now deserted clubhouse, in the early hours of the morning, Dave was beside himself with anger. This was a conspiracy, and the security detail were accomplices, so he had made them stay until the police arrived. The facts were, that an enterprising young mechanic had made a copy of the remote locking device whilst the car was being fitted with a security system, and knowing where Dave lived, he and the syndicate had followed him to the club, waited in the street until he was happily entertaining his after golf buddies, and had simply walked into the car-park, climbed into the car and driven off; A fact the vehicle theft unit would never uncover, but which the Insurance Company had no interest in either. They would cut their losses, even after a very pro-active Dave had managed to locate the vehicle in Maputo. The syndicate had driven it straight across the Mozambique border, and the vehicle had been sold to a wealthy Indian businessman. Dave had found out, through the random checking of engine and chassis numbers done by the parent company, who sent officials to the various emerging branches of dealerships all over Southern Africa. This guy, just happened to know Dave after a game of golf at a BMW sponsored tournament. He phoned Dave to let him know where his BMW was and Dave phoned the Insurance Company, who, having settled the claim was in no mood to have investigators sent out to locate their lost property.

It required too much work, and the already over-burdened investigation team, had little incentive to follow up on this case, along with the thousands of other reported stolen vehicles. What was evident, however, was that their risk was limited, by the market valuation on a one-month old car that they would only pay out to the bank, based on the depreciated value. The rest would be for Dave's account! To say Dave was incensed was a gentle reminder to those who knew him that he could get extremely angry. He turned that anger on those poor retched car guards, whom he had every intention of implicating. They had gone from a first name basis, "Sawabona Sipho," to a cold stony stare every time they approached him for a tip. He would give them a tip alright, "Stay the *%#@ away from my car. Dave's anger was taken out on the golf course, and his game suffered, and so too did his customers. Dave was falling apart at the seams and he felt powerless to act. No one else cared about his damn car, and whilst he would now buy himself an even more expensive and sports variety, luxury Mercedes, to counter his dented ego, he still raged within.

In Dave's mind, it was a conspiracy against the whites. The reality, that the Insurance companies were owned by whites, and the Vehicle Protection Unit was still predominantly Afrikaner, was a fact which eluded his deteriorating logic. Dave would get even, at a system that was grossly unfair, and which Dave, in his indignation would remedy! The over-burdened systems were failing because Government were now intent on enriching themselves, and not spending the hard earned tax payer's money on the security of the nation. The Police force were hugely underfunded, and private enterprise were too intent on generating massive profits, for sinister Investors, like his father, who demanded more and more returns on their share capital, so that those lives of luxury could be further enhanced. It was a vicious circle, and Dave felt he had to act. But how? He could not become a vigilante, because he was intrinsically lazy. He could become involved in the system and become a member of Block Watch, but that was under funded and a white elephant, typical of the old order system. No! In Dave's mind, he would require to get even, with whom, he was now not sure? The Police had investigated the car guards, who had been fingerprinted and harassed maliciously at Dave's insistence. Nothing! So Dave was now plotting, and it would be his own drunken declarations that would prove his undoing.

Dave had been chatting to some mates, who having heard the story a few more times than was necessary, had humoured Dave just to satisfy his ego, but had secretly resented his ability to go one under par, even with all this baggage he now carried.

"I put a rubber snake on the back seat of my car!" Offered Mike, who had been Dave's mate through thick and thin.

"Yeah, but no one would want to steal that old squadron, retaliated Dave." They would have to pay someone to steal it!

"That would be pointless," ventured Ralph. He had heard that the syndicates were made up of 'coloured's from Coronationville, who had been employed in workshops across the city. "The people who steal these cars are not superstitious like the old blacks!" A voice of reason in a changing environment.

"Yes, they only drink and get wasted on Zol," added Mike. That lay heavy on Dave's mind. The thought that his thirty percent loss was now being pissed against a wall in the western suburbs of Johannesburg was irritatingly clear.

But the thought sat with him, whilst the others all conjectured over varying degrees of crime, until it naturally trailed off into thoughts of food, and celebrations on a winning four-ball.

But it remained in Dave's mind for just long enough, for him to formulate a plan.

"Why don't I get a bottle of Klippies, fill it with rat poison and leave it under the front seat. If they steal my car this time, they can drink all the way to Hell." Dave's sudden and unexpected remark came half an hour later, with the general conversation already turned to skirts and the cute ass on that blonde in the four-ball ahead of them. She had played a satisfactory game, despite the fact that she had the advantage of the Woman's Tee. They had just stared blankly at Dave. He was beyond salvation!

So it was to be that Dave set a trap for his antagonists, who would deserve nothing less than their comeuppance. He left the three quarter full bottle of golden coloured liquid just visible beyond the edge of the passenger front seat. This would tempt, but show an attempt to conceal. It was perfect! He would spring surprise retribution on anyone who had the gall to attempt to steal his new car. Dave lived in expectation of his self-serving justice.

It would however come in a manner; he could least have expected. One afternoon, having taken his ready-made family with him to the golf club, he and the team had ventured out to the First Tee, and Dave had catapulted himself into celebrity status once and for all. He had played a truly meteoric game and posted an outstanding and unbeaten individual total which eclipsed the course record. Dave was a stunning success, and in his mind, had truly arrived. The lads toasted his success with the enviable aplomb it deserved, and Dave had taken them through to a winning score, which would forever be etched on the club scoreboard. They toasted him with award winning Johnnie Walker Blue, and they settled in for the evening with respective spouses in celebratory style. The day was a complete success and Dave was at the pinnacle of his fame. No one would or could wipe his name off the winners' board, and the course record would stand for many years to come; a stark reminder to his father who would soldier on through ill-health, for years to come and eventually succumb in complete isolation in his grand Mansion on the hill, having died from neglect.

Dave would never inherit the estate as he badly wished for, and could not have ever predicted his fate when at the zenith of his colloquial stardom. No! Dave was to spend an inordinate number of years fighting the justice system which he believed was weighted in favour of criminals, and he would lose his job, his reputation and his pre-packaged family, when suddenly and cataclysmically his world would be turned upside down.

This all happened unexpectedly, when his brilliant idea of retribution went so horribly wrong. His wife, newly married and mesmerized by Dave's glittering success, and potential inheritance, had arrived with him at the golf club earlier that morning, to watch his round. Carla of course was a somewhat stern but aging beauty, who had a teenage son and a myriad of social dilemmas like Dave. She had sat dutifully for the first time ever, and played the doting spouse. She would countenance Dave's rages, for long enough she predicted, to win a handful of that esteemed inheritance that stood forlornly on the hill, a magnet to all the avarice that 'old money' in Johannesburg could attract. Dave had swept into the members parking area, with his sports car roof down, and his smiling effusive family in check. Carla with her already wind swept look, was gushing, and Matthew her delinquent son was chuffed. He sat in the jockey seat behind, his skinny over grown, gangly legs squashed sideways into the sports car. Dave parked in the bay reserved for the club professional, and parlayed with the less fortunate members who arrived with golf clubs in tow, from the parking area across the road. They had all envied his brash manner, and the trappings of a lifestyle they could only yearn for in those glossy covered magazines in the members' lounge. Dave need not bother putting the roof up, as twenty-seven degrees and blue skies were predicted for the day. He would leave the roof down so that the committee members could all lust over this silver toned statement of intent. Dave would be after their positions soon enough, and with his family connections would get the required votes to upstage one of the committee members. For now, they just had to recognize his phenomenal talent on the course, and respect the arrogance of his private school education.

Dave, having left the roof down, had overlooked the inquisitive nature of youth, and whilst the players and spouses were celebrating the enviable round, Martin was helping himself to quick gulps of that smooth looking golden liquid that passed for the real thing. He had purloined the bottle and its contents while conniving to ask Dave, his new step-father for the keys so he could get his jacket from the boot of the sports car. The jacket retrieved, he slipped the three-quarter full bottle of whiskey into the folds of his jacket, and headed across the road and the solitude of the tree-lined golf course. They would find his lifeless body, contorted in excruciated pain later that night, when the car guards would show Dave and the posse now in pursuit, where that teenage delinquent queen, had disappeared. The bottle and its half-finished contents, complete with Dave's finger prints were recovered for analysis.

The Insurance Scam

Jacobus Stephanus Marius Andreas Van Niekerk had been sitting at his desk in the relatively opulent offices of Sassurance International. The company was a massive conglomerate of every conceivable financial services concern, that the old Nat party had been able to accumulate under one huge umbrella. The company had started off by being a rival to one of the oldest companies in South Africa, and had quickly surpassed it, by having the privilege of unlimited resources thrown at it in the form of Government tenders and surreptitious loans. Because it was not a listed company, there was no way the public could hope to know the extent to which this company had grown, utilizing the boundless resources of a very buoyant economy. Gold prices had surpassed the thousand-dollar mark, and revenues for these hard won resources flowed in the form of tax profits and foreign currency reserves.

To say the company was flush would be to understate the case. Money oozed from every conceivable department that the financial gurus who headed the mega-corporation, could dream up. To work for Sassurance had always been a dream of his, but now 'Andre', as he was known to his friends and work colleagues, but not to his mother, was happily ensconced in his twelfth floor office. But there was a small problem. Andre, who had left the National Defence Force after serving four years in the permanent forces; just long enough, that he was able to secure a degree in Psychology from UNISA, and earn his Captain's ranking, before seeing the inevitable turn of events in the country, that would require him to get a jump start on all those other millions of South Africans.

It was 1992, the Mandela era was upon the country, and the start of an attempt to forge a Constitution for the new country was under way. Andre had seen it coming, with the un-banning of the ANC, and the inevitability of a democracy based on 'one man one vote'. He knew it was a recipe for disaster, fully appreciating the workings of the human brain, and that this dispensation only offered one thing. "An opportunity for an emerging class, to manipulate the mass proletariat with promises of land and of dreams of owning their own homes!" He had told his friends that the great drive to democracy would falter on the one thing that the 'Nats' had succeeded at.

"Education." By educating the vast number of the Afrikaans speaking population, the old Government had managed to uplift the voting public, and ensure their success within any new dispensation. When the kids of the townships were busy burning down their schools, and setting fire to their books, because they did not want to be forced to learn the Afrikaans language, they had done themselves a disservice. Andre was very sure that a future in the New South Africa could only be attained through education. "No amount of spewed liberation politics will make a difference! If people are not educated they will fail."

So Andre, resigned from the Army, and having a degree, was a firm candidate for Sassurance. He had heard the discussions in the officers' mess, when the annual visit by the Sassurance man would stir a mass debate of how much they should all be putting into the policies that would be their future. It was ingrained in their twenty-year-old brains. When the Insurance man had visited 'Oom Piet' and 'Tanie Joey' at the plaas, the kids were all packed off to the garden, whilst the adults sat on the stoep and discussed the savings plans they had made. It was an Afrikaans tradition, and had stood them in good stead. When Andre had needed the money to buy his books for the first year of his degree, his policy had been accessed, and the Insurance man had delivered the two thousand Rand he would need from his Endowment plan. This was how wealth was created, and how the commitment to good fiscal policy had been drummed into their lives.

It was 1992, and Andre now sat in his comfortable office, with its standard regulation chipboard office furniture, covered by a bland looking fake oak veneer and high backed red dralon chair. There was only one problem! There was nobody sitting opposite him at his desk, which he would require if he was to sell life insurance. He had a choice. The business could either walk into his office, off of the street twelve floors below, or he was going to have to get out and start knocking on some doors. This was a conundrum, because although studious, Andre was an intrinsically lazy man. He had opted for a degree, rather than serve at the front, like so many of his schoolmates, who had been sent to Angola. This had exonerated him from having to get physical, but had ensured his survival, and his success. The thought of having to walk around knocking on doors was unappealing. He would rather use the phone, and pick up appointments by calling, but who knew him? He was a young man from a Dorp outside Bloemfontein, and who would give him the time of day? Andre needed his own strategy. He was astute, and could recognize opportunities if they presented themselves. But none had. He was getting desperate. This office in downtown Johannesburg was a far cry from the Officer's Mess at 'One Mil', and would require some cultural acclimatization.

The phone rang! It had only ringed twice since he had been in his newly appointed office since Monday. The first was when 'Tannie Joey' had called to wish him every success, and 'Oom Piet' had shouted from the kitchen, 'Vat hom fluffy'. Andre had smiled. The world was his oyster, and these oysters would be the big plump ones they had scavenged on Luderitz beach all those years ago. He was going to make his fortune, and not disappoint the family. This was the second time it had rung. He snapped it up in inimitable fashion, an assertive strain to his voice.

"Good morning, Andre Van Niekerk wat praat!"

There was silence. The phone had gone dead. He held the old plastic Telkom handset away from his ear, looking at it as though by some miracle the silly twirled phone cord might have snapped. Why did they design those stupid cords like that? It only meant, one had to unravel them every few days, by holding the unit by its base, and dropping the head set, so as to allow it to untwist itself, before being able to use it again! What was the point? He held the head set away from him, about to do just that, when suddenly he heard a faint voice from it.

"Hello?" He had the head set to his ear once more. There was a stutter, when the 'poppie' from the reception desk spoke again. "Andre, there is a man at reception. Can you see him?"

"What at reception. That was entirely unusual! He had not invited anyone to his office." Who could it be he wondered? Her voice trailed off. He could sense she did not want to say too much.

He put the phone on its cradle, and lifting himself two handed off the chair with a catapult action from its arms, he headed for the closed office door, and left, to the reception desk. As he entered the open area, he saw a black man sitting on the sofa, but no one else in the reception area. He walked straight up to 'Poppie' who smiled a lopsided grimace of a smile. He furrowed his not so unsubstantial brows. The question was in the quizzical way the two brows met in the middle, and contorted his face to a seemingly obvious answer. "Who was here to see him?"

The 'poppie' grimaced again, and with a not too subtle shrug of her shoulders, and a slight inclination of her head, which seemed to bobble off the top of her elongated neck, she indicated the visitor on the sofa behind him. Andre was now standing between them, and when he furrowed his brow once more, she just shrugged her shoulders. This was very peculiar!

Andre turned, not having said a word, smiled broadly at the man on the sofa, who was now looking expectantly at him. He approached the man, who now got up as he reached the other side of the room.

"Goeie môre", The man offered. Andre could sense the inflection in his voice, and was sure Afrikaans was not a familiar language.

"Good morning!" Replied Andre, offering him an escape from liguistical suicide.

"Hello, how may I help?" Continued Andre. He would be intrigued as to why this man stood here, in this company reception, in 'this day and age', in South Africa. Had the release of Nelson Mandela, so radically changed peoples' perceptions?

"Yes please. May I speak to you about insurance?" The golden ticket! The one sentence every insurance person would ever hope to hear.

"Yes. Of course. Come with me please." Andre lead him to his office, with not so much as a cursory nod to the receptionist. That would have been too unprofessional. He would thank her later, when he got to know her better at the office drinks party they held every Friday evening.

"Please sit down." Andre ushered this man into his office. He had not yet introduced himself. He would do this formally with his business card. The man sat without introducing himself, and waited.

Andre opened his desk drawer pulling out a cardboard box with his business cards still firmly intact. He had not thought to open them previously but this fact might be lost on...." Aagh Ya", he had not yet got a name.

"Andre Van Niekerk", he offered, proffering a card from the box across the desk." The man dutifully got up again from his chair, and replied. "Nkosi. Nkosi Tshabalala." They shook hands. Nkosi's grip was withdrawn and not a full handed grip like Andre's, so he appeared to take hold of only the fingers.

Andre continued, smoothly rectifying the social abyss. "What type of insurance are you after?" The two weeks of intensive training had geared him for the plethora of terms that the instructor had bandied around, and which had their mass of abbreviations. To make one's way through the minefield of insurance terminology, he had figured he would need to know 'each and every one'. There was no doubt these terms would bamboozle the majority of people, but he guessed that Nkosi, may well have not had the same education opportunities he had. Their culture was different he assumed. No one on the course had broached the idea of selling life insurance to 'blacks'. He was in unchartered territory.

"Yes. Replied Nkosi. I want life insurance." He was adamant that he wanted it!

Realising that he would have to dispatch the acronyms into touch, Andre began with the very simple terms. "Yes, life Insurance is there to cover your life and disability is…"

He was interrupted, "No I do not want life insurance!"

Andre stopped in mid-sentence, he looked deep into Nkosi's eyes. He thought he saw a cloud just above the left pupil of his peculiarly dark iris. The other was slightly opaque.

"I want insurance for my wives!"

Andre almost choked. There was no denying he was in completely un-navigable waters. All the years of dishing out his rudimentary psychology to young white serviceman, back from the ravages of Angola, and dealing with post-traumatic stress syndrome, had not unfortunately prepared him for this. A young Afrikaner, with a sense of rage, elicited from seeing one of his buddies blown sky-high by a land mine, was not a patch on what he could encounter here. Those conscriptees would be whipped into shape, slapped around with basic rehabilitation psychology, fed lots of anti-depressants, and packed off back to the border.

"Okay. How many wives do you have?" Andre would now determine if this was a genuine attempt to get insurance, or whether he was just a charlatan looking to bump off his wives, one at a time, and claim the insurance.

"Five wives!" He stated with pride in his voice. The cultural divide had now shrunk just a millimetre.

"Five?" Andre was impressed. He had often wondered, if those men who had multiple spouses in South Africa, then made it more difficult for the other men who had not yet married. He was embarking on what would be an interesting journey. "That must cost you a lot?" The financial ramifications of even having one wife, had ensured Andre had not yet popped the question to his school sweetheart, who had remained his full time girlfriend.

"Yes. A lot." Replied Nkosi. But I am a Shangaan, and that means I must have many children, so that my ancestors can be proud of me." Andre had not known too much about African Religions, "or is it one Religion?" he thought. All African tribes follow the same ancestral worship; he had learned at school. Andre had never given it much more thought! He was a Christian through his upbringing, but was his moral standpoint any different to this man sitting across the desk? That desk may just as well have been an ocean? He resolved to find out more. It was his inquisitive brain that drove him.

"Okay." The formalities now dispensed with, Andre would begin by getting more information. "What is the insurance requirement? How much do you wish to insure them for?"

"One hundred thousand Rand each." He had clearly thought this through already. Andre was relieved, it was not a big amount. He might not have been too happy to assess this one had it been.

"Okay. Is there a reason for why you feel they need to be insured?" Insurability issues were vital.

"Lobola!" The answer was obvious, but had not even been something Andre would have considered.

"Lobola?" Andre needed to know more.

"Yes. Lobola costs a lot of money. Each cow is Two thousand Rand. Each goat is three hundred. The house I must build for each wife is very expensive!" He was making sense for sure.

"So why would you feel the need to insure your wives? Are they sick?"

"No! No sickness." He was quite persuasive. "But if they get this sickness and have many children, they will have much expense."

Andre was not sure what this sickness was, unless Nkosi was referring to HIV and AIDS.

"Yes. If they have this sickness, then I must find another wife. More lobola!" Andre could see that to Nkosi, this was a financial transaction. Nothing more, nothing less!

"Okay. So we have to get them to complete a form. And medicals for the blood test."

"No!" He was adamant again. "I am the husband. I must do this for them. No forms for women."

Andre was not sure if this was going to be possible, but whilst Nkosi explained that his family village was in a remote area and to bring all his wives to Johannesburg would be a big problem, he began to formulate a plan in his head.

"Okay. If they cannot come to Johannesburg, we can go to them." The forms would have to be completed.

"No!" Nkosi was not someone Andre would be able to satisfy easily. "What do you need? I will bring it to you." Andre could appreciate that this was to become a questionable deal, if he did not physically complete the forms with each client. What Nkosi was after was illegal.

"I know what we can do!" Andre was eager to please this man. "If you can bring me a specimen of each signature, and you make copies of their I. D. documents, I think there is a solution to this problem."

Nkosi smiled. He could see that in Andre, he would have a co-conspirator. But he would play this one carefully. Andre was a 'boere', and they were not people to be messed with. "Can I see you again next week?" Nkosi did not want to appear too eager.

"Yes." Andre was keen to get his deals on the books. Next Wednesday same time?"

Nkosi stood up, shook his hand, a more forceful and confident grip. They would soon be making a good living; he had a strong sense of this.

It took all of Andre's enthusiasm to keep this transaction to himself. He did not want branch managers and other colleagues questioning what he was doing, until the deals were on the board, and they would be ringing bells and toasting his success with Sparkling wine next Friday at the weekly drinks session. He would have a Klippies and coke, and raise his glass to a job well done.

The rest of the week dragged on, with Andre making the most of his time by hood winking his manager into thinking he had been cold calling. A schedule was being prepared with all those phantom calls, the referrals, and potential deals lined up. This would satisfy Gerrit his new manager, a bit of a sissy he thought, but would not verbalize. Not yet! He had dealings with the recruits who at 'One Mil' had been assessed as queers, but separated in most instances from the battle hardened recruits, who saw them as a threat to moral. Andre would wait until he was ahead of the game. Deals on the board were the currency of Life Insurances houses. He needed the advantage of a few good life policies, a commission stream, and a willing conspirator, and Andre would be able to hatch his plan.

'His Plan?' "Ahh ya," he thought, 'this was a plan no-one in his office, at least, would be thinking of." Andre had been thinking about how his father, Koos, had run a Stockvel on his farm for many years, before he was forced to abandon the farm due to ill health. Andre and his siblings had been moved to the local dorp to live with his Oom Piet and Tannie Joey, just whilst his father, the oldest son, recouped. He never did, and his mother devastated by the loss, soon followed. She literally, willed herself to death, he thought. The possibility of living without her 'Koos', too much to bear. Andre had not forgiven her, but in Oom Piet, he had found an affable and supportive father figure. This was the strength of the Afrikaner community. They would support family without question. He had found strength in this fact, and later when he decided on psychology as a degree, he realized that he would have the advantage of understanding all these things. He had endeavoured to bring a sense of normalcy to 'One Mil', the military hospital built near Pretoria to handle the medical needs of a growing South African conscripted army. He figured, if he was going to have to serve in this army, he would make the most of it, and rather than spend his days in some God forsaken tent city, on the border, he would study and get ahead.

So the plan was to get as much knowledge as he could, but working as a medic on the 'Psycho Ward' did more to assert his understanding that it was the Jews in South Africa that were part of the problem. They all seemed to have a fit of conscience, when their turn came to head to the border, and some had told him in confidence, that they just wanted to get out of the army, so they could start doing what they did so well; 'Making money'. It was Andre's assessment that the majority, would just want to stay in South Africa, to make their fortunes, then retire to the relative safety of Australia, or back to Israel. The problem was that the SANDF, which was still firmly resolved to fighting the black scourge of communism, in the late eighties, had a zero tolerance of Conscience conscriptee's and Andre was effectively in charge of all of those that found their way to the 'One Mil' hospital, and the psychiatry ward. It was early days, and not a lot was known of these people. Andre, may not have understood their lack of integrity, but he did recognize that all-consuming desire to make money! It was what drove them, and it made sense, when he came to realize, that the only way to survive this harsh world was to be empowered by money. It was the one thing that had destroyed his family, and forced his Uncle to sell the farm, when his father had died of 'bad debts'. His father, 'Koos' had died of a failed life, because the farm he had inherited as the oldest son was uneconomical. The bank had foreclosed on him, taking his family inheritance and their future away from them. Instead of finding alternative ways of supporting an alternative crop cycle, or advising 'Koos' on better farming practices, they simply shut him down. This was as a result of 'El Nino', which had ravaged the Northern Free State, and rendered their farm useless. It was 1986, the writing was on the wall, and the Land Bank was in no state of financial strength to bail out another failed white farmer!

Andre was adamant he would not suffer the same fate as his father, and with a drive, which would hold him in good stead, he determined to make his fortune and save the families reputation. This was his opportunity! He would talk to Nkosi about the Stockvel idea, and he would plough his first commissions back into the Stockvel. The weekend dragged on with the usual rugby to watch and his friends down at the club, partying up a storm. Andre was distracted. He would wait patiently for Nkosi's return, and had prepared a business plan he would show him. Andre had not felt so motivated, since he matriculated, and now he could see his destiny calling. It was tangible; real, like some physical presence in his mind, not a distant mirage, but a tactile realizable goal. He could taste it, feel it; even smell it! It was success, and no person or circumstance would stand in his way. Nkosi was his trump card.

With Monday, easing into Tuesday, and Tuesday seeming an interminably long drawn out series of re-hashing and then again more rehashing of his business plan, Andre had thrown himself into his work. Gerrit had left him to sit in his office with the door closed intent on working it seemed on all his leads. If he had bothered to look at Andre's out going phone calls, he would have seen a problem, because Andre had not picked up the hand set once that week! Other than to answer the 'poppie' at reception's call, to come through to see if there were any sandwiches, from the sandwich lady, that he would like. No, the only other time Andre would pick up the phone, was to answer a call from Nkosi, who had called Wednesday morning, early, to reaffirm their appointment. He was back in town, and staying at his brother's place in Hillbrow. He would be in the city at ten to see him.

"Great," thought Andre, "he is even keener than he had realized." Andre would await his arrival.

When Nkosi arrived, with a briefcase and a stash of money, to pay the premiums, Andre was in business. The specimen signatures were in place, with the identity documents which would need to be copied for his file. All the other necessary details together with a wad of notes, which Nkosi would pay in advance, were handed over to Andre. The plan was hatched, and with Nkosi signing all the forms as the payer, and Andre standing at the window, as he had seen done by one of his fellow doctors at 'One Mil', he copied the signatures onto the forms, by allowing the light behind to shine through and illuminate the signature so it could be traced. Unlike his fellow doctor, Andre was forging these signatures to ensure his financial success, whereas his colleague had done so to forge the signature of a patient who was being sent back to the border, and 'who knows what'! He could justify this in its blatant hypocrisy.

The forms were completed in good time, and Andre would take them downstairs to the 'New Business' department to be assessed and the rudimentary blood tests, which would be required to be arranged. Nkosi would have to handle that function, but that would be a simple process of getting some surrogate recipients of his brother's very profitable rental business in Hillbrow, to take the I.D.'s down to Hillbrow Hospital and get their blood tested for HIV. This would work handsomely for the first few years, and while the nurse in attendance had her back turned, an already completed Indemnity form was switched, and the nurse happily would take the sample and form to be submitted to the laboratory. No one asked any questions in those days!

The number of multiple married men on the books of Sassurance seemed to increase alarmingly, but whilst the premiums were being paid annually in advance, everyone seemed to turn a blind eye. Andre was the toast of the office, and soon was catching the attention of the 'big bosses' in Cape Town. This was splendid, and was just the profile of customer they needed to see them through to the new dispensation that was now in place. Every company director worth his salt was positioning themselves to be seen as leading the transformation of the new fledgling democracy. It was just what Sassurance would need to bring more previously disadvantaged customers and employees into the company fold, and be seen to be empowering the New South African population.

Andre was toasted regularly at the Friday evening drinks sessions and Gerrit, now seemingly invincible that he had the leading salesman in his branch, descended even further and more destructively into his drunken binges, during which he would become extremely hilarious and mince around the office with the appropriate shrill in his voice that alcohol induced. Andre always left early after the awarding of his now insurmountable collection of crystal glasses, of which he had more sets than he would, or could ever use.

The insurance was rolling in, but it was not this that interested Andre. Every last cent he made from the sale of his insurance policies was going back into his Stockvel, and Andre, who had been working full time to bring the Stockvel into the modern age, was spending more and more time with his burgeoning clientele. The Stockvel earned thirty percent interest, at a time when interest rates hovered around twenty. This was not usury; it was good business sense! The clients borrowed the money from them, for new business projects, to buy more cattle, or to send emergency funds to family in need. It was always paid back in a short time, always with the interest and was probably the best business model Andre could ever have hoped to devise. With no realistic limit to how big they could grow it, Nkosi and Andre continued to expand it beyond the family clan, and into the neighbouring villages, with similar success. It was 1995, and the democracy was on a high, with the winning of the World Cup Rugby in Johannesburg. Everyone was on a role, business boomed, and the infectious euphoria could not be maintained. This attracted more and more people to the cities, and Andre was swamped with customers for insurance, who were now living in one-bedroom flats in Berea, and the quickly deteriorating Hillbrow Microcosm of crime and violence. It was human nature at its worst, and the urban decay had begun.

Profit was the motive that drove these new citizens of the Utopian society that had emerged from the middle ages. There was no limit to their ingenuity, and despite the Councils banning Hawkers, the street traders descended onto the streets of Johannesburg and surrounds, with the demand driven informal sector economy firmly entrenched. This microcosm of society was not understood by the authorities but none-the-less was here to stay. Andre was providing the loans to get them started, and with it, the system mushroomed. Andre's business could not have been better. He had now built his dream home into the granite rock of the southern formations of Bassonia, and life was grand. He was engaged to marry, and despite his beautiful 'bride to be' having a rather peculiar pre-disposition to the aversive practice of religion called Jehovah's Witness, he was only too happy to accommodate her, despite certain misgivings. After all, he spent most of his days with people who worshipped their ancestors, and revered ghostly images of dead relatives in frankly grotesque rituals where animals were sacrificed like the ancient Jews had done thousands of years before. Andre had attended his first funeral, feeling incumbent on himself to hand the proceeds of the insurance cheque over to the grieving family, and this would make it alright. He vowed never to attend another when the screams of the bleating goat, sent a demonizing shiver through his body, and the gathered crowd had erupted in union with glee. The ancestors satisfied, Andre handed over what he now considered blood money, and returned to Johannesburg to extricate himself from the web he had manufactured for himself.

In keeping with his desire to make his fortune, Andre now had a dilemma. He could either turn a blind eye to the proceedings that had disgusted him, and given him pause to think beyond what his role was in the premature death of Nkosi's most senior wife; or he could resign from the company, which would cause a storm, and result in an investigation. He could go 'broking' which meant he would give up all the proceeds from his existing business, and if he was lucky, he could convince Nkosi to allow him to stay on as a shareholder in the Stockvel. Fortuitously for Andre he was spared the ignominy of having to resign.

Albeit, that the insurance industry was in a state of euphoric growth, he felt life insurance was not something he had a passion for. It was the same reason that any accountant worthy of any acclaim leaves the Auditing business once they have seen through their training. Andre saw the life insurance business as a de facto form of gambling. No one should ever have to base their future on the possibility of a loved one's death, but he was convinced that it was done, so as to alleviate the pain of financial ruin, that would and had in his case, left families destitute. Andre would change that by moving into endowment policies, as 'Oom Piet' had done so and had proved to be so effective. But not the endowment contracts that were signed for a lifetime so as to maximize the commissions paid to the broker. He would develop a new policy that could be renewed every five years, and which would create real wealth. So as Andre was about to begin processing the changes that would require him to have a change of direction in his insurance business, something happened, which would change his life forever!

Whilst he was happily ensconced in his office Monday morning, working on a new formula for his five-year endowment contracts, a commotion was ensuing in the reception area. 'Poppie' was screaming, there were shouts from unknown voices, and two heavy booted footsteps could be heard approaching his office, down the corridor. Andre's heart skipped a beat. The door was flung open, and two uniformed officers stood in his doorway. They looked him up and down, then turned, leaving the door open and preceded further down the passage. Andre was on his feet in an instant, and popped his head out the office door. The first armed officer had stood at the door of a recently recruited insurance agent, and had requested him to follow him. The second officer was standing with a flak jacket and two pair of handcuffs. This was very peculiar! Andre had not known these new recruits, but the one whose office they were standing outside, was a chap called Andreas. Is that possibly why they had opened his office door so unceremoniously. His nameplate outside his door read, 'Andre Van Niekerk'. Andre waited whilst the second officer stepped into the office, and then two handcuffed men were escorted down the passage past Andre, their heads bowed in shame.

When they were effectively out of the building, and the gawking bystanders had watched them being dispatched off in a heavily armoured vehicle, Andre returned to the reception, and a visibly shaken 'Poppie'.

"What the hell was all that about?" He asked her with incredulous concern etched over his relieved face.

She just stared up from behind the wooden reception console. Another woman was holding her shaking form, but it was not helping. She was suffering posttraumatic shock, so Andre guided her with the help of the other lady, and sat her comfortably on the sofa, whilst he asked the tea lady to bring her a strong, hot cup of tea. A crowd was now emerging from behind their bunkered office doors, slowly peeping their heads, one by one, out of their doors, and walking aimlessly around, asking questions and getting no answers. There was no one who knew what had gone down, and no sign of Gerrit. He was probably hung over and suffering post weekend addiction blues. Where was the management of the other office branch? Andre would go and ask them.

He headed down to the floor below, looking for some management staff. There were hushed voices from behind office doors, and the main administration office was deserted, and there was an emergency meeting being held in the back office of one of the managers. Andre knocked, and popped his head in. They all looked around as he stood in the doorway; ashen faces told him this was very serious.

"What's going on," Andre voiced his concern. They all stared blankly at him.

The manager of the admin department ushered him in, and the conspiratorial meeting ensued.

"We are going to be audited by Head Office," the manager continued. "It appears that two of our new sales staff had been selling life insurance to a random number of black people, with whom they had some employment arrangement. The two in question have been caught in the act, due to their own negligence and greed. It appears that a mini bus load of black workers, whom they had arranged insurance for, had an accident on their way to Mpumalanga, and the mini bus taxi ran over the edge of the road and down a hundred-foot cliff!" He seemed shocked.

"What has now transpired is that the mini bus doors had been locked from the outside and despite the fact that the back was filled with gas cylinders, the bus did not explode. Eleven men have died, but one survived. It appears that he was able to tell the police that the bus had been pushed over the cliff, by these two insurance agents!"

Andre was visibly shaken. He stood at the back of the room, and listened to how the policies had apparently been sold through this office. All policies sold in the last two years, would now be investigated. Andre was panicked. His pulse was racing, as too was his mind. He would now have all his policies reviewed, and the purpose of the insurance investigated. He would have a hard time explaining Nkosi's senior wife's death.

Andre emerged back onto his floor, to the raised eyebrows of all in attendance. They would all need an explanation, and he would have to deliver it. He played it down, in not so dramatic a tone as the manager had delivered the bad news, and in his audience was a few, 'I told you so looks' as the more experienced salesmen could justify why they had not done as well as these two new recruits in the previous months. It was all ego driven, and with this, Andre turned his back on their enquiring eyes, and trooped back to his office, to make sure his files were ready for audit.

Two weeks passed, with no audit, and when Nkosi called to ask why he had not heard from him, Andre simply said, he had been busy. Nkosi wanted to know why the police forensics team had been to his wife's grave and exhumed the body for further testing. He was furious. Andre explained that the police had arrested two guys in his office for insurance fraud and manslaughter. Nkosi was silent.

"What did they find out about your wife's death?" Andre had asked in an absent-minded way.

"She died, in child birth of our seventh son," Nkosi replied matter-of-factly. "She was too old for it, and the baby died."

"Oh!" Replied Andre, expecting the worst. He had fully expected those heavy booted footsteps outside his office door for the past two weeks.

"What did you expect?" Nkosi was inquisitive. "She was not the young woman I married so long ago. But now I can afford the Labola for a new young wife, and many more sons." He laughed uproariously.

"What are you doing next weekend? I am having a big wedding ceremony. I want you to give away the bride. She has no father, and her family will be honoured if you would do this favour!"

The Weekend

"Its lekker man!" Maggie had commented from the front passenger seat. "There is nothing better than my old man with a big fat hairy butt! It's really quite endearing." Rhona laughed, one of those long 'knowingly' shocking, guttural laughs.

"Yes", replied Thomas. "It gives you something to plat whilst he's making love to you." A wry smile on his face.

Maggie screamed with laughter. Prodding David with her long finger nails. He seemed irritated, and kept his focus on the road ahead. The trip would be a long one, and he was now having serious doubts they should have made it.

Maggie could have cared less, she continued chatting away animatedly, her torso half twisted in the big comfortably armchair of a seat, that wouldn't have looked out of place in her big plush Edwardian home in Saxonwold. She would look over at him, every once in a while, looking for his face to contort to the serious non-committal grimace that showed her he was disapproving this conversation. Then she would descend again into the depths of the conversation with Rhona in the back.

The two woman still baited and bayed at their men, unravelling their most private weaknesses, and having a good old fashioned gossip which would keep them entertained for the entire weekend. Thomas would be their co-conspirator, but would spend the days with the men.

The two men just stared ahead. Their thoughts were on those cool mesmerizing beautiful ponds on which the winter Eastern winds sent a refreshingly rich breeze to ruffle the water, but just enough to give it life. Those ponds were their hunting grounds and their seemingly only source of joy right this minute. They imagined the eastern bank with its bramble of foliage, in hues of yellows, tangerine and verdant thickets. They stared ahead and focused on the fish they would catch and the proud display of their boyhood trophies over a good glass of Johnnie Walker late into the night. No! They would talk about 'men things' and leave the idle gossip to the women.

It was funny, but David and David had been colleagues for years, working together on the General ward of the Johannesburg hospital when doing their internship. Their paths had constantly met during those years of adventure, when their prize as young interns had been to bag as many of the young nurses from across the road. Their Friday nights were intent on getting laid, and the Sunnyside hotel was their rich hunting ground. After a binge on beer, whiskey and shooters, they would head back to the club house, in its old Victorian splendour on the hill. Here was where they would frolic naked in the pool, with the girls howling with delight every time one of the doctors in waiting had leapt out the pool to continue chasing the protesting but obviously delighted young nurses, naked around the edge. Those were the days when nothing was sacred. Bare bottoms meant naught, except to the prudish, and they were not in attendance.

Yes, David had met David on the general wards, and together they had been let loose on an unsuspecting public. No amount of platitudes to the expectantly eager faces that stared up at them from their hospital ward beds could reduce the severity of a misdiagnosis based on the exuberance of youth. Luckily, there was always the Doctor in attendance who would remedy any unsavoury attempts at surgery on a gout induced inflamed toe, which may be cancerous, and require immediate surgery to remove it! The men had become instant friends, and they had hit it off despite their different backgrounds. They also hit it off with the young nurses, and they had the pick of the crop to choose from, as the nurses, intent on finding themselves a rich doctor to settle down with, would be easy pickings for the twin David's, who would bed them with the alacrity of rutting stags. The 'Gen' was their rich hunting grounds then!

David had winced once more when Thomas had asked indiscreetly who the better lover was. Their love lives now scrutinized, they would be laid bare by one of their own. But Thomas was a not really one of their own, he remembered! Thomas had never married, and despite that, he was an 'G.P.' David and David had chosen to become Anaesthetists and to spend another five years specializing, so that they could spend the rest of their careers helping to solve the problems of a quickly deteriorating public health system, which was now becoming privatized. The Hippocratic Oath had been largely forgotten by the time these two men had specialized. Now that their private practices based at the two hospitals that had kept them apart for so long, after they branched off into the world to make their fortunes, were doing so well, they could afford to spend time away at the various weekend retreats they had individually invested into. Strangely, despite their geographical separation, they had maintained contact telephonically, keeping in touch to let each other know when they were engaged to be married; when they would be tying the knot, and when their first born was brought into the world. Other than that, they had remained apart, despite the fact that they literally were only a stone's throw away from each other across the Westcliff.

David had chosen to remain on the western side of the ridge, at the local hospital, remaining within the haunts that had been his happy hunting grounds for so long. The Country club, where he had played squash, and where he had met Margaret, who he would marry now he had sown his wild oats, was his domain. They had settled in the family home in Saxonwold, after his father's untimely passing. They had married in his family parish church in Parkview and never been apart since. The second David had chosen to work from the other ridge hospital near Linksfield, where he too had gone to school, and close to where he worshipped. He located his practice close to family who had been at his graduation, and then at the wedding to Rhona.

The two would lead completely different lives, but the camaraderie was still there. David and David had kept in touch telephonically during their rise to prominence in the various communities that housed them. It was their camaraderie and their sense of right and wrong that had kept them in touch. Both had seen the errors of the privatization of all the hospitals, but neither with politically leanings, would be inclined to comment. The large emerging private sector health companies were buying up all the old hospitals, face lifting them in garish blue glass panels, and selling the souls of those that worked in them, for all that the private market could muster. The medical aids were an untapped reserve of revenue, and all that was available in private contracted rates was being charged to placate the needs of the alarmingly high rentals exacted from private practitioners. The system would implode on the very premise that it was designed. The expansion of private medical aid companies into the emerging middle class, who would afford the premiums initially, but find the excesses of the capitalist system too much of a burden to maintain in years to come. David and David had stood steadfast to their oath, and unlike many of their colleagues had determined to make a difference. It was 2004, when with their children now finished their respective schooling, and having ventured to pastures greener, in the First World economies of attractively professional working environments, that the two David's had met by chance at a restaurant in the north. They had struck up a conversation over a combined after dinner coffee with the gals getting to know each other, and had been together ever since. They became soul mates again, understanding the nuances of an ethical life of dedicated service to the medical fraternity, but gaining the strength from one another that the system seemed to have failed to deliver.

They had met regularly since, choosing a restaurant of their choice on neutral ground to entertain their respective spouses. Their bond increased with each passing dinner, and the semantics that this lifestyle afforded them, was what reflected back on a bankrupt system, which was paramount in their minds. Whilst the men spoke of their changing environments at work, and the pressing necessity for a voice of sanity, the two woman, now firmly bosom buddies, chatted about family and friends, and each with the enthusiasm of mothers about to become grandmothers. The distances between them and their children, and the possibility of an annual visit to see their imminent grandchildren paramount in their minds!

The men discussed Governmental policy, the talk of a National Health Scheme, which would exact another tax dollar from an already over-burdened taxation system, and which would supposedly end the misery of an impoverished and failing public health sector. All the good hospitals were in the north, and not even the billions of Rand of taxpayer's money would stem the haemorrhaging of a system devoid of management skills, and intent on self-profiteering of the administrators. The system would implode, but so too would the private health care system, as more and more of those eligible for medical aid cover, but unable to afford it, would opt out and choose hospital cover only. The private funds would be reduced to curtailing the expenditure of the beneficiaries, by introducing co-payments and limiting the payments of badly needed chronic medication. The system would falter on the greed inherent in any system that regarded its rights to fair payment, as a necessity and not a privilege. The private doctors, forced to limit their claims by a shrinking medical aid base, would then find ways of charging for their time, which would challenge the Hippocratic Oath, once and for all. There would be no honour amongst thieves, and no room for the gradually aging medical aid members, whose memberships were not being subsidized by younger healthier members joining. They were all overseas, or unwilling to join a system intent on self-destruction.

Unless, that is, they had agreed, "some alternative system was put in place, or a miracle occurred!"

Both men were devoutly religious in their own way. David being an Anglican, had grown up in the belief that the Catholics were too conservative and corrupt, that the Methodists had no method to their mundane madness, and that the charismatic churches needed their charisma, because they were devoid of all salvation, due to their outwardly obsequious show of devotion. The other David believed. That was enough, and he needed no inducement to go to synagogue because it was his faith, and although he was taught to question everything, there were certain 'sacred cows'. They both recognized the Muslim faith, but neither understood it. Had it been given a bad rap by the American media, intent on finding scapegoats for their own inadequacies, or was it just unfathomable in this modern era? They both understood how religions evolved, both being quietly cynical that their respective religions were often driven by profit motives.

But in truth, their faith was in the miracles they had seen performed in surgery virtually every day of their lives. Not in the neat incisions of skilled surgical operations but in the actual miracles their God had performed. These miracles that had lived, to get up out of bed and had taken themselves home, after unrealistically elaborate surgery! Those were the miracles that had given them their respective religions. Religions which for the sake of society were in the visible pilgrimage to Church and Temple, but that were in 'their' hearts though, more visibly etched in their souls. Perhaps there was something to be said for the grotesque displays of Spiritualism they saw in the decadent shows held at charismatic Church's neither had seen, nor ever wished to, but had heard of?

Those very visual displays of faith often came with ritual healings, and this, in of itself was to be applauded. But were they really what they seemed? No one knew for sure, but faith had a peculiar healing property. As it was, anyone in faith ministries would attest to the power of 'faith healing'. Why was it then that the Hospitals no longer offered the services of Priests and clergy, or even Rabbis and faith healers? These were important aspects of the healing process! Was it that our modern society had become too secular and that the interests of the patient were no longer a consequence of faith, because modern science had all the answers? Or was it, as they believed, that the function of faith and miracles in a business, cut to the very heart of the process of determining a profit. The two were somewhat at odds with one another, or so it appeared.

David and David would sit and debate these issues at length, and over this weekend, they would find in their mutual beliefs, a very pressing issue which needed attending to in the Health sector. The issue of the profit motive versus the very visible display of wealth that came with the private healthcare sector! The vast array of expensive Porsche and BMW motor vehicles that inhabited the 'Doctor's parking' bays at the private clinics. These often could differentiate the worst and the least of the offenders, but in a social hierarchy, theirs was a grand display of everything that was wrong with Capitalism. Where the majority of private patients would have a medical aid cover, they were nonetheless still left with shortfalls after expensive trips to these clinics. No! This was a systemic display of corruption, which required fixing, but how was this avarice to be weeded out?

"There would have to be a complete transition to socialism if we were to see any of that change in the future." David had been standing on the low bank of that tranquil pond, as the mist had hung like a draped woollen shawl over the still water. The reflection off the water echoed the green and brown foliage of the eastern hill, not a ripple evident. A mirror image of tranquillity.

"Yes, but that in itself would be unrealistic!" David had agreed that socialism was a far more beneficial system for Healthcare. "But we have seen enough of a brain drain away from South Africa. That would lead to a mass exodus, like the Jews of Egypt had done when Pharaoh had granted them freedom. His hand was forced by plagues and pestilence in a society that was overcrowded and under-fed! It was that systematic break down in health and wellness that had left the Kingdom in a state of decline."

That was true David had agreed! They had also lost all their skilled artisans and that had led to the ultimate failure of the state. "What would this Government do if that happened?" They knew that Cuban doctors were already being brought in to work in the rural areas, because none of the locally educated doctors wanted to be assigned to those areas. There was definitely no sign of social uplifting in the New South Africa, and that was because of a demand driven society. The skilled surgeons were needed in the Private clinics because the demand was there, and not in rural areas where people were dying from AIDS and related illnesses, and not from cancer. Cancer was a rich man's disease; or was it? There was convincing evidence that as social dynamics were changing in South Africa, the prevalence of 'stress' in society was increasing. Women in particular were becoming affected by breast cancer, and this seemed to be directly proportional to the number of women now seeking medical advice. Where ignorance had once ensured that women folk in the old Apartheid days, never had the opportunity to seek medical opinion, they were now empowered to do so. Where once women would return to their clan, and remain there until they died, they were now finding ways of dealing with health issues, in a vastly under-staffed hospital system.

"But we should be doing more for the poor!" David was in agreement, and they had spoken of a yearly secondment to the area in Limpopo Province, where they had both had an itch to visit. Mapungubwe! Now there was another civilization that had died out! Why? They had a very sophisticated society based around Iron Age craft, with an infinitely more organised social structure than that which had greeted the Voortrekers in their quest to escape the British yoke. The great burial sites that had been unearthed showed a system of communal living, where the dead were treated as the ancestors had dictated. Their gold and precious wealth had been buried with them. The tools and artefacts of an emerging agricultural society had been evident, and there was a definite order.

"The Government must at some stage force the hand of the medical fraternity! There needs to be a system like they have in Israel, where community service is enforced. Otherwise, young interns will just opt for the cushy private practice jobs, we both enjoyed. We should enlist and set a good example!"

"Yes. I would like to do that. Then we could spend some time studying the ruins, and learning about their society." David was an adventurist at heart.

"What on earth would you want to do that for?" They had not seen Thomas emerging from the cottage behind them in a pair of grossly overstated fishing waders.

They both turned. He had his fly rod in one hand and a cup of freshly brewed coffee in the other.

They both looked at one another. They could not be sure how long he had been standing there.

"Because we feel we need to put something back." David had answered him. They all were aware of the shortages of skilled doctors in those rural areas, but somehow the two David's could not imagine Thomas working a locum anywhere other than Sandton. They dismissed his raised eyebrows with the contempt the question deserved.

"Ohh, and talking about putting back, if you do catch anything below a half a kilo, please release it!"

"How will I know that?" Thomas was a very evident first timer. He had no idea what a half-kilo Trout would look like.

"If it's smaller than the span of your hand." Offered the other David. He could see it was going to be a long morning.

"What difference does it make?" Thomas would see a fish as a fish. Good for eating and that was about it.

"Because for sustainability reasons, anything larger than a two pounder is game! Nothing below" He reiterated. They had both snuck out the cottage in the hope that he was still asleep.

"That's it! Isn't it?" David offered again.

"What?" The other David asked. Fully expecting to see something David was looking at.

"Sustainability! That was why those civilizations died out. It is why the Healthcare system needs revising!"

"It is already dying out!" Thomas was at his cynical best. "The fact that modern science is moving so quickly to find cures for everything, is the one factor that will secure its demise!"

The two David's looked blankly at him, and then at each other.

"You see, the point is, modern science is finding ways of curing every ailment with a tablet, or will eventually find an inoculation against every disease possible! With the mapping of the human genome, and genetic modification, every potential disease will be known before it has a chance to kill."

He had a point they realised.

"Soon any cancer will be curable with medicine you can buy over the counter at the pharmacy. People will be vaccinated against dread diseases. Diseases like Alzheimer's will be a thing of the past. Like everything, modern medicine will evolve, and it is just a matter of time before doctors and health practitioners become obsolete! You, on the other hand will always be needed, because until they have found a scientific way of predicting accidents....," his voice trailed off, allowing the thought to settle like so small a speckle on that pristine pond. Its ripple however was yet to be shown!

The Property Guru

When is a property deal not 'a property deal'? This was the question paramount in the mind of Izaak. He had been awaiting a call from the bank, intent on securing the guarantees that would allow the conveyance attorney to proceed. It had not happened!

The office was quiet, and only the constant hum of the traffic on Sandton Drive gave evidence that there were still business activity and people out and about. The winter chill had really set in and there was an air of frigidity that sent a shiver through his spine. The heaters were on, but Izaak knew he was not feeling the shivers of Johannesburg's winter snap, but the shivers of an expectant demise to the business he had helped his good friend and cousin to set up. They had left school with the prize of revolutionizing the property market in South Africa, and wrestling it away from the large Institutions, who controlled the acquisition of land and the issuing of property mortgages. Theirs had been a dream of empowerment and rise to media acclaim, by emulating the great property guru of New York, Donald Trump, who had revolutionized the way developers looked at property into the future.

With the dreams and expectations of youth, they had set out to claim their territory in a society controlled by large Insurance companies and bank CEO's who could dish out their shareholders' funds with the dexterity of an Oprah show. They knew that to get ahead they would need the benefit of a 'leg up', and that was forthcoming from the finances of their uncle, who had given them the deposit for their first building purchase, and with that came the hard work. It was not easy in the early days of pre-revolution economics in South Africa's property market. Group areas restrictions and the limitation of other colour classes to purchase property in 'white' areas had limited their chances of succeeding. After the death of Chris Hani, who had been murdered by fascists who saw his attempts at bringing communism into the political fray, an assault on everything the 'old South Africa' had stood for, it was open season. With the demise of Hani, the door was open for premeditated rabid capitalism, spawned by the returning 'Liberation Struggle Comrades'. With the intention to deny the rampant poverty that existed in post-independence South Africa, they embarked on their self-enrichment schemes. The corruption was rife, but then they had seen the workings of the previous Government of whom, large departmental heads were still in place, to ensure the ease of transition to the new regime, and they learnt from them. It was not long before the corruption and nepotism had filtered through most Government departments, and the process of wealth redistribution was happily ensconced.

This was where deals were to be done, and fledgling Government departments created to dish out the huge reserves of cash that Government exacted from the corporate and middle class taxpayer, had now officially clicked into action, like a faultless Rolex timepiece. The opportunities were there for the taking, and if no one else was empowered now to do so more, Izaak and his cousin were going to make sure they benefited. The tenders for Government buildings, required for the new offices created for the civil service were the first prize. Where large corporate entities had given away buildings they no longer needed, or would have owed too much to the various councils in back taxes, Izaak and his cousin saw the openings for a get-rich-quick scheme. Their tenders were always lower than the other companies who initially bothered to submit, but when it became evident they would not have a chance competing, would not bother wasting their time. So the bulk of the building projects were awarded to Zwangendaba Investments Limited.

Their projects exploded onto the streets of Gauteng, and with ten and twenty year leases being signed on prime property deals, the various banks who had denied access to loans from property developers like Izaak and his cousin, were now falling over themselves to grant loans. The feeding frenzy was well under way, and there was an ironical twist that would render Izaak's cousin raucous with glee. The banks were calling him to get business, but the one bank which was falling over their own coat tails to grant them loans, was a private bank owned exclusively by Izaaks' rivals. Izaak could not have cared less, but to his cousin, it was a point of pride. The property market was booming, and they were growing their business in multiples, with the large signboards popping up all over Johannesburg north. This was their pay back for all the doors that had been slammed in their faces before. Izaak was the first to admit, that he would have preferred to have not had to grow up in a suburb, where he could not venture out at night for fear of the gangs. His uncle, a wealthy businessman, with spazas all across the country, and large stockpiles of cash, from the tax-free proceeds of the informal trading sector, had lent his father the money to buy a house in the new emerging area of Carstenhoff in Midrand. This was where the large family of twelve children had moved, and where Izaak had finally learnt about the segregation of communities in the old South Africa. The property had been purchased in a Trust, so that the true ownership of the land would be hidden from the authorities. Here Izaak had finally made peace with the old system. Not so his cousin!

No! He had a bone to pick with the old system that had deprived so many of his ilk for so long. He was going to get even and he would do it at the expense of all those in the bank, who had been unwilling to see his potential until it suited them. The 'old guard' was to be put in their place, and if he had his way, he would rub their noses in it big time. No expense was spared, in the pursuit of obtaining every conceivable luxury possible. From the homes he built his family in the previously exclusive Sandhurst, to the luxury motor vehicles that caught his fancy, only long enough that they would lose a reasonable value, before being traded back to dealerships who saw these purchases as the excesses of a corrupt system, but which they had no problem trading-in. The whole, ubiquitous process was systematic of another failed system that had only provided benefits to a select few, and would have to be prized loose from their grasping hands at all costs. From the diamond studded cufflinks which emblazoned his initials across his hand made silk weaved shirt sleeves, to the latest Armani sun glasses which gave him the appearance of a bumble bee, but which hid his devious eyed intentions from all those who could not recognize the pursuit of his retribution, he would show them.

There was obtuse excess in everything he did, and he would not let anyone forget it. The majority of his employees saw the brash display of consumerism as his God Given right, and there was no one who would stand in his way. The outward show of bravado, belied an inferiority that was evident from the ceramic 'Glock' sixteen shot handgun he kept on display on the sideboard in his lavish private suite of offices. With bullet-proof plexi-glass looking out onto the towers that paraded themselves on the hilltop above his company, almost appearing to 'Lord it' over him, he resolved to not stop until he owned the lot. To say he was driven would have been to understate the obsession he had. Those Rolls Royce and Aston Martin sports cars were a statement of intent. If to be associated with the wealth of a privileged society of 'old money', meant he had to forego the blatant display of nouveau riche Italian sports cars, then he would do so by opting for the staid, grossly conservative English brands. If he had a chip on his shoulder, it could not be seen below those five thousand Rand dress shirts. Izaak's cousin was all show. For a trader's son he was without exception someone to be respected. But with respect comes the occasional envy. It would not have been human for them not to have been at least partially envious. The bank extended loans that were far beyond the limit of what would make good business sense. They were destined for a big hit, and it would not be Izaak's cousin who would be taking that hit!

By now, he had managed to make serious inroads into the most powerful channels of Government, and it was not unlikely that these contacts extended right to the very top. There were dinner parties at the estate in Sandhurst, and chauffer driven dignitaries whose identities were unseen behind the black tinted windows of large SUV's that would get the neighbours all a twitter. This was the life that had become his domain, and which led one deal to the next to become accepted norm. The expectation was that no degree of failure would be possible, but of course, that had been the case with Trump as well. Izaak's cousin had a saying, each time he secured a new deal, from the rolling hillside golf estates to the large mansions in Sandhurst being developed for business rights. The saying he had coined was "Now trump that," and this became his signature call. The champagne flowed and for a good Muslim boy from the south, he had a lot of thanks to give, when he could on the off chance of a spare moment, answer the calls to prayer Friday lunchtime. No, in fact, he was too busy for that, but Izaak would say his prayers for him, and redouble his efforts to maintain a sense of balance.

The year was 2008, the banks had come under considerable pressure from Government to reign in the issuing of property loans, with the introduction of the new National Credit Act, and there was a sense that the property market may have overheated, with demand being driven by avaricious property tycoons, intent on making a quick buck. Auctioneers plied their trade on every street corner, like the harlots they procured for wealthy landowners at the lavish dinners held in Sandton Hotels.

The market was being driven by greed, and Izaak's cousin was leading the charge. Every auction was attended by his Lieutenants with Gucci sunglasses worn indoors, and slim-line cell phones attached to their overheated ears. These deals were going down with regular monotony, and those with real vested interests watched as properties were snapped up for unrealistically high prices, and auctioneers rubbed their hands in celebration. The 'high fives' were almost as popular a sight as the comrade fisted salutes at a Cosatu rally. The juxtaposition of these signalled the turn of events which would see the exalted being brought down to earth. There was a change in the perception that had driven the euphoric rise of property as a time-honoured investment against inflation. The bubble was about to burst, and it would be a catastrophic bang!

It required a man for the moment to step into that breach, and Izaak's cousin was to be him. The property loans were immense now, and the bank was starting to get the jitters. The Board of Directors could see their annual bonuses being used to fund the non-payment of loan interest, which along with the multitude of unpaid levies and rates for those properties, were becoming a cause for concern, not only with the bank, who owned the titles, but to the councils who were not able to collect much needed revenues. The realistic thing to do was to recall the loans, but they were now in too deep. The only way out was to subsidise the loans by means of a property loan from elsewhere. But who, and what would pay the debts of a property company which had created so much paper that to get an investor interested there would need to be a miracle of sorts. It would come from an unlikely source, but only for long enough to buy the much-needed time for Izaak and his cousin to extricate themselves. It was their contacts at Government level to which they turned, and it was that phone call that Izaak now awaited. His cousin was happily off, playing a round of golf at his estate in the mountains, and would be reached by cell phone once the necessary guarantees were in place.

It was a fait accompli, and if nothing else Izaak had to admire his cousin. He had managed to salvage every deal possible through his undivided belief in his 'God-Given' right to be the man for the occasion. "Cometh the hour, cometh the man," he would proudly announce, with his inimitable sense of humility. But the clouds were gathering on the horizon, and it now appeared that there were some who were not convinced his deals had the merit of a credible Trump deal. It took more than mere belief for his detractors to consider he would pull this rabbit out the bag. It was now that the time was here, that Izaak needed more than ever to convince those around him that they were still buoyant. But it was the mid-winter depression of a cold blustery August wind, that blew the discontent through those offices and which Izaak could feel in his bones. He would find himself waiting by the phone for no ostensible reason. The call was not to come! It was a Friday afternoon, and he should have been at prayers, if not for the strict instruction from his cousin to stay there until the guarantees were in place.

The phone rang! Izaak grabbed it with the brevity of a child let loose on a bowl full of sweets.

"Hello, Izaak speaking!" He was relieved.

"Ah, hello Izaak, it is Martin Brenner from Earpiece magazine. We spoke yesterday?" The question was rhetorical; he knew only too well who this meddlesome journalist was.

"How may I help you," replied Izaak, his sense of disappointment evident from his resigned sigh.

"I was wondering if I may get your comment on the August issue of our magazine, regarding your company's involvement in various questionable property deals." The man was a bull terrier with an attitude and Izaak had been chased by a few of those in his day.

"What dealings are those?" Izaak could play dumb for now. The bank had assured him that no information would be made available to the media.

"Well, it has come to our attention that your company is not too happy about the article we have written, and that there may be a cause for concern from your Directors that has given rise to further questions being raised." Martin was stringing him along.

"What questions might they be? I was under the impression we had answered all your questions in writing?" Izaak would not suffer the temerity of this confounded rumourmonger.

"We just wanted to get your comment on why you have had your employees phone every magazine store in Northern Johannesburg to buy every edition of our August issue? It is very flattering, but we have reason to believe you may want to suppress freedom of expression for some reason!"

"Why would we waste our energy doing that?" Izaak knew only too well that this article could do serious damage to their attempts to secure second mortgages from a select source.

"Well it seems that the Hyde Park, Bryanston and Sandton outlets of our biggest distributor were contacted by a gentleman with a specific agenda!" Martin might not get the answers he was looking for, but he could possibly provoke a newsworthy reaction.

"It might occur to you that we have been very visible in the local press of late Mr. Brenner. If that is any consolation to you, it is possible that one of our rivals might find your magazine of interest? Frankly, we are too busy to concern ourselves with such things. Besides, Mr. Brenner, have you considered someone else might have been inclined to buy your magazine" Izaak had personally instructed his young assistant to collect the magazines he had ordered.

"Yes. It could well be that as I first considered. My attention however, was drawn to the fact that a very erstwhile investigative journalist had reason to call me this morning. He had been notified of a refuse bin marked with your company address, which was pilfered through yesterday evening!" He paused to give Izaak time to consider his remark.

"The contents were alarmingly of interest to me. It appears that our August edition was prominent amongst the refuse. Which in itself is cause for concern? However, it appears that all the magazines were missing page seventeen. Ordinarily I may have ignored this, but that page in particular had a very striking, if not somewhat telling picture of your cousin!" The facts were self-evident.

Izaak remained silent. His reaction would only prove to incriminate them. He would have to talk to his cousin to coax him down off his self-righteous pedestal. That ego would be their undoing.

Nancy's Necessity

Her name was Marilyn, and she could talk the hind legs of a donkey. Well she could converse with any one more than eloquently for sure. Interestingly, the plot she had bought came with its resident donkey's next door, which would suddenly and unexpectedly bray and send the shivers of a ghostly chill down the spine of all those in residence. "The house was haunted", so it was said, and Marilyn had been in residence two years off and on. It was the old Anglican Rectory down at Bathurst, which had fallen into ruin, and Marilyn with the courageousness of her fifty years of life experience had bought the property on a whim. This was where she would retire in relative luxury, and would take time out from her very busy schedule to smell the roses.

"They were an Historical monument, and cannot be dug out at any expense," she informed me.

The Rose bush in question, was indeed two hundred years old, and had very evidently and extremely well laid down its roots in the healthy soil of the Eastern Cape. This was where a thriving community of egalitarian people were living a life that only time and fortitude could deliver. It could be said of this brave and varied community, that there was very little that they could not do. The Sunday morning market sold everything from homemade jams to the phenomenal healing ointments, which would heal anything extraneous. Administered liberally and a good prayer or two later the blemish was gone. In fact, that was the reason for Marilyn to put down her own roots in the eclectic society of Bathurst. The community had flourished in various numbers for two hundred years, and if nothing else, the quaint little town on the road from Port Alfred had given more to the fame of the Eastern Cape, than could be said for its metropolitan areas of Port Elizabeth and surrounds. Bathurst was where it had all started, and Marilyn was keen to show that those intrepid adventurers had not done so in vain.

The 'old Rectory' was somewhat ramshackle, and no one would have ventured into its leaking roof interior, without some sense of adventure. Rumour was that it had been a Witches Coven, a site where dark and unnatural practices had taken place, and where there was a resident ghost. 'Nancy' was her name, and she had been a Nun who had been sent to Bathurst to help as a nursing sister, during the Frontier War with the local Xhosa, who had resisted the settlement of Bathurst and wrought fear and devastation amongst the tiny community. It would have been her duty to tend to the wounded amongst the British soldiers who had been the mainstay against the marauding natives. Nancy had herself been murdered, and it was this legend that had spawned the rise of her ghost. To Marilyn, however, she was no simple legend. Nancy was indeed a co-habitant of this beautifully restored home. It had taken her the better part of five years, but Marilyn had dutifully and diligently restored it to its former glory, at the bequest of Nancy. The home was once more the place where all in Bathurst could focus their energies, and it became the talk of the town. If nothing else it was a symbol of the returning spirit of a town that had fought through native wars, and suffered at the hands of the Boer General Jan Smuts, during his foray into the Eastern Cape to rout the British once and for all from the land. The British had been the scourge of the nation from its birth, and South Africa would have truly been a healthier and wealthier society, had it not been for the confounded British who had laid waste to the Boer settlements in a futile attempt to rid the country of their nemesis.

However, it was just this conflict, which would bring this community together once and for all. Because they had strived and fought for the land on which they now laid claim to their organically grown vegetables, which were in abundance at the local Sunday morning market, the locals had somehow contrived to build a stronger sense of being. This was how communities should exist, and it is the very nature of a community spirit that had allowed this mix of well-meaning town people to co-exist until now. It was their differences that had brought them together, rather than driven them apart. That was what had attracted Marilyn to the area, and had inspired her to seek the assistance of a Spirit Medium in Durban. The woman had convinced her that the decision to resurrect the old Rectory would be well received by the spirit world. Should she renovate the house to its former glory, she would be rewarded by friendship, laughter and good company for many years to come? This was enough enticement for Marilyn, who was a gregarious soul, with a fountain of energy and indeterminable Spirit.

Marilyn had dived into the rebuilding project with the tenacity of a woman possessed. Or so the local town people may have thought, but never voiced as an opinion in those first few years. Marilyn would have made the ultimate martyr, having made her pact with God very early on in her life. She was the inheritor of a family of great acclaim, but had married into the worst of possible circumstances. She had met and married her first husband and conceived her two children in isolation of any true affection, and it was this failure in her life that now haunted her. Marilyn would appease her own ghosts with the ultimate sacrifices of her mammoth fifty years of labour. Marilyn was a Saint to all she came into contact with, and lived an exemplary life, so as to show others around her that her God would forgive all sinners regardless of their indiscretions. She accumulated friends, as a magnet might attract iron filings, but instead of her solid exterior being sullied by brittle and sharp pieces of superfluous metal, she would somehow mould and melt those people she attracted into real and valued forms. Marilyn was the eternal optimist.

So, having spent her entire life's savings on buying and renovating this less than remarkable shell, with its boarded up doors, and dilapidated windows and floors which would have to be re-sanded, she moulded the most historically accurate and magnificently restored piece of Colonial History; but for what reason?

It was said of the little town of Bathurst, nestled in the rolling hills of the Eastern Cape, that the early settlers had arrived there under the leadership of Sir Rufane Donkin, so as to commit an armed force to the eastern extremes of the Cape region, to prevent the Voortrekkers from attempting to settle the area with the help of the French, whom Britain was then at war with. They had disregarded the local San, who had roamed the area, foraging for roots and berries that naturally occurred in the region, and which had been their prized medicinal potions for a millennia and more. No! They had driven the San out, never thinking to learn from them, and instead of embracing their knowledge and expertise, they had harried them away with the pestilence and diseases that they carried ashore from their ships. Rats, which had not been known to the area previously, scurried ashore, like the dirty soldiers that accompanied them. The area beyond the coast, with its cooler climes, and westerly winds, had provided rich soil, and ample rain for their community. The British intent on securing this little known Eden from the rest of the world, ensured their own demise, by settling an area which was in the midst of its own cultural upheavals. The Xhosa tribes, who like the British, had only recently settled the area, had assisted with wiping out the local San, and their thousands of years of history in a matter of years. The Xhosa, of whom Nelson Mandela is a descendent, were war like and as with their Zulu cousins to the north, had been at the forefront of many tribal wars with each other, for the land that was now to become, under dispute. Marilyn, having been born in the Eastern Cape, knew this history only too well, and her love for the Spiritual ancestors that had made this part of South Africa the most spectacular mystical area of the country. People were attracted to Bathurst by the energy that surged from within her myriad of home industries, and the faith of her small, but devout Christian enclave.

The two cultures blended well to provide a history that despite the obvious ecumenical differences of Ancestral worship versus the Christian faith ideal of the resurrection, had proved to Marilyn, who first determined, that her Christian faith, was not at all at odds with the ancient customs of the San. They had worshipped the land, and faithfully tended to their Earth Mother, in their rituals. Whereas, if taken in the context of a Jewish Faith, which evolved through circumstance, to worship a Jewish man named Jesus, who had died for his differing opinion with the Jewish authorities, and then later had been returned to an earthly realm, in a Spirit form, and then ultimately raised to an eternal life of Spiritual existence in trinity with God. Was there any difference with the San? Marilyn could not determine, if there was! After all, the San had spent a long time painting some of the most impressive forms of Rock Art in the world, pre-dating the arrival of the Xhosa, and the British, by almost twenty-seven thousand years. That was twenty-seven years, a long time in any ones' existence, and multiplied by a thousand. That is a considerable period in the history of the known human race, let alone the tribal history of South Africa!

So it was that Marilyn determined to integrate the wealth of Spirituality in her world, with the life of a fundamental Spirituality of the Ancestors. This would go against the very beliefs of a Church stepped in a two-thousand-year-old tradition. But notwithstanding these perceptions, she was convinced that man and spirits would, and could co-exist. But how could she take that perception and change the way people looked at their traditions? It would be a long process, but it required the unravelling of the baggage that a history of unrepentant ignorance had wreaked havoc on her African Brethren. But as with her own ancestry, Marilyn believed categorically that she was a Whafrican, and that her place on this continent, was as integrally linked to the ancestors, as was her Xhosa brothers and sisters. Marilyn would have to prove to them that they had a common destiny, and she would do it with the help of 'Nancy'.

If the cultural worshipping of ancestors was so entrenched in the Xhosa culture, like her San forefathers, then what was so divergent from the truth of where her beliefs came from? The only difference was that Marilyn did not slaughter a goat every time she would have a wedding. She would not sacrifice a cow, each time there was a funeral. No, her ancestral worship was based on the risen body, and the spilt blood of a man who the world knows categorically, had lived and roamed the known world of the time, healing and giving comfort to all those in need. Of that there is no dispute, but what part of that history would people wish to disregard, or which part of ancient Jewish custom would the early Church Fathers, determine to include in the rituals of sacrifice? In other words, Marilyn determined to make an analogy between the two cultures of Faith, that would bring healing and kinship together amongst a society previously divided by the colour of their skin, rather than their true beliefs. This was her mission and her destiny!

The thriving Mecca of Bathurst was to become the centre of a Faith Healing Foundation, and Marilyn would put her heart and soul into helping those lost souls, whose circumstance and hurt had manifested in their frail human forms, a systematic destruction of their bodies called 'dis-ease'. Marilyn would heal them and provide the basis for their renewed Faith, turning her Rectory, once more into the venue, once a year on her birthday, where hundreds, then thousands would come to camp in the fields beyond that grand imposing house, and her friends and family would provide help feeding those in need. It was her Mission, and God had called her to minister to the needy, healing them through the resurgent strength in their own belief in their God. It was her calling and she had waited her entire life to arrive at this point. The little town of Bathurst became the focus once more of a return to sanity in a society that had once defined themselves as the Lords of the land, and negated an entire history of a people, who once roamed these lands in solitude with nature. Two hundred years later, the knowledge of those people would be returned in a delightful show of pilgrimage, and the town people would welcome them with open arms.

Marilyn would finally settle, down a dusty road, at the heart of a land which was recognized for its abundance. It would be this simple act of Faith, which would bring the People of South Africa together to rid themselves of the Ghosts of their past. It would be Marilyn and 'Nancy', who would show them how!

'Nancy' had indeed been murdered, after an illicit affair with a black Xhosa man, who had been imprisoned in the dungeon below the main house. When her impropriety had been uncovered by the soldiers, they had strangled her, then hung her lifeless form in the upstairs room, where she now roamed at night, maintaining her very visible and energetic presence. Instead of chasing away Marilyn and her family, she had embraced them, and now would ensure their safe passage to a place of retreat. Nancy would heal those 'old wounds' of a society divided by social norms, and where her faith had kept her prisoner in that old haunted home for so long, she would finally fling open the doors to a new and revitalized energy in that home she had once loved so passionately. The Nun had returned in the form of Marilyn, who would tend to the sick once more. It was the ghost of a past that had once been responsible for murder and mayhem, where a lonely gravestone stood, to commemorate the murder of a young soldier, "Treacherously murdered by Kaffirs in a time of peace". No wonder the country and this quaint society had been divided so long! It was now time by necessity, for 'Nancy' to offer her healing once more and it was remarkable that everyone who visited Marilyn, was healed of their illnesses.

An Explosive character

There was no one who could doubt the very explosive character of this man. He was never late, but would always ensure his arrival into a room, was timed like the destructive chemicals he purveyed. His name was Oswald, an unfortunate coincidence, but he commanded a room, with his mountainous presence and his unflinching belief in himself. His father had said to him as a child, "There is money to be made in other people's shit." This would be his calling card, and was how Oswald would get started in business and ultimately lead to the chemicals game.

It all started, when Oswald, an out of work school dropout, had seen an opportunity from his father's farm in the Free State, to deliver a trailer load of manure once a day to a market where he would bag the stuff, and sell it onto homeowners who needed mulch and manure for their gardens. Johannesburg and Pretoria were veritable Gardens of Eden in a land, where once nothing but grassland and the occasional acacia tree existed. Now it had become the largest man-made forest on earth, and literally had generated its own climatic changes to the Highveld. It was the sustenance of his manure that was so badly needed in the gardens that proliferated in this vibrant biosphere. Winter rains, and summer deluges often arrived without warning, and weather forecasters had their work cut out predicting the arrival of these weather systems. Because Gauteng was perched on the edge of a natural physical divide, from which the summer rains would either wash southwards several thousand miles to the Atlantic Ocean, or northwards a further thousand to the Indian Ocean, it was considered a proverbial watershed and an example of the most phenomenally diverse region in the country. This was where fortunes had been made and lost, and where Oswald would seek to make his.

The gardens were in abundance, with all manner of invasive plants now growing in the extravagant stretches of suburbia and reaching ever upward into the ether. The sun, which drew them with sustained voracity, was prevalent almost three hundred days of the year. The soil although considered to be capable of sustaining only a Savannah type ecology, had been altered by the addition of these manures and chemicals. The invaders into an ecological system, where ground water had cleaved the deep furrows of the Braamfontein Spruit and where the other tentacles of river systems, had leached through the shallow top soil, now found their way into the underground river systems. This was aggravated by the run-off water from the considerable low cost housing developments that proliferated in the demand driven post '94 jubilations.

Gauteng was simply sitting on top of a veritable 'powder keg', and the various underground water channels, were fed directly into the vast network of tunnels that ran for thousands of miles under the heart of Gauteng. The mining companies had left this sinister web of tunnels unattended when the gold reef had naturally run out, and now these tunnels were slowly filling up with water. Instead of pumping the old disused slurry from the mines back into these deep cavernous warrens, the mine dumps were being reclaimed for whatever gold could still be extracted. The waste material was being used for building material and the mining bosses, who had taken the necessary shortcuts to ensure their own financial gain, now watched as Gauteng sat on top of a neatly primed explosive den.

Unbelievable as it may seem, these gold mines had managed to extract a total of one thousand five hundred million tonnes of rock from the earth since 2000, which was in itself a remarkable feat. Compared to the building of the first Jumeriah Palm development in Dubai which was ninety times more in volumetric weight, this was extraordinary, because the mines were digging to levels four thousand meters below ground where rock temperatures were sixty degrees Celsius. This was why the scale of this endeavour was all the more notable. The mining industry was now reaping the rewards of a high gold price, but the industry in South Africa was nonetheless in decline. Compared to thirty years ago when South Africa produced two thirds of all the worlds gold, it had now reduced to only nine percent, and even Australia was producing more gold in tonnage. The heyday of South Africa's gold mining was over and she was no longer the strategic power that commanded the economic world's attention. Subsequently profits were paramount and costs needed to be cut. This was where the problems started.

The Government had little incentive to force the mining companies to attend to these obvious procedural failures, because the revenues they garnered from the thirty percent taxes these mines offered had given them reason to turn a blind eye. But the problem was that these shortcuts were now feeding into the water table of the area, and Gauteng was literally sitting like the 'old Houses of Parliament', on a ticking time bomb. Despite the concerted efforts of environmentalists, Gauteng which housed ten million souls from the eastern extremes of Nigel, where the reef had disappeared deeper than any mines on earth, to the western towns of Krugersdorp and Westonaria, where the vast array of tunnels ended, some hundred miles in length, was a disaster waiting to happen. The city was perched on top of a 'Mechanno set' labyrinth of these tunnels, ready to collapse, as more water percolated into them. Even the hard granite rock of the Gauteng ridge, that stretched across the breadth of the megatropolis and cordoned the north from the south, could not indefinitely contain this morass of soup-like chemicals, ready to poison the city.

The authorities had never acted, because it was not their dilemma. They had inherited this mess from the previous Government of which, Oswald was an ardent supporter. He had tried his hand in politics, but most people had found him too abrasive, and his manner had divided the supporters of the 'old regime' rather than gather them together. Sticking to his business ethos, like a proverbial piece of excretion to a blanket, he had continued to make his fortune in a demand driven society, where no limits were formulated. The city expanded and attracted more people from the rural areas, and as with the fables of 'city streets lined with gold', they kept coming. From everywhere in Africa they came, and the demands placed on the infrastructure was untenable. Sooner than later it would implode, but that was not his problem!

No! Oswald was not the man who had created this dilemma, but his myriad of Business trophies awarded over a newsworthy business career, attested to his ability to think laterally, and he began to add to the problems that would impact on this future geological catastrophe. When he had founded his chemical company, off the back of his manure business, Oswald had seen the potential for the mining industries requirement for explosives. So with all the ingredients of the greed that spawned this race for financial gain, he set up a factory in the industrial area to the east of Jo'burg and with his contacts in government soon found, he had a captive audience. The company thrived during the years of Apartheid, when it was difficult to get the required explosives, from an international community, only too happy to buy the gold. Where their explosives had helped render the gold from the guts of Gauteng, all remained equal, but they were unwilling to become embroiled in the politics of supplying a Government of the day, which shot and killed its detractors, with ammunition which was manufactured using their gun powder. So Oswald slipped into that breach with the inimitable flourish of a visionary and soon had large contracts with all the mining houses. They procured his explosives, without fear or favour, and the financial reports kept everyone happy, including all the offshore investors.

Oswald was certainly no apologist for Apartheid, and he believed that the Government of the day had been given a bad rap by meddlesome journalists, looking to profit from negative publicity, and he could not care less, who knew it. He simply took these meddlesome journalists head on, when an opportunity arose, and with the faith that an education in the 'old South Africa' afforded him, simply blew off his detractors. He was going to make his fortune no matter how badly the international press deemed his Government to be, and how badly his business practices might be. It was 1986, and the writing on the wall foretold a somewhat different story, then that which Louis might have wished to portray. Any attempt at re-writing the history of Apartheid, was not going to help this larger-than-life business mogul. With the infamy of his namesake, he was going to make his mark on this world, and no one or any factor was to stop him.

From his forays into politics, to his brazen attempts at laying claim to a sporting heritage, he could neither understand, nor emulate; Oswald was involved. He made it his mission to paint the Apartheid picture as attractively as an 'old Thomas Baines' landscape. But no matter how, his attempts were met with the incredulousness that a history of neglect would instil, in a population just intent on getting on with the process of living. They wanted to get to work, make an honest day wages, and get home to their families. The 'Utopian' picture that he wished to portray was a figment of his own imagination. What was not, was the real crisis that lurked beneath his feet, and filtered ever further into the sub soil and deeper even to the places where men had toiled in staggering heat and confined working environments for so long. It was where lives lost in the pursuit of that golden treasure, now haunted the darkened tunnels. There where, their rotting timber posts, and the ever rising ground water levels, which crept ever upwards, awaited a day when it would wreck its vengeance on a society lost in the pursuit of profit.

Oswald had a lot to be thankful for. He had retired happily to his coastal palace, and with a lifetime of achievements, would now be partially responsible for the devastation that would ensue. No manner of Apartheid Reparations would or could ever make up for the destruction, still to be wrought. The entire Gauteng infrastructure was about to be laid to waste, by the greed that had allowed these entrepreneurs to wrestle the profits from that ancient soil. On the surface the utopia of a forest, as seen from the ridges that formed the backbone to a geological treasure, seemed to belie any undercurrent of discontent. But nature was staging its revolt, and the environmental destruction that bubbled and festered below, would soon begin to raise its ugly head.

Peter the Pumpkin eater

He had a nose that reminded one of a beak. Not a short sharp beak like those on seed eating variety birds, and not quite as long as the 'Common Ibis' or 'Hadeda', that frequented his Northern suburbs garden. More like the carrion eating, flesh tearing beak of a predatory bird. In fact, that was exactly it; his nose reminded Gillian of the 'Bald Eagle' caricature of 'Muppet' fame; the baldhead, descending into those sharp, narrow set eyes and that aquiline beak. It was hard to look past it, and this had always been a major source of embarrassment to the firm. So much so that they had kept Peter away from the clientele, and particularly the young male recruits, who had joined the firm so as to sit out the next two years, write 'The Bar' and hope to reach stratospheric careers in the world of 'Law'. Gillian had seen past the physical deformity but although working for Peter as a legal secretary, she knew how complex a person he could be!

It was this environment of law that was to be their practical learning ground, but it was a far cry from the glamorous, sexually explicit soap dramas evidenced on prime time television. The truth was not as sordid as those one hour long, advert filled 'soapies'. In fact, the relative truth was that the real world of 'Law' was about as action packed as a mid-afternoon siesta on a winter day, in the seclusion of a wooden cabin in the Underberg. There was about as much substance to 'real law' as there was to those soapies. Take away the advertisements and there was probably about half the time crammed into that one-hour show that actually dealt with the story. Take away all the sexual innuendos, the snide remarks, and the searing looks intended to melt adversaries in their tracks, and there was probably about half as much again in dialogue and content. But that was the point, wasn't it? Law in the real world was a fine line between the barbed comments of 'combatitive' attorneys, and the humdrum daily paperwork of an over-stretched legal system, that favoured the rich, who could afford to employ firms like the one which Peter worked for. With its troops of loyal clerks, who would trudge away each day in a series of paper pushing exercises, determined to knock the incentive out of any well-meaning aspirant attorney. No! The system was about as effective as the dinosaurs who created it, and it was time to revolutionize it!

How could it be, when the legal system had been installed all those years ago? It was designed to deal with a Colonial heritage, that was favourable to a privileged class, intent on ensuring the 'status quo' of their dispensation. It was exactly this scenario that had allowed the systematic failure of one culture to understand this legal process. Whereas, a select few were able to profit from the complexity of these practices, the vast majority could neither understand it, let alone afford its 'so-called' benefits. It needed to be overhauled, and in a country on a continent, which had its own ancient legal system, the advantages of overhauling it would be staggering. Over fifty million people would finally get to be part of the arrangement, and not remain some disempowered spectator. Like those millions who sat glued to those television sets, for some titillation on a boring Monday night, so too did millions of South Africans sit in cold lifeless courtrooms, blankly watching proceedings, while a bunch of less than inspiring actors, mumbled their words, usually to a litany of terminology they also vaguely understood.

This was not the arrangement that would, or could ever hope to work in a country, populated by a majority, whose ancient traditions were learnt in the rural area, and where that system had worked effectively, if not somewhat brutally for thousands of years. The 'old Bantu legal' system had been scrapped, in favour of a 'Roman-Dutch' scheme that offered the ordinary citizen no real benefits. The legal process was too arduous, its machinations too unwieldy, and the sheer weight of the legal backlogs threatened to swamp it. Like his 'old caricature', Peter understood, along with all his cronies that they were grasping onto the remnants of a structure which threatened to topple over under its own inefficiencies.

The rising number of retributive mass justice cases was soon beginning to overwhelm the system. Day after day pockets of a population of disenfranchised South Africans, took their wrath out on the very system which the colonials had instilled to protect them. They felt the burden of a slow and inefficient legal system which operated to profit a select few, and they revolted. It was becoming common place in South Africa to see clandestine vigilante groups burning down the houses of known criminals that the legal authorities could not seem to come to terms with. The corruption was rife, the justice system top-heavy and the people frustrated. They began to seek their own communal form of retribution and normal peace loving citizens themselves became judges and assassins. All the while Peter sat in his opulent office, with a private bathroom and the trappings of a 'made for Hollywood' set.

But 'cometh the hour, cometh the man', and he was there in all his bluster. The two would now stand toe to toe, sparring with jibes, insults and bravado, in the only way they knew possible. They stood, juxtaposed by a history that had cleaved a division between the two fundamental principles they stood for. On the one side was the 'old time honoured 'legal system installed by the Colonialists, represented by Peter, and on the other, the ancient Bantu system of 'village courts' that had been used for centuries before the arrival of the 'white' man in Southern Africa. Those ancient judicial systems were not without merit. But John, who had been a powerful advocate of some transformation in the legal system, was going to have to use all his guile and every ounce of his bluster, to remedy it!

The two were worlds apart in their thinking, and for John, who represented the 'black majority' who had never been given adequate representation in this archaic system of Roman Dutch Law, he felt it incumbent on the judiciary, to change it from the top down. For him it was a matter of principle that the system he now fought against be rendered obsolete. The problem was that the society in which he lived had also transformed itself during those years he had spent studying the law, so that he could become a High Court Judge. From there he had laboured under the immense pressure of a legal system bankrupted by the avarice of its proponents. It was no longer possible to get a credible defence without the cost of a plethora of legal advocates. So with his objective in mind, John set about bullying and manipulating those around him to achieve what he desired. The way forward was to fight the 'Peter's' of his world with the only power he had available to him. "Intimidation!" Everyone who came in contact with him could see the makings of another megalomaniac. But try as they might to discredit him, they could not. He had received a favourable seal of approval from above and this would stand him in good stead.

Problem number one for his detractors! The system John so vociferously wished to transform could not be done so easily. The legal system was so entrenched and people like Peter had too much to lose to allow it to be reformed. No! If there was to be a way forward then it would have to be done surreptitiously, with John calling on all his political favours, and ensuring that the message was filtered down from the top. The judiciary was supposed to be 'Independent' of the State, but that was in an ideal world. Like Mugabe to the north, the legal system was designed in just such a way, that through political coercion, incentives and all manner of politic-mongering, the 'Swiftonian' idea of the Law being a process of "the ability to argue that Black is White, and White is Black", had never taken on such a real meaning until now. They stood in their 'proverbial' corners, and it became a very racial issue. John was the archetypical 'reverse-racist', if ever there could be one. His attacks on his judicial colleagues took on a very specific racial slur. John had a chip on his shoulder and no amount of rationalizing would be adequate to contain it. The barbing and slandering continued, and in the time-honoured tradition of egotists, John would finally get his voice heard, making it clear that with the help of a system he despised, he would find every way of beating it. The saga continued like a typical 'soapie' and John and Peter took their opposing opinions as far as any satirical 'made-for-TV' series could!

It was episode twelve, in the third season before the two protagonists would meet again in the very public domain of the media. John, in the one corner representing his African roots, and Peter in the other doing his best to appear professional. Like two leotard resplendent wrestlers, they were now going to have their day. But it was not to be in court! The bouts were laid out in the media, one day at a time with a division being drawn, ever deeper and ever wider between the respondents. Peter would not yield to the racial slurs, and John would not succumb to an age-old tyranny. The fight was a bitter wrangling between two superior beings. One with the confidence of a three-hundred-year old antediluvian legal prowess, that only education and elitism would countenance; the other with political support and a very visible prerequisite from above. The system had to be transformed, but how would they do so, and would the winner take all the glory, or have to find some adequate compromise?

Peter it appeared, would have to concede in some way and eat humble pie, whilst John would brazenly continue with his vain attempt at transformation. But Peter was the epitome of a lawyer, and also had his price. He could switch allegiances and with the suppleness of an octopus. He had learned in his time to squeeze in and out of any crevice, and this would not be any different a scenario. John on the other hand was becoming, not only an embarrassment, but a political liability. Unlike the dispute resolutions of the ancient Zulu Nation, where Dingaan had been forced to abandon his attempts at unseating Chaka, there was no such room for a solution to this impasse. John had become such a liability that it would be necessary to dispense with him in due course. The prized seat he sought was on the Constitutional Bench. Here he would be able to barb and bully his opinions through the highest echelons of the legal system, and where he could have his opinions heard in a very real way! But with time-honoured petitioning, he had had his 'day in court', and like the 'good ol' boys' that maintained supremacy over mere mortal High Court judges, he was not welcome. So, with the creative genius of a drama filled weekly episode of Law and Disorder, the screen writers and Director would have to side with the incumbent, and side-line the challenger, for now. Would he receive the benefit of a 'Golden Handshake' and go quietly? Or would he have to be removed more surreptitiously? Only time would tell, and season four beckoned.

Craving for mud

The French have a lovely saying, 'Nostalgie de la boue' which literally translated from French, means 'craving for mud'. The meaning is an attempt to poetically explain why someone would long for a depraved way of life, instead of an accepted value based system that is universally accepted by the majority. It is in the new frontiers of society that these ideals and social norms have evolved. Sometimes I think back to the nostalgia of that homeland, stretched across the vast, perennial Limpopo, where the first Pioneers, had forded the river, at low tide, during the months when the river ran low. They had stretched the limit of their known world, in an attempt to seek more land for the Queen and the British Empire. Under the guise of a forward expeditionary force, funded by Cecil John Rhodes, the pioneers struck across that wide Limpopo River in an attempt to create this new frontier. That land was where men had gone before, but they had settled there, hundreds of years before in a very similar turn of events. Displaced by his disagreement with Shaka, Dingaan had taken his Ndebele, and followed a very similar route. They had settled, just as the tribes from North Africa had done for countless centuries before, not as some historians subscribe to as typical land invasions, but simply by acquiring land that was arable, on which to plant their millet crops to feed their clan. They would then move further and further south as the Sahara Desert expanded and their shifting cultivation methods rendered the land fallow. Until the arrival of the settlers with their more sophisticated farming practices, the land was being eroded by a number of significant factors. The slash and burning methods employed stripped the top soil of its natural vegetation and the resultant crop planting stripped the sub soil of all its nutrients. The land devoid of life became valueless and so the clan moved on. The Ndebele displaced the tribes that occupied the south of Zimbabwe, bringing their cattle with them and they in turn were displaced by the Pioneers. So it was that the new Zimbabwean Government would feel justified in displacing the farmers who now occupied that land. Some would enter into agreements with Mugabe to trade part of their land for a portion thereof, transferred into some Government official's hands, while most would be forced physically from their land by greedy opportunists simply backed by an unregulated system.

It is a natural accomplishment for man and woman, to seek beyond their recognized parameters of endurance. It is what keeps us sane, and prefers us in the realm of natural selection, to stretch ever further into the void. The pioneers were just such opportunists, dealt a low blow by a Government which traded on racial intolerance as its hall mark of power retention. The majority of these settlers treated their employees well and the diseases that had kept the populations low were erased from a land of great prospect. Instead of embracing the evolution of the country and greeting its history with the merit it deserved, the leaders of post-colonial Africa had simply tried to erase any vestige of the past. Denying any of the ills that had occurred, those leaders also ignored its contributions. Left to his devices Mugabe would drag that once 'bread basket of Africa', to becoming the begging bowl of the region.

William was just such a man, but would not countenance any detractors, and he cared less for the political correctness of that age. It was cash that dictated his morality, and invariably everyone he came into contact with, bowed to his greater determination. It was not sufficient that he stretch himself, but needed to stretch everyone with him or dispense with them if they resisted. Circumstance and time would erase his detractors, yet William would forge ahead and meet his challenges head on.

Who was this man, I hear you ask yourself? This is the age-old question. He, or she, is that one person who lives down the street, or across the road, and in one monumental moment of inspiration, or more acutely, aspiration, had got up, picked themselves out of their average lives, and followed a destiny of notoriety. How can we now criticize them so irreverently, after a lifetime of achievement led them to the goals they so desired? We cannot, because by doing so we simply give into our weaker innate sense of fear. After all, we are all human, and to fear is perfectly normal. It is the rationale that kept us timidly ensconced in our caves, until the early dawn, evoked our pride, and set us free from our cave-mentality. It was just such a sense of freedom that invoked the Pioneers, to go beyond the great expanse of sand and rock, with horse and Royal Enfield, their only advantage. But go they did!

So why are they criticized and given so little acclaim in our post-independent Africa. Is it because we secretly fear the ill that was wrought on the tribes that resisted them, was so unconditionally evil. Was it really? It was not the early settlers to whom we should look for the blame that recent leaders must attach, but the system that had installed them for their thousand-year reign. No! It was not those intrepid adventurers that should take the blame, but the malice of administrators who came behind. In every society, you have your Courtney Selous' and you have your Wrathalls'. They equally should share any blame, if blame was to be apportioned, but they all are now reviled in a system, that itself is so obtuse that the world can barely stand back one second longer, and watch its implosion.

But watch they must. This is because it is repugnant to try to criticize a system which once had the moral high ground. Mugabe was once above reproach; a liberationist whose ideals were to enfranchise his fellow Zimbabwean's with hope and dignity. That failed dream was due to the corruption of his mind. Where once he had held lofty ideals of a resurgent Zimbabwe, he now, held onto whatever hope he had of keeping power, in the vein chance that a miracle might occur. The real power brokers were the men who had corrupted him with money and power. They were still pulling the strings of this puppet regime, thirty years after liberation. The resident 'Lucifer', we all so fear, was not Mugabe, but the men like William who held the purse strings and piped the tune. They are the shadow that lurks beyond the flickering fire light, to which we all retreat. But it was no coincidence that Mugabe should be the one we should all fear, for he allowed himself to be dragged into that mire, and his face now covered in mud, he had no possible way of escaping his reality. Behind every failed state, there is something or someone that must have benefited. No the name that hung on lips in testament to his enduring reputation was William, who would seriously fit the 'bill'. It is he who now dictated through his influences the process which governed the failures of that country. It is he that would live larger and more obscenely than any other in the history of this hundred-year-old tragedy play.

William was the one man that had recognized the opportunity that so many of our lost countrymen have so aspired to. He would stretch out his hand in return for a similarly returned acknowledgement of favours. This man who had lived large and above the law for so long! But who was he really?

William had been born like any other South African, in a land where opportunity abounded. His name somehow evoked vilification by some, and admiration by others. He had lived the life of the great explorers, in a modern day setting, and he would either be remembered fondly by those who recognized his true determination, or he would be shot and his reputation sullied by his detractors. He was like the treacherous General Frohm, who would turn on his allies, and like the predecessors of Hitler's Europe, would condemn Colonel van Stauffenberg to a military court martial. Mugabe was the Hitler of Africa, and the Corporate World which hung in the wings waiting for the inevitable 'suicide', were the Valkyrian Inner Circle. They had time on their hands, but were not the admirable heroes of Norse Mythology, who would be conducted to an afterlife of feasting and heroic deeds. No! In point of fact, there was no Odinian maiden, much less twelve! The heroic deeds were not to be found, but there were twelve 'Corporate Big Shots' who were about to get their justice. They schemed and plotted from their lofty offices in Johannesburg's financial district, but they were not to know the extent to which William would engineer their demise. Were 'Frohm' had been the loyal General, who took his opportunities and prospered under the old regime, so to would William. It was just such a scenario of treachery and deceit that would lead to Court Martial of the 'Twelve', and their destination would not be Valhalla.

William had made fortunes in the old South Africa, and his family were well heeled. The thing about William was he truly encapsulated the pent-up dreams of a nation of intrepid pioneers, who secretly would want to emulate him. He lived the rich and fruitful lifestyle of aggressively pursued wealth, but it always came at a cost. For William to succeed, he had to have the support of highly influential individuals. It was this reputation that would ultimately seal his fate.

William had spread his influence throughout Southern and Central Africa, and his freight and haulage company would do business with anyone prepared to pay the 'ferryman'. But as with the lyrics of that great Chris de berg song, it was wise to, not pay William, until he got your goods to the other-side. He would double-cross anyone who stepped irreverently onto his territory. There was no Van Stauffenberg in this story, no hero to copy! The only similarity the story had with its Second World War heroic actions, was that Mugabe, like Hitler was their all-consuming focus.

William shipped anything, anywhere and was intent on expanding his trucking empire far afield. He had been in transport, and it was not a far cry for him to get his hands dirty in any other deal that might come his way. So it had transpired that a large Eastern car manufacturer was looking to make 'inroads' to the Southern African market, which with its extensive road networks, and burgeoning economies, was plum for the picking, for any new motor car manufacturer. William could sense an opportunity, and with the courage of his convictions, stepped up, to make his mark. The manufacturing plant for these 'SKD's' or semi-knock-down vehicles was going to be north, and in a prospering area of Southern Africa, which had offered worthwhile tax incentives for this new employment opportunity. The crates of SKD's would be shipped north, and reassembled in this dust bowl society, governed by true Capitalistic ideals.

William's partners were nameless and faceless, but had no idea that behind William's profit motive, laid yet another sinister ploy. The SKD's were destined for a South African market, but in order to get them to the south, they would have to be transported by large carriers. This was easy, as William already had the transport company to make that possible. What his partners-in-crime were not to know, was the true extent to which this crime would pervade the South African market. William was the epitome of a racketeer, and those assembled vehicles were to him, merely a convenient way of smuggling all that contraband that was destined for South Africa and the lucrative markets it represented. From uncut gemstones that would find their way onto the streets of Johannesburg and the Jewish quarter of the north, to the drugs that shipped in through Central African Airfreight terminals, and then were repackaged for the club scene in Sandton; anything contraband was transportable. William was making his fortune and the new motor vehicles were speeding out onto the slowly over-crowding city streets. Along with the millions of refugees displaced by the unflinching Mugabe regime, South Africa was becoming overloaded. But overloaded or not, William continued shipping!

It was only when a very senior police official, funded by a less than salubrious business tycoon was side-stepped in this feeding frenzy, that William's activities were uncovered for convenience sake. The treachery was insidious, and those that had attempted to unseat him took full advantage and the Asset Forfeiture Unit stepped in and William's South African assets were impounded. This remarkable turn of events just inspired him all the more, and in Hitler, (sorry Mugabe – one can tend to get carried away!) William found a common ally. Mugabe had turned to William and offered him sanctuary in return for his unfailing loyalty, and thereby history was rewritten. William would re-write the colonial relationship between monster and morality and William would ensure all of Mugabe's desires were fulfilled. From the

Italian marble staircase of his new insanely decorated Villa in Harare's wealthy north, to the luxury jewellery turned from those uncut gems that found their way into questionable craftsman's workshops in Sandton, William was living the life he had always dreamed of. No one cared anymore! He was no longer a blight on the skin of a fledgling democracy intent on showing the Western world how educated, industrious African's should live. William was a faded memory, but his influence still persisted.

So it took the greed of an erstwhile trader in Johannesburg, who had seen an opportunity to trade in Cobalt from the 'democratic' Congo. William had seen it coming. Some get-rich-quick entrepreneurs in Rosebank, had determined to get out of a financial hole they had dug for themselves. So with the brave, but stupid Greg as their patsy, they set off for the DRC, and a contact in Kinshasa. Arriving in the late afternoon, with a simple transaction to complete, Greg had met with a rather unwelcome reception committee. A go-getter with a failing career as a Merchant banker, and a failed career as an accountant, Greg was willing to try his hand at anything. With one lawsuit against him for a reverse take-over and asset strip of a listed company, Greg was in good company. But it was not the company he would have settled for in his gentile lifestyle home on the Braamfontein Spruit. The meeting was a set-up, and Greg, with a briefcase full of dollars, was soon a target for William's accomplices. They would take the money, have Greg arrested, and walk off with the loot. No cobalt was to change hands, yet Greg's partners had known that all the time. It had been a set-up from the beginning, and the partners who were in banking, had provided a wad of counterfeit dollars. Greg was incarcerated in a dingy cell and given one phone call. Luckily, for him he was released, when he had a nervous breakdown and could never again look anyone in the eye.

William was furious. The cash found its way back to his plush office in the Hotel in Harare. "Was there no honour amongst thieves?" Those responsible would have to watch out, as they would get their come-uppance. However, William had bigger fish to fry, and his dealings with the South African's could wait. He was monomaniacal and this obsession would eventually be his own downfall.

However, William was a patient man and he would wait to seek vengeance on those who he believed had double-crossed him. He would bide his time and pick them off, one after another. It was his inability to remain neutral that had brought him in conflict with the South African authorities, and his memoirs would tell a sordid history. But like all good memoirs, it would tell an insightful story of the past, which would incite a mass hysteria amongst those businessmen who had tried to profit from his alienation from South Africa. It was still his homeland, and where he would wish to return one day. They were ironically, on the other side of the Great Limpopo River and were untouchable for now; but were they? As much as they might feign disapproval, William knew the sleazy truth of their involvement. It was the Police Commissioner and his involvement with one particularly disreputable businessman that had evoked his ire. William had time on his side, and a bucketful of money.

Chris was the first to go. William had found a way to get to him, and this particularly unscrupulous man had attracted his attention, because of his willingness to double-cross one of his own Lieutenants. Either he was a stupid man, which was doubtful, or he had no level of integrity. Either way he would have to be eliminated. William knew he could rely on the cadres in his army of loyal ex-fifth brigade members. They had wrought destruction and fear on the Zimbabwean population once before, and William could rely on their support by holding the purse strings. The diamond fields of the Congo, and the new Murowa Kimberlite cluster to the south and the Marange deposits to the east, had proven to be very lucrative. William knew by controlling the illicit proceeds of those diamond deposits, and the transportation of the stones southward to the diamond cutting workshops of Gauteng, that he could lure Chris once more. He would wait for an opening, and then reel him in like the small fry he was. This time however, he would not allow a 'catch and release' program. Chris would be reeled in and bumped off like the mud-sucking Barbell he was.

So William set the trap, and it incidentally had a very peculiarly humble beginning. This, William realized would be a potentially simple way of luring Chris. The South African diamond market was awash with uncut gems from the north and these stones came from all sorts of sources. Tanzanite was a particularly lucrative proposition for many. Enterprising Zimbabwean businessmen were setting up scams all over South Africa, and finding ingenious ways to sucker greedy dealers into the fray. The scam operated undetected by the SAP, because there was a lack of interest in prosecuting what turned out to be a very innovative marketing ploy. Particularly when the 'victims' were always white, greedy and naïve. The Zimbabwean syndicates run by William, would somehow contact South Africans, who would be spun a yarn as long as a, Tiger fishing reel full of twine. Sceptical prospects were disregarded immediately, but those who showed even the slightest interest were then reeled in with alarming enthusiasm. It was the cleverest marketing angle devised yet. Innate human greed, and an opportunity to show a quick profit, was what drove this particular scam. These modern day prospectors, usually relied on a hit and miss philosophy. If a prospect showed interest, a meeting was arranged. When the eagerness of the prospect was ascertained, the Tanzanite was offered as the lure. Uncut gems, particularly diamonds were illegal to trade in South Africa and all diamonds had to be traded through a central buying cartel, which controlled the price. Tanzanite however could sometimes slip through undetected. The trap was laid, and victims were ensnared.

When William's men had done their typical offer, the victim would then be fleeced unceremoniously for a few thousand Rand. It was quick, easy and the victims invariably made no fuss because their involvement was equally wrong. These scams usually went unreported. It was a great way for usually unemployable Zimbabweans to make a great living in South Africa. They were seen as the scourge of South African society, but in truth, it was always the guilty that adopted that attitude. Now Chris was too clever to be attracted by a simple scam of this order. William needed to formulate a more intricate plan. Some research had shown that Chris had never married, and his lover had a particular penchant for diamonds. This was the opening! The lover would be lured, but instead of passing off a few blue stone rocks and departing with a minimal profit, William would arrange real Tanzanite from his contacts 'up north'. The trap was carefully set and the lover contacted. When a meeting was convened at a coffee shop in the well-heeled Rosebank Mall, William's men had the lover followed to make sure there were no surprises. The one surprise was that Chris had turned up as well. This would work splendidly. The meeting went ahead, and only when the Tanzanite was offered, did the foolishness of Chris become evident. He was not the astute businessman William had given him credit for. The deal was concluded in the parking area, outside, where video cameras could not detect the boot-sale activity. Chris who knew his diamonds, could also recognize good Tanzanite. The trick was now to lure him into something bigger.

Diamonds from the north. This was the enticement William needed, but to ensure it happened, he would have to make certain Chris did not suspect there was any involvement from players other than the two Zimbabwean accomplices in Johannesburg. Any hint that there were bigger players would raise suspicion, and Chris with his self-preservation firmly attuned to the wider dangers of his nefarious activities, had been very cautious up until now. William wondered what may have changed his usual trepidation. After all, he had sent Greg on his own to the Congo, and left him to wiggle his way out of that hole! Why would Chris get involved in this deal? When the final analysis presented itself, it was uncanny how simple the basic desires of man could be! Chris was doing this to impress his lover. As with the businessmen who stop alongside the Oxford Road haunts of the street hookers for a quick blowjob on their way home, Chris had needed to be involved, because it was not the money that attracted him; he had plenty. It was the excitement that drew him there. Like the suspicious circumstances that led to the hit on another mining magnate, on a dark lonely bridge over the M1 highway, Chris was being lured in just such a way, for the sheer ecstasy of the illegality of it all.

William had his accomplices arrange another meeting, but this time the subterfuge was heightened. Having got away with a handsome profit which Chris had turned with his lover on the Tanzanite, he now needed more and William knew just how to spring this trap. The meeting was arranged for a very busy restaurant in Hyde Park. With the ideal setting for a deal like this, the two Zimbabweans met Chris and the now indulgent lover in the restaurant, which could be casually observed from above by two more accomplices, casually relaying text messages to their colleagues below. When the uncut diamonds were exchanged under the table, but prior to Chris and his lover finishing their grossly excessive meal, the two Zimbabweans feigned another appointment, and retreated just before the arrival of a pre-arranged squad of the Fraud Squad. Clad in uniform, they asked Chris to stand whilst the contents of the package were determined. The humiliation was complete. William need not have concerned himself with anything more, as the damage done to Chris's reputation would far outstrip anything that William would have been able to render with a suitable, but uninspiring shot. Vengeance was sweet.

However, despite the fact that William had now made it clear that he would not suffer the fools who had ratted on him all those years ago, he still had one score to settle. William would wait until the new Police Commissioner was installed, and the protection of a previously loyal force was no longer afforded his archenemy. William would pull the strings from the safety of his rambling ranch in the eastern lowveld and the likes of those who had turned him in would suffer the consequences. This was his destiny, and no man was above the law. As with the farm invasions of Zimbabwe, and the deals that were struck between corporate giants in South Africa, and the Mugabe regime, the double standards were rife. Where mere farmers were expendable, those corporate players in South Africa had guaranteed their property holdings and mineral rights in return for favours. William was not immune to this treachery, but having been the victim of these deals himself, he more than anyone could appreciate the irony! He would return to his homeland one day, free of the sinister speculation relating to his reputation and then he could continue a righteous life with his family and loved ones. In the meantime, he had some scores to settle. One down and eleven to go!

The Muti Murderer

Granny Anita had picked up the phone. She was a concerned citizen. She had heard the rumour now, not just from one friend, but from a second, very reputable and vitally significant source. Her own daughter had phoned her five minutes before, to say she had seen the email circulating through her office, and which had immediately grabbed her attention. It had read, "Muti murderer in Gauteng".

She had immediately opened the document, there was no attachment, just a bland and unsolicited bold face type email, which laid out the facts in three paragraphs. Her heart skipped a beat. The document went on to read.

"Summit Shopping Centre management staff today reported that a black man and his accomplice, a black woman, who had subsequently escaped, had been arrested in the family cloakrooms of the mezzanine level. The two had been monitored on CCTV and they had been subsequently detained after it appeared that the woman had attempted to kidnap a child in the access corridor of the cloakroom facilities. The woman had been wearing a green uniform with white pinafore which resembled a 'maids' outfit. She has dark hair, dark eyes and a dark complexion. Anyone who has seen her or someone resembling her description, was to report it immediately to the local Linden Police station." The report went on to describe the activities that had raised the suspicion of the management office.

"The woman had escorted a little boy, about four years old to the woman's cloakroom. There she had taken black boot polish and covered the boy's face with it. The man had been seen loitering outside the woman's cloakroom door, which had raised some suspicion. When the young boy emerged, the woman was holding his hand, and he appeared distressed. This was when the Centre's management had reacted, and the security guards had cornered the woman and her accomplice in the narrow passage near the Centre Management offices."

"It is suspected that they were going to attempt to kidnap the child, and the man's identity matches the description of a man wanted on charges of mutilation of a child in a 'muti murder'. The management staff detained the man and the woman, pending the arrival of the Police, but the woman managed to slip away whilst they were waiting for Linden Police Station to respond. Be on the lookout for this woman and report any suspicious activity."

The report had not mentioned if the little boy was safe!

Granny Anita had just returned from her shopping foray, and she was certain she had seen the woman in her area. It was important that she report this immediately. When Arita who was the 'Gogo' of two grandchildren of her own, had seen the woman, she had not recognized her. She knew all the local domestic servants who worked in the area! They often took time off from their busy schedule to sit on the corner of Rooibok and Carnation Avenue, where they caught up on the day's gossip, over a game of 'Farfie'. It was their way of unwinding, and they would sit, legs drawn up sideways under their rather large posteriors, in the fashion that their ancestors may have done for a thousand years. They looked comfortable sitting there on the grass verge, and always waved at 'Gogo' when she passed. They were a happy go lucky clique of woman, whose lives revolved around the domestic duties of their suburban incarceration. Their lives were based on the early morning rise, dishes to be washed and morning porridge to be made, before heading back to the one bedroom quarters at the bottom of the garden, steaming galvanized iron tea mug, with its chipped yellow paint, in one hand, and a plate of brown bread cut into large square pieces in the other. The day started with this ritual, and never varied, unless the routine was broken for some reason.

'Gogo' always waved back, with a cheery smile and a warm acceptance of their vital contribution to her day. Gogo would then head off on her shopping errands, and the local shopping centre was where she tended to get all her provisions. This was her suburban bliss, and she was as regular as a skinny model on morning infomercials, eating her all bran breakfast cereal. Nothing could upset her routine, and one could set your watch by her ritual passing. It just so happened that Gogo had been turning back into Rooibok Avenue, when she had seen this woman, in a green maid's uniform, and waving as she usually did, she received no response. This was entirely unusual, but because she was in a rush to get back to her kitchen to prepare the rusks she was baking for the afternoon visit of her two granddaughters, she had dismissed it out of hand. The afternoon would be filled with games and activities for these two spirited girls, who kept Gogo busy and active, chasing after them to keep them from mischief. The house was one of those sixties style suburban 'hacienda' homes, with peach coloured earth coat walls, and burglar bars on all the steel framed windows. It was Gogo's dream home and where she had raised her two daughters and a menagerie of dogs, cats and parakeets. Gogo had contentedly lived there whilst her husband had worked his twelve-hour day job, and Gogo had ensured he had his breakfast before work, and his sandwiches packed in their greaseproof paper every day for nearly forty years. The mortgage was paid, the house somewhat ramshackle now, was comfortable, and Gogo very content!

But it would take very little to upset that suburban delight. This was one of those moments, and Gogo sat on the phone waiting for someone to answer from the management office. The phone rang three, four and then five times, then a loud click interrupted her impatient vigil over that synthetic handset.

"Good morning, Summit management office." The voice trailed off as the recipient of this anxious call seemed to be distracted by a third party. 'Perhaps it was the Police who were now investigating?' Gogo would wait a second.

"Yes!" A slightly impatient voice queried. "Can I help you?"

"Ahh, yes please." Gogo was back. "I just wanted to report on the woman in the green uniform. I think I have seen her here in Rooibok Avenue!"

There was silence on the other end.

"Hello? Sorry?" A very South African, South Africanism. What was this woman on about?

"This is Summit Shopping Centre management office! How can I assist you?" The man's voice sounded irritated. Perhaps he was in the middle of filing a report?

"Yes." Repeated Gogo. "I am phoning to report that I have seen that woman you are looking for!"

"Hhuuh?" The voice sounded incredulous. "What woman? This is Summit Shopping Centre. Who did you want to speak to?" The man's voice was young, irritated and now becoming rude. Gogo would have to explain the email, and her suspicions. 'Maybe this man was not a manager, and had not been informed yet?'

"My daughter called to let me know that she had seen the email on her computer and that I should keep an eye out for the black woman who had been seen on your TV with that poor child."

"I don't know anything about a woman and a child?" The young man replied. "What email are you talking about?" He seemed concerned now. Maybe he might ask his manager and get the manager to call her back!

"My daughter works for the Opti Group, and they have an email sent from your offices to warn people to be on the lookout for this woman?" Gogo was now beginning to sound unsure of the facts. Her voice was not as assured as when he first picked up the phone. He was a pleasant sounding young man, maybe she could appeal to his better judgment and get the manager on the phone.

"Would you mind calling the manager and maybe I can explain it to him?" She wanted to get someone to react, but clearly, this was not the man for the job.

"You see. I have just seen the woman walking down my road, and she definitely does not work here. I know all the ladies in this street and she is not one of them." Gogo had seen the desperate look on the woman's face when she had waved. There was guilt written all over it.

"My manager is not here currently," the young man replied. "Can I take your number and ask him to call you when he returns to his office?" The young man was now taking control of the situation, but he would need to hurry. Gogo would try to give him a description. Maybe that might help! In her mind's eye, she could see the black woman's face. It was like a simulacrum imprinted on her brain. Gogo could see her wide set eyes and her quite full lips. No makeup! Not exceptional she supposed, but nonetheless a plain face with very little identifying features. But then she remembered they had CCTV coverage. Maybe her description might help to provide some assistance when they send the police?

"Okay, but I should also call the Police. The email said to call Linden Police station if we see anything suspicious!" Gogo was now rationalizing her behaviour. She sounded stressed.

"Okay, that would be the better thing to do," the young man could see an easy way out. Maybe then, he could return to his computer screen and the game of solitude he had been playing.

"Yes, I will give them a call so long. Perhaps you might take my number?" She reminded him.

"Yes, of course Ma'am." He responded, and dutifully took down the number which Gogo repeated to him for good measure, and then had him repeat back to her.

"It's just that you really can't tell one black woman from the next," she admitted. "They all look the same!" There was silence on the other side of the phone.

"She was definitely medium height for a black woman. You know not too tall: not too short!" Gogo continued. She needed to relay the information. I would help her to remember the woman's features.

"Yes. I see." Replied the young man in his most understanding manner. He could not have cared less, but she had begun the description. Gogo was on a roll.

"Yes. And she had her hair in a braid. You know! Like the black woman do with their hair! She was not wearing her dook, which goes with her uniform. That's what I noticed more, because I could see her hair. It was very fancy. Not like the ladies in my area, but more fashionable. Like you see on Isidingo." Gogo might not have been the world's most observant granny, but she knew her TV programs.

"Yes, I see." He repeated. This would take a long time and the game awaited.

"She was wearing running shoes like the ones they wear on the Comrades." That was another show she watched. Glued to the TV set from six in the morning until the final stragglers come in eleven hours later.

"Yes. Most extraordinary, because I have seen the ladies wearing sandals and the leather slip-ons they wear. But never those running shoes." She had now convinced herself of this woman's guilt. How would she be able to sit sideways on the verge with those? Most peculiar!

The young man responded as if he were writing all this down. Then there was silence again.

"I think I will get onto the Police now, and give them the details of where I saw her." Gogo was sure she could help the Police re-arrest this woman if she acted swiftly. 'How long had it been since she saw the woman. Perhaps not even an hour ago! Even with her running shoes on she might not have gotten that far.'

The young man was non-committal. "Okay, thank you," he offered respectfully. She had not thought to ask him his name, and it would be important when she spoke to the manager.

"What is your name young man?" She asked in her most caring of manners.

"Simphewe." He responded. "Simphewe Mathlana."

There was silence on the other end. She would not ask him to spell it. The phone clicked.

The 'Importance' of being Margaret

Margaret was 'eighty-something' and had lived a full and exceptional life. Not one of those lives that are written down in the annals of history in some lengthy autobiography, but nonetheless exceptional. She had arrived in 'Jewhannesburg' as she playfully referred to her new home, sometime in the sixties, an immigrant with a large Pharmaceutical company her employer. It was the 'Age of Aquarius', the age of the sexual revolution, but Margaret had never seen it. She was too busy doing what Margaret did well; looking after everyone else, and every stray dog and cat in the neighbourhood. In fact, Margaret had not married, and had never intended it to be so. A woman of similar independence you would never meet. Margaret had bought the house, in a little cul-de-sac, in the quaintest of villages in the suburbs of the city.

"There weren't any trees here," she would remind all who cared to listen. The suburb had been tilled from the farmland that had once stretched beyond the river into the rolling hills beyond. The encroaching suburban creep, emerged upon the Braamfontein Spruit and erased those picturesque fields with urbane squalor. Well, squalor would be a harsh term to use, if it were not for the importance of the community that would be housed below those refined mansions of northern Parktown. The meandering spruit acted as a natural barrier. The authorities had originally built this quirky little village to house the returning servicemen and women from the 'war' but Margeret, although having served as a WREN, had never been part of that community. She was a loner who danced to her own piper's tune, never once feeling the urge to conform.

The suburb had then been usurped by the Nationalist Government to house the Afrikaans speakers who would swing the vote for the Ward Council in their favour. It never happened and Margaret an ardent Unionist, remained faithful to her English heritage, claiming her little piece of England in the thundering storms of South Africa. She had befriended most, and through her dog walking, had met almost everyone in her street. Margaret loved her confined community and would not have traded it for any of the opulence that existed behind the twelve foot walled gulags to the east. Each plot was neatly divided into rows and matrixed across the gently undulating fields. From the safety of the reserve set up across the Spruit, the suburb of Victory Park was a mere stone's throw, but may as well have been a lifetime and a world away. From the lofty reaches of their hill, they would look down upon their lesser 'brethren' with contempt, having scant regard for their neighbours with whom they shared little in common. The city was divided between the 'haves' and the 'have-nots', but in an ironical twist, the value of smaller, easier to maintain homes became evident. This was Johannesburg in the midst of the social unrest which occurred in every suburb and would ultimately roll out onto the streets of Soweto. Margaret had bought her little three-bedroom house, with its corrugated iron roof, then another and then a third. Margaret was no entrepreneur, but she could see the need for a roof over one's head, and rented out the two, to support her secretary's salary. Her inheritance in Sterling securing a very worthwhile lifestyle and the development continued.

Margaret was a petite four foot eleven, but no shrinking violet. She had travelled alone to South Africa, during the heady days of 'Apartheid', unflinching in her belief that she may make a contribution. And make a contribution she certainly did. This diminutive lady made up in integrity far more than her body weight. Leading one of those exemplary lives, she neither imposed her beliefs on others, nor asked for opinion. She simply lived. It was this 'esprit d'corp' that had seen her through the trials and tribulations of the next fifty odd years, and never once considered her homeland and the refuge of a gentler climate. No! Indeed, Margaret would never consider Britain her home again, keeping her old friends and family; but at a distance.

It was Margaret's attitude that had set her apart from the avarice that had attracted most others from abroad. She would never take more than her fair share of the rental, and as long as the mortgage was met, she would happily befriend and entertain her tenants as one would host a family of Glossy Starlings, on a bird feeder. Along with the trees that were planted, originally to act as a windbreak, the starlings and all manner of bird life appeared. These trees protected the new residents from the harsh dry north-westerly winds that descended on the suburbs during the August months and the dust that followed. The blustery days would pre-ordain the coming spring, and a respite from the winter cold snaps that snuck up from the spruit. The dust covered everything including her family heirlooms, but Margaret along with her other good qualities was impervious to it, and the haughtiness of her western neighbours. Margaret set down her roots in this enclave with only one thing in mind. She would make a comfortable life for herself, and spare the rod that others would yield, in self-sacrifice to her community. She did so willingly, never asking for anything in return.

The summer rains came and went, and the spruit overflowed and gouged a ravine through the brittle granite rock of the Highveld escarpment. The Braamfontein Spruit, from its source on the ridge to the south, wound its way through the now leafy suburbs of Westcliff and Parkview, then on into the nestled village through which it paused not, before continuing unabated into the North-East. This tiny tributary would find its way to the vast Indian Ocean, seeking lower ground as all torrents of water must. But Margaret would strive for higher principles and higher ground, in an effort to make her mark on this society. The beggars came and went from the suburbs, looking for handouts and Margaret never failed to deliver. There was however, a myth that if these fellows left a coke bottle laying outside your property, it was a signal to their accomplices that the property was vacant, or that the silver canned lemonade was a signal that the occupants worked during the day. Or the most sinister was the brown wine bottle, lying empty on its side with the neck of the uncorked vessel pointing in the direction of the house, which meant that the occupants were elderly, and an easy target. Margaret did not believe this trivia, and came and went at all times of the day and night in her 'little yellow peril' which she had bought despite everyone's advice to get an automatic. She had not, and Margaret was into her third clutch, and the yellow doors and bumpers had been replaced so often that the chequered panels resembled a New York taxi cab.

To Margaret it was not the amount of money that determined the value of her friendships. She would live in modest circumstances among a comfortable existence with her two dogs and her cats. She always picked up strays from the SPCA and Margaret was a sucker for anyone who would be lost in their quest for bigger and better things. Margaret always took in their un-wanted, or seemingly inconvenient pets. To Margaret it mattered not that these animals might be a nuisance, because somehow she would win them over with her mild manner and her unbridled loyalty. They in turn would calm down from the unsociable beasts that found refuge in her home, and with time, they would offer her their unwavering faithfulness. Margaret remained unmarried and content in her solitude because she had her dogs and cats. She would often remark, "I don't trust anyone who does not have an affinity to animals! They are usually treacherous and I am usually right!"

Well, she should know having outlived most of her contemporaries. Margaret had taken her Pension from the firm, and retired, never having had a day of sickness in her forty years of work. She paid her taxes, paid her rates and utilities, and never once short paid her gardener. She had a live-in domestic and fed and kept her with the same affection she had for her animals, but Violet, would never quite earn the same respect as her pets. It was uncanny, but nevertheless true, because Margaret was happy within herself, and had no need of shared human emotions. For Margaret her socialization revolved around a busy post-retirement schedule of Bridge games, coffee outings, of which there were numerous, and the occasional fag, over a glass of wine and a cross-word puzzle. She was neither frugal nor spendaholic, but Margaret managed to make her pension stretch beyond some luxuries from 'Woolies' and a yearly outing to Hilton in the Natal Midlands. No! Margaret was your typical pensioner, but had successfully managed her finances so as to outlive her colleagues at the firm, and share her modest income with all and sundry.

Margaret was the epitome of a Christian, but her unflinching distrust of basic human nature, had rendered her immune to 'its' inherent failings. She believed that, to 'outwardly' show ones' ideals was to place oneself on a pedestal, and Margaret was not familiar with shows of communal expression. So to Margaret public displays were unnecessary because she knew her ideals were held firmly within her own comfortable desire to co-exist.

Charities were her hobby, and she would happily drop her loose change into those cylindrical charity boxes, with no favour given, but she had one particular doubt. It was the charities that came knocking on the door. Someone would invariably ring her door bell on a weekend, and if it was not the men with their wooden handled brooms, it was usually an individual with a hard-luck story and a pre-scripted reply to any objections. These individuals would have made excellent Insurance salesmen, because they had an answer for every protestation, and a reason she should part with her hard-earned cash, with very little substance to back it up. When Margaret would ask them what they needed, if she could see there was a modicum of genuineness in their ploy, she would invariably help. To her, the sales pitch was the key, and anyone bold enough to think up some of the stories they concocted, was worth a loaf of bread, or a dip into her lose change. This particular day, was to change her outlook forever!

The dogs had alerted her the moment the doorbell had rung. But she had taken a moment to place the back page of the gossip column magazine, with its check board black and white squared reliefs, on the couch in her living room, before getting up to see who it was. The man stood at her gate silhouetted by her green palisade fencing. He eagerly looked through, eyes dissected by the iron bar that framed his oddly shaped head. Margaret called from her open door beyond, as the man appeared about to leave, unsure if anyone was home.

"Can I help you?" Margaret called out in her inimitable croaky voice. Fifty odd years of social cigarette smoking had defined her vocal cords.

The man continued to walk away, apparently having not heard her. She called again.

"Is there something that you want?" He seemed to hesitate but then slouching forward in the gait of one who had been dejected as a human being for so long might, and devoid of all hope, he continued his hapless amble.

Margaret feared he may be deaf, so instead of turning and closing the door, she opened it and leaving the dogs inside, strode after him to the gate in a brisk walk. Her concern would enable her to pursue him with ease, despite the intoxication of a glass of wine and her slightly rheumatoid legs and recently operated knee joint.

"Hello!" She now stood at the gate, he some ten meters from her, but still sauntering dolefully away. She repeated, now slightly concerned.

"Hello, is there something you wanted." Past tense now being opted for, as he had clearly changed his mind. She looked through the still closed gate, her remote control in her left hand. She could still press the button and pursue him if he was unable to hear her.

As she followed his departure from the security of her gate, she made a mental note to pick up the discarded litter on her front lawn. The council would never pick it up, so she would.

Margaret now unable to raise a response from this rather dishevelled fellow, then turned her attention to her lawn. She opened the gate, and emerged out onto the street below the oddly shaped tree, which the Parks people had cut, so as to avoid fouling the telephone lines. All the way through the leafy suburbs of the north, these peculiarly shaped trees stood a testament to the practical necessity of maintaining telephone lines which were income generating; but also to the complete lack of aestheticism which created the hideous deformity that resulted. Margaret made her way to the litter that now fouled her lawn. She stooped to pick up the newspaper and found an old disused wine bottle, which the chap who had now vacated the area would have had as his supper the night before. Perhaps it may well have been the old chap she had just seen! As Margaret went after some more paper dispersed by the wind, she saw her neighbour appear from the cloistered garage beyond Margaret's property. She owned a little bistro up the road, but Margaret had unusually not befriended her. Some in the area said she had unhappily split from her husband, but that was as subjective as the rumours she herself proliferated. Margaret knew she was not a pleasant agreeable person! She had heard the midnight tirades from the sanctity of her East facing bedroom, and knew that she and her delinquent son were up to no good. 'Perhaps' her friend Sue had noted, 'it was the ready cash from the second till at the restaurant, that fed her drug fuelled episodes, or maybe just the ravages of age and the loneliness of a failed marriage'. Margaret not prone to rudeness, looked the other way.

She remembered to look down the street once she had retrieved the bottle and newspaper, but she could not see the old boy. He must have turned the corner somehow, whilst Margaret was busy. She shook her head. He certainly could move if he needed to. Margaret rounded the tree to see if he was still in view, but there was no sign of him. Her dogs barked, and Margaret now intent on getting back to her cross word, turned and returned to her gate. She made sure there was no further litter before closing the gate and heading back to the front door. The dogs barked again inside the house, a more insistent bellow. She would hush them and closing the door behind her, she made her way back to the living room. The dogs followed tails wagging.

The glass of wine lay on the side table next to her magazine and spectacles, so she lifted the magazine and sat. She would coax another ten sips from that glass. "Six across, silver - white metallic chemical element." Margaret thought, if only she had a tuppence for every question she got right. She would be an exceptionally wealthy woman, but then what? She would end up spending it on unnecessary things. Margaret only had a cell phone because her friends insisted she should be contactable when out and about in the 'yellow peril'. Grand, if only she knew how to switch the thing on. Not to mention how she would remember the pin code!

The dogs barked again and shot out the living room, but not to the front door as usual. They careered down the passage to the kitchen and the back door. 'That's peculiar,' Margaret thought to herself, 'Violet was only due in the following day. Today she was doing some piece work at Sue's.'

Margaret dutifully followed them through, once more discarding her efforts to finish the puzzle, and check on the disturbance that had invoked this uproar from the dogs. It was probably that son from next door, playing his loud music again. If only that woman had opened her, nickel-and-dime shop somewhere else. 'That's it.' Margaret was pleased as punch. "Nickel", she proudly mouthed to herself!

She lifted herself carefully off the couch once more and remembering to ease her not so significant weight onto her left knee, she headed for the kitchen. The dogs barked uncharacteristically. 'This was very peculiar she thought.' The dogs might usually bark once or twice when roused by the Common Ibis that frequented her mulberry tree. They left their purple coloured uric acid deposits all over her garden furniture, despite having removed it to a safe distance from the tree. How they managed to foul the chairs and table continually, was anyone's guess? They had one benefit she always argued, they were good at clearing the garden of insects and the ghastly 'Parktown Prawns', which she reminded herself were far more objectionable. The kitchen was down the hall and to her left. She hurried, those dogs were kicking up a storm and that appalling woman would be on the phone with some complaint before long. Margaret had never given her the number, preferring to forego good neighbourliness for the possibility of having her house ransacked whilst she was away, but somehow she had obtained it nonetheless.

As Margaret turned the corner, she suddenly stopped dead in her tracks. There was an unknown silhouette outside the open kitchen door, and the dogs stood between the two equally horrified looking protagonists, barking incessantly. Fortuitously, the wrought iron gate held him securely on the outside, whilst the two dogs seemed intent on scaring him half to death. He had obviously entered the property whilst Margaret was outside, and made his way dutifully to the back kitchen door. If it were not for that gate, he may well have been inside, and who knows what! Getting over her initial shock, Margaret quickly assessed the situation. She would be safe, but the poor fellow outside was about to be mauled by the dogs. The expression on his face gave her a sense of his sheer terror. He stood, with his worn canvas cap in one hand, raised in submission to his breast, but held the other hand out in panic, the dogs now a mere six feet from him, and now that Margaret was there, performing all holy hell. Margaret could see that the lower bars of the gate which allowed the dogs access to the garden, whilst safely ensuring no intruder into the house, was now precariously about to offer the suitably crazed dogs, access to this poor old fellow. Margaret moved deftly to the glass-door, closed it securely, then calling the dogs to follow her to the passage, ushered them out of the kitchen and closed the door. They faithfully did her bidding, and with some manner of sanity restored, Margaret re-entered the kitchen to attend to her beggar.

He stood patiently outside the door, un-phased by the abrupt closing of the door in his face, and a more relieved expression in those eyes. Margaret re-opened the wooden cottage-pane door that she had resisted converting to those ugly steel doors, pertinent to the sixties and seventies. The mood of fear among South Africa's white population was gauged by the number of houses fitted with these unattractive steel doors during that momentous period, but now post-Madiba and the return to civilized co-operative existence, the doors of these homes had been converted back to normalcy and wooden frames. Margaret could now hear herself think, the dogs banished to the front part of the home. The 'old boy' stood, an odd expression of recognition etched into his yellowing eyes, and sallow brown features, enfolded by years of leathery skin creased by sun, age and hardship.

"Hello!" She offered, having been somewhat surprised by his intrusion. "Did you want some food and water?" Her congeniality returned despite an initial trepidation.

"Hello Missus," he returned in an eloquently subservient tone. "It is me, Alfred, you don't remember me?" It was more a question of the years having altered his features so, more than his expectation that she should automatically have recalled where she knew him from."

Margaret knew the voice. She smiled. Her memory was vivid, and there was no fading of her acute recollection of their first meeting.

"Yes! Oh hello Alfred, how have you been?" Her response instantaneous and welcoming. She recalled the circumstances as if there was no interim period of forty years.

"Yes madam." He smiled a crooked teeth smile, two left on his upper jaw, and his parched dry lips covering who knew how many on his lower. "It is me Alfred, from number ten. I came back to find you but you had moved." It was more a case of good fortune that now wiped away those forty years, more than a reminiscent return to recounting the times he had looked for her. He had been devastated by her move, having worked for Margaret for nine years, then having had to return to his home in Malawi on a family errand. He had returned some months later, only to find that Margaret had moved, and he had spent the next forty years looking for her. Margaret remembered him exactly!

"Hello Alfred, do come in." She offered, and turning to extricate the key from its hook on the kitchen wall, she opened the gate, and welcomed him in. The years flooded away, and his yellow eyes, glazed by the start of cataracts, and a hint of emotion, seemed to return to life with an infused delight.

Traffic Violations

The function had been held at the Casino complex north of Johannesburg. This was where the company could get everyone together for a night of casual discussions over an awards evening that celebrated the best of the industry. Bill and his second wife Esther had attended the evening, Bill said, "Just to show my face and make certain those other agents are aware that I am still working for the company." He had been contacted by too many loyal clients over the last five years since his medical procedure, that had called to complain that some guy had just told them that he was no longer working for the company, and that they would need to see the client urgently to review their Insurance Portfolio. It was a grudge activity, and Bill had not been keen. He would however make that twenty kilometre pilgrimage to the north, because he still had a few mates working for the branch.

When they had arrived, it was early evening and the crowds were slowly filtering into that den of iniquity. He was a devout Christian, but Bill, a practical man had told Esther to have a flitter on at least one of the machines on their way to the function.

"It will do no harm to put a hundred Rand into a machine. You never know!" He had told her. Esther did, and within three spins of the ornately decorated wheels, she hit jackpot. The wheels had turned and whilst the jackpot was a plethora of different symbols, all in Bill's mind sacrilegious, the sevens had appeared above and below.

"Four thousand three hundred and fifteen Rand." That had certainly paid for the evening, although he reminded himself, the evening was a black and white tie occasion with no expenses spared, and they would not need to put their hands in their pockets.

Esther had somehow been born with uncanny luck, and since having met her, Bill's run of bad luck had changed. The divorce had been ugly, dragged out through the High Court, with Bill having to pick up the entire legal bill, and his 'Ex' walking away with the house in Sandton, and his dog and the children, which the lawyers had argued over.

"The children would be devastated," her Lawyer had remonstrated, "if they are separated from the dog as well as having to suffer the loss of the break up as well."

Bill knew that this was just his 'Ex's' way of getting at him. She had harried him into working for the company, because she had seen her friend Sheila living the life of riley off of the proceeds of her husband's frenetic sales activities at the company. Those were the heady days, when commissions were paid on the length of the terms of Insurance policies, and Bill had witnessed the plethora of Retirement Annuity contracts sold full-term unnecessarily. Bill had neither wanted that exposure to future legal wrangles, nor had he felt the client should ever have to make a choice later to have their RA paid up because of exorbitant annual contribution increases that rendered the contract unaffordable. No! He had maintained that the client should be able to retire at sixty, or sixty-five according to their needs. "What was the point of selling them a RA to sixty-nine." The only benefit that had was to maximize commissions paid to the Insurance Consultant.

So with his reputation unsullied, Bill had decided to kick back after nearly twenty years of working for the company. He no sooner had done so, when he had a medical emergency, and as bad luck would have it, he ended up with cancer. "Operable, but nevertheless a concern!"

It was Esther who had saved him from a world that seemed to have its hand out at every turn in his life. The 'Ex' had fortunately taken her settlement and disappeared into her own sordid debauchery, with the kids. Bill had taken the path of greater resistance, and continued with his Church work, and now had a thriving community of refugees, working on several farms out in the Hammanskraal area. He had met Esther whilst on a Church outing, and she had immediately seen his hurt. She befriended him, working with the refugees as an outreach program from her congregation in Centurion, but had been a rock, during the ugly break up and subsequent illness. Bill had been grateful for her support, but would not immediately commit himself to anyone other than the 'Lord'. Esther had won him over with her hard work, diligence of action, and a steadfast belief in what they were doing was 'God's' work. She had been a re-born Christian, but her zeal was tempered over the years by a practical knowledge of God's limitations. She would temper that faith with love, and it would be evident in her commitments.

Bill, now stood on the threshold of a greater existence, and being a fairly good salesman, had sold his concept of 'Farming Community' projects to some of the more rational minded Supermarket chains. They in turn sponsored his projects for just long enough, that he was able to get the refugees out of the urban squalor of Hillbrow, and onto the land, where they could 'lift a spade and learn a trade'. It was this practical application that had led to Bill initiating an 'organic vegetable growing commune' which now supplied those same food stores. He had learnt in school that to give a man a fish, would feed him for a day, but to give him a fishing rod would feed him for life. This philosophy was what inspired Bill to now continue full steam ahead with his work. The Insurance business would have to take a back seat, but anyone who cared to join him, was welcome to volunteer. Bill knew that most did care, but had no concept of how to apply it and spare the time from busy working schedules. Bill would start a training program and eventually lecture on self-improvement and hygiene, the more practical side of fulfilment. Those self-actualization courses, a planet and culture away from reality!

So, it was only the need for an income to supplement his charitable activities that had forced him to stay with the company. 'That and the loyalty he had to his clients, who still needed his considerable financial expertise'. Bill felt the need to change the program. He could see that a numbers driven Insurance industry would ultimately be its own failing. Greedy shareholders wanted bigger and more aggressive returns, to substantiate their capital investments, but gave little recognition to the impact that organization could have on an emerging South Africa, in a despondent and largely devastated African economy. The company needed to branch out into Africa, and with his refugees from Zimbabwe, the Congo and as far afield as the Ivory Coast, Bill recognized that a truly international Insurance market in Africa, would need to change the focus of what made it successful in South Africa. Bill had spent many days chatting to the refugees and finding out what their aspirations were. This was a wakeup call, because although living from hand to mouth, their dreams and goals were exactly the same, as those of his. They all ultimately wanted to retire with a family, grandchildren and a monthly Pension. Bill now knew how to achieve this!

The evening had been pleasant, but in Bill's mind, he could not see how this culture of commission driven sales objectives would, or could possibly fit the model of an African Renaissance. These guys would ultimately be spending the next ten years churning their client's money, and all in a vain effort to fill their own pockets. Bill had other ideas. The main course came and went, and conversation flowed, but the effort exceeded the reward. Esther was glowing, her success over the gambling and a far cry from her usual hands on soup kitchen activities. She was enjoying her moment, but as Bill knew, it would be short lived. Esther, not needing that money, having been the fortunate recipient of her father's estate, and her previous husband's tragic death, had been left with more than adequate resources to pursue her goals as a care-giver. There was, no doubt, a lot to be said for Risk Insurance, but Bill felt it was a little bit like the gambling. Families gambled on death, instead of spending the fortunes that would ultimately be lost, on expenses that are more practical. 'Imagine', he had thought, 'if every last cent spent on Insurance cover, was put into a fund, that was there to support families in need, and the more practical applications of funding community projects!' The system was the wrong way around, he thought. 'Instead of funding huge egos and selfish returns for greedy investors, a truly African Insurance Industry would need to be funded by the community, in a more practical way.'

It was these thoughts that drove his future plans, and it was the very essence of the failings of his twenty years of endeavour, that had led him down this path. Well, it was not truly all failure! He had managed to achieve a significant amount of wealth creation, that certainly helped the families he advised. Over twenty-odd years, he had generated over two hundred million Rand in revenue for that company, and the vast majority of this had been in the form of savings, not flittered away on risk cover. Bill was confident that this would hold him in good stead for the next twenty years of his life. Each time there had been a change in his career, he could almost certainly gear it to the day, "seven-year itch got you," his mother would say. Bill had literally had life changing circumstances every seven years, and the number seven was his lucky number. It was not only a spiritual number, but it seemed to evoke the kind of favourable response that a 'God' rewarded period of time might. Bill had been able to count on his seven-year itch, as a property tycoon might use it to buy and sell. The world turned in cycles, and every time there was a momentous occasion, the numbers could be read like a proverbial calendar.

"Gosh", he thought, he could not believe it had been seven years since the divorce. "Mind", he did know one thing, the boys had now grown old enough, that they recognized that their father was not the ogre their mother had painted pictures of, in the fitful sleep. They had contacted Bill, asking if he would take them out to Hammanskraal, and they wanted to help. They were in their teens, but despite the 'mall rat' behaviour of their school peers, they had no design on the incestuous groping of the tarts who frequented 'The Square' on Friday nights. Thankfully, Bill had somehow managed to father two very intelligent and discerning children. Perhaps it was in the genes?

Esther was the life and soul of the party, and bill had no designs on dragging her away from the proceedings, so he sat for a while during a lull in the presentations, which he had dutifully clapped through. He was seated with some of the longer serving members of his branch, and they in turn could sense the jadedness of it all. Bill was cordial, but made no attempt to conceal his boredom. The festivities would proceed late into the evening, but Bill needed to be up early as he had a feeding scheme that was being commissioned the following morning. He would politely say his good-byes, and hopefully escape with Esther, before the fanfare of the 'big writers' who almost always had their glory spared until the culmination of the evening's awards. By the time, the one-man band that sufficed for entertainment got going on his take of the Beatles, Bill and Esther would be long-gone, and hopefully spirited away to earthlier matters.

By ten, Bill was raising an eyebrow each time Esther would catch his attention from the other side of the round table. She could see it was time and slowly extricated herself from the hilarity of a gaggle of wives. Their spiritedness raised by free drinks and a modicum of success. They all had husbands who were colleagues of Bill's, but none truly knew each other. Insurance salesmen seemed to keep their clients and their wives at arm's length from their colleagues. This was the nature of their industry. It was definitely time to go. Bill reached back for his jacket, draped across the back of his chair, and rising with a deft shrug of his left shoulder placed one arm, and then the other into the silken folds of his dinner jacket. "Hugo Boss", it had lasted him twenty years, and still looked as good as the day he bought it in that men's apparel store in Sandton City. It still looked good, despite the years, after all, it only surfaced twice a year, for the awards evening and the Christmas charity ball at the Church. Either way, it had served its purpose.

Bill realized, that he was ready for his next grand adventure. It would be twenty-one years since he started in the Insurance industry, if he counted the one year he worked as a sub-agent despite the industry rules and regulations of the time. Those days were a long forgotten memory of client analyses done on the back of a piece of scrap paper, or in some instances, by some Insurance guys, on the back of a 'thirties packet'.

'Whatever had happened to packs of thirty'. He could not recall having seen one for years, but being a non-smoker, he probably paid no attention anyway. He and Esther shook some hands, a peck or two on some cheeks, and they were making a hasty retreat back through the bar where the smokers had gathered in a plume of bluish smoke, whilst earnestly touting ideals on disclosure and 'Replacement forms'. Bill whisked Esther safely through the haze, that a lifetime of Insurance claims and death statistics had still not erased. They were on their way to the car park and the safety of Bill's old Landcruiser. It would be safer travelling at night in such a vehicle, as it gave him a considerable vantage over other road users.

As they turned left back onto the double carriageway, heading for the motorway, they chatted amiably over discussions of 'old friends' who now had forgiven Bill his previous indiscretions, and had not seen nor heard from his 'ex-wife' since the divorce. Esther was indifferent over those events, because Bill had transformed his activities and now had an office at home, which was his refuge from the petty office politics of his former working environment. Esther now assisted him with his administration, which with all the new regulatory requirements was not too inconsiderable. They had a beautiful thatch on the ridge overlooking Menlyn Park, and a safe distance from their projects in the North. Now the emphasis was on how they could offer support to the hundreds of clients that called Bill on a regular basis to illicit his opinion on the down turn in the markets, and how they would be affecting the values on the Insurance Portfolio. The company should be paying him to keep those reluctant clients from cashing in policies, or switching to the new emerging, and hungry company's that waited cravenly in the wings.

"Fat chance of that," he thought. Everyone was out to make a quick buck, and the industry was not for the faint of heart. Insurance salesmen, were only second in terms of reputation, to their distant cousins, "Estate Agents". Bill would not demean the twenty years he had spent creating his business, by constantly 'churning' the policies he had sold to clients, some of whom had become long term friends.

The on-ramp appeared ahead of him. The lights were red, but the slipway to the left was somewhere in the dark up in front. The street lights were not working again, and the on-ramp was very poorly lit. Bill indicated and turning into the far left lane, made sure he kept a safe distance from the edge of the tarmac. Even with his big off-road tires, those sharp bitumen gravel rocks could easily slice through the rubber. The place was falling apart. He had seen the steady decline, much like he had witnessed in Zimbabwe over twenty-eight years before. Bill had arrived in South Africa and started his first job after school, intent on getting a degree part time, and somehow making ends meet with part-time work in a restaurant at night. The Accounting firm paid him a pittance, but he had justified the move, because the tax rate for his meagre salary was twice the rate in Harare as it was here. Besides, who would have wanted to live under that dictatorship? Who indeed. He felt a little nostalgia for the Les Brown pool, and the lunch time sessions he had continued for that first year. The firm had transferred him when it became evident the studying was not working through correspondence. No! Bill had needed to get out of Zimbabwe for his own peace of mind. He was feeling as though this was a warning. Bill had always followed his gut instinct, but now he was too committed to his refugees and his new life with Esther. Déjà vu was written all over those cascading rubbish tips that passed for township living. He had never understood it. Those blacks who lived in abject poverty, would never lift a piece of litter from the ground, and why should they? They had no ownership of their circumstances. It drove him mad. Their emphasis was on existing, so why would there ever be any attempt to bend down and pick up the litter? Fourteen years of so-called democracy had not changed a thing. Nor would another fourteen!

As Bill hit the on-ramp, he put aside his negativity. He was homeward bound and the motorway stretched out below him, with his pulse already geared for the forty kilometre journey and a night cap with Esther. She had been quiet. Too quiet! This had raised the sense of the eerie quiet similar to that silence which descends before the sudden calamitous thunder roll, pre-empting the summer showers. The ridge at Menlyn was particularly bad, as the valley through which the thunder rolls, projects the easterly thunder claps, like an amphitheatre. The house perched atop the sharp granite cliffs, was cantilevered and east facing. The noise was alarming. As Bill turned onto the on-ramp, he saw a torch light pointed directly at him, and what looked like a traffic check. He slowed even further, and pulled over as the traffic officer wielding the torch came into full view in his headlights.

"Damn." He muttered under his breath. He felt, more than saw Esther look across at him through the dim interior light afforded by the orange luminescence of the dash board. Esther was on the edge of the big comfortable seat, constrained by her seat belt.

"Careful Bill," she warned as another traffic officer came into view beyond. She was panicked, he sensed, having been high-jacked outside their driveway years before, but the experience still etched in her mind. Then she had screamed a shrill blood chilling scream which had alerted him from the comfort of his armchair in the TV lounge. That shrill cry may have alerted him, but nearly resulted in Esther being shot by the attempted 'high-jackers'. Fortuitously he had reacted instantaneously and opened the gate which was still closed as she had approached the entrance. She had been busy digging in the centre compartment of her spacious, compact Mercedes. The subsequent opening of the gate had distracted the high-jacker just long enough that Esther had sped deftly through the opening gate. Had she been in the Cruiser, she would have taken it clean off its railings. The High-jackers' had fled as the flood lights on the driveway had erupted into full blown activity. Bill had made a point from that day on to never allow Esther to approach the gate without first opening it. She had an angel who accompanied her, and this experience had given her greater faith, but had left its obvious scars on her conscious psyche.

"Bloody vermin." Bill had muttered again. He pulled over and deliberately wound down the window with a concerted effort. The Traffic cop was at his door waiting.

"Good evening officer," he smiled broadly. "How may I assist you." Courteousness written all over his broad chiselled features.

"Driver's license and veh'icle registration," the man announced. No 'Please' or 'Good evening'. Just aggression!

Bill waited patiently after turning them over. He had them strategically placed in the sun visor sleeve above his head.

The Traffic cop, without comment went around the front of the vehicle. The registration disk was attached to the front left lower corner. The cop was able to see the disk easily despite his large paunch. He leaned over, placing his large belly against the side of the Cruiser and on tip toes used his torch to read the disk. He prowled back around the hood of the car looking for an opening. Bill and Esther waited.

"Your license is expired," he declared without even further comment. "You have been drinking! Come with me." He turned without offering a good reason for his abrupt behaviour. Bill had seen this before. Aggressive attitudes that intimidated, and then the 'softly softly' approach of the expected bribe. He wasn't going to play this game. Turning to Esther, he said, "Close the window and the lock the doors. I won't be a minute." She looked anxiously after him as he climbed down from the front seat. The officer was already half way across the on-ramp, on the right hand side of the wide approach to the motorway. His squad car sat on the verge, in darkness. Something he recalled in the past brought out the warning bells. The other two traffic cops were up ahead, molesting other motorists.

As Bill crossed the precarious on-ramp, he thought the situation was a bit peculiar. Like that time, he had been driving through down town Johannesburg. That time he had been in his old Chevy Blazer, with its wide running boards. It was a left-hooker, which was difficult to drive around Jo'burg. He had found himself in one of this bus lanes demarcated for taxis and buses. The last time he had been there, he had been able to drive through from Diagonal Street from the old Stock exchange, to Braamfontein. It was now unfamiliar territory. The Traffic cop on that occasion was a young smiling coloured chap. He had slowed and stopped when the guy had stepped in front of him, signalling Bill to stop. There was nowhere to go. The lane was restricted by large cobbles on the right and due to the camber of the road, Bill's driver side window was inclined left to the pavement. The cop had sauntered around to his side, and with pad and pen ready, was about to write out the fine. Bill had stopped completely, but the large block motor was still goggling and the beast was still in gear. Foot on the brake Bill had again smiled back. As the cop approached Bill greeted him.

"Good afternoon Officer, I think I am lost." He was all decorum.

"Ya. I see that," the young cop replied. "I am going to have to give you a ticket!" He waited for a reply.

"Oh, okay. It is just that I have not been down here for a while." Hoping to appeal to the man's better sense of fairness. None was forthcoming.

"Your name?" his question was rhetorical. He would rather have not known that, and simply passed Bill by with a cursory nod and twenty Rand note in his sticky paws. Bill would not countenance bribery.

"William Henry Poster," he pronounced clearly.

The cop looking for a solid surface to hold his pad against, lifted his left leg from the vantage of the higher pavement, and rested his foot on the running board of the Blazer. He was about to start writing the ticket, when Bill resigned to now having to wait while the ticket was written, took his foot off the brake, but just enough that the torque engine, now unrestrained by the brakes, lurched the Blazer forward and sent the cop sprawling into the gutter. From the pavement ahead, Bill heard the uproarious laughs of the fellow officers, and replacing his foot on the brake, he looked out through the open window in time to see the poor chap, lifting himself out of an oil stained pool of stagnant water that had accumulated in the gutter. The young chap was all bravado, jumping back to his feet, but his pad was history. He wasn't going to be using that again in a hurry.

"Oops, sorry Officer," Bill smiled down at the crest fallen chap. "I was putting the car into park, whilst you wrote out the ticket!" Explanations unnecessary.

"No! It's okay. You may go." The cop was beetroot red, below his dark complexion.

"Can I pull over up ahead, and get you a towel from my gym bag?" Bill was trying to be helpful despite his desire to scream with laughter.

"No. NO!" The chap was devastated. The sooner he could get over this one, the better. "You can go. Please go!" The chap implored.

That was then, now Bill found himself running the gauntlet across a two lane on-ramp, with no street lighting. He managed the precarious shuffle without mishap, but could not help but think to himself, that this was extraordinary. The Cop waited for him on the driver's side of the squad car. From across the roof, he commanded Bill.

"Get into the passenger seat." No please or reason.

Bill quizzed him, "What is this all about?" He had not yet given Bill his License and registration back.

"I am going to give you a breathalyser test!" There was no attempt at providing adequate explanations, just a rude badgering attitude. Bill was now thankful he had left the cash with Esther in the car. Suddenly he was concerned for her safety. Could it be possible that they were followed from the casino? This might be a set up? He looked across at the Cruiser. Esther was seated in the dark, the vehicle locked and imposing on the far verge. Bill opened the door. It was beginning to feel like a JM Coetzee novel to him. The white man no longer the aggressor in this depraved society, was now on the verge of being hounded out of the country by intimidation. He could see the irony despite his predicament. This country of vast foreboding treachery, was more like the frontier societies of the Wild West, than ever before. Or maybe it was just his perception from the recipient of the aggression. He may have not seen it before, had he dared to look.

"Get in and close the door." Bill could see the bribe coming, long before the obvious result. He had only had two beers. But, there was always a nagging doubt. He looked over his shoulder one more time for good measure. Esther was cocooned in the Cruiser. He opened the door and slipped in. He could have requested blood tests at the clinic, if he had felt so inclined, but this was going to be easier, and quicker. He would get the breathalyser over with, and they could get on their way.

As Bill closed the door behind him, the door of the German sedan, did not shut properly, but clicked once, and remained partially closed, but not secured. The interior light remained on.

"Close the door properly," the cop barked an order, like so many others may have done to him over the past twenty-five years. Bill looked across at him diligently, searching for the spirit that drove his wickedness. He caught a glimpse of what looked like evil in his narrow slit pupils. The man's eyes were hooded by too many nights of no sleep.

Bill instinctively smiled. "You wait here!" His voice assured. He climbed out having leaned on the partially closed door.

"Get inside," the cop was now belligerent.

"Just wait here," he had just about had enough. "I am going to fetch a witness!" Without looking back, Bill walked calmly back over to the Cruiser. He motioned to Esther to open the door.

"Come with me sweets," he asked. "I need a witness." Esther just looked blank.

"The guy is about to try to get me to pay a bribe." He motioned to the cop who still sat in the now darkened interior of the sedan.

Esther did not need another request, and leaping out the passenger side she rounded on Bill, and clutching his hand, the two walked serenely back across the two traffic lanes.

Bill opened the rear passenger door, and introduced his wife.

"Hi Officer. This is my wife Esther."

He climbed into the front and closed the door with a 'thunk'.

"Good evening ma'am," the cop was all manners. "How is the madam tonight? Did you have a good evening at the Casino?" Warning bells rung. Bill looked back across at the Cruiser. Perhaps this was the ploy, and while they were distracted the passenger window was being broken, and the cash lifted!

He could not see anyone near the car. 'Had Esther remembered to lock the door?' He remembered hearing the door close, but there was no central locking. As they sat, the cop, pulled out a kit, and with a grand smile, and a cherry lilt in his voice that now sounded too contrived, he explained to Bill that each plastic wrapper contained an unused mouth piece, attached to a small plastic device. The years of procedure kicked in, and Bill could hear the forced recounting of hours of training. He would now play it by the book.

Bill took the proffered mouth piece, and taking a deep breath, gave it a solid blow. The cop retrieved the device from Bill's still pouted lips. He nodded. Then turning the device around so that they could both see it from their respective seats, he displayed a faintly lit white glowing analogue reading of zero point zero one five. Bill could certainly hold his liquor.

"Does the madam want to try," the cop was now playing the clever role of facilitator. He would woo Esther in an attempt to ingratiate himself, just in case this incident was reported. Esther declined gracefully.

"Thank you Officer," Bill took the initiative and opening the door climbed out. Nothing more was said as he opened Esther's door and headed straight across the tarmac, and the safety of the Cruiser. They did not even look back once, whilst they sped off into the night, and a calmer, relaxed evening over a ruby coloured Port.

Esther was wearily quiet the whole way back, giving Bill time to reflect on his thoughts. They entered the safety of their garage, with no other vehicle in pursuit. Bill climbed out, walking around the large spacious garage, before opening Esther's door for her. The garage was eerily quiet apart from a motor that hummed somewhere off in the corner of the garage, as the door made its final descent in defence of their anonymity.

As Bill closed Esther's door, he looked over at the disc on the corner of the windshield. The date showed '31/03/2008. It was two months prior. Petrus had forgotten to replace the old disk with the new cut out disc Bill had given him. The vehicle had been illegally operated. Bill made a point to remember to replace it in the morning. He would have to do everything himself, it seemed!

The Medicine Man

Wellington was a well-educated man, much like all those fortunate enough to have been afforded a Christian education in the thirties and forties in that period of turmoil that pronounced the end of the British Empire. The British had held on for dear life to what political power they could, having been afraid of the losses that an upheaval in a system that generated huge revenues for their State coffers would have. The system favoured the British, and it was why they fought so diligently through the Zulu Wars, then through the Boer War, only to ultimately concede to the population group, who did not want them nor needed them in the first place. The Voortrekkers had escaped their clutches, braving wild tribes and hostile territory, to cleave a place for themselves in the interior of South Africa. The Boer Republics had been founded, and relative tranquillity restored, until, that is the discovery of Gold on the Witwatersrand. When that occurred, every prospector and opportunist arrived. They benefited from the brave onslaughts of the Drakensburg and the laagers of the early settlers, arriving only after the hard work was done. The 'Uitlanders' were a thorn in the side of a Boer Republic of Transvaal, who had tried in vain to escape the clutches of the British. Their role as master and tax collector had driven the 'Volk' northwards. However, once the Boer Republics found that giving up Natal had rendered them isolated and land locked, they returned the favour and taxed the 'Uitlanders' in an attempt to rid them from the land. It would not work, because the land contained the biggest reserves of gold ever encountered. Much the same way the Rhodesians had been strangled by the geographical limitations of their own position, the British Government had bullied and cajoled the Boers into War. From then on it was simply a matter of 'Might is Right'. No! No one wanted nor needed the British in Africa.

So when Wellington had arrived at his mission school in the Natal Midlands, in the early part of the thirties, the British had created a system of education which would drag the local inhabitants out of their hut mentalities, and offer them a British Christian education. This would solve all their problems! Or so the authorities thought. Wellington had been one of those astute scholars, who had grabbed every opportunity to learn, and he did so like a sponge, soaking up every available piece of information with alacrity. His education was honed on a willing and receptive mind, but even from a young age Wellington knew exactly what he wanted to do. He was to become a doctor of medicine. This would empower him to provide the much needed services that his village needed, and with the help of the diminutive, bespectacled Father Hampstead, he would rise to prominence in his village. Wellington would learn the grace that Christian servitude to the community offered, and Father Hampstead would elicit in him a sense of the forgiveness that countless generations of Bantu men and women would need in the coming decades. All his education was centred on the sacrifice of the individual, to the common good. Wellington's education proceeded well. If the early Christian Fathers, had brought a much needed education system to the vast plains of the Natal Midlands, where communal living had always centred around the large herds of cattle, then Wellington would evaluate everything he learnt, and extract the good in each system, and consolidate it all for future generations. These cattle were the tribe's wealth, and it was a system that had worked relatively successfully for many centuries before. It would take the British and a pioneering spirit to render the entire system defunct; that is until the release of Mandela sixty years later, and the rise to prominence of Wellington, as the most revered 'doctor' in the country.

When he had qualified at Natal University during the post war period and before the disbanding of the Christian based education system, there had been an expectation that now finally, black men and women in South Africa, could finally achieve the great successes of their erstwhile white brethren. South Africa was alive with possibilities, but that all changed when the Calvinistic education system of the Boers, superseded the British system, and the whole education of the country would flounder for the next fifty to sixty years. The Christian missionary schools were eradicated in favour of the large double story clicker-brick facades of education facility pre-ordained by the Apartheid Government. They, the 'Old Nats' truly espoused the belief that their religion, their education, and their strict moral codes would drag these people out of their loin cloths and into civilized apparel. They believed that the system of discipline that had worked for two hundred years since the Cape Colonies were wrought apart by the Great Trek would prevail. After all, it had worked for the Afrikaner! Why not the African? Why indeed?

Wellington graduated with distinction from medical school, and preferring to remain among his people, had chosen a clinic within the Tribal area of his forefathers. From there he would oversee the births and deaths of three generations of his clan. Wellington was the epitome of a selflessly serving General Practitioner. The Pass Laws came and went, but nothing deterred him from his calling. He had a wife and seven children and kept them and educated them all on the meagre salary of a Government doctor. No possible cause would distract him from his goal and Wellington made provision for a retirement with his seven children, forty-two grandchildren and a multitude of hangers-on. This was the African tradition and no endeavour to change the attitude of families through family planning would stop the children and grandchildren from having these conglomerates. The historical wealth was in the number of children one had, to help with the family affairs when reaching retirement. This was the extended family base and would prove the only solution to a crisis which began enfolding as the population exploded. The myth was that large families provided support, but in truth what was occurring was the opposite. Tradition meant that Wellington would first have to provide the Lobola for his three daughter-in-laws, then ultimately the next five granddaughters, and then again through a system of un-employment among his grandchildren, the next seven grandchildren as they came along. Unemployment in theses rural areas was sixty-five percent, and the jobs all these children and grandchildren required for economic prosperity were a thousand kilometres away, and would result in the family unit disintegrating. Only Christmas holidays and Easter would bring them together as one. So, thankfully, if nothing else, the Christian education and non-secular calendar had allowed the three generations of Khumalo's to again congregate at the little village of Kwa-Thabunachu outside Mooi River. This was cattle country and the land was generously apportioned with every conceivable plant and insect species which grew and prospered in abundance. This was a land of Eden, where countless generations had grown up and where many more would. But Wellington had known something was missing in their education!

They lived on that is, until the early eighties, and the work related migratory habits of its inhabitants, had rendered Kwa-Zulu Natal, the leading protagonist in HIV and AIDS transmissions. Wellington was now slowly watching the retardation of his community, in much the same way as he had seen its earlier explosion. The virus was prevalent amongst the young men, but no one was truly safe from its passage. The local tribes would call it the 'sleeping disease' because so many would succumb to lethargy. Coughing would often pre-empt the demise of many and tuberculosis was often attributed to the ultimate death. The medical fraternity were unable to explain successfully to the millions of poorly educated blacks in the rural areas, who had not had the advantage of the Missionary schooling system. They had fought against the Apartheid Government and rendered themselves illiterate and uneducated in the process. Wellington would see the ultimate sacrifice that came hand in hand with ignorance. The spread of the virus could never be contained, unless the people once more became educated. Many of the men had abandoned the clan system in favour of the highly exploitative society that met them in the Big Cities. Consumerism was everywhere. Billboards, advertising everything from cars, which lay way beyond the reach of most, to the furniture that displayed what their lives could be as long as they lived long enough to qualify for and see the completion of their RDP home. Government bureaucracy was rampant and nothing ever seemed to get done. However, the virus was spreading its way through one community after another, and NGO's were trying desperately to cope with all the problem that should have been the domain of the clan elders, and ultimately the chieftain. If not for the break down in this successfully tuned system, HIV and AIDS would have never been the pandemic it had become.

Wellington, now effectively that clan leader, was extremely aware of the dangers of this sleeping giant, and every holiday he would sit with his people around the open fire, and recount the stories of his ancestors, drink his millet beer, and warn the children of this scourge. The family would listen intently as spirits were evoked, and Wellington gave them the benefit of his eighty years of experience. Other clans were not so fortunate, and one by one the villages around them disappeared along with their occupants, and the traditional lifestyle became a thing of the past. This was evolution and progress, and the elders could not stop it. Wellington however, had other ideas. Medicinal properties of locally grown shrubs and roots of trees, contained within them the healing ingredients that no modern science experiment could hope to replace. Westernized medicine had largely become the way forward for a Government intent on eradicating disease and pestilence among the population, and restoring the status quo. The problem was as Wellington could see, "They had forgotten the land, and abandoned the age old traditions of a way of life that had been brutal, but nonetheless successful."

Wellington knew the only way forward would be to teach the younger generation the benefits of the herbal remedies of the past. They had provided all the necessary solutions to their needs for countless generation, but were now being overlooked in a solution to this AIDS problem. He had been fortunate enough to be the recipient of these well-worn herbal remedies, from an old San elder. A woman whose knowledge of these things, had been living in the Eastern Cape for many years. She was reputed to be well into her nineties when he had been to visit her outside her original wooden branch hut, covered by leaves and animal dung, which kept out all the unwanted insects and pestilence. Wellington had sat with her and learnt the values of her Shaman lifestyle for forty days, whilst the full moon returned through its cycle. Wellington was keen to learn all he could because she was the last of her kind, and the ancient traditions would die out with her. This was part of the tragedy of the Southern African continent, and instead of preserving these practices for posterity, the succeeding educationalists had implemented their styles of education on a people who had survived these conditions, since Stone Age times. The San would have the last laugh. They would all die off, and take with them the secrets of their medicine. But Wellington would try to honour them as best he could, in the traditional healing that he could learn from the old woman. This would stand him, and the clan in good stead.

Wellington believed as many would come to realize, that the huge jump in population from the tailored numbers of their ancestral clans, was not good for the country as a whole, but it was due in part to peacetime. No longer would the young men lift their short stabbing spears, scream 'Byete' and run headlong into the awaiting Swazi and Xhosa tribes that threatened their borders. No! Wars were a thing of the past, and the Great Trek, had ultimately brought with it the civilization that those intrepid Boers had yearned for. As with every great migration, there was a value to be had in the positive attributes associated with cultural symbiosis. The Boer would teach the tribes the value of their God, and the tribes would in turn show them the value of a cultural heritage that had stood the test of centuries of cruel but effective authoritarianism. They both had merit and would be a grand symbiotic solution. The fear of God, as portrayed in those ancient forms of pulpit bashing, Calvinistic tirades, and the fear inducing evocation of the spirit world which elicited response from the ancestors, were needed to keep the people in check. But, the other side of this conundrum was the fact that Wellington knew they had fought Apartheid, only to relinquish power to the

Multinational Conglomerates, who now controlled the supply of everything in their 'New South Africa' including medicines. These medicines were not, however, necessarily good for the health of the country. The place in society for the traditional healer had been usurped for adverts on Television for everything from Headache powders to women's sanitary pads. The rate of coronary artery diseases among men was increasing at a phenomenal rate and Pension Funds were finding it difficult to cope with the increasing number of claims. The Medical facilities were being swamped and the hoards who descended on the cities like some ancient Impi phalanx, were now in desperate need for the remedies that they would have gotten from men like Wellington. Analgesics superseded the traditional root crop 'Ngumbe' and cough syrups containing alcohol, were substituted for the herbal remedies of the ancients. The alcohol in the syrup sedated and pacified a nation of children, but their health would suffer later in the shebees of the old Sofia Town, and the new bars and clubs that made their way into the townships after the demise of Apartheid. The 'People' once more became subjugated and the whole system turned on dependency. For them to be truly free, they would have to shake off the shackles of consumerism and return to the 'old ways'.

Wellington was sitting at his kraal in the dusty sand driven off the escarpment, that preceded the coming spring, when a large black SUV pulled up on the dirt track that lead to the homestead. The men in suits, all dignified and cultured, climbed the kopje above the lake to his cluster of traditional huts, where he spent his Sundays, away from the clinic that had been built across the valley on the hilltop opposite. Wellington had expected them, as they came from the city of Pretoria, in that Province carved out of the granite that had been home for two hundred years for the boere. But these men were not Boeres, and their disregard for the humidity of the valleys of Natal had rendered them to sweating, puffing hulks, by the time they reached him in front of his hut. They were now carrying those tailored jackets, and they had soaked through the white linen shirts which had looked so resplendent on them a mere ten minutes before. This was Africa, and they had been born here, yet they had already forgotten their traditions. As the first of the group stooped to catch his breath, the others caught up with him. The traditional hospitable thing to do would have been to send his younger daughter to them with the gourds of water, so they could refresh themselves, but Wellington wished to see them sweat. These were the same bureaucrats, who six months earlier, had reduced the funding to his clinic. Now half a year, and one political upheaval later, they were here to see him to request his help. The new regime was planning to implement a National Health Insurance scheme, and they would need his help to disseminate the role of traditional healing in its implementation. These were the very people who had sold their heritage down the great Limpopo River, with not so much as a glance back at the old ancient buildings of Mapungubwe. The chances were that they were now here at the behest of their new President, who was embarking on a radical change in attitudes towards the ancient traditions. Being a traditionalist in every sense, and having six wives with a seventh for good measure on the cards, he had determined through the various policy strategists, to bring back some form of traditional healing to a nation intent on destroying itself from within. The ancient ruins of the Mapungubwe and the Zimbabwe civilization, were testament to how easily one dynasty could make way for the next. He would, with Wellington's help reclaim that fading dynasty.

The men stood now before him, their pride in tatters, and the humility of their predicament etched across the broad furrowed brows of those ancient faces. Wellington would give them a good lesson in the ways of the ancients, and when they were finished they would be humbler and wiser for it. They were all introduced, and friendships restored. This was the way of their forefathers, and sitting on neatly arranged wooden stools they whiled away a few minutes in introductions and polite conversation. When this meeting convened they sat under the broad acacia, whose buds had sprung in the weeks before the first thunder showers. The stratocumulus would ride in from the North West, like dragons of mythical magnitude, billowing expectantly on the far western horizon, then sweeping through the escarpment the air would sour first with the driven dust storms. The sky would turn blood red like the Rivers of the Zulu Wars had done, then with three days of unrelenting humidity, and no show from the rain God, the air would frizzle with the electric anticipation, and them, one drop would land on the dust layered area and the scent would be as sweet as the nectar of the African honey bees that built their wild hives in the boughs of the fallen Gomagoma tree. This was the precursor to the next and then the next. The dust jumped in a million splashes of an Irma Huntley canvas, alive with three dimensional rainbows as the oblique rays of sunlight refracted off the waters below, reached up the hill and swarmed with the innumerable buzz of a horde of committed Angus Buchanan devotees. The smell was of ozone, as the electric storm jettisoned its ultraviolet light into the melee, and the oxygen particles were wrought apart, only to reconnect with other oxygen molecules, forming the O3 compound of ozone. This gave the air a sweet sickly smell but which hung on the dust particles it attached itself to, and suddenly the ground was statically charged with the promise of a million other such storms. This was the omen that the wise old Sangoma's looked for in their cursory predictions of the hope of a good yield in the autumn.

Wellington would move them into the hut, where he would celebrate the rain and thank them for their arrival, which he would explain had pronounced to the world this austere occasion. Their Westernized educations and materialistic lifestyles did not preclude the innate sense of superstition that still abounded in them. Wellington would play on these fears and leave them gaunt and haunted by their lack of belief, now turned eerily fable oriented. Those ancient stories still told in hushed conversations by aging grandmothers was their only link to their past. By the time Wellington had finished with them he would have them suffering the ailments of their ancestors, and miraculously having healed them with his potions, he will have them eating out of his hand. For Wellington this was his way of introducing the herbal wealth of the thousands of years of historical verbal relating. Of these remedies that one faith healer to the next would relay, Wellington would now commit to paper, so ensuring that it would become part of written knowledge. They sat with him in the confines of his hut, drank his millet beer, and by the time they had spent an afternoon and evening with him, he would be co-opted into the framework of the NHI planning committee, and marrying off one of these men to his youngest unmarried daughter.

Wellington would divulge his successful remedies for all the common cures and some for more severe doses of the maladies that young men brought back with them to the village after excursions to the cities. But it was not this that these bureaucrats sought. It was through the statistics of his clinical studies that he had drawn the attention of the authorities in Pretoria. Amongst a population of millions with an infection rate of over forty percent among men between eighteen and Forty-five, Wellington had managed to produce a statistical incongruence. This was what they were after, and the prize that held the lofted opportunity for salvation for their battered Medical Health Care system. The cost of introducing the vaunted cures, and even potential inoculations against its rampant spread, had bankrupted most medical departments. This was a short term pipe dream, as the ARV's were not a cure, but a long term noose around the financial neck of the country. They would have to embark on that form of treatment for the short term, but what was needed was the kind of proactive treatment campaign to address the root cause of the problem. Wellington had been their hope in the trials and tribulations of a systematic destruction of basic healthcare through an implosion of service delivery swamped by need. He would be able to assist them to claim victory over a disease of the twenty first century that had been introduced to do exactly what it now potentially would. Lay waste to the population of Kwa-Zulu Natal, and in so doing render the Zulu Nation a spent force, and a lost nation, subject to incursion from the banded hordes that now stood waiting in the East. The nation would have to fight off this pandemic with the gusto they had fought at Isanladwana. The stakes were high and Wellington knew only too well what was at risk. It was the long term survival of the new nationhood of the Zulu, and at eighty, he would rise to the challenge, and like so many of the wise men that were his peers from a similar era, he would fight diligently with all the knowledge his years had afforded him to take the number 46664, and using numerical supremacy, turn that number into 8 which was the sign of infinity, and success of their cause.

Golden Treasures and forgotten fables

Bart or Bartholomew as he was known to his academic colleagues was a man who time and nature had gifted with intense intellect and a grand sense of purpose. Working on the Witwatersrand's campus, he had grown to love the great melting pot of ideas that formed its very core. The noetic sciences of the great thinkers of the day, had achieved great things through the academia of Wits University, and Bart had been at the forefront of that thinking. It had taken a combined effort of great intellectual focus, to change the mind sets of that myriad of students that had passed through the esteemed establishment, but that great broth of egocentric thinking, had slowly changed the morality of thought, that had once been the central purpose for individual study. Bart had thus helped contribute to the global thought process that had shaped the minds of our future leaders.

The campus had seen many great thinkers come and go, but each great thought, each comprehensive debate, had formulated the universal consciousness of those students. They would join economic activities of corporate and parastatal endeavour which ultimately would lead to the prosperity of South Africa, and re-shape her political landscape. From the broad-based elitism of an ANC government, who once handed the reins of power, had selectively sought to enrich themselves, the university would reclaim lost ground. Through the massive contributions of academics like Bart, future thinking would provide hope for the landless and politically ostracised. This was his domain, but now that he was reaching retirement, Bart had found a new sense of purpose for his empathic energies.

The growing conscience of human sciences had made the concerns of fairness and equitable distribution of resources a major focus of his energetic contributions. But it was a chance visit to the newly opened Origins Centre, along with a display of the famous Mapungubwe treasures that had provoked his latest project. Whilst listening to the young curator of the recently created Pretoria University exhibit, talking about those ancient South African artefacts, a thought had occurred to Bart.

"What had become of the hoards of gold trinkets removed from the site of the early archaeological digs at Mapungubwe?"

The attractive, but diminutive woman curator, had made mention of the history of that great prize of South African heritage, yet there were still many pieces of ancient gold treasure, which had not found its way into the display. It was believed that they were in the hands of private collectors, and Bart was going to make certain they 'gave them up' before the ancestors could finally be put to rest.

In their culture, the people of the Limpopo Province had been very aware of the powers of the ancients. This was why the country and particularly that region had not found peace in over one hundred years. It was believed that when Jameson had famously ventured north with his expedition, at the behest of Cecil Rhodes, he had passed by the ancient Mapungubwe ruins, a magnificent natural defensive position where the tribe had been located during that period between the eleventh century until present times. The first evidence of Iron Age technology, some thousand years after the Northern hemisphere had been through their Iron Age, was a fantastic example of the ancient technology of these people. Jameson had admired its ancient reaches but had glibly passed on believing that the riches he sought, lay beyond the Limpopo River, and his destiny with Lobengula. What he failed to understand was the reason for why this ancient tribe had needed such impressive defences in such a sparsely populated region! He had crossed the Limpopo, and struck an agreement with Lobengula, for the prized land under which these precious mineral rights lay. It was these mineral rights that the British South Africa Company desired and Rhodes would need to press Lobengula into bartering the wealth of his land, for some cattle and a few trinkets. But it was Mapungubwe that was the real National Treasure and something that needed to be preserved for the heritage of the country. The Pretoria University had done a splendid job up until then, but Bart felt a campaign of, 'name and shame' might bring this famous history to conclusion.

The last visit he had made to the area, had been as an academic exercise with some friends some five years back, and Bart knew the rich history of the people needed to be complimented despite years of being lost to that other monumental history that was Southern Africa heritage. The importance of Mapungubwe had been disparaged by Jameson, and he had simply ignored the warning its vast ramparts presented. Jameson was a surgeon, having studied in England before settling in South Africa. But despite his knowledge and academic prowess, he had ignored the basic fundamentals of warrior wisdom. The Limpopo had presented not only a source of water for the tribe, but its natural course had provided the delineation between the land that would be carved up by the BSAC, and the Boer Republic of Transvaal. Rhodes would negotiate with Lobengula to have that land renamed 'Rhodesia', but the desired one-thousand-year history he and others had sought would be foreshortened by circumstances and a disregard for the ancient ancestors. It was now time for those ancestors to sleep, and to ensure that, the prized artefacts that lay in these private collections would need to be returned. Until then, the people would not rest.

Bart had decided that a small expedition to Mapungubwe would be required. He knew the locals, spoke their dialect, and would find out from them who had the last remaining golden treasures. Their customs preserved in ancient fireside stories, ensured that those who had taken artefacts from the site, would be remembered, and so Bart would go to speak to these private collectors first.

The sand coloured, sun bleached Land Cruiser stood outside his driveway with the roof rack sporting all the necessary equipment he might require for a month long expedition. The tyres inflated for the extra weight of equipment and provisions, sat at a peculiar angle at the curb-side, incongruously silhouetted against the sunrise of an early spring morning in the suburbia of Johannesburg. Bart's ramshackle estate on a tributary of the Braamfontein Spruit was an enigma in modern day Johannesburg. One hundred years before, when Rhodes had stood on the Parktown Ridge, before deciding on a location for his new offices, he had turned northwards towards the still visible Spruit that snaked through the barren Highveld brush and acacia, and he could see as far as the Magaliesberg range, with not a tree to obscure his vision of the land that lay to the North. Today, that view from the Parktown Ridge was met by a canopy of green trees that blanketed the entire Northern Suburbs of Johannesburg. This forest had started explicably in 'Forest Town' where the first mining magnates along with their subordinates had settled. By 1896, and before the ill-fated Jameson Raid had severed what little trust there was between the 'Uitlanders' and the Boers, there were one hundred and forty thousand occupants of Johannesburg. The city spread like wild fire east, and west along the extent of the Gold Reef, and along with it, this man-made forest which now created its own climate.

"Yes," thought Bart, as he looked up at the rising sun and took in her demonstration of brazen colours. This was the new South Africa. It was from there that this modern day explorer would set off to reclaim some of this lands rich heritage, and put some of those ghosts to rest.

Rene waited patiently in the passenger seat. His live-in-lover of some twenty years now, had recently completed a post-grad degree in Archaeology at Wits, and she was keen to get going. The two were waiting for their travelling companions to arrive. They would embark on their journey with fresh coffee brewed and relative air-conditioned luxury, on an epic journey which would hopefully be the last expedition to Mapungubwe needed in the pre-2010 euphoria that was South Africa. The government and big business were so focused on the profits they would make from the World Cup, that they had forgotten the richness of their past. Bart was determined to change that, and finally put the cliffs of Mapungubwe firmly on the map. Only now, in the post-apartheid era of affirmation of historical correctness, was it possible to see those chiselled, weather-worn fortifications for what they really were. With his Garmin tuned in to Mapungubwe, and pictures from Google Earth now firmly configured into his travel arrangements, Bart was ready to conquer the last remaining lost legacy of South Africa.

Strange, that in a country so intent on reclaiming land and lost wealth, that the benefactors of the Mapungubwe Treasures on display at Tukkies, had been a private individual who did not even live in South Africa. The newly resurrected Mapungubwe Rhino had been pieced together with great care and diligence in the hallowed halls of The British Museum, but yet the new South African Government had never understood the value of their own birthright. The new Zulu lead faction of Zuma's camp had not been interested in a history of some ancient tribe that had pre-dated them by almost five hundred years. Why would they? The tribalism of politics in Southern Africa was still firmly part of the culture. Until those in positions of power could put aside their regional differences, and colloquial inadequacies, they would never appreciate the true history of their country. The new power block was not interested in riches from the past, only contracts for lucrative merchandising agreements for the future. Bart would change the way they perceived Mapungubwe, and put it on the map forever.

The group joining them were running late, and Bart had received a SMS message to say they were 5 minutes out. Imagine if those early trekkers had been so co-ordinated? Imagine if South Africa had not had Gold. "Would we even be having this expedition?"

Bart was conscious of the modern diaspora of a xenophobic society. It was ingrained in their psyche and needed exorcising.

Bart was only concerned about the traffic on that run through to Pretoria. He had arranged they leave on a Saturday morning early, so as to avoid the long lines of traffic that commuted daily between Johannesburg and Pretoria. He suddenly had an idea. "Just as the 'Uitlanders' had arrived in Johannesburg to seek fortune and fame, imagine if those commuters who had settled in Pretoria, but commuted to Johannesburg, and vice versa, could do a simple exchange, like the 'Uitlanders' who arrived to work on the mines. Their lives had been fraught with hardships that even now, our refugees from Zimbabwe and the rest of Africa, could relate to. But their lives had been simple. Shacks had been their residence, whilst they sought their fortunes on the Gold Reefs. When a new reef was struck, they would relocate to a new area, in hope of that 'new' fortune. But it had always been the 'Big' mining companies who would dominate those Gold Fields."

Bart understood this only too well. The refugees he worked with in his AIDS projects, and the people he had met during the xenophobia violence, were exactly the same as the 'Uitlanders' of the 1890's.

"They had been ostracised and victimised by the Government of the day, paying huge taxes to the Boer Republic of the Transvaal." However, they were the same as the refugees of today. Just as the Boer Republic had tried to tax them to death, so to now, was the New South African Government intent on ensuring they register so as they may become contributing members of our society and not a tiresome burden on the infrastructure. One thing they could be certain of, was that the majority of those Zimbabwean refugees were hard working, educated people who had been displaced by their own kind.

"These people needed homes, they needed jobs, and the local South African's had not understood that in just one decade, they had gone from victims, to victimisers", Bart had told Rene.

This was the irony of economic prosperity and the innate human need to dominate that existed.

"Once they had received the benefits of their 'Liberation Struggle', they were none too happy to share it with anyone else."

This was why this trip to Mapungubwe was vital. Bart wanted to put this historical site into perspective. The ancient tribes had settled in the area, intent on their lives of cattle breeding and iron-mongery. The relative hardships that they encountered were not as arduous as one would imagine. They had a plentiful supply of water, as the Limpopo, although perennial, had a good catchment. They remained in their settlements, not having too many enemies, because they were the first to settle the area. The 'Great Zimbabwe' settlement was far enough north as not to be a threat, and there were some scholars who considered them to be related. However, they alone had forged an identity for themselves in the harsh environment that was the Limpopo Valley, and they had left their legacy there for all to witness.

"What would become of the modern refugees from all over Africa?" Bart considered this. He hoped that on this expedition he might find some answers that would give hope for those in the future.

But his idea, although quirky, remained with him. "What if those who commuted to Johannesburg for work, simply swapped their homes in Pretoria for one in Johannesburg? The commuters, who worked in Pretoria, would then live in Pretoria, and those that worked in Johannesburg, could live in Johannesburg. Commuting was such a wasteful expense! Imagine the saving of resources if the people could simply swap their homes. A three-bedroom home in Menlyn for a three-bedroom home in Craighall! A two-bedroom duplex in Pretoria East for a similar one in Edenvale. That would simply economies of scale. The commuters would not have to commute, and life would be as simple as it was in Mapungubwe!"

The idea, once formulated in his mind, began to emerge more and more during his trip. He was thoughtful and Rene could sense he was in his own little world. She made small talk with their late arrival fellow expedition colleagues, and Bart drove. The freeway to Pretoria was already busy. The Gautrain earth works, and large concrete pylons made it a tricky journey through the eastern suburbs of Pretoria. Bart remained focused on the road ahead, and kept his thoughts to himself.

He wondered, "Imagine what this trip must have been like on horseback, with slower oxen wagons trundling along behind. Today it would be a twelve-hour journey up through the old Pietersburg highway, and then once they had reached the Limpopo Province, left along all those scarred tarred roads, and eventually onto the dirt tracks of the farming communities that nestled on the border with Zimbabwe. A border that was so porous, that when Mugabe had chased all his Murambatsvina refugees away from Harare and the larger towns of Mashonaland, he had effectively forced them under those barbed wire fences, almost as sure as those who escaped the Nazi concentration camps, must have felt it their obligation to get away from the horrors of that repression. Then it had been a war that had driven men under those barbed wire enclosures. Today it was a war of attrition, and Mugabe seemed intent on winning at all costs.

The victims of that war were the Ndebele of the south, who like their early ancestors had fought the Colonials, then the Rhodesians, and then having finally achieved their much sought after Independence, were to be victimised by Mugabe and the Fifth Brigade. All this manic history was relevant to the woes of the New South Africa. These men along with their predecessors had failed to understand the fiasco of the past, and were deliberately forging ahead down a road which they neither understood, nor could control for themselves. That 'figurative road' was being manipulated for them, in some peculiar twist of fate. Mugabe had remained staunchly in power, but how? He had been forced to concede his International standing as a Liberation Struggle hero. His Government and their cronies had simply ruined a perfectly good economy, in less time than it took to build it. The 'so-called' 'War Veterans' were so young that they were not even born when Mugabe came to power. And in all of this, his own supporters had turned away from his paternal guidance, sensing that his true motives were somewhat selfish. But in all this mayhem, he clung onto power. How?"

The conversation in the vehicle had turned to scholarly discussions on the 'Iron Age' culture of Mapungubwe, so Bart turned his thoughts further inward. He had heard all this before.

"What would Mugabe have done, had the big mining companies not discovered these new reserves of diamonds in the Archean Craton of Zimbabwe? Those diamond fields of the Murowa kimberlite cluster, and more recently, the Maranga reserves of Manicaland, were the most lucrative of all the current reserves in Southern Africa, yet none of that wealth was able to find its way into the Zimbabwean infrastructure! Harare airport housed the most sophisticated Diamond cutting and polishing facility in the Developing World. Only The Netherlands had more elaborate factory's, yet in a country impoverished and dependent on hand-outs from the World Bank, this little nest-egg of sorts, sat in full view of arriving dignitaries from all over the world! The irony was palpable.

Imagine if Rhodes in his heyday had set up his diamond cutting business on the outskirts of Kimberley, amidst all the poverty that existed in the slums around that bourgeoning town. He would have had a full scale riot, and the natives would have butchered him! But, there in Harare, twenty minutes from the open-sewers of Harare Township, in the midst of the worst health epidemic in modern history, is the most expensive, most elaborate diamond cutting facility in the southern hemisphere. Those 'Blood Diamonds' despite all the lip service paid by the exponents of 'the Kimberley' process, were finding their way into the markets of the east, with India, one of the most rapidly expanding economies next to China, gobbling them up faster than the Zimbabweans could cut them! The funding for this elaborate smoke screen had to come from somewhere! Who stood to gain the most by investing those huge sums of money into a defunct rogue State?"

Bart's thoughts were interrupted by an obstacle ahead. It was a toll road! "Heaven forbid", he thought, "having just filled up his tank with petrol, that one hundred and seventy litre tank, had solicited a hefty four hundred and twenty-five Rand tax to the Government! Now they want more indirect tax, for a road which was paid for by the tax-payer anyway!" He smarted at the injustice of it all.

"Oh, for the simplicity of an ox-wagon, and a horse, and the freedom of a Highveld barren of modern day clutter!" Bart was feeling a sense of foreboding. The country, the region and the world, was headed for damnation, and all he wanted to do was to get off. This trip would secure his faith in humanity, and return his thoughts to a more honest time. What he was not to know, and nor too, did Jameson all those years ago, was that from Mapungubwe, all the way north-west along the Botswana border, lay the most lucrative 'Orapa Kimberlite Track'. So intent had Rhodes and Jameson been, to get their hands on the wealth of the north, that they had literally tripped over these massive diamond reserves, in an attempt to find the gold, they knew lay somewhere to the north. It was down to who owned the mineral rights to these areas!

Suddenly, it all seemed clear. It was not the land, with its rich sub-soils that had fed a nation of cattle breeders that held the key! It was what lay below, and who owned the rights to those mineral reserves? When Rhodes had deviously struck his accord with Lobengula, it was to claim the land which Lobengula valued highly. But for Rhodes, it had all been about retaining the mineral rights that lay beneath the ground. Whoever controlled those mineral rights, held the power!

Then Bart remembered the legend of Lotrie. He had supposedly been the first 'white' man to see the Mapungubwe. It was around the turn of the last century, that a loner called Francois Bernard Lotrie had found his way whilst on horseback, to the grand Mapungubwe. "Lotrie was the key", he thought. This enigmatic man had lived with the local tribe for over a decade before Gerry van Graan. It was this fact that had gone unaccounted in the discovery of Mapungubwe, as the farm Greefswald on which it was now located was in fact a neighbouring farm on which van Graan's father had settled. Bart now knew who he needed to search for!

The clues would be in the history behind Lotrie and what he had come to learn about Mapungubwe in that time. Had he secretly found other graves and secreted the gold treasures out and re-smelted them for sale? Or had he been the curator of these treasures, until the rumours and legends of the 'City of Gold' had found their way back to Pretoria?

"What had happened to the gourds of diamonds, emeralds and other precious stones that had been seen at the site?" Along with the Kruger Gold, this legend of the 'Lotrie Loads' would become as popular a story for grave robbers, archaeologists and the like! The history would reveal itself to him on this journey, and Bart felt a sense of purpose. Whilst Rene and the others searched for more burial sites, Bart would search for the stories of the ancients. It was in these stories that the truth would be revealed, and the ancestors put to rest.

He would seek out the family of Mowena, a young Venda speaking man, whose forefathers had lived on the Mapungubwe. With the verbal stories handed down from that period, Bart would also follow the trail of the 'Lotrie Loads' and with the trail still hot, it would lead him to a bank vault in Amsterdam, where the hoards of emeralds and uncut diamonds still lay. It was somewhat ironic, that the oldest geologically known areas of Africa, which had survived the past 2.5 billion years, and which were the most immobile area on the earth's crust, were home to the singularly most unstable economic and political upheavals of recent history. It was time these treasures were brought home, for the benefit of all Southern Africa's people, if their ancestors were to rest in peace.

The Nightingale Robberies

Des awoke in a cold sweat, like so many times before. But this time it was different. He had been dreaming, but it was a dream unlike any he could remember. It was difficult to put his finger on exactly what had just happened. The perspiration clung to his forehead like tiny beads of mercury to a magnate, but he lay motionless, staring up at the ceiling. Judging from the dim light that filtered in through his hessian style curtains, the hour must have been that dull twilight just before dawn. Somewhere at the bottom of the garden he could hear the weaver pair calling to one another. It was the frenetic call of the male, harkening to his mate to come see his latest attempt at building a home. She had dismissed his three previous attempts, and all three lay in the pool, forlorn and decimated. Des remembered vaguely how his mother had packed up the family home and left their Durban suburb in the middle of the night, ashamed and devastated by the arrest of her husband for a crime she was unsure he had committed, yet nonetheless to protect young Desmond and his siblings, they had absconded in the middle of the night. It was this memory of his father, he now lay trying to recall. He had been a young boy, but had loved his father adoringly. His last valid recall of his father's face had been the one he had seen, the night they came crashing through the windows of their fifties style designed, clinker brick house in Addison Drive. It had been the middle of the night, and ten very heavily armed policemen had literally smashed their way into the house, through the front door which had remained hanging at an oblique angle on the only hinge that had survived, attached to its wooden door frame. The others had shattered the large window panes of the bedroom windows, and climbed in through the cavernous openings left by their forcible entry. After all it was the seventies in Apartheid South Africa, and anything was allowable. He recalled his father's desperate pleas to those burly Dutchmen, as they hauled him out of the marital bed, and how his father had looked harrowingly scared. Those men were going to kill him for sure, and this would be the last time Des would see his father alive.

Then Des remembered what the dream had been about. It was very peculiar! He had been dreaming, that he was lying in bed asleep, dreaming of his father. In this dream of his dream, Des was standing in the large doorway of an unfamiliar church in a strange suburb, and he was howling with grief. His little body shuddered with fear and trepidation of the unknown, and he sobbed uncontrollably. The tears flooded down his freckled face, and his body heaved with each passing sob that wracked his ten-year-old frame. It was peculiar, because when Des had woken now, he could not sense any of these tears he had shed, and yet his body had been wracked by the same uncontrollable emotions that he had dreamt. It was one of those out of body experiences. Des was dreaming of his father and shedding the fictitious tears he should have shed all those years ago. If he could try to psychoanalyse his dream, he would have put it down to the fact that he had never shed those tears in reality. He had been the oldest of four and now, as a ten-year-old he was elevated to the position of 'man of the house'. Accordingly, Des had a hard time showing any emotion. He felt it incumbent on himself at that tender age to show all the fortitude his pre-adolescent brain could muster. His mother had fallen apart, and he needed to be strong for the sake of his younger siblings. His childhood devastated like so many young South Africans of the day, he felt a familiar pang in his stomach as he lay in bed staring at the fly shit on the ceiling. This was his edge! This fear was what drove him to live a full and meaningful existence.

Des was now a well spread forty, and his life had taken some unexpected twists and turns. He was nonetheless doing well for himself, and alongside his dark Irish debonair looks, he had an easy charm that flowed with all he met. Despite his harrowing experiences as a child, Des had grown to be a vigorous 'man-about-town', and yet there was something missing? He knew that it was the ghost of his late father that haunted his every move now. Each time he would sit back to relax, Des would be spurred on to achieve even more. If one thing, his father's death had given him a decided benefit over most young men at the time. He had an uncanny sense of the spiritual void his father's death had created, because he knew that his father was with him in spirit. Des was an easy-going gregarious sort, with an eye for the ladies, yet he had a very real, sensitive side. Unbeknownst to all his friends and work colleagues, Des had a tender spot that the abrupt end to his childhood had not removed. Des had the ability, in private, to become quite emotional at the mere mention of his father. He remembered the sense of loss he would endure when he heard the words to that song, "When I was a child" by Luther van Dross. Those words were poignantly charged for Des, and he now knew why he had dreamed that re-occurring dream again. Des had stayed up late after the rest of the household had gone to sleep the previous evening. He had sat on the internet and tuned into X-Factor. There was a young boy, who had sung a powerfully moving rendition of that song. Des had almost teared up, but had marvelled at the sheer capturing of those words in the timber of that hauntingly beautiful voice, and wondered how that youngster had been able to capture those feelings so expressly? Had he also suffered the feelings of devastation that those words evoked?

As Des lay in bed recalling the song, he felt his father's spirit driving him once more. Even the dull headache, from one-to-many whiskeys, could not blanket that sense of purpose. But this morning he felt peculiarly different. Des could sense the calling he had tried so hard to ignore before. He knew his father wanted him to put those demons to rest, but there was a strange comfort in knowing his father's spirit was with him. He also knew that to chase those demons and find out exactly what had happened that fateful night, would somehow erase the advantage of his spiritual guide. But he knew he was destined to try. All that he had ever achieved was pushing him in that direction. It was time!

That day while waiting for his ten-thirty appointment to arrive, Des began to Google the story. There were some vague references to a robbery in Krugersdorp. His mother had never spoken of it, but he recalled, overhearing a whispered conversation of his mother's, with his only living relative, an elderly Aunt, who had visited them at their new home in Mondeor. Des had heard the 'old lady' arrive late one Sunday evening, and had leopard crawled all the way along the parquet passage floor, sliding over the smoothed wooden bricks, to hear the mooted conversation. The fear that his mother now lived with was palpable in her hushed tones, and Des knew intuitively, that his life would never be the same. So having only the possible recollection to a bank robbery, a tunnel and the unsolved mystery of a long forgotten conversation as his frame of reference, Des abandoned thoughts of his ten-thirty, who had clearly forgotten their appointment, and began his research in earnest. Clearly, according to what information was available, the heist must have occurred sometime during the late seventies. Well that would tie up with his age. Des had turned ten in the early winter of 1977, and this heist had apparently taken place during the early part of May. He could recall how his father had been away on a 'contract' in Johannesburg and how, when he had returned from that lengthy working contract, their lives had been somewhat different. The house in Addison Drive, on the hill overlooking a picturesque north coast, was a single storey farm-style building, with a porch that ran the entire length of the east facing facade. The wind from the sea would ruffle through the sugar cane plantations below, and Des and his siblings would run through the neighbouring farm, war-like and unperturbed by the cutting slashes of the stems of sugar cane and unconcerned about the venomous Green Mambas that lurked within the fields, preying on the Cane rats and Indian workers alike. Des's father was a larger than life, Ex-Rhodesian, who had seen the folly of the war against Zanla and Zipra, and the Communist backed liberation forces. He had turned in his Reservist camouflage fatigues, and the rifle they had allocated him, and dragged his young family away from the horrors of an escalating war. They had found themselves in the 'Last great British' outpost of Natal, like so many other Rhodesian families, and Des's father had set about trying to make an honest living. It had been around about that time that a man whom they had known in Salisbury, had arrived with a bottle of scotch, and he and Des's father had taken to spending evenings in the study, discussing business. Shortly afterwards, or so it had seemed, Des's father had been seconded to Johannesburg. His mother had been provided with plenty of provisions, and whenever his father returned, in the following months, it was always with gifts. He had adored his father.

Then came that fateful night, and the screaming and heavily booted storming of his family home. Des had only just turned ten, and his father had bought him a brand new Raleigh Chopper. It was purple, with polished silver handle bars, and a smaller front wheel, that made 'wheelies' a real possibility. Des had taken to the fields with abandon, his siblings tearing after him on foot, in hot pursuit. His father had really loved him, and this bicycle was his parting gift. But like so many of those memories, his one a grievous recollection was having had to abandon his beloved bicycle in Umhlanga, when they had left so abruptly in the middle of the night. With only suitcases, and the stench of his mother's perspiration filled fear filling his ten-year-old nostrils, he sat upfront and had finally fallen asleep after Mooi River, and the early hours of the morning. When he had awoken, it was mid-morning, and the cold wind which had rolled in from the Drakensberg had settled an eerie mist about the car, which was blanketed in this cloak of serenity. It had been an 'other worldly' experience, and he had recalled how he had dreamt of his father then, and every night since. When the mid-day sun, had finally burnt off the last of the winter fog, they found themselves parked outside the quaint out buildings of a truck stop in Van Reenen. With his siblings stirring from their exhausted back seat slumber, and now emerging in ravenous expectation from beneath their hastily organised sleeping bags, Des was sent out into the cold to obtain breakfast from the truck stop. His mother never left the car, and he had smelt the urine soaked cushion on which she had slept. Exhausted and drawn, she had never left the car for a second; not even when her bladder had nearly burst! She would shepherd them all into adulthood, like some 'mother hen', and Des was grateful for her love.

But now Des had to complete this mission. He had made it his obligation to do well, and his family had been there when he graduated from University. Having remarried, Des's mother had settled happily into relative peacefulness in Mondeor, and they had continued to live a rather uneventful life. However, for Des, there was something missing! It was the ghost of his father, and his unsolved death that had driven him thus far. If he was to put that ghost to rest, he would have to follow all the clues to where ever it may lead him. He tried to think of all the speculative conversations he had ever heard.

"The robberies were known to the authorities as the 'Nightingale Heist'. "This he knew because later on when his step-father had passed away, he had heard his mother mention the Krugersdorp affair for the first time since that muffled midnight conversation. Whatever had happened, the robbers of that bank had never been caught. "Or so the rest of the world was supposed to believe!"

There were sinister forces at work here that had buried the truth for long enough. This affair should have been brought to light during the Truth and Reconciliation hearings of the early nineties. Des had been un-prepared, and his mother had still been married, so there was no chance this event would be brought up! For the sake of her happiness, Des had let 'sleeping dogs lie', and there was some ironic twist in that. If the authorities had arrested his father for the robbery, why was this now such a closely kept secret? Surely if his father was the culprit who had 'tunnelled his way under the bank from a property next door, and safely entered the bank vault over the weekend', then this should be common knowledge, and his real family name would have endured the ravages of notoriety!

"No. There was some subterfuge here!" Those so-called 'Nightingale Three', had disappeared into oblivion. Or was that what the authorities of the time wanted everyone to believe? There was speculation that a blond woman, who was one of the accomplices, was now safely living out her retirement with all those other Nationalist refugees, in a remote part of South America, and that she had been the 'Mrs Diana Spicer' who had rented the property next door. "Was she related to the famous family of the same name? Or was this an ironic pseudonym intended to be 'tongue-in-cheek'?

"Who was the third accomplice, because Des had a definite inkling the second was his father? Who was the Rhodesian who had arrived so salubriously that weekend, and disappeared just as easily?"

These were all questions that begged the asking!

That evening, with laptop computer and 3G card, Des spent the entire time at his desk. The party raged on in the social club he called his lounge, but Des had asked not to be disturbed. His house mates knew this was serious. Des had some work to do, and whereas the free-spirited man would never deny himself the opportunity to live out his greatest fantasies, this evening he would forego the three nubile young strumpets his house mates had towed home with them from the local 'Jolly'. This was deadly serious, and they would have to quiz him in the morning, but tonight one of them was going to get lucky and have two companions to wile-away the late evening.

Des remained locked in his room, and he uncovered a bounty of information. It was interesting that the mastermind was supposedly a 'Peter Harold Nightingale', who had been the brains behind the whole heist. Yet Des knew that those hushed discussions behind the doors of his father's study had been initiated by the third shadowy character. It made sense that this character was the' Peter Rohwein' that had implicated his father in the conspiracy. There was no doubt that his father must have been the 'Nightingale' of the newspaper reports of the day. It was his father's favourite book that had presumably invoked the name. "A Nightingale sang in Berkley Square" was a title that Des recalled having seen on his father's book shelf! There was a reason Des felt so confident it was his father! He would explain it to his mother that weekend.

The Peter Rohwein referred to in these new reports was definitely the German with the slight accent, who had come to the house in Umhlanga. It was obvious to Des, that he had used his father as a patsy, and then disappeared himself, into thin air. Only to emerge as a suspect after his arrest in the failed Seychelles coup in the November of 1981, four years later. Des had an idea that the money from the bank heist had probably been used to fund that failed coup, and that the Colonel Mike Hoare, whose name was implicated in that debacle was again the 'front man', but that there were again sinister minds behind that event. After all, who served to gain from the Seychelles being wrestled from the grip of an Indian Ocean quasi-dictator? It was 1981; talks were already being orchestrated by Van Zyl Slabbert and other forward thinking Afrikaners, and the unbanning and eventual rise to power of the ANC in South Africa, meant that certain people in positions of authority, who had been instrumental in repressing the Liberation Movement, had a lot to be weary of. What better way of disappearing, but to your own secluded island paradise, and no potential extradition agreements! After all, they had all the loot from the heist, and that unofficial loot was far more than any amount that had ever been reported!

The bank had claimed the amount to total about six hundred thousand Rand, but then there was the matter of all the safe deposit boxes! There had been some suggestions by the investigating officer at the time, that there was a fortune in undeclared assets that had been elicited from those boxes. 'Martin 'Cowboy' Saunders', a celebrity policeman, who had investigated the robbery was known to have suggested that the true value of the assets in those safe deposit boxes would have been enough to buy anyone their own country! Go figure! Then this was where Des would need to look?

The protagonists in this affair had been the very owners of all that illicit wealth stashed in those safe deposit boxes. There was no hint that the very person who had masterminded the robbery, had in point of fact been one of those bank account holders. After all, what better way of enriching oneself, than to have knowledge of all the other people, to whom those safe deposit boxes belonged. The true mastermind would have been able to identify all those who had secreted their fortunes away from the tax authorities of the day, and would have bumped into those victims regularly, in the normal course of their weekly visits to the bank. Only those who used the dubious deposit boxes would have been known to one another, and they would have been too embarrassed to come forward afterwards. No wonder the real value of the heist was never reported, and that there was need for a patsy.

'The Nightingale Robberies' were a smoke screen for the real culprits. Those responsible had orchestrated the death of his father, and now Des was keen to find out who they were! The bank would surely have handed over the identities of those account holders who had registered safe deposit boxes? That information should be a matter of public record now that the TRC had done its work, and the bank would be obliged to make available that information. It was this fact that had been covered up and that had smelt of conspiracy, according to Saunders. The real culprits had stolen those fortunes from the very people they met regularly at that 'Old Boys Club', just off Commissioner Street, in downtown Johannesburg, and as surely as Taunnenberg and Madoff had seduced investors into parting with their ill-gotten wealth, so to had the real mastermind behind 'The Nightingale Robbery'! Desperate times call for desperate measures and so he had stolen from his own people.

Des was confident this was how his father had been duped into believing that it was just he and Rohwein, and the attractive blond, who were involved. Peter Rohwein had maintained his stony silence, even during the 'wrap on the knuckles' six-month prison sentence he served after the failed Seychelles coup. He never let on about who had been involved in the funding of that coup. Some believe that it may have been a greedy hotel magnet, who might own a string of hotels and casinos and who had a lot to gain from a potential change of Government. 'A more lenient tax regime, and a friend or two in Parliament, would have secured more lucrative concessions for building bigger and better hotels and casinos! Was it possible that the very man who had masterminded that robbery, had in fact been able to provide enough information to Rohwein and his accomplice, the aptly named Di Spicer, and that the whole purpose of bringing Des's father into the fray, was to send the police off on a wild goose chase to Natal, while the real culprits headed off to a paradise hotel on a far off Indian Ocean retreat?

One thing was certain! Des's father had been the patsy, and the reason his involvement and the disappearance of the third accomplice had never been solved, was that his untimely death in police custody, had never been reported. The fingers of the real mastermind, had reached into the dark caverns of the 'old Apartheid' system, and palms had been greased as easily as memories had conveniently faded. The answer to this mystery as far as Des knew, lay in the bank records of who had owned both hotels and safe deposit box!

Retribution from the grave

His was a world derived from division! He had been the notorious self-proclaimed 'Bomber', who had taken pride in his self-styled retribution on a society that had not recognised his talents as a human being. He made them pay with those near and dear to them. But it was a scar he now carried, like that bottle of brandy with its uninspiring label. It was ironic that he should eventually turn to alcohol for solace, from the demons that now raged in his mind. He was after all the one person every social drinker in the old Apartheid system had feared, yet they had not truly understood his motives. He had claimed at the time that it was his own motives that had forced his hand. But in truth it was an orchestrated crime against humanity. Every war has them in perpetuity, because it is the nature of war. As the scorpion had famously told the crocodile in that lovely African Mythology, as he tried to cross the river on the back of the crocodile. When the going had become too arduous, he had stung the crocodile and when asked why, he said, "Because it is in my nature!" Yet this was precisely why the old system had taken such umbrage from his crimes. He was half them, half other, with a massive chip on his shoulder, which would never be healed. Not even a belated post in 'high authority' would solve that problem, because he was inherently devious. It was how his mind worked, and the passage of time and the settling of his demons would bring justice.

Nowhere was safe to go anymore and he had single-handedly ensured that the message got through loud and clear. Why no one had thought to write his story was more reason for him to turn to drink. No one could be bothered, as he was just another so-called minority, marginalised by the class barrier, that neither recognised him as one, nor the other. Was it that his father's tirades against his colonial masters had instilled such hatred? Or could it simply have been that Thys would never have settled for a simple life! He had not been justified, like so many of those crimes against humanity that abounded in the old South Africa. But because he knew he would earn the kudos of an over eager Government in waiting, his notorious actions had set him apart from the rest of his fraternity. Yet it was exactly them he had turned to when in the moment he was rewarded for his actions, he then began the systematic empowering of his social class. If they had been deprived in his mind, by the one system, then maybe, just maybe the new class would recognise their talents. But history was the bearer of ill-omens. The reason his grandfather before him and his lineage had failed before, was a direct consequence of their dependency on the bottle. It was legalised euthanasia and the Government taxed it with the merit that was befitting a systemic social parasite. But to many like him, they had turned to that golden liquid in an attempt to deny the ravages of a social class system that had squandered great opportunities.

It was a late evening of just such revellery that had landed him in trouble. The questions still abounded some years later, and he had done his best to secure his innocence by manipulating the system he himself now controlled. If ever there had been a quirk of fate that had rebounded in anyone's face, this was it! The charges had been levelled against him by those he had once sworn to protect. It was the ultimate betrayal of the support he had garnered in a turn of political events. He surely had enemies, and there were those who had made it their vocation to ensure he suffered similar retribution for his crimes. But to Thys, whose lineage was half Afrikaner, with San ancestry, they would surely not approve of this violent act! So he lived with the demons that chased him for all he was worth. Faster and faster until....... ?

The Golden Mile had lost its lustre. It was on that avenue of high end luxury hotels and apartments that Durban had forged its early success. But it was now a far cry from the mesmerizing metropolis that had greeted so many holiday makers in the past. It seemed to Jacques, that it was a lifetime ago that he had stood with his family at the memorial service, where they had tossed their wreaths into the surging Indian Ocean from the granite pier on North Beach. Now the streets were cordoned off in a stark reminder of the new desperate society that had emerged from the remnants of Apartheid, and taken up residency in this once exclusively 'white area'. The place looked more like a picture of the Beirut of the seventies, where large concrete chevrons now sought to cordon off the main routes in and out of this burgeoning demographic time bomb of urban squalor. The passers-by looked on Jacques as he may have viewed a stray black man in the heady days of Durban's glory. Some suspiciously glared in outright disapproval of this incursion, whilst others looked on approvingly as he cruised through boulevards that once teamed with holiday makers and late night revellers. Now he guessed correctly, this would be a 'no-go-area' for tourists on their way back from festivities. The Apartheid system had been replaced with urban decay, and where the Golden Mile had once hosted the cream of South African society, it was now a sprawling example of why those barriers had once been in place.

The bakkie drew both admiring glances and distrustful glares. He knew only too well the poverty that seeped through these streets, having worked in the Police force and been into the township of Umlazi. Never having realised his full potential in that understaffed service post-1994, he had realised that his only hope for promotion was to change his skin colour. Instead he had taken the offer of his uncle Koos and had headed for the sublime serenity of a Free State grain farm and the obscurity he so wished he had been able to attain before his sister had died. They had both been away from their working class home on the Bluff that fateful night, but whereas Jacques had been on duty, manning the Central Durban control room from the comfort of a brick block fortress, his sister had been with her mates from college and they were pub crawling the 'mile'. She had been outside when that car bomb had ripped through the inner sanctum of their Apartheid comfort and torn the family apart forever. He hardly recognised the place where he had lost his sense of identity eternally, having had the guts torn out of his relative contentment. This single act of brazen hatred, had forced many, to look inwardly at their lives and determine what purpose they represented to a failed system. It was now as he tried to find his way along the beach front from Addington Hospital, where he had once waited in vain hope on that fateful night more than twenty years before, that he realised he did not recognise this place anymore. The bar had now been converted to a nondescript restaurant, with its lifeless facade and bland walls which had once displayed the pock-marked shrapnel wounds of its calamitous past. Now all the bars and clubs had moved north with the moneyed population to the evermore opulent Umhlanga skyline. Her guts ripped from her, Durban was now a sad reflection of her previous magnificence. Jacques found a parking on that chaotic beach front, and walked along the avenue, looking up at the towering, tiled monoliths that sold their hearts and souls for the hope of a past dream. Those once pristine white tiled facades now stood as a testimony to the rot of an evolving dichotomy with which the new owners had to contend and a system that was failing from ground up. Maintenance was a long way from the minds of empowered entrepreneurs eking out a living, from a low budget holiday experience clientele. Feeling somewhat depressed, Jacques turned before he reached the corner where the large car park area had facilitated the bombers' access. Jacques resisted the temptation to go back to the site where this urban decay had started. It was symptomatic of the failed state, and he had no desire to face his demons again. He had moved on, but had the mind of the killer done likewise?

It was that momentous night that he had received the call at the 'ops room' and despatched every available unit. Then grabbing his R1 rifle from his locker, he had raced to the bar, fearful of the inevitable. His demons had visited him that night, and had continued to do so for countless nights after. This had been a bad idea, so he retraced his steps back along the beach front to his car, and climbing into the cab, had two dishevelled street urchins to deal with before he could extricate himself and his brand new American import, from the ravages of that social abyss.

"Hey man, is that a V8 under there?" The dirty unshaved homeless man had asked.

"Yassus boet, listen to that engine!" He continued, as Jacques had turned the ignition. Jacques was in no mood to entertain these guys.

"Meneer. Do you want an air freshener?" The gap toothed man had persisted, having taken Jacques non-committal as an opening. He proffered a cardboard cylinder with a ribbon bowed around its centre.

"Thank you. No!" He was now quite forthright. He had no time for these scoundrels.

Jacques turned the bakkie away from that heaving pot of 'pojkified' humanity, with the street markets that employed hawkers from every conceivable cultural background on earth; and it seemed 'hell'. He headed back up through the back streets past his old unit, and the hill. He would stop at Florida road and having just driven the four hundred kilometres from his farm on the flattened plains outside Kokstad, he would need to eat soon. The afternoon was getting more humid as the warm onshore winds brought the precipitation of her tropical anti-cyclones in from the east. He found an airy open veranda bistro, and settling in for a cool beer and some hearty fare, he began to relax. The cricket was on the monitors. It was the 'Boxing Day' test at King's Park and he would take some time to watch the cricket during his trip. Jacques unwound on the stoep of that cosmopolitan eatery, and after ordering, sat and watched the cricket on the monitor. A group of four couples, of well-dressed blacks sat at a table between him and the television distracting him from the cricket. They were nearing the end of their luncheon, and as each had a Blackberry or equivalent hand held cell phone in both hands he watched as they performed a communal misnomer. Not one communicated with the other, unless it was via that technology that now posed an obstacle to verbal communication. It was an interesting interlude which he realised was symptomatic of this emerging class. He hated the things, and had resisted having one, until his boys had gone off on their trip. They needed to keep in 'comm' with him and this devise was a useful tool. He reluctantly agreed to buy one which they taught him to use.

The cricket was labouring into a hot, sticky end to the second session's proceedings, and Jacques unobtrusively watched these eight people spend the next twenty minutes before paying their bill. It was a far cry from the shouted hysteria of the beach front markets. Jacques felt somewhat disillusioned that the trip down had met with such an anti-climactic ending. "Still", he considered, "it was a far cry from the sight that had greeted him on that frenzied night so many years ago!"

But he could still see his sister's lifeless eyes, glazed by the trauma of that event and staring straight up at him, searching his soul for help. He had resuscitated her there at the now abandoned bar, with its mangled iron and wooden benches and accompanied her to the emergency room at Addington.

"God forbid any such occurrence now," he thought. The ambulances would never be able to find their way through that maze of streets and cul-de-sacs. It would be a catastrophe, and the Soccer World Cup was on its way. He secretly feared for the authorities. He had once been there!

Jacque put aside his thoughts and decided to enjoy a solitary afternoon engaged in that mindlessness of pursuits. Watching cricket! He would wait for the inevitable early rain induced close of play, then head for his hotel in Ballito. There was no rush. He had no timelines to meet, no agenda and nobody waiting for him the other side. The thought sent a pang of fear through his soul for the second time that day. He had recently lost his wife of twenty years. The 'Big C' had taken her from him, and his two boys were now living in London, having taken a gap year and stayed for the northern winter. He guessed they would be back soon, but this was going to be the first Christmas and New Year alone for as many years as he could remember had passed since losing his best friend and adored sister.

Jacques allowed himself the pleasure to wile-away the afternoon to its steamy conclusion with his Castle Lager and the large flat screen TV. Then with the close of play and nothing left to watch, except the inevitable replay after replay, he decided to leave the commentators to gabble on about nothing, and paying his bill, smiled a thank you to the young Indian waitress. He headed for his vehicle before the constant drizzle became a flood. As he approached his bakkie, a young man about the same age as his oldest son Stefan, stopped him. He was very well spoken for a car guard and having seen Jacques approaching, had looked up from his conversation with his colleague. They were both well dressed and decidedly better fed than the two he had been accosted by earlier. Clearly even the car guards were in a different league to their cousins on the beach front.

"Excuse me Sir, Jacques waited for the inevitable request for money! None came. Jacques turned to the man whose accent was a mixture between well-bred Zulu and elite education Durban High School good manners. He did all but doff his hat at Jacques to get his attention.

"Ya?' Jacques was feeling mellow and was in no hurry.

'My friend and I are having a problem. Jacques still awaited the obvious question about money.

"We are arguing about love! He says it is not possible to fall in love with anyone unless it is the right person!"

Jacques raised his eyebrows, his weather beaten furrowed brows arching in surprise from the question.

"No! No!" The man seemed to be visibly embarrassed. "I mean can you fall in love with a woman at first glance?" He had clearly understood that his question may have been misconstrued.

Jacques observed him suspiciously. He was still waiting for the 'close'. All sales pitches had them!

"I think it is possible," offered Jacques in his best English, "to fall in love ten times between here and the next block," he intonated, pointing to the adjoining street corner.

"The difference is whether you are 'in love' or 'in lust'!" He smiled playfully as the two men now nodded approvingly. He climbed into the cab, retrieved five Rand from the unused ashtray, and handed it to the well-spoken man who had watched him to his bakkie. He somehow suspected that the implosion of the economy had created many unnecessary casualties to this economic war. Jacques handed him a card, with his cell phone number on it.

"If you ever need work, you phone me and I will happily employ you." The man smiled graciously taking the offered card.

"Thank you I will," he looked down a Jacques details. "Farming hey?" Hard labour and early mornings sprang to mind. Jacques knew the guy would toss the card along with his advice the moment Jacques turned the corner.

He returned to his colleague and began a further lengthy discussion in English. Jacques started the bakkies engine and as he pulled out the two men were engulfed in another heated debate. There would be two more casualties in this crisis, but it would be up to them as to whether they could adapt and evolve with the changing world around them. The new Government had simply changed the way business was done and Jacques guessed that these two were not in the correct clan. Natal had always been a bit cliquey, which he had first-hand knowledge of. It mattered not who you were, but who your family were related to! The sense of Nepotism had surely taken hold on this society, as deliberately as that other band of brothers had shaken up the system and infiltrated every last vesture of the upper echelons of power. It was an illness which would ultimately drag this society to its knees if left unchecked. Jacques knew the value of family, but he was now ever more aware of how fickle life was. The ironies that were dealt as cards on a table were like the time he had ventured to the 'old Howard Hotel' where they had a gambling room. His mate Chris who had served with him in the police, before turning his appreciably intellect to making his fortune, had played the tables relentlessly. When Chris had exhausted the last of his months' pay, he had turned to Jacques and asked for a loan. Jacques somehow knew this could only end badly! Taking his card, he had drawn one thousand Rand, which he lent to Chris. The next two hands went badly; then all of a sudden, with his next hand, he was dealt two eights. Chris was not someone who would stick on sixteen, so he split the two. What happened next is the stuff of legends. His next two cards were eights! The two had to be split again, then with his chips on the table, four eights in a row and his ego pulsing, the dealer dealt two picture cards, a ten and an ace. This took care of the high cards and all four hands were winners!

Now after being dealt that kind of hand, one would expect Chris to have been a runaway success and cash flush he would have wanted to share his gift and the proceeds of a great hand. No! He simply handed Jacques back his original capital, and with his hoard of winnings continued to play and ultimately lose it all. Jacques had learnt a valuable lesson and never again accompanied Chris on his gambling forays. They were still friends, but the experience had left a bitter taste in Jacques mouth. Human nature was thus derived from greed and lust! He had opted out of that lifestyle and settled in the calm extremes of a Free State. Here he had the run of the farm and the love of a tender woman. He realised now, that he too had escaped the rigours of a challenging life. He was one of the lucky ones!

At the robots ahead, Jacques had bought the Mercury, and read the headlines.

"Poor Matric Results" These matric results would show a litany of problems that were still to face this fledgling democracy. The list of failed matriculants that would have to be given further financial assistance from Central and local Government read like a stuck record player.

"M..... M..... M....." It would go on endlessly. Taking the average of failures into account, the 'M's' had it by a large margin! They would have been the future on which the ruling class had pinned their hopes. But like the game dictated, they had become so dizzy from their euphoric success, that they had no sense of direction on which to hope to pin that donkey's tail. The failings of a system that now prided itself in the grand Stadia that had taken countless billions from education, social welfare and the potential future of the next generation, was about to unearth a multitude of problems that would ultimately see the ANC defeated in future elections. Jacques was not political, but he knew the power of education, having been the recipient of a concerted effort by the 'Nats' to raise their level of education. However, by forcing learners to study Afrikaans in schools throughout South Africa, the 'Nats' had secured their own demise with the school riots of '76'. An uneducated and illiterate population was a huge risk to future governments. The revolution was still to come, but it would be driven by class wars over who was entitled to that large pot of tax-payers money. There was still to be a division drawn between the clans, but as Jacques had seen from the wars between the residents of Umlazi, there were no survivors when a system consisted of the 'Haves' and the 'Have-nots'.

On the inside page there would be an article about the trail of a convicted murderer, who now stood accused of drunken driving and defeating the ends of justice. It was sad that a society that had healed itself miraculously at the Truth and Reconciliation Commission in the 'nineties', was still fighting its demons even now. "Why had the very beneficiaries of the grace offered by that remarkable commission not lived up to the expectations of a forgiving society?" He thought.

Maybe it was that they demanded too much of the system, having overhauled it for their own benefit, and not seen to raise all and sundry from the depths of poverty along with themselves. The one thing was for certain! It was not a lack of education that had forced the hand of those who had conducted those heinous crimes in the past. It was in fact the opposite. The system had offered a first rate education for most. But revolutions being what they are, there would always be room for improvement. It was the demands of that changing system that had ensured that a middle class emerged from the Apartheid era and thankfully they had side-stepped a brutal meltdown. But through the imploding education system now, the war of attrition was still to be fought. If the wanton greed that reeked in every hallway of the Government were not addressed soon, it would be a new revolution that this country would be facing; lead by the youth leaders who had been entrusted to calm the very people who were being disempowered by the system. They still had a sense of entitlement and it was vital they be offered a chance to succeed. Jacques could see that the cards were on the table and it was now up to the 'new generation' to see to it that they played their hand correctly.

The Tanzanite Scam

Kerry was livid. She had been scammed and she had only herself to blame for being duped out of Seven thousand Rand! This was her university fees to the 'University of Life'. For every Rand that she lost, she would make certain that she would never fall prey to her own greed ten times over. Yet what she had been sold was not any different to any other pyramid styled scheme that was legitimised by glossy brochures and dreams of rich pickings. Her mother had always warned her, "If it sounds too good to be true, it is usually too good to be true!"

But Kerry was a 'start you up and fire you off' kind of gal. A self-starter and someone willing to go the extra mile to have an opportunity to make a success of her limitless gifts. Kerry could not believe that she had just been relieved of her monthly takings from her very profitable marketing business. However, she had worked for that money, and these guys had not! She was livid. But who could she call? As Kerry sat in her blue Ford Focus, and gazed unseeing out through the window into the depths of the Sandton City parking garage, she began to laugh. It was a whimper at first that soon became a full bodied howl. She was a fool for having been taken in by this scam, but it was not necessarily her greed and desire to succeed that had motivated her, but there was undoubtedly mitigating circumstances. She would allow her own chastisement of herself to take its course, and then once fully self-effaced, she would call her friend Paul. He would know what to do! She had called him countless times before to bounce ideas off of him. It was a pity that she had not done so before being taken by the hard luck story she had just paid seven thousand Rand to listen to.

"Mind you," she thought. It had all happened so quickly.

The phone rang, once, twice then was answered on the third.

"Hello, Paul speaking!" He had clearly not recognised her number on his screen.

"Heeloo." She always tended to disguise her voice when speaking to men. She wasn't sure why, but maybe it was a way of playing sultry and seductive. Heaven alone would know why!

"Who is that?" Paul sounded quizzical.

"It's me, Kerry", she announced. "Why don't you have my number on your phone?" She was sure that he must have it.

"Oh, hi Kerryster," he had a fondness in his voice that reminded her of her dad. "I think I saved more than one number under your name. That is why the caller ID does not work!" He was sure he had her number because he had phoned her regularly.

"Oh, yes." She remembered her previous phone had been stolen. She had changed her number.

"How are things going?" She wanted to suss him out. Make sure he was not in one of those business conferences he was always having. There was, however an edge to her voice!

"All well. Have been busy putting together a new deal on the Australian front. How are things with you?" He had intuitively picked up on this.

"Ahh. The marketing company is doing well as usual. But I need your advice on something!" Too little too late she thought to herself. She should have called him yesterday morning after she received the first of the many phone calls. This was the irony of technology. Whereas landlines could be traced, once these cell phones were out in the black market, there was no hope of finding someone. Even though she had called fruitlessly five times, suddenly 'George' was nowhere to be seen! His cell phone just switched to an innocuous message system. He had been so confident that he had not even switched off the cell phone!

"Okay. Fire away!"

"Have you ever heard of Tanzanite?" It was a peculiar question, because he clearly knew what Tanzanite was. She wanted to pre-empt telling him the whole sorry saga! "I have had a run in with a marketing company who sells the stuff."

"Ohh! What do you mean by run-in? Have you lost money?" It always came down to the money. He had been fairly shrewd with the stuff, but knew the value of it, having had to work all his life, without the aid of a family financier, or a role-model. For Paul, his centre-of-influence had been his gut instinct!

"Seven thousand Rand!" She would be candid. Cut to the chase and limit any further explanation.

"Ohh. Okay! I think I get the point? When did this happen?"

"Right now," she was still sitting in her car, shell-shocked and had not moved. It had been an hour since 'George' walked off with her money, and the two accomplices had been in the parking garage with her. She had been given a jewellery bag, made from a chintzy bluish-black suede material, its tie-string knotted and the contents clearly of value. She had been told to wait in the car and they would be back once they had agreed on a price. Her 'cut' would be the ten percent that 'George' was paid by the dealer. He was an overweight man, balding and a hooked nose, with wire-rimmed glasses, who went by the name of Sheldon. He had been the epitome of a jeweller, so stereo-typical of every Hollywood movie. There was even an air of confidence in the way he had scurried into the parking garage to greet 'George' and Kerry. Why had she not insisted on going up to his store?

The whole event had been tainted with an air of subterfuge, but just enough to heighten the expectation, but not enough to scare Kerry away. It was only once she was sitting alone in the car, that she realised the futility of her situation. She had believed 'George' when he had told her that the dealer was a well-respected business man who had a shop in Sandton City. That made sense? The other accomplice had waited with her in the car then made an excuse to go to the loo. "He would be back before 'George' returned." It was only as he disappeared into the maze that was Sandton City, that she realised she had been duped. But, like all victims to these 'cons', she had sat in earnest anticipation for their return. First, ten minutes, and when the second accomplice had not returned from his ablutions, she began to get a knot in her stomach. By the time half an hour had elapsed, she began to feel a sense of concern. "What if they had been arrested while doing the transaction? What if they had been under surveillance since arriving at the parking garage? If she had any sense, she should just reverse her car out of there now, and head for the pay-point on the lower level?"

When she had tried 'George's cell phone after forty minutes and then subsequently the next four times, she had tried to find an excuse for her distrust each time. She had no address for the shop. There were twenty jewellery shops in Sandton City! Kerry had explained this all to Paul.

"Kerry. You have definitely been scammed! Listen to me! Go and sit at the Mugg & Bean on the top level, and I will be there in twenty minutes."

It was music to her ears. He hung up before giving her a chance to respond. She climbed out the car, nervously anticipating a tap on the shoulder, and headed for the entrance, electronic beeps assuring her the car was locked.

Paul arrived just as she was getting her Cappuccino.

"Hi Kerry. Got here as soon as I could!" He was spot on time.

"What have you done since we spoke?" He needed to be clear on things.

"Nothing! I just came straight up here, and waited for you."

"Good. I have just gotten off the phone to a mate of mine who is with Liberty Properties, who own the centre. He put me in touch with the security manager, and they have cameras on each and every entrance, so we will be able to get a video of these guys, and track their movement through the centre. He is going to meet us here."

She felt a sense of relief, like the time she had fallen from her bicycle and her dad had been there to lift her up. Paul was organised, efficient and put up with no nonsense.

'Ahh, here he comes now!" A tall man in a double breasted jacket and grey flannel trousers was walking towards them. He looked concerned. The management took these events seriously, not wanting the centre to be implicated in any form of crime.

"Good afternoon," Paul stood as the man arrived at the table. He was tall. Almost a head taller than Paul! He towered over Kerry.

"Paul Schweiger. How do you do?" The man regarded Paul suspiciously, in a way only twenty years of Koevoet training could do. He extended his hand. The palm of his hand would have snaffled a rugby ball as likely it may have done all those years ago, and Paul's returned grip was lost in the immensity of it.

"Danie. Danie Hendricks." He repeated his first name so as ensure they knew it. "What's this all about?" He eyed Kerry who was still sitting. His suspicious nature had overtaken his manners.

"This is Kerry," he was informed. "She has had a run in with a pair of fraudsters, who have stolen seven thousand Rand from her." Paul felt that too much information now would not help his cause with Danie.

"Good afternoon," he repeated to the sitting Kerry. She had just finished her lukewarm frothy drink, and the milk had left a fleeting mark on her upper lip. It looked quite comical, so Paul gestured with his hand to his upper lip, and then made a similar gesture with his index finger, so to warn her. She looked at him quizzically then shot her hand over her mouth and removed the milk and coffee stain with a simple wipe.

"Good afternoon." She offered in return, milk moustache dispensed with.

"I believe you need to see footage of the security cameras?" He was not happy to have to entertain civilians in his nerve centre deep in the bowls of that mega-city.

"Yes please." Paul was respectful. "When I spoke to John, he mentioned that you may be able to assist us!" There were technicalities here that Paul would need to be conscious of. John Ashcroft might be the senior director of Livprop, but this man was the 'General' in charge of his own world. Here, his authority was not subject to the whims of a civilian with a personal issue, unless it impacted his customers and potentially compromised their safety.

"Okay, come with me, I will show you to our security hub." Niceties dispensed with, Danie had become all business. He had a good sense of judgement, which had been honed over the ten years he had been in charge of the underworld that allowed the centre to run seamlessly and efficiently. He had a knack of being able to position his foot guards in places where potential threats were defused. He could react to an attempted robbery of one of the stores with a masterful precision that left the culprits unable to escape, and common pick pockets were no match for his infra-red video cameras that showed heightened levels of heat patterns just prior to the crime, and he would swoop with the speed and dexterity of a hawk, his guards picking up the suspect before they could filter into the maze of corridors and atriums.

They followed him without a word, all the way through the warren of stairwells and service corridors that ran via the far retreats of the centre. Paul kept pace with Danie, with Kerry tripping along behind, having to hurry her five-foot frame earnestly to keep up. They descended further and ever deeper into the depths of the building, and emerged at a large security gate in front of a plush series of brightly lit offices. This was the hub he had alluded to, and no expense had been spared.

"I will sign you in, and there is an indemnity form you will have to complete." He was matter of fact, but they seldom had visitors down here. Somehow he was enjoying this. He could finally show off his kingdom!

With the forms completed, Paul and Kerry were ushered into a room, where a plethora of plasma screens were arrayed across the walls. In the centre of the room was a semi-circular command desk, with five smartly dressed security personnel at their posts. Danie walked over and surveyed the screens.

"Right! Which entrance did you use?"

Kerry looked lost for a second. She had parked on the north side, on level three. It was close to the Mezzanine level. She informed Danie.

"Section five, level three." He pointed to the screen, and one of the operators immediately drew the screen across to the main command facility which encompassed a screen the size of a small movie theatre. The controller swung into action, presumably having been briefed, but more than likely through repeated procedures, similar to a military operation.

"There!" Danie pointed. On the screen was Kerry emerging from the brightly lit garage, onto the mezzanine level.

The operator followed her through the centre, down the flight of stairs, into the main concourse, then up two flights of escalators. Danie spoke in Afrikaans, and the operator reversed the footage, and Kerry descended all the way back and then the screen froze on her somewhat frail looking form, as she emerged again from the parking area. Her face looked contorted. She was stressed, and she looked repeatedly over her shoulder.

"Parking section five, green level three." Again the order was barked out in commanding form.

A sub-screen with footage of the parking garage appeared onto the same screen, and the camera followed Kerry back to her car. She seemed to sit in it unmoving for quite some time. The operator sped up the rewind. Then a man emerged from the left of screen, walking backwards and slid into the back seat of Kerry's car.

"That's Lovemore!" She was somewhat shell-shocked. "He was the second guy."

"Time?" Danie noted the electronic timer on the bottom left of the screen. "11.48.45. Note that." The controller made an entry on his sheet on the desk in front of him. Immediately he keyed in the time, and switching to the other half of the screen, he back tracked to that time on the first camera.

Lovemore or whatever his real name was, appeared into the opening of the mezzanine level, and made a bee-line for the service entry on the far side. His head scanned the area looking for the camera, but he had not seen it above and slightly behind him. As they were following him on the coverage, the young operator was making snap-shots of his face, wherever the camera angle allowed.

"Sub-level M, corridor twelve." With military precision they switched to the corridor. He was caught like a rabbit in the glare of an on-coming pantechnicon.

"Got him!" Danie shouted victoriously. He loved his job passionately. It was all that he could do to ensure that those who used the centre were kept unmolested by these vermin.

The camera followed him briefly. Then he disappeared.

"Shit, I don't believe it! He has gone down to Lower level two. Pick him up as he comes out of entrance six."

The cameras picked him up as he came through level two. They were able to follow him down into the parking garage on the north-west side. Then Lovemore disappeared out through the garage and caught a taxi on Sixth Street.

"Sorry, we can't trace him any further!" Danie looked crest fallen. He had hoped for more.

"But he was the second accomplice. There was 'George' and the other guy!"

Danie turned accusingly towards Kerry. The words hung on his lips, but he said nothing. He quickly mumbled something again to the operator. The footage returned to the parking garage. There was a brief rewind as the camera could pick up Kerry's car. Then again, as before, the camera picked up movement from the left. But this time, two characters appeared on screen, and arrived at the car. The digital clock showed 11.32.18. The whole transaction took place in the car, so no footage was available of money or goods passing hands!

Danie and the controller then followed the two back out into the mezzanine level.

"Hymie Cohen! That bloody con-artist." Danie knew this guy from some other dealings. "He was kicked out of the centre for trying to fence stolen jewellery to a store."

Danie had every reason to now be excited. Finally, he had a suspect he could monitor.

"Let's follow him!" The camera showed him turn right, and he and 'George', exited through the parking garage. They stood as calm as you please while the woman in front of them negotiated the ticket vending machine, and once she had paid, Hymie placed his ticket into the machine, rummaging through his pockets for change. Eventually 'George' handed him some coins. He was getting nervous. The camera then tracked them to the disabled parking area, to the left of the entrance, and Hymie unlocked the door of a large Jaguar XJ6, older than most of the other swishy vehicles that adorned Sandton's precinct, but nonetheless a status symbol to him. 'George' then pulled the envelope containing Kerry's money, and deliberately counted out some notes, which he then handed over to Hymie sitting in the driver's seat.

"Get the registration on that vehicle." It might help, because if Hymie was this careless, then he might well have presented an opportunity to finally identify him.

The footage then showed 'George' disappear into the cavernous garage, and Hymie reversed somewhat deliberately from his parking. As he manoeuvred into the direct path of the camera, the operator was able to zoom in on the back of the vehicle.

"Shit!" Danie was unapologetic. The Jag had no rear licence plate. Just an empty space below the boot lid, illuminated by the little yellow lights that made the red paintwork look slightly pinkish. The operator seamlessly changed to another camera angle. He knew Danie's requirements before he needed to ask. The same! The camera showed no front plate either. Unperturbed, they followed Danie out into the street, and then followed 'George'. Same routine! He simply exited the parking area, and slipped out into a waiting taxi.

"Sorry, I can't help any further. What I can do is provide you with copies of the three on a disc, and you are welcome to take that to the Police.

"Yes. Thank you." Paul was very appreciative. He was not sure if Kerry would want to follow up on this evidence. If nothing else, it would give the Police some evidence of what was going on. Whether they had the manpower or the inclination to pursue it was another matter!

"What about the footage of when Hymie arrived?" Kerry spoke again. Danie rounded on her for the second time since they had been in the hub. He did not appreciate women showing him up. It was obvious however!

211

"It will only show him arriving and nothing more!" Danie had already spent enough time on this.

"Are you sure?" Kerry was now on dangerous ground. Danie would evict her from the office if she was not careful.

"When he paid for the ticket, he put an awful lot of coins into the machine! He must have been parked for well over an hour!"

Danie looked at her again with those eyes that must have surveyed human spoor, as effectively as he would have tracked a wounded buffalo through the dense bush of the Etosha. He blinked once, convulsively, swallowed his pride, and then gave the go-ahead. The operator went back 11.32.00 .....11.10.00.....10.30.00.... then finally the footage stopped as the Jag had pulled into the parking at 10.13.19!

He has been here since then? Danie found himself asking what he had done in the interim! Without further adieu, the operator traced his movement through the centre, with Hymie, this time hobbling down two flights of stairs, moving slowly through the concourse and then sitting with a younger, smartly dressed man at a small bistro on the lower level. The two sat discussing something that became quite heated when it seemed Hymie opened a small bag with a draw string. Kerry immediately recognised it! It was still in the cubby hole of her Ford. She had been too nervous to bring it with.

"What is that? Focus in on the bag." Danie was getting excited again. If he could prove any contraband was being traded, he at least had an opportunity to open a docket with Morningside Police. They had a close relationship with him, and he was good friends with the station commander who had been in the Koevoet with him. Danie peered at the bag. The frozen screen was enlarged and from what he could see the contents were small, but unsighted. Neither Hymie, nor the younger man actually retrieved anything from the bag. They simply looked into it, confirming the contents with one another, and then began arguing. Kerry kept quiet. This was no time to bring up illicit Tanzanite, or the possibility she may have to go to the Morningside Police station to lay a charge.

The controller then began to speed up the coverage of the spat, focusing in on a very aggressive man's face, who sat opposite Hymie. Across the table they traded insults and then there was a brief moment when a third party approached them from inside the restaurant. It was the owner. Danie recognised him from the time he had been to see the owner because of a trading irregularity. That had been an issue they had dealt with and 'Chico'? That was his name. He was of South American extraction. He was a short burly little man, who stood as tall as Danie's chest. They had resolved the problem, and the late night revellers were despatched and the coffee shop closed for the evening.

'Focus on the owner please." He was beginning to get really interested. The owner, 'Chico', seemed to calm the two down, and then after a hand shake with the younger man, he disappeared. A minute later, he reappeared, and then as the younger man stood, Chico shook hands with him a second time. There was a brief delay as they clasped each other's hands, but then suddenly and unexpectedly, the younger man disappeared.

"Go back to the handshake!" Danie was tense. He could smell a deal going down from where he stood over the operator. The TV monitor clawed back time for the umpteenth time. Then as Chico approached the table, he dipped into his right trouser pocket and for just a moment, Danie saw the cornered edge of a packet. It was opaque in colour, not visible without a trained eye.

"Quickly! Freeze frame on the pocket of his trousers." The video shuddered back ten seconds.

"There," Danie pronounced elatedly. "There is the contraband." He pointed at the very obscure corner of the plastic bag that glinted in the fluorescent light of the centres lighting. The operator froze the video. There on the enlarged picture, was the evidence Danie needed.

"Capture that onto a disc." He was no longer interested in Tanzanite deals. He had his 'smoking gun', and armed with the evidence, he would make an application to management to have 'Chico' chucked out. No slimy Diego was going to trade in narcotics on his watch. The evidence, if not fool proof, was enough to embarrass and threaten 'Chico'. He would leave the centre of his own volition, and the owners of the centre would be spared any unnecessary bad publicity. Danie would get the acclaim, and his team would receive Christmas bonuses.

Paul and Kerry had watched the whole process in utter silence. They innately understood that the heat was off of them, and now firmly on the culprits. Kerry began to relax. At least some good would come of her lose. They eyed each other, and Paul motioned with his chin and a twist of his head. This was the time to leave!

"Thank you for helping." Paul shook Danie's immense paw. Danie smiled for the first time that afternoon.

"My pleasure," he motioned to the security officer at the door, who opened the it, and lead them through to the large gate. Danie followed them. As they slipped out through the gate, for the first time in several hours, Kerry began to breathe easy. She suddenly realised that she had been holding her breath, and her neck muscles were almost in spasm. She had done a stupid thing, but had got caught up in the moment. Drug dealers, and con-artists aside, she realised that this was a lucky escape! As they said goodbye and walked quickly away down the brightly light corridor, she suddenly stopped in her tracks.

Turning she looked back at Danie who was watching them. "Where did the other man go?" She had needed to know.

Danie smiled again. "Oh! Probably to the bathroom to get his fix! I will have the bathroom he used scoured for evidence. Maybe we can get his identity from the Police?"

"Thank you," Kerry was relieved she did not have to deal with criminals any further. This had been an expensive lesson, and she had paid her dues.

"No! Thank you Kerry!" He used her name for the first time that day.

Three years later, Paul was reading an article in the newspaper about a Tanzanite scam. There on the second page, under an article headed Tanzanite Scams, was a picture of the young man with the cocaine, they had seen on the video monitor. He was slightly older looking, but nonetheless distinctive in a well-tailored suit, and although drawn and twenty kilos lighter by the looks of him, he was distinguishable by his short cropped hair and distinctive jaw. Paul had read the article, and then with a grin and a chuckle to himself, turned the page. The suspect in what was being called the 'Bosch game', had been through purgatory, and having blown all his ill-gotten gains on drugs, had been through rehab and serious ill-health. He had now turned to the 'Lord' and having become a re-born Christian, was now plying his new trade in the 'Ministry'. "How convenient," Paul thought. Three years of stealing off the gullible and worldly ignorant and 'shnarffing' the proceeds up his nose had left him destitute. Instead of resorting to an honest living, he now was preying on innocent Christians too forgiving to chase him away.

Paul had read somewhere, that the genesis of the word jewellery, had come from the word jewel, which had its early origins in Old French, from the word 'jue', which meant a 'game' or 'play'. That in turn had its birth from the Latin word 'jocus' or 'joke'! How ironic he thought. It was all a game to them, but unfortunately many people had been left financially ruined. Paul would give Kerry a call and let her know!

The Flower Lady

Standing with the pinkest, Fuchsia coloured two-piece outfit on, her body language belied her distress. This business meeting had been hastily arranged whilst she had been away on compassionate leave. Her boyfriend had discarded her like any one of those cheap paper pie packets, which littered the northern suburbs. She, unlike those wind-blown trappings of a modern day emerging class of cash empowered South Africans, had substance, but she was having a difficult time establishing herself in a peculiarly male dominated industry. The advent of Resource driven demand from the economic power houses of China and India had made the deposit rich resources of South Africa a magnet to every conceivable mining guru in the world. Management companies had set up offices in the extravagant towers that lorded over the Sandton landscape. These businesses had a crucial part to play in the development of a bourgeoning society, once dependant on the leftovers of a mal-administered system. She could have been a success anywhere in a community that prided itself in the power of achievement over the age-honoured dependency on family ties. But to Meredith, her boat had sadly been missed, when the jetty on which she should have departed for success and self-fulfilment, had been whisked away from under her land lubber feet, before she could embark. Meredith was a symptom of her total dependence on the decision makers in this largely unglamorous industry, which had not yet learned that the substance of veneer may not necessarily belie the qualities that lay beneath. So, like the geological formations that they sought through highly sophisticated ground radar and satellite imagery, the visible beauty that Meredith was, somehow managed to detract from her own talents. She was a visible lesson of what not to wear, if by all accounts that substance was to be considered of value. Her tall, leggy exterior, and blonde attractive looks, were in complete contrast to the industry and the man who now accompanied her. He was a slob! A middle-aged overweight and sadly unkempt slob! But he held the keys to that gate that held her access to those mining treasures, and he clearly had surreptitiously arranged this mine visit, with the intentions of furthering his own romantic quests.

What had she been thinking when she agreed to accept that offer to visit the mine in Zimbabwe? The contract had not yet been signed, and to Meredith, the offer to retain the services of their company was a promissory request that even she knew was subject to no specific obligations. Why then were they going to Manicaland Province? What possible good would they be able to offer? She knew about the Marange strike which had caused a massive diamond rush that left Kimberley's diamond digs, almost ludicrously small in comparison. First and foremost, the site was dangerous and was no place for a young attractive girl of twenty-five, to be spending an hour, let alone a week! When she had signed her contract of employment, she had been grateful to Hans for taking her on, after a brief but failed endeavour with Amatito. That company had been too large, too cavernous, like the Great Kimberley hole, they simply were too structured and too bureaucratic. Meredith had been swallowed up in their Corporate head office for two years after Varsity, going nowhere. In those two years she had watched the fast tracking of several black male middle managers, and Meredith had kept quiet and made no waves. It was fundamentally a systemic re-ordering of corporate mentality, with large B.E.E. requirements a prerequisite for the empowerment of top middle management. This arena was no place for a dynamic lass with top honours at Wits, and a sense of destiny unlike any of her male colleagues. Meredith would have been a modern day Cecil John Rhodes, if her industry had been able to cater for a hungry aspirant, female mining mogul. Like so many young people in South Africa, who saw the opportunity, Meredith was destined for greatness, but it would have to be in alternative employment. After three failed project submissions, she had realised that she too was destined to be a B.E.E. statistic, and her position at the company was merely one notch in a requirement based hierarchy, where black skin colour, and female gender facilitated the necessary twenty-five points in an Employment Equity facilitation. She handed in her resignation the day she had worked her two-year term. Having been head hunted whilst in first year, by one of the recruitment drives the big mining companies facilitate, Meredith had seen stratospheric stars. Having completed her first year as only one of six young women in her class of one hundred and fifty students, she had been offered a bursary with the company. She had finished top of her year, with all the young men whose only first year quest was to 'get laid', having spent the better part of their Matric years in lonely or group Onanism!

Meredith did not need to suffer that humiliating fate of self-fulfilment, because she had her hormones firmly in control. But to Meredith, the next three years and an honours degree, were now of major historical importance. She would not have needed the bursary, but having lost her dad at sixteen, she knew it was one more important way of showing her independence from the family Trust. Meredith was a fortunate recipient of an enviable education at Parktown Girls High school. To her the bursary would have given her the recognition she deserved having excelled with all seven of her Matric distinctions. But Meredith had done something completely unexpected, and caused a riot in the Carter family home, when she had chosen Geology and Mining engineering as her two majors. Her mother still grieving the loss of her husband had wished for Meredith to study medicine, become a doctor and tame an unflinching world through her passion for humanity. Annabel Carter had been a doctor, and still ran her successful practice from her home in Galway Avenue. But her wishes to see Meredith do likewise and eventually take over the practice fell on deaf ears! When she had made it clear she wanted to follow in her father's footsteps, and reach the dizzy heights in a mining sector wreaked by personal greed for far too long, her mother was devastated. She had already seen the effect of this industry on her husband's health, and was only to aware of the negative impact the mine dumps had on the health of ordinary South Africans. That was why she now set aside one day a week to work on a locum at the clinic in Daveyton. The August winds brought with them the residue off those huge burnished yellow mine dumps, and as a consequence Tuberculosis became the single largest killer among the poor, whose homes surrounded these monstrosities. Her mother had wanted her to do something of value but Meredith was single minded in her efforts to make a mark, where her father had left off.

In point of fact Meredith had one major advantage over her peers. She was capable of segregating the sex and skulduggery by the skilful use of Socratic irony. It was however her constant attempts to show her naivety and other-worldly experience that had attracted Hans. He was a typical Taurean. A proverbial 'bull shitter in a bull pen'! He was the embodiment of someone who could walk the talk and appeared to be knowledgeable on most topics, bamboozling all who held his repertoire in high regard. To Hans, the fact that Meredith played these games of sad conjecture inevitably had the reverse effect. Where all her colleagues saw her as boring and contemptuously naive; Hans saw this game as a challenge to be honoured, and the cudgels taken up, for posterity and the furthering of Mankind. Meredith had now got herself into a rather difficult situation and Hans was now beaming from ear to ear. He had his secretary make all the travel arrangements, but had made no effort to hide his agenda from the office. The rumours had already begun circulating long before they had even left. This was the basis for which corporate mentality had become so inefficient. It was far easier for those whose own work performance was questionable, to concoct a good story when one of their colleges seemed intent on success. That way at least they could justify their own mediocrity. Meredith had hoped that she was out of that environment, when she moved to D.M. Aitken and Partners, but she knew this was how the business world worked. Sex was as integral a part of the Corporate mentality, and no hiding from it would further her career. Hans may have made the arrangements, but Meredith held the key. She now had the power, and with a week to go, she would literally have him begging. Perhaps his marital maladies might prove to be a quick step-up for her? She would need to gauge this one carefully!

The flight to Harare had been delayed, like so many internal and international flights at O.R. Tambo. This work in progress was becoming a nightmare for business people. The increase in the volumes of flights required, even in this economic downturn, had somehow caught the Airports Company off guard. Even with the planning for 2010, and the Soccer World Cup, they had somehow underestimated the demand for air travel. South Africa had become the powerhouse of Africa, and with all its mining riches, was in great demand for businesses all around the world. It was a legacy of the political expediency of a past, which had been run remotely from the offices of Representative Companies in small enclaves all around the city. With the democratisation of the country, and the wholesale redistribution of those mining assets to a select few empowered blacks, the necessity for running Sanctions-busting businesses from obscure offices in low key destinations around Johannesburg, had been negated. Now it was essential for opulent emerging class extravagance to be shown to the whole world. These Corporate offices had popped up all over Sandton, and instead of Main Street in downtown Johannesburg holding the key to all the mineral wealth of Southern and Central Africa, it was now possible to see the lavish offices and the very visible wealth that those mines elicited. So, despite a supposed downturn, the economy had forged ahead, and the revenues somehow slowly filtered down to the poor, although intangible by the time they could benefit from it. In pride of place was the mega-nouveau riche, who had easily forgotten their own roots. It had taken less than a generation before it was clear to the working class that they had not benefited in the slightest by the change in political dispensation. It was a matter of time before South Africa, like the Velvet revolutions in the Eastern Bloc, after the fall of the Iron Curtain, would be unsettled by the mass movement of its voting public. When the majority of the post '94' generation were old enough to vote, the tide would turn, and thankfully those who had claimed racism as their lasting excuse for lazy mid-morning breakfast meetings in lavish surroundings, would suffer a similar revolt from the youth. Disempowered by the self-enrichment of a few at their expense, it was inevitable they would rise up. In the interim, Meredith could see her opportunity to make her mark.

Meredith now waited patiently for their flight to be called and made small talk with Hans. To any observer looking at this odd couple standing in the queue, it would be easy to see who had the controls of their destiny firmly in hand. Meredith feigned indifference, but deep below that elegant exterior, she fidgeted and waited, but kept herself proudly upright. She could feel the burning looks of enquiry that judged her. She would pray for the flight to be called and the anonymity of the packed passenger cabin to envelope her and hide her obvious embarrassment. In the meanwhile, Hans fawned over her like a rutting Peacock, but the juxtaposition of this mating ritual was vastly evident by her loud display of colour and fusion of good looks and graceful repose. He was the bland and uninspiring suitor, trying too hard to ingratiate himself.

Once the call came across the announcement speakers, she dived for her bag, and hurried forward. The bag was an understated grey Venturian; but it was packed very neatly and strategically. Into the confines of that hard exterior, were a change of outfit for each business day, but Meredith had brought only one casual outfit for an expected dinner in Harare with their contacts. This was to be a working week, and no distractions would be countenanced. The queue moved forward gratefully, with Meredith hurrying forward to avoid any further glances. They were on the plane before long and Meredith and Hans sat in silence. He in quiet anticipation of a week with no specific outcome required for business, but a wild and steamy escapade of extra-marital bliss, and she in lurid loathing of what she may have to resort to, in order to get what she finally felt she deserved!

They waited for the usual polite instructions from over-zealous cabin crew, and the young woman with a British accent attended to them with the required respect expected of business class travel. This BA flight was about the only remnant of a history of Colonial subjugation by an elite class, over a society that had not been able to muster too much resistance, against a superiorly armed and equipped fighting force. If the only permanent mark Britain could leave on the country was the name of the seventh natural wonder of the world, then a hundred years of history was not worth the brave men and women who had died to discover it. But like that brief history, this flight would be in and out with no lengthy stop over, and the British flight crew would not have to countenance the hectic ride into Harare central and the pot-holed roads to get there. Amazingly, the despotic Mugabe regime had chosen to wipe out any visible signs of their Colonial past, with road names, suburbs and cities being changed to suit the victorious liberation mentalities. Yet the one visible sign of that Colonial heritage stood, as it had done for a billion years, and would probably do so for another. Yet its name, 'Victoria Falls', was in stark contrast to the renaming of all other signs of Britain's subjugation. Meredith knew that the reason was to do with the fact that Mugabe had soon realised, that the revenue generated from its tourism potential, surely outweighed any possible negative aspects of its name. It was one of Africa's ironies, that the name changes that took place after 1980 in Zimbabwe, had seen a plethora of changes back to the native spellings. The Zanu PF Government had argued that the British had 'bastardized' the language, and that they were simply replacing incorrectly named signs. It was poignantly remarked. "that if Mugabe who was abandoned by his own father, and who had orchestrated these name changes, had been entirely honest, he would have not changed the name of Fort Victoria to Nyander, after the famous mountain in the area surrounding the Zimbabwe Ruins. Shortly after, he then changed it once more to Masvingo, with the intention of erasing an entire history of a people who had lived there.

The official version of the story was that the name Nyander did not translate well, in a society who had been accused of flagrant racism and objectifying the native people as inferior. To have a name which could be thus objectified so as to relate the local people to 'Neanderthals', was not a wise move? This was a joke among many of Mugabe's detractors. After all, in the final analysis, who would travel with much required green backs to visit an isolated part of the world, in order to gaze upon the 'Mosi oa tunia' Falls, much less the 'Mugabe Falls'? However, the later had an ironic ring to it, worthy of consideration!

As the flight dipped its wing for approach to Harare airport, Meredith recalled her father sitting her on his lap as a precocious six-year-old, and telling her the stories of his visits to Zimbabwe. It sounded like the adventures of Allan Quartermain and the legends of King Solomon's Mines, and to Meredith the excitement of sharing these stories with her father whom she adored, were the makings of another legend. She would grow up in the relatively sublime sanctuary of a middle-class lifestyle in a suburb below the 'ridge', and dream of visiting these places. She would badger her father to take her with him, but the country was no place for a young girl, and her mother had no desire to visit. She was originally from there and had disposed of any willingness to return, if even for a fleeting holiday. There was a history that had not been told, but which her mother would someday relay to her! Meredith would now get her opportunity to see the country for herself and she felt the excitement rise as they started their descent. Her father had told her about a flight he had taken some years before, and when they had flown into Salisbury as it had been named by those intrepid Pioneers, the flight had literally fallen out of the sky over the city. This, he had told her, was to avoid the potential 'Sam 7' missiles that had already downed two other commercial airliners. These incidents had helped to bring the Smith Government to a so-called negotiated settlement at the Lancaster House agreements. Meredith suspected that agreements were all about give and take. What had the British Government of the time managed to negotiate in their favour? She presumed the answer lay somewhere out in the mining districts, where companies with Anglo Saxon ties still owned the mining rights!

The plane touched down and began its taxi into the grotesquely shaped International terminal. Mugabe had ordered the rebuilding of Harare International Arrivals hall to rival the sight those ancient traders would have seen as they approached the 'Old Zimbabwe'. A sight for sore eyes! The ancient ruins had rested on a strategic hill above the plains on the ancient rock of Masvingo Province. What history Meredith knew was all about how the Arab traders had cut their way through the desolate Savannah shrub of the eastern lowlands, only to find themselves in the midst of an ancient geological formation of granite hills, which a billion years of erosion had left uncovered. This conical tower and fortress was what the ancient traders would have seen, and they would have stood in awe of the massive ramparts that stood fifteen feet thick at their base, and constructed of free-standing granite bricks, which towered above the plain. An awesome sight which deserved more of the historical recognition than had been allowed until now! Those grand walled enclosures and strategic towers were constructed for a reason. The ancient Zimbabwe nation was war-like and fearsome. The structure would have sent a message to their trading partners, that they were in hostile territory, and they would have been firmly in control. Not dissimilar to the message Mugabe would be trying to send even today. There were synergies in his thinking. However, as those ancient tribes had done six hundred years before, their nation thrived on trade. The Arab traders came in pursuit of the gold and ivory that was as plentiful then, as the diamonds were today. Those precious cargos were borne through a thousand miles of unrelenting African bush, by manual labour. The slave traders and Arab caravans had wound their way north and east through wild and dangerous terrain, to the port cities on the east coast of Africa. It was these trading ports that had sprung up all along the eastern reaches of the modern Mozambique and Tanzania, and which now were still populated by the peoples of Arab descent. Meredith somehow knew those ancient slave traders would have been severe task-masters. It was no different to the subjugation of the minority tribes of modern day Zimbabwe, at the hands of the modern Shona!

Mugabe was no different to them, but where they had traded worthless glass beads and shiny polished objects, for the gold and ivory, today the trade was in illicit diamonds, considered by the Kimberley Process to be 'blood diamonds'. Yet somehow they still found their way to markets. Mugabe had lined his pockets and built a modern day castle, resplendent in Italian Marble and crystal chandeliers and 'Lorded' over the people of Zimbabwe. But in a slightly different way, he had held onto power whilst the country starved. The ancient Monomotapa had lost their hold on the power they craved because their gold had run dry, literally. They no longer had the plentiful reserves that had seeped through the water table and into the rivers and the reserves of gold in the ground were too deep to be effectively mined. They lost power when their trading partners lost interest in them, effectively leaving the Monomotapa to become a lost civilisation. Modern day sanctions aside, the diamonds from the DRC and more recently from the 'Marange strike' were what was keeping Mugabe in power. He was the 'King' and all trade had to be approved by him alone. But, like those ancient Kings, he had to have trading partners?

Meredith and Hans now found their way into the large reception area of the arrivals hall, and as most visitors to Zimbabwe felt, they were watched by eager customs officials and even more eager police. This was a 'Police State' that terrorised its subjects, and ruled by fear. It was not surprising that her father would have been sceptical about taking her. The sense of intimidation was palpable. It hung in the air of the cool Highveld winter like a fog. Despite the mild midday temperatures of Harare, on a cloudless day, the air in that terminal building was heavy. Meredith stood in the queue with her suitcase retrieved, and waited patiently for the customs officials to ferret through the suitcase of an elderly white man, who looked like he had spent too many years in the harsh sunshine of a farm on the Mashonaland plateau. His craggy exterior, and folded skin, bore the remnants of a hard life of living off the land. His lungs, probably blackened by the tar of a million cigarettes gave an audible but choked strain to his voice. It sounded like the large gravel centrifuges they still used to sift the diamond bearing shale from its soil. His hard weather-worn looks, belied his gentle calm character. He had survived the purges of the farming communities by Mugabe thugs, hell-bent on destroying any vestiges of economic activity the 'old Rhodesian' population had created, because of his cool, unruffled demeanour. After these 'custom thugs' had rifled through his belongings and emptied the contents of his suitcase, they summarily dismissed him to a cold stainless steel table, to repack his worthless belongings. Meredith took pity on him, as she looked on, and when they had been ushered through the queue, she turned despite Hans' insistence they meet their scheduled driver, so that she could help the old guy close his hastily repacked suitcase.

"Let me help you there!" She reached over and leaned on the canvas top as he clasped the two metal locks down.

"Thank you," he welcomed her intervention. "This is a welcome respite from a rather unglamorous humiliation!" There was still a section of his old white cotton briefs sticking out at an angle. "I don't normally let young ladies see my underwear!" He lifted his powerful jaw just high enough that Meredith could see his grin. That jaw had once been a potent symbol of an immensely powerful physical exterior. Now it resembled the craggy features of a Matopos hillock, the skin drawn tightly over the bone in a series of rugged angles outlining the chiselled bone.

"My pleasure," Meredith grinned back. Hans was waiting expectantly a few meters away, dancing on his pudgy feet, unwilling to be the centre of what was becoming a scene.

"Where are you staying," the old man asked, clearly identifying them as tourists.

"The old Monomotapa?" Meredith offered.

"I will meet you for a drink in the sportsman's bar, on the ground floor." He smiled broadly.

"To thank you for your charming assistance!" He winked.

"That would be nice," she would love to hear his story. She waved over her shoulder and headed off for the waiting shuttle. This was going to be an interesting trip.

The old Monomotapa Hotel, had been big businesses contribution to a modern tourism industry that had flourished in the seventies. From her room, Meredith could look down on the Les Brown swimming pool, which was abandoned during the winter months. Too cold on a Highveld winters day to swim, the open air venue had seen some famous champions. Pity, she thought, it would have been nice to have a swim. Meredith had swum provincially and had met some of the Zimbabwean swimmers during swimming meets in South Africa. They were amazingly good, for a country that only had facilities that allowed them to swim for half of the year!

Meredith had managed to arrange her own room despite Han's attempts to book them into a suite. His secretary in the Jo'burg office had pulled her aside, and showing her the travel arrangements had warned her, "There is only one room booked."

Meredith had surreptitiously arranged the change without Hans knowing, and now she had a room at the opposite end of the crescent shaped hotel, away from his vain attempts at familiarity. She was due to meet the old man downstairs. They had not made a specific time, but she imagined a one o'clock drink would be on the cards. Hans had kept the afternoon open for his own indulgences, so now that she was free from his clutches, she could do her own thing.

The lobby of the hotel was in stark contrast to the rest of the unseen narrow corridors that swept in a convex arch across the northern stretch of the Harare Gardens, the only lasting tribute to Jameson. These corridors lead to the bedrooms in a subtle reminder of the walled entrances to the Great Enclosure at 'The Great Zimbabwe Ruins'. They hid a multitude of the sins that had laid waste to a once powerful Kingdom. Standing in the central area of the corridor, from the lifts that deposit visitors on their relevant floor, one could not see the extent of each passage leading off to the bedrooms. It was in these rooms in the late seventies, that deals had been brokered on the future of Zimbabwe's mining industry. These rooms were the only physical remnant of those shady, illicit deals. Meredith wondered if any similar events occurred now. Whereas, the lobby had been redesigned to catch the visitor's eye and the granite stone tiles were constant reminders that Zimbabwe was built on the back of its great mineral wealth. The large cavernous entrance with double volume ceilings that lead off into Mezzanine levels, echoed the open enclosures, and had an eyrie sense of being watched over. In occasional groups there stood smartly dressed men, discussing deals, but in amongst the few clusters there was the shifty eyed reminder that Mugabe had a strangle hold on this society. Like those old rulers of the past, the Great Enclosure had been designed to greet visitors and conclude deals. Meredith saw the irony in that design, because once they were inside, they would have been a prisoner of the King. Here and there, stood

Chinese and various other Eastern looking men; strangely, she saw no other women. She disregarded her thought, and with her expectations high, set foot into the bar.

Meredith was not disappointed! He sat alone in the far corner, near the large glass windows that looked out onto the well-tended gardens. He cut a lonely wizened figure and she was immediately drawn to his plight. Probably widowed, and abandoned by family, who had moved onto greener pastures, in America, Canada, or other foreign climes. She made a beeline for him. He saw her coming in the reflection of the large plate glass windows.

"Good afternoon! I am pleased you could join me." He stood as she approached.

"Oh, my pleasure! It is not often that I get a chance to meet a real gentleman." Her attempt at endearment working! He offered one of the chairs, pulling it back with amazing ease. Meredith could see his sinewy arms belied a hidden strength.

"Your travelling companion is not joining us?" He looked towards the open bar, somewhat relieved.

"No, I left him in his room to unpack. I did not need to." She smiled with all the charm of her twenty-five years.

"Oh, excellent!" He swung around motioning to the barman. "What can I offer you to drink?" He was halfway through what looked like a glass of coke, but Meredith would imagine it contained more than that!

"It is not often that I have a beautiful young lady all to myself." He smiled ruefully. If ever, she reflected!

"Why thank you!" She mimicked a damsel in distress. "It is wonderful to meet you, but we have not been introduced!" She glibly offered.

"Yes, but what is there in a name?" He grinned, that lop-sided grin again. "My name is Kevin. Kevin Murphy!" His Irish accent just a hint away from the sixty years he had been here since leaving home.

"Pleased to meet you Kevin." She extended her warm hand across the wooden table. "Meredith Carter." She made no fuss of her name, as if it were an inconsequential adornment. Meredith could sense though, that to Kevin, his name was the last vestige of the Murphy clan in Zimbabwe, and he would hold onto it with all his eighty years of stamina and strength.

"What brings a lovely lady like you, to a dump like Harare?" He was inquisitive.

"Business" She explained. "I am a mining engineer and we are looking at one of the mines in Manica Province." His raised eyebrows, unwrinkled his eyes for just long enough that Meredith could laugh into his opaque blue eyes.

"Yes. I get that a lot." She smiled. "I was the only female to complete the honours course in the year I graduated!" A proud achievement!

"Yes. And so you should be proud of that!" Kevin would have flattered many a maiden in his time.

"And, Mr Kevin Murphy? What is your story?" She felt a familiarity; like that she would have had with her father.

"Farming. Unsurprising as it may seem. I have a maize farm in the Marandellas area." He took another slug of his dark concoction. The barman hovered. There were no waiters.

"Edward," he announced. "I think the pink lady would like a pink gin!" He grinned sheepishly having reminded himself of an old joke!

"I have never had one," Meredith was on a voyage of discovery. "That sounds interesting. Thank you."

"So what would you want with those cut throat pirates out in Marange?" He looked deeply into her eyes. He saw her surprise.

"How would you know that we are heading for Marange?" She smiled nervously.

"Well it is the only mining area of any interest in Manicaland, which could have any economic value to a South African business." He had obviously seen them come and go.

"What do you know about the Marange strike?" She was being direct. She had a sense that in Zimbabwe, honesty was going to be a refreshing quality.

"Enough to tell you that every young able bodied man in Zimbabwe is heading for the area, and that they are shooting them faster than they can bury those bodies!" She looked shocked.

"Really? I heard that there are illegal miners, but I had no idea it was so bad!" She seemed uncertain of herself for the first time since meeting him.

"Meredith?" He let his next sentence hang while he framed his words. "Marange is no place for a young lady. And this is not some old chauvinist talking. I lost my wife of sixty years only last year, and have since then spent several weeks with my daughter in Durban. This is no place for young people! The only future here will be achieved when old 'Bob' meets his maker!" He pleaded with his sun chiselled eyes. Eyes that had seen a lifetime of events degrade a society to the brink of extermination. She could see his sincerity, but knew although fore-warned she was still going to enter the Lion's den.

She smiled; flattered that he would care. "Thank you for the heads up Kevin. I will speak to Hans. I don't know what the security detail is like, but I will ask!" She knew his pleas would fall on deaf ears. He knew this too!

"So what is there for lunch?" She quipped, changing the subject. "In a sportsman's bar in Harare?"

That evening Hans finally caught up with her in the lounge area. She was sitting calmly making some notes. Her several gins, elating her and providing her with a time to reflect on what Kevin had said. She was writing the opening gambit to her report. The geological aspects aside, Meredith knew this mine was not going to be an easy picking. She would need some other angle! It was in the legends that she would find the pitch she needed.

They settled for dinner in the large restaurant on the upper level, and having a meal quoted in US $'s she was able to do a quick conversion to Rand. Not unreasonable she thought, although the steak was a little tough. Those beef cattle had probably suffered the same fate as Kevin, and a hard life of harsh environment and lack of good sustenance had given the beef, a stringy texture. A far cry from the plump beef she had enjoyed at her mother's birthday party, at a famous beef restaurant in Parktown North. Strangely they were also an export of sorts from Zimbabwe, although the beef was not. Meredith felt the sadness of a system which had failed all but a few well positioned elites. This was a travesty of modern day justice, and it was clear that Mugabe's clinging to of power, was being orchestrated from high levels in the business community. How else would he be able to stay in power for so long, when the whole country had turned against his authoritarian rule! He had become a two-bit dictator. A sad reflection of the once educated man! Like Hitler, who had written a largely meaningless mish-mash of psychological 'Munbo Jumbo' in 'Mein Kampf', Mugabe had also become a parody of his once powerful liberation struggle image. What was once a real attempt to regain the inheritance of this beautiful land, for his 'People', had turned into a litany of abuses and self-enrichment for some in the higher echelons of power. All good leaders will lead by example, so it is not surprising that the country had fallen into ruin with the excessive greed of a few. But Meredith had a sense that this was where the story started. Who paid these Government officials, and where did the Generals find all their military hardware, in a country Sanctioned from the rest of the world, and isolated for so long. The answer she knew lay in the deals that were brokered in the bedrooms of this very hotel. She could see the surreptitious dealings that went on over these dinner tables, and the backhanders that flowed in the envelopes that passed hands. But away from all the schlentering and wheeling and dealing, were the mining rights that existed. Who owned them, held the key to those who pulled the strings!

Meredith had studied the deal which the Khumalo brother from Durban, who had invested largely into gold mines in Zimbabwe, had tried to orchestrate. He had lost his investment when the gold extracted from his mine, was requisitioned by the Mugabe Government to earn much needed foreign currency. He had lost everything when the Zimbabwean Reserve Bank had refused to pay him out for the gold. The twist to that tale came when it turned out he had acquired the mining rights through somewhat nefarious activities. The mining rights were owned by a third party, and he had not paid for them. Small consolation, when the title deeds to that mine became the subject of a criminal suit. Ultimately the whole system fails when Government officials, have to be bribed to allow a commercial company to mine those riches. The system becomes uneconomic, when there are too many snouts in the feeding trough. That was why the security details at Marange had their work cut out, and why armed military personnel roamed the area with trigger-happy fingers.

Meredith instinctively knew how they could win this tender! She would need to contact Kevin again, and get more information on the farms on which those mines were now located in Marange. The farmers had been removed along with countless other commercial farmers. But, who legitimately owned the mineral rights that lay beneath those farms? It was in that answer, that Meredith knew she could win this contract!

Despite the forced removals of those commercial farmers over many years since Claire Short, and the Labour Government of Tony Blair had renounced the terms of the Lancaster House Agreement, and Mugabe had claimed, "That if the white man had come here and taken the land from the blacks, then why can we not simply take it back from them."

Well, it was clear that his argument fell well short of his theory when the purchase of half that land occurred after 1980. This was a legal specific which he glibly ignored. He had tried to put pressure on the British Government, by countenancing the farm invasions, but the Blair Administration could not have cared less. It seems he had his focus on bigger issues with the illegal invasion of Iraq. The farm invasions had no legality in International Law, yet the G8 and mostly northern hemisphere governments of Britain and America, had stood back while they continued. Now that these farms on which the reserves of diamonds were found, were the subject, yet again of forced removals, it was easy to see who was again involved. Mugabe simply ignored International law and flouted every principle of human rights. Not bad for a leader who came to power on the strength of those same emotive foundations! Those ancient ruins of Zimbabwe now stood as a testament to how yet another leader had created a ruined Zimbabwe through greed and stupidity. But was Mugabe stupid? By no means was he stupid in the traditional sense. He had orchestrated this unrest to maintain his iron grip on power. However, he had impoverished an entire nation because of his inability to do what 'Madiba' had been capable of doing. His notoriety would stand as a tribute to all that is wrong in African politics, but he was not alone in his fundamental greed. Who were his happy bed-fellows?

However, this time the farmers were not the white commercial farmers who had supposedly usurped the land from the Shona. No! This time it was the local subsistence farmers, whose wealth lay in their cattle and the maize crops that they grew in the same old ancient shifting cultivation patterns. Looking at her file of the schematics of the area, Meredith had done one simple thing that evening, whilst in her bedroom. She had used the hotel WiFi to log onto Google Earth. It was amazing! There scattered amongst the new structures that were visible from satellite pictures taken one hundred miles above the fragile earth of Manicaland Province, were the tell-tale signs of a farming community which had been there for hundreds of years, if not over a thousand. It was evident from the small hillside pockets of arable land, that these farms were small scale peasant farming communities. These farmers were the descendants of Mbire and the ancient Rozvi Nation. They were the forefathers of the Shona, however, in a culture where traditions were not written down, the true descendants of the Manica were still being debated. In the seven-hundred-year history of this land, the tribal wars between the original migrating Zulu from north of the Zambezi, to the uprisings that finally unseated the Monomotapa King, there was debate as to who could claim real ownership. Mugabe like the British Colonialists, was busy usurping this land because of the worth of what lay beneath it, and not for its arable value. However, there was one major flaw in his strategy. The land could be traced back to the ancient Chieftains of the early thirteenth century through the wealth of archaeological artefacts that lay in caves and burial sights all over the area. The value of these sights would be destroyed by the current mining operations, and Mugabe would single-handedly destroy yet another treasure of the African continent. He would have to be stopped! Meredith would find some way of getting the International Community to force him to halt the mining, until these ancient burial sites and caves could be mapped and recorded!

The next morning, they met their driver down at the lobby at six. He waited under the large contemporary thatch theme of the reception desk; as many of his tribe would have done for countless centuries before. These were a patient people, and it explained a great deal about why they had allowed Mugabe and his henchmen to get away with what they had for nearly thirty years. The world had forgotten Zimbabwe and until the new Marange strike, most countries around the world had largely ignored this dictatorship. The ancient chief Chengamira, who was a BaRoswi, and related through royal blood to the ancient Monomotapa nation, had ruled over the land when the Portuguese had tried in vain to claim occupation in 1693. Three hundred or more years later, the land had stood, un-mined and unclaimed until now. The disputed farming communities lay in the region which were the trade routes between Monomotapa and the port city of Sofala. Those trade routes had existed in relative peace, whilst the Arabs had traded their glass beads and fabrics of the Gujarat. This had been a thriving community of traders and wealth abounded. The ancient port of Sofala still exists to this day, its old stone walls and ancient wharf, still visible in the sea driven sand banks that now covered the area. Those Arabs had traded with the Monomotapa Kingdom, unmolested for hundreds of years. It was the arrival of the Portuguese that changed it all. The greed that was their driving force, had ensured the demise of the Monomotapa and eventually those old mines that had been covered up were lost; until now. The gold that occurred in the rivers had been exhausted, and the only remaining wealth lay buried deep below the surface and awaiting the arrival of sophisticated mining techniques like the ground mapping, radar systems available in orbiting satellites. Technology might be changing the way mining now continued in this part of Africa, but to Meredith, it was the systematic denial of basic human rights that she saw as the real problem!

The trip to Marange, along the old tarred roads, badly in need of maintenance was going to take them a while. Meredith settled in, on the comfortable front passenger seat of the VW Combi. Their driver, Simba, who was related through royal lineage to Nyatsimba, was to prove to be a mine of information. Meredith sat up front, largely ignoring Hans, and questioned a very cooperative Simba for most of the journey. Two hundred and fifty kilometres through Africa's heartland and along rutted roads to the new mining complex, gave Meredith a sense of the complexities of this nation. Meredith would determine, during that trip, and whilst touring the secretive mine; that she would stay on under secondment to the Mining company and begin a lengthy fight to have those mineral rights, and the wealth of the region returned to its people. It would be a long fight, but she knew she had the support of the people on her side and the rule of law firmly behind her. Meredith was going to use her knowledge of mining and her God given conscience, to make those who held the reins of power and wealth, realise the futility of their greed. Like those ancient Monomotapa, if the wealth of this nation could not be shared amongst its people, then she would expose those who were the protagonists in this human tragedy. No longer could mining magnates sit in their ivory towers and dictate the outcome of people thousands of miles away on another continent!

Gangster's Paradise

The clouds hung like pregnant haemorrhoids. Anyone who had spent any amount of time outdoors on the Transvaal Highveld knew exactly what they looked like. It was the summer clouds that gathered around four or five o'clock in the afternoon that made such an impression on everyone, especially the un-initiated. Those dark morose formations that brought the hail that sounded catastrophic on the tin roofs of those northern suburbs homes. This was the way summer arrived in those early days when Roderick had just arrived in the city of Johannesburg. Head-hunted by his Canadian based company, with a two-year contract in the mining industry, Roderick was going to be in for a rude awakening to the Gauteng. This was where all the crime and violence was reported, and where the base human rights of hundreds of thousands of refugees from all over Africa, were systematically stepped on. The City of Gold was no place for the weak of heart. A frontier society akin to the famous gold rush towns of the West, where men actively carried guns to protect themselves and their families. This was a city which had not lost its frontier mentality, despite one hundred years of progress. But that progress had been there for the taking among most 'white' people, but was sadly missed in the townships and ghettos of the power, impoverished and homeless. Here, unlike their more well-heeled neighbours to the north, the shanty towns of the south had mushroomed on land left vacant by farmers, unable or unwilling to deal with vagrants. Unlike the regulated distribution of land in the 'Wild West', South Africa had missed its one opportunity to level the playing fields of discrimination, even after the euphoric 1994 elections. The ANC came to power, unable and incompetent. Victors in a grossly over-crowded society, they were swept to power by that jubilation, without the means or will to take responsibility for the ease in which they had won their 'Liberation Struggle'.

Perhaps they would have done better to win by the barrel of a gun! But that, like the revolutions of countries like Vietnam and Cambodia, would have meant a long protracted wait by all, for the deliverance from Marxist policies doomed to fail by the sheer stupidity of it. Disbelievers need only look northward over the Limpopo River, if proof was needed! Roderick had left his home in the winter of 2008, in minus twenty-degree weather and snow drifts ten feet deep; only to find himself in the sweltering heat of a mid-summer shower on his arrival at Johannesburg's newly named international airport. Liberation always had a way of re-writing history, but could never truly erase it. The international airport had been renamed O.R. Tambo after the father of ANC politics, Oliver Tambo. But this honour had been made posthumously, with the name first changed to Johannesburg International, then again to its current name. The previous name struck a chord with some in the ANC, but if they had truly understood the history of General Jan Smuts, they may have recognised that this one individual in South African politics had done more for the international profile of the country, than any other man with the exception of Nelson Mandela. But politics being what it is, there were still rival groups even within the ANC that had favoured one tribal heritage over all others. It was this ugly rivalry that had reared its head at Polokwane, and would continue to do so for some time to come. Roderick arrived with no pre-conceptions of what to expect, other than what he had seen on Liberal Television stations in Seattle. His life was to change from the moment of his arrival, and with the tenacity of his Native North American Indian blood, he had determined to not allow this to change his outlook.

Roderick White-Eagle, had hired a car and a 'sat-nav' from the local hire company at O.R. Tambo. His destination was Morningside, and a small but comfortable express hotel which was to become his digs for a month. He had acquainted himself with the technology, like his forefathers had acquainted themselves with the gun. This was a frontier society, much like the one which had greeted his grandmother's family from France, three hundred years before. The strength of their society had been born in the assimilation of the various cultures and traditions into one. Just as the ancient Moors had assimilated themselves into the southern European societies all those hundreds of years ago, so too was it possible for progressive societies to do so today. It was the cross-pollination of that blood, which would strengthen the future generations of North America, and it was the eventual acceptance of all these cultures that built a harmonious and healthy society. South Africa had still to pursue that course and it would take hundreds of years before they could reach a state of symmetry. Unlike Zimbabwe, where Mugabe had stated, "There was no place for the White man in Zimbabwe!" Countries which had embraced cultural diversity were bound to succeed. Those that did not were doomed to fail.

So Roderick had set off for his hotel with his two suitcases and a sense of elation. Unlike many who arrive in Gauteng which is affectionately known as 'Gangsters Paradise', Roderick had no fears because his expectations were of success. His warrior blood had provided him with an innate sense of courage, and this was no place he should fear. He had spent many weekends in the wilds of Northern Canada, and sleeping out in the wilderness had prepared his mind for all sorts of savagery. He could sense danger like a wild animal smells fear. The road to Morningside lay stretched out ahead of him and the 'sat-nav' guided him on his way. He had no reason to check his rear-view mirror and the four 'tootsies' who now followed him in a white Toyota Corolla.

As Roderick joined up with the R21 highway and headed off towards the Gilooleys Interchange, he saw the traffic slowing ahead. He slowed accordingly. This gave him a chance to get his bearings. The highway dipped down towards Gilooleys and the 'sat-nav' was telling him to merge towards the left to take the old on-ramp to the N3 north bound highway. The massive road works left no room for error. There were concrete culverts and large earthworks machines everywhere. 2010 and the Soccer World Cup were on their way to South Africa, dragging this already sophisticated society further into the First World. As he filtered left, so the backed-up traffic fed him unexpectedly towards the merger with the N3 South and before he could get back far enough to the right, he was forced into the traffic heading towards Germiston. The 'sat-nav' immediately adjusted to allow him to see his next calculated route. It was telling him to take the Van Buuren off-ramp ahead. But where was it amongst all those chaotic earthworks. He was looking for a way off the motorway, so instead he pressed the reset button and the 'sat-nav' readjusted to calculate his route via the M2 West and around the old CBD of Johannesburg. He knew that would take forever. There was no way back until he reached the Germiston and the M2 intersection, and he would have to follow the busiest road way in the entire country, with the imposing walls of the motorway cutting impeding his escape. He would have to follow them south before being able to turn around in the right direction. Roderick's anxiety levels rose. The Toyota dutifully followed!

As Roderick reached the next major intersection, the 'sat-nav' gave him directions right towards the M2 West. He decided to break left and turn off at the next intersection. If only he could get back into the north bound traffic, which had calmed as he took the Germiston off-ramp and he began to relax. There was no urgency, but Roderick was beginning to wish he had now taken the map book offered him by the Avis lady. He was not certain of his exact position because the deep cutting of the highway had hidden the Johannesburg skyline from his view, and he had no landmark he could use to ascertain his position. The 'sat-nav' now took him east away from the highway. Somewhere up ahead he would have to make a U-turn and head back to the N3 highway. There was a grassy verge in the middle, which he could see had been used by many a lost motorist in the past to turn around, but at this time he could only imagine that Johannesburg lay somewhere behind him and in the direction his rear-view mirror was pointing.

"If you can see where you are going in your rear-view mirror, you're probably heading in the right direction." He recalled hearing his father quip, when his mother, who was notorious for getting lost, had phoned him from her mobile phone. Mom was not of First Nation extraction, and her Anglo-Saxon blood had not prepared her for the traffic of a metropolis like Seattle. She had been born in England and met her husband during the war, when he had arrived with all those other gum-chewing American and Canadian forces prior to D-Day. England was like living on a giant aircraft carrier, which had been used as a spring-board by the Allies to gain a foot-hold back on European soil. Having French heritage as well, his father had known the sense of pride his people had, when invaded by the Nazi's. Yet his First Nation blood also gave him pause to reflect on all those who had stood against the French and lost their lives. The palpable sense of destiny and time was etched in his blood, and Roderick knew he had inherited those ideals. But there were no wars to fight in the First-World, so the new frontier was now being explored in countries like South Africa!

Roderick contemplated using the central verge, which he could have done easily were it not for the fact that his regulated and stereotypical education taught him not to flout the law. Besides, this would endanger other traffic users, but might have just provided the opportunity to his escape the tailing Toyota. At the end of the highway the road intersected with a T-junction and the 'sat-nav' was now telling him to turn right through the traffic lights, and this would allow him to find a route back onto the highway. Unfortunately, he was in the left lane, so he ignored the devices advice and turned left, feeling he could just as easily find his way back to the on-ramp that way by finding a side road, turning and affecting his escape. However, there was a large truck right behind so he followed the tar road north and at the first opportunity he turned into a little dirt road which was part of an industrial area. As he slowed and negotiated the rutted dirt road, he was suddenly met by the blaring of a horn, and a car pulled up alongside him and forced him off the road and into a shallow ditch to the left of the road. Roderick braked violently and came to a halt in a cloud of dust!

He was completely disorientated. The whole accident had happened in a split second. One second he was looking for a place to turn around; the next he was stationary as a plume of dust enveloped the car. Fortunately, he had his seat belt on because as he came to such an abrupt stop, the harness had burned into his shoulder, but saved him from a more fatal injury. He looked up in time to see the other vehicle that had caused the accident slew to a stop up ahead through the cloud he had created. It was only then that his military training suddenly and unexpectedly kicked into gear after laying dormant for twenty-five years. He remembered the Sergeant of his platoon screaming obscenities in his ear, and it felt as though he were there again. His pulse was racing from the adrenaline of the accident, but it was not the unexpected result of that accident that now sounded warning bells. Through the dust which had blown forward from the accident scene, he could see two hooded men suddenly burst from the rear doors of the Toyota. The one slipped as he leapt from the vehicle, his track shoes not holding his eager feet long enough for him to gain a purchase on the dirt road. He was still partly obscured by the dust. Roderick heard the Sergeant bellow again.

"Get out! Get out!" But this time it was not the Sergeant's bellows which alerted him to the impending danger. It was the balaclava'd man who now sprinted from the left hand rear door, as he had probably done in training countless times before. The window of opportunity hung in that dust filled air for a further second, and suddenly and deliberately Roderick's instinct and training synchronised. He flung the driver's side door open, and in the following seconds that it took him to roll commando style into the dust and back up onto his feet, the second man had regained his feet and was sprinting also to the car. He reacted as he saw Roderick slip seamlessly from the door, but in the moment that he reacted for the second time in as many seconds to change his direction, he slipped. Roderick now back on his feet, saw the gun that was being wielded by the man to his left. He was raising it as he ran, but the car suddenly and fortuitously blocked his shot. The shot rang out, but it flew off to the right and ricocheted off the roof. Roderick pounced on the fallen man, lunging for his right hand that now held a second gun. He was busy trying to lift himself off the ground with both hands, and the gun was presenting a problem for him in the slippery dust of the road. Roderick was on him in a flash and had his large vice-like grip around the hand that held the gun, in an instant. He dragged the smaller man to his feet and as he did so a second shot rang out. It was deafening as his heightened senses were now being driven by pure adrenaline. The man in his clutches screamed a blood curdling child-like scream. He had clearly never experienced pain before, always having been on the other end of that gun. The man's leg collapsed beneath him and Roderick felt his weight transfer to the left leg. The bullet entered his knee cap, shattering the patella and literally cleaving the knee joint apart. His hand let go of the gun, just in time for Roderick to prise it from his numbed hand. The man went into immediate shock, and presented a dead weight to Roderick, who was now tracking the second man around the back of the hire car. In the instant that he emerged to Roderick's left, having spun around with the body of the now limp form still in the bear hug that held him aloft, Roderick had slipped his finger onto the trigger, and fired. There was a second scream. The second man nose-dived, head first into the dusty road, the gun from his lifeless form spilling out of his hand, and cart-wheeling off about twenty feet ahead of him.

Roderick made a mental note of where it had landed, but now had two others to contend with. As he spun, he saw the Toyota ahead, begin to wheel-spin in a trail of dust, and head off away from him. He went down onto one knee, took aim and fired a second shot, then a third, and finally a fourth. The left back tire of the Toyota exploded in a flailing of rubber, and the car catapulted off to the left, hitting the ditch and spinning around so that Roderick could now see the whites of their eyes. The two men who sat in the front driver and passenger seats were staring open eyed in disbelief. They sat for a second, before ducking out of sight, as Roderick's aim was centred on the driver's head. The dust enveloped them once more, but this time they took advantage of its screen, and they both wrenched open their doors and made a dash for safety. Roderick took aim once more on the driver who was now to his left. He fired and the man went down in a heap next to the car. The fourth man now sprinted as fast as his chubby legs could carry him, a paunch and twenty years of swilling beer, no match for Roderick. The Toyota was now masking his escape so Roderick raised himself from his right knee, taking the weight on his left leg, and skirted to the right so as to take aim once more, but the man was already a good forty meters away. Roderick shouted a warning.

"Get down! Get down now!" The man kept on running, his comical legs now seaming to pound away on the earth laden road, like a cartoon character from the seventies. Roderick took aim once more, and as he did so with the man firmly in his sights, he eased the trigger back, and instead of a loud bang, he heard the gun click. It was a miss-fire. He pulled the trigger once more, but more firmly. It clicked again. The chamber was empty. Only five bullets had been used. He remembered thinking to himself that he had only used four, and the fifth one was in fact the first that had hit the dead man.

He watched the fourth man sprint away. He would not be back in a hurry! Suddenly Roderick was aware that the man who had shot himself in the leg was still screaming. Roderick turned and seeing him lying on his side, his injured leg pulled towards his chest in a howl of anguish. He looked almost infantile. The knee was drawn up in a display of foetus-like submission. His screams seemed to echo down the dusty lane, and bounce off the building site to the right of the road. Roderick now realised he was in an old dilapidated Industrial area, and there was a large crowd of spectators emerging from the building next door, and suspicious faces appearing from the corner where a taxi rank jettisoned its passengers and retrieved them from their work. The large crowd began to swell. It was a re-run of 'Blood River". The faces seemed inquisitive and alarmed. The on-lookers surged forward sensing the battle was over.

Roderick knew he needed to get to his hire car and call the police. He headed straight to the car. The cell phone with its 'sat-nav' still active, sat on his centre console. He lifted the phone to call, but was alarmed to see the crowd descend on his vehicle. The mob looked intent on some retribution! He could not tell if the anger that now appeared on those faces was aimed at him or the man who now lay in the road. As Roderick raised the phone to call an emergency number, a loud shot rang out. He instinctively ducked. There was a second shot. He wished he had now picked up the gun that had lain in the road. "Where was it?" He thought, but in that instant the third shot rang out, and there was an eerie silence that followed!

The mob, now milling around his car looked upon him with glazed eyes. He could see women with infants wrapped around their backs, with the towels that held those children firmly to their bodies. He could see older men with eyes that were yellow from the kidney failure of a thousand cigarettes and too much 'Cachasu', a raw liquor favoured by the older generation. He looked into the eyes of children about to reach puberty, whose child-like expressions belied their near-adult status, and then they were gone. As quickly as they arrived, they dispersed. But for one!

There was a wrap on the window. Roderick looked up from his cell phone. The man was knocking on his window. He was in his sixties, Roderick imagined, and looked like any one of the others who had descended on the car. He smiled a gap-toothed smile, his eyes expressing kindness.

The ignition was still on, but the engine had stalled. Roderick instinctively lowered the window. The window eased down allowing Roderick to see his visitor more clearly.

"You must go!" The man calmly announced. "It is time. The police will be here soon."

Roderick looked at him uncomprehending what he meant. The look on this kind old man's face gave Roderick pause for thought. What could he mean?

"I am about to call the police!" Roderick felt duty bound.

"No worry about the police." The man stood his ground. "Go now before they come. There is no place for you here now!"

In that instance, Roderick knew he was right. It appeared from the still quietness of that now semi-deserted road, that any justice had now been exacted. He looked into the pleading man's eyes and could sense that the Africa of today was no different to that of yesteryear. Mob justice had taken its toll and there was no place for this 'white man' in this isolated place.

Roderick could see the other now lifeless body lying in the road, his right leg protruding at an oblique angle from his body. This was not what he had expected on his first day in Africa. It was some initiation, but somehow Roderick knew this sage old man was right.

248

"Where is the gun?" He remonstrated to the old man. He had discarded it in his haste to get to the car.

"No worry." The old man smiled again. "She is gone." As was the other weapon, which now it appeared had been lifted from the dusty soil, and used effectively, but brutally.

"Yes. Then I must go." Roderick nodded. No evidence of his passing would be known. To the Germiston police, this would be another Taxi war crime, and the statistics would be skewed once more.

"What about the damage to his hire car?" He had not even noticed the small dent in the roof line made by the passing bullet. He had not even noticed the sixth bullet which had flown past him and lodged into a tree behind the car. This had occurred as he had rolled from the car. That magic bullet had missed him by inches, and this whole drama may have had a completely different outcome!

But, the man was right. This was no place for Roderick!

Fat-bellied Cops

It was the joke of the New Millennium. The Internet had brought people closer together than ever before. Global consciousness was now a mere click of a mouse away from reality. As more and more humans became familiar with the computer, the idea of a Global Thought Wave was nearing its obvious conclusion. The more power exerted on this common conscience, the greater was the world's ability to cure its ills.

"Have you ever stood in a queue and while the person in front of you is waiting for service, you stare into the back of their head and repeat the words in your mind, over and over. 'Turn around. Turn around'. Guaranteed after a very short time, the person in front will do so!" Jaryd had said.

"But that is not an exact science!" Nkosinathi smiled, dismissing the thought. "There are too many external factors, like the conversations around, the length of the queue, and the relative familiarity of the people!" He was not convinced.

"Nonsense. It is the way you focus your mind on that person. Invariably your thought patterns create an energy field which will resonate with the person in front of you. Especially if you are close enough." Jaryd had tried this at the supermarket.

"I don't believe that." Nkosi, to his friends was a sceptic. "I have stood in many taxi queues and the people hardly ever talk to one another, as they look straight ahead waiting for the taxi." He would try this theory out the next time he was waiting to get home.

"That is my whole point! It is because they are focusing on what they have to do when they get home. They are thinking about family and are anticipating the next meal. There cannot be any interaction on a Global Conscience level, if people are only focusing on where their next meal is coming from!"

"You're probably right about that! It is why Dictators keep people hungry when they want to hold onto power. In the past when my ancestors made war with their enemies, they slashed and burned the crops first so as to starve them into submission. Food has been used a weapon of control for many years. It is why the people of Zimbabwe cannot get that monkey off their back. Mugabe will dictate to them forever because he holds the key to food supply. He controls the distribution of food through the 'Grain Marketing Board' and the army and youth militias are on his side because they know they will be fed if they control when and where the food is distributed!" Nkosi had seen first-hand on a visit to Harare, how the militia chased anyone away from the large grain depots around Harare.

"Exactly. If they are constantly thinking of their stomachs, they cannot become an effective force for change!"

"Maybe that is why those with a moral conscience have moved to South Africa, the UK and anywhere else that will take them. Did you know there are more political refugees living outside Zimbabwe, than there were South African refugees at the height of Apartheid. Mugabe has starved them into submission and they would rather live elsewhere than be starved to death." Nkosi had family there. He was confused!

"Why had the Zimbabwean's not risen up en masse and overthrown that dictator?"

"Yes. It is symptomatic of any society that goes through large scale hunger. They will emigrate when the crops fail, and when disease drives them from their land. The Zulu nation found their way to Zululand five hundred years ago, at the height of the Monomotapa dynasty. They moved south when they had land disputes with the ancient Shona. But it was all about food. Mugabe has done the same with the White farmers, but his problems are worse still. He has orchestrated the forced removal of commercial farmers, so as to ensure the food supply remains firmly in his control. Those farms which once supplied the rest of the region with grain have been lying dormant because there is no one willing or able to farm them. Then when the World Food Program steps in, Mugabe steps up and says 'thank you, we'll have that'!" They were sitting in the Cafeteria on Rhodes Campus, a million miles away from Zimbabwe, or so it seemed!

"Do you think that they have done Zimbabwe an injustice?" Nkosi had seen how food was used to win elections.

"What? Those organisations don't discern between dictators and democracies. The problem is Mugabe knows how to manipulate public discourse, and every time there is a mention of human rights, he is very quick to throw 'Racism' into the fray. He has history on his side and his own demented personal issues to deal with." Jaryd's dad was an ex-Zimbabwean.

"Don't go down that road again!' Nkosi had listened to the discussions on Mugabe's personal quirks.

"Why can't we just call him what he is? A dictator, who has clung onto power for too long and now, cannot get enough of it. He is an ardent Iconoclast, who wants to break down the accepted norms of a society that has rebelled against him. He believes by destroying all the basis of the 'old system' and eradicating the White man from Africa, he can go back to his trusted Chieftain roots." Nkosi was a Ndebele.

"God, imagine Zimbabwe without him." The thought of returning to Kariba with his dad and the Tiger fishing off Spurwing Island, too much for Jaryd to hope for.

Nkosi remained silent for a moment. His kin still lived up near Bulawayo. The city had fallen into ruin and yet Mugabe still clung to power. They had gone through the trials and tribulations of the food shortages and the Cholera out breaks that had killed his cousin Tulani. They were Ndebele! Descendants of Dingaan and a once proud Zulu nation! Their ancestors had driven the remnants of the Monomotapa's from their land and had shown that the Shona were a spent force. It was only Mugabe who had resurrected the power of the Shona, despite his chequered roots. Mugabe was a two-bit dictator who had clung onto power, after the referendum in 2000 had shown that the majority of Zimbabweans were not happy with his rule. "How had he managed to stay in power?"

"We should start a website called "ZIMISA", or Zimbabwean's in SA. We could begin a million-man-march, through Pretoria and raise so much publicity for the Zimbabweans living here. Then finally the South African government will sit up and take notice!"

"It has been tried before." Nkosi had attended the walk to Parliament Square in Pretoria when the police had prevented them from marching further. "There is no political will among the Zimbabweans in South Africa. They are too relaxed in their relative security here now, and the SA Government has begun to come to terms with them staying."

"Yes. I heard Zuma saying that the other day. Xenophobia was not cool because the rest of Africa had welcomed the ANC in the seventies and eighties. This was an example of blatant double standards."

"But in those days the ANC was not taking jobs from hard working Zambians and Zimbabweans. Now what is happening is that the average South African has become too comfortable and too lazy in their new found democracy. Where less than a generation ago they fought for jobs and a livelihood, now they have an expectation of entitlement that transcends Democracy. B.E.E. has made them aware of how easily they can become wealthy and they have forgotten where they came from." Nkosi was a likeable guy with a great personality, but even he had seen resentment from local black people.

"Hey. That's why the average traffic officer is a fat bellied cop on a motorcycle!" Jaryd grinned.

Nkosi began to laugh. A raucous bellow which drew attention from a table next door. The girls, all freshmen and not yet been introduced to these seasoned third year students, began to titter among themselves. The two on the table with their backs to them, brazenly turned to look in their direction. Nkosi's laugh was infectious. Like a child with the hiccups in a Sunday morning church service, one could not help but look over, whilst the pulpit bashing continued unabated. His laugh made one stop in mid-sentence and look.

Who could have such an unsolicited effect on a social gathering? It could only come from a soul whose passion for life had made him thankful for the small mercies of an education system that favoured none, yet gave full credit to talent and ability.

"Yes, it is the most obvious sign of our growing democracy." Nkosi was trying to catch his breath between the modest belly rolls of his chuckles.

"How long do you think it takes them to get into those trousers they wear?" The thought of this guy rolling out of bed and having to somehow confine his large posterior into those polyester jodhpurs which made them look ludicrous, was too much for them all. They all burst into fits of laughter, all the while smiling appreciatively at the table of freshmen, who were now beginning to feel uncomfortable with the attention the laughter and stares were invoking from the surrounding tables. They began to look sheepish, fearing that the laughter was directed at them. The gaggle of young women closed ranks, they leaned forward over the table and disapproving looks between them became more frantic, until the inevitable happened.

"Can you imagine them trying to take a shit? They would have to be released like some champagne cork, never able to reinserted into those breeches again." The double-entendre was lost on the others, but the image of those chubby thighs being unrestrained from skin-tight trousers was enough to evoke another round of boisterous laughter.

The girls had now had enough. For the sake of their self-respect and honour, they would not countenance any further mud-slinging from those boys. Regardless of the fact that they were third year students and that they were cute. They all stacked, packed and stood with files of notes and with one unity, left the communal eating area. The boys, all too intent on their hysterical conversation missed their opportunity. But they would meet them again, individually or as a group, and those freshmen would be lambs to the slaughter.

Nkosi watched them go, unaware that their conversation had antagonised this evacuation. The boys continued their merriment in earnest.

"Hey, why don't we start a website with pictures of 'fat bellied cops?" The idea would be hysterical.

"Yeh, and have a picture of the month with the winner being posted onto Facebook!" Nkosi used his FB account like a little black diary. He notched up the girls and posted their pictures like trophies for the others to see. The girls all rivalled each other for his attention. It was the most visual and accurate account of student life, in this burgeoning education system, where social norms were being re-invented every day. Nkosi spent each Christmas holiday up at the 'Falls' where he worked on the rafts as an oarsman. The Scandinavian girls had always taken a somewhat salacious liking to the Ndebele men who worked those river rafts. It was something almost exotic for them to bed a virile black man, and they came in their droves to experience the adrenaline surge of the river and the forbidden fruits of this savage continent. Nkosi would not need to work too hard to bed these freshmen girls either. His was an enviable ease, which his more Calvinist educated brothers at Rhodes University would have to contend with. Nkosi was very comfortable around women and his experiences were legend. However, he had one major advantage over his whiter, puritanical brethren. He had been taken into the confidences of an older Matriarchal mother-figure, who had, as the Ndebele custom dictated, chosen him to become her lover, and she had taught him his seasoned love-making prowess. Because he was the oldest, strongest and better looking of his clan, Mama Tandi had invited him to her hut at the age of sixteen to become a man. His ritual circumcision had been dispensed with, and now that he was old enough, she would teach him everything the clan needed for him to become a source of much needed fertility for the next generation of Ndlovu's. Nkosi had been a keen and eager student and his sixteenth summer had been spent in the sweltering heat of Mama Tandi's hut, whilst her husband was away in Johannesburg working.

Things had however become uncomfortable when she had unexpectedly fallen pregnant, and Nkosi had been shipped off to school in Bulawayo, where a private school education sharpened his intellect. He had won this bursary to Rhodes to study a Bachelor of Science, and Nkosi had not failed his benefactors. A father at seventeen, to an illegitimate child, Nkosi could not return to his village outside Plumtree. He would have to remain away from the scandal that had left Mama Tandi having to explain her actions to an irate husband. All would have been well, if he had been introduced to the use of condoms then, as he was later by the erstwhile Scandinavians.

The conversation had continued between the others at the table. Nkosi was in a world of his own. He had been thinking of Mama Tandi, and his thoughts were for his son. He would grow up in the clan and be accepted as one of them, but he would never really know his father, just as Robert Gabriel Mugabe, had never known his real father. Growing up as a bastard would have very negative influences on a child, and Nkosi knew that when he had finished his BSc, he would go home and collect his son and bring him to South Africa. There was no future for him there and being a Ndebele, even less chance of him surviving the food shortages and the purges that still occurred. Mugabe would decimate his old enemies the Matabele before he himself died, and drive them to the point of extinction; or drive them back south where they came from two hundred years before. No! That was no place for his son, so he would bring him home, and Nkosi would take that job offer with the large Pharmaceutical company in Natal; the original home of his ancestors.

"What do you think?" Nkosi was being drawn back into the conversation. He looked at his best friend Jaryd and smiled. He was holding up a mobile phone and a picture of a 'fat-bellied cop' which had been taken on one of their excursions to Port Alfred, Bathurst and the famous 'Pig and Whistle' pub, where many an exuberant weekend had been spent in the past.

"Brilliant," Nkosi smiled. He had been there when the bus had been pulled over by a 'fat-bellied cop' on a motorcycle. The cop had suffered imperceptible abuse at the hands of the students, with Nkosi leading the fracas. Eventually the traffic cop had given them all a stern talking to, and they had humoured him, with talk of behaving and keeping their heads and shoulders inside the bus. The guy was a world away from the reality of their situation. They were rebellious students and he would have done better to have let them pass on their festive way. Instead, his instinct had been to show them all the power he held, by giving them a piece of his valuable philosophy on life. The students lead by Nkosi had howled with delight, and even in their inebriated state he was no match for the verbal platitudes that followed. He eventually relinquished that power when he realised that the laughter and derision was aimed at him and his rather awkward strut. Those leather padded breeches were filled to capacity, and whereas he looked quite important when on his big Yamaha motorcycle and his ego intact, now he just looked a parody of everything these students railed against. As they became the ardent anarchists they espoused, when alcohol and free-spiritedness gave them the courage to speak their minds, there was no match for the jest that followed. The poor guy reclaimed lost territory by climbing onto his motorcycle, which brought only more howls of laughter, before heading off for Port Alfred.

"Yes. Let's start with this picture and build an interactive site, where anyone can post their pictures."

This was Jaryd's forte. He was a computer whiz-kid and it would take him no time to develop the idea. "We'll call it 'Fat-bellied Cops.com', so we can get posts from all over the world."

He was certain that the rest of the world also had many examples of these guys. It seemed a consequence of their career path and their lifestyle that all these cops should look the same.

Nkosi agreed, as it was symptomatic of their way of life. What central thought process went into becoming a traffic cop, was only evidence that once they became one, there was a universal law of 'fat-bellied cops'. They did not start as one, but had to earn the right to become one. Nkosi smiled to himself. He had just had an epiphany. That was why he was here at Rhodes and not stranded in some God forsaken country to the north. Mama Tandi had done him a great favour, when she had taken him for her lover. Her husband had become the beer swilling, excessively rotund man that wealth and custom accorded the head of the clan. His girth gained from excessive nights and weekends of beer drinking and starch intact at the Jo'burg 'Shebeens', had left him with a less than vigorous sexual appetite on his return to the village. He would not satisfy Tandi, despite her willingness, and so it became the accepted norm, that she should take a lover. Her position and power accorded her by her Matriarch status meant that Nkosi would become a man. This was the way life imitated those old legends, and jealousy and intrigue would eventually lead to Nkosi becoming the leader of that clan. Life had a way of levelling playing fields, and Nkosi knew he had just been offered the position of 'Grounds Keeper'. He could control his destiny, and with it an opportunity to make a difference. The changing political dispensation in Zimbabwe would eventually lead to 'Bob's demise, and hopefully long before his 'son' was old enough to be handed the reins of power!

But surely there was an anomaly in all this. 'Bob', was already in his sixties when his 'son' was born. Having lost his first son through cerebral malaria, there had been no heir apparent, until that is, Sally Mugabe had succumbed to the cancer that she had suffered. Grace Mugabe was thirty odd years younger than 'Bob', so she would have automatically been able to provide an heir. But was it the legitimate heir, he expected?

Genuine Bling

What was it that immediately drew his attention? He could not be sure, but Tristan had seen them arrive, catching their entrance into the restaurant, for long enough to notice their self-confident strut. The assuredness of their walk, a tell-tale sign of the package that they represented! In the corner of his eye he had seen them approaching, and as he had turned to look, what had greeted him made him sick to the stomach! It was everything he loathed about this new found society of excess! They had become a reflection of his own misgivings, and this was what had made him decide to marry an uncomplicated woman who made his life complete. He could not help it. He had worked all of his forty-six years, creating and re-inventing business ideas, then selling them on for a reasonable profit. This restaurant was a new one, and like all good new venues in Umhlanga, he had seen the locals arriving cautiously, testing the food and his excellent service. This was a good sign, because Tristan was not someone who would invest his hard earned cash easily. He knew a good venture when he saw it, and this little venue was prime position. He had had an eye for detail and had liked the clean uncluttered lines, the simple form and the bright colour green, which in any other venue would have looked garish. Here it did not. Yet they did!

What he immediately noticed was the 'bling'. He had wanted this to be a family restaurant, and had pitched the decor, the menu and the prices in such a manner, so as to appeal to the greater spectrum of families that would find their way along the board walk to his neatly appointed, gastronomical paradise. Tristan knew only too well that after three weeks of being open, he could hardly turn anyone away at the door. Paying customers were 'paying customers'! He would not have the luxury right this minute of being too selective about his clientele, but he certainly did not wish to encourage the likes of these two women in his family restaurant. One could immediately see that they were on the payroll of someone important. Looks aside, it was the way in which they exuded that air of righteous pleasure when looked upon in the way Tristan now found himself looking at them. They were both in their twenties. Both clearly from good breeding stock and both had the self-imposed sense of expectation that their careers had handed them on a plate. Tristan would stand back and allow them to be seated. But he certainly would not have been too happy to have them parade up and down for too long. The family of Christmas revellers seated at the entrance had turned to gawk as these women had entered, and they were paying a large bill for their lunch!

The waitron attended to them without too much fuss, so the dust settled and everyone returned to the normal activity of general eating and merriment. Tristan could see from the overall turnout for his Christmas day special, that the marketing had not yet sunk in and he would have a half empty restaurant on a very busy day. This was not too much of a concern, but he knew the value of word of mouth, and this was valued in the restaurant trade far greater than any 'knock-and-drop' campaign and certainly would be worth more to the success of the business in the long term. Good word of mouth marketing was what put all good restaurants on the gastronomes map, and so inevitably the value of keeping the standards of his restaurant high, went as far as ensuring he did not attract the wrong crowd. That approach would stand him in good stead, but he would have to be very selective. How should he deal with 'these woman'? Ignore them, thereby not drawing any further attention to the obviousness of their position, or entertain them with polite greetings and gracious courtesy, thus ensuring he could never be accused of blatant discrimination. He decided to pursue the former. By the time they were seated and ordered drinks the family had settled down and everyone was enjoying a grand Christmas lunch of Peking Duck, Prawn and noodles and followed by a deep-fried ice cream which exacted several "Oohs and Ahhs" from the family. They were having a very 'non-traditional Christmas lunch' but seemed intent on their meal none-the-less. This was Tristan's forte! He had the ability to recognise the trends in a society which was re-inventing itself in a continual evolution of norms and vogues. For now, he would remain tight-lipped.

When the sound of a distant rumble reached that inner sanctum of peace and good will, Tristan looked up in time to catch a very sleek Italian sports car with a solitary driver, and no passenger arriving outside the restaurant. From where he stood attending to the next order of food, Tristan noted a very dapper dressed individual climb from the cock pit of this futuristic looking machine. Its driver side door lifted like some alien module might look to an American about to be abducted into space. The occupant had slipped effortlessly from the car, and was easing the door smoothly back into place. As he turned to face them all in the restaurant, he looked like some latter day 'Don Johnson' character with his over-sized Armani-style sunglasses and enlarged ego. He calmly walked towards the restaurant, the family at the large front window seats, looking up from their main course in time to see his arrival. Heads turned and obvious remarks were made. The man seated directly in view of the approaching well-groomed man, raised his hand in acknowledgement. He knew him personally, or so it seemed. They exchanged a casual gesture of greeting, and the new arrival walked straight past Tristan into the restaurant without so much as a greeting to him, and headed straight for the two women dressed to the nines, and adorned with very expensive looking jewellery. They stood on his approach, and dutifully shook his hand and kissed him seductively in a manner that hinted of intimacy but displayed more of a sense of duty. Like some royal underlings, they stood on ceremony as they chatted amiably and smiled as they returned his remarks animatedly. The conversation was limited to a few remarks from the debonair man, but mostly consisted of brazen displays of opulent hand gestures with diamond encrusted bracelets, mimicking European royalty. All the while the debonair man looked around the half-empty restaurant gauging the reaction they evoked from other patrons. This interlude lasted a few minutes and then he was gone. Out through the front door he swung left and away from his illegally parked car.

The mood changed again as he retreated, and then with a momentary lapse of conversation, the table of family members with their tongues wagging more eloquently, followed his swagger down the street. Tristan made a mental note to ask the host of this family lunch, if he knew who this guy was!

The lunch progressed and the outcome was a monumental success. Great hilarity, festive goodbyes and the group were ready for their well-deserved after lunch siesta. The host came personally to the reception desk to thank Tristan, and when he was paying, an opportunity presented itself.

"That was a spectacular lunch! Thank you for providing such a wonderful feast." The host offered.

"It is all my pleasure Sir." Not too obsequious but just enough dutiful service. "Did everyone enjoy the food?"

"Yes. Brilliant! I must add that it was very reasonably priced." The host was only too happy to settle the account. "Have you been running this restaurant for long?"

"Not too long. Just about three weeks now, and we are still getting the service levels right." Tristan was a stickler for the finest detail.

"Yes! The service was excellent. Who is the young Thai woman who served us? Is she your wife?" The host had made the obvious connection.

"Yes. We have been married seven years." Tristan offered with pride. I met Maileen when I was in Thailand on a chef's course. I married her there!" She was a very simple but proud woman, who carried herself with the Asian dignity that her culture dictated.

"Yes. I could see she is very assured. A truly beautiful woman!" The host was genuine.

"Thank you. She works very hard and has been a fantastic asset to me."

"I see that. It is a pity that some South African women do not share those same values!" The comment was directed towards the table of two who still sat drinking a bottle of wine.

Tristan followed the direction of his sideways glance. He knew immediately what the host was referring to.

"Yes. My apologies. I have no idea who they are. But they have never been in here before!" He felt it incumbent on himself to clarify that he was not partial to the lifestyle they represented.

"What do you think they are doing in here on their own on a Christmas day?" The host was inquisitive.

"No idea!" Tristan quipped. "It may be possible they are not Christian and do not celebrate Christmas!" He had converted to Buddhism as part of his marriage vows to Maileen, but that did not prevent him from opening on Christmas day for his guests.

"I know the guy who came in here earlier to greet them!" The host offered. "They must be on his payroll for all accounts!"

"What do you mean?" Tristan had suspected so. "Do you mean he is their pimp?"

"Yes. But I have a feeling it is a little more complicated!" The host remained cryptic.

"Ohh! You mean he shares the pleasure as well as the profit?" Tristan could only imagine what these women did for a living.

"Yes. Sort of! But I know that the pimp makes a lot of money by facilitating tenders for the local Government, and that he is married to a woman in Government. Perhaps he keeps these two women on his payroll for purposes of easing the tendering process a little too conveniently!" The host had made his point.

"Oh. I was wondering who gets to afford a car like that!" Tristan gestured to the Italian sports car still parked across the way. Who indeed? The car probably cost more than the average family home.

"Is that the guy who has been in the papers recently?" Tristan suddenly put two and two together. He had read an article in the local newspaper.

"The one and only!" The host held no respect for his ilk. It was all too easy to make large sums of money at the expense of the taxpayer. There would always be some sucker, who would happily supply the necessary criteria for the tender, and then the cogs of municipal, local Government and then finally central Government kicked into action. The chain of events shifted down into low gear, as the local Government official was bribed or coerced into providing the competitive tenders with an undisclosed benefits package. Then the rival bidders used this information to submit a more competitive financial offering, and with that the cogs all shifted into place and the well-oiled machinery of local Government continued in seamless efficiency. The percentages were siphoned off at an alarming rate, and all along the food chain someone benefited until eventually the sucker who had to physically carry out the work, ended up with all the risk and the lowest share; whilst our 'pimp' walked away with the 'lions share'.

As they stood waiting for the credit card machine to spew out its paper receipt, the oddest thing occurred. There were three traffic officers happily enforcing no parking zone violations in the street. They sauntered along checking the registration disks, and writing tickets as violations dictated. But to the women who chatted amiably to each other as they progressed up the street, the Italian sports car parked in the tow away zone opposite the restaurant seemed to offer no contest. The three were oblivious to its stealth design and for all intents and purposes it may have been invisible to them. The personalised KZN registration plates were perhaps too much of a give-away, but they avoided this shockingly red car with all the tenacity that their basic wage income would afford them. Perhaps they understood only too well that their Christmas bonus may well hinge on the evasiveness of their pursuits. They stood very happily ticketing a large SUV parked with two offending tires on the pavement and chatted about 'what, who knew?'

Tristan and the host watched this performance then turned silently to each other. It was symptomatic of an evolving society, in which the hunter had become the hunted. In which social normalcy no longer offered retribution from sideways glances. Those large Armani sunglasses shielded a multitude of sins, and deflected the obvious stares like a 'futuristic force field'. His basis for a life of accepted values was being challenged every day and Tristan knew only too well what that meant. He had struggled for five years to arrange Maileen's permanent residency, so that they could live their dream of a demanding but fruitful life with their two children.

Those other two women stood, having finished their bottle of wine, and headed for the cashier desk. The host saw them coming and shaking Tristan's hand, thanked him for a wonderful meal, turned and followed his family outside.

Tristan took the proffered cash from the one with a genuinely outrageous diamond bracelet, and without being offered a service fee from the change given to add to his staff wages, the payer slipped the money into her Gucci hand bag, and they left with not so much as a word. Tristan took no offence from this. He simply made a conscious decision to effect his 'Reserved Right of Admission' should they ever return. Perhaps, he conjectured to himself, "They do not have service fees added to restaurant bills in Nigeria?"

The Valindaba Tragedy

It was a cold winter's evening, even for the Highveld, that blew a chilling breeze through the suburb if Alberton on the South Rand. Albie had been at his computer terminal again. It was that game Warcraft that had entrapped him in his room for yet another night of obsessive games playing. It was like an addiction. He found himself up late that evening despite very little sleep the night before. Albie found the strategies and subterfuge of the game intoxicating. His brother had eventually shouted at him from his bed, to switch off the computer and let him get some sleep. Albie had acquiesced to the demand, aware of his own exhaustion. He had an ability to stave off the desire to sleep, going beyond the eyelid drooping moments of pre-sleep, somehow able to maintain his concentration for one more level.

That previous night had been an unusually fitful exhaustion induced slumber. His mind had remained active despite his REM, which had been particularly frenetic. The dreams had come and gone throughout his four hours of sleep which would provide enough physical rest, before he would rise to read through his set book for the day's lectures. Because he had been so exhausted he had not been able to recall the dream. Or was it a nightmare? Either way he had a sense of foreboding, and it had remained with him the entire night. Albie had woken with the birds, their early morning routine a ritual of tentative chirps, which woke him, then a crescendo of calling and raucous activity in the avocado tree above his room. The tree had been planted when he was a child, when his parents had moved into the clicker-brick family home on Prinsloo Straat. The tree had grown with him and had soon outstripped his sprouting adolescence and had heaved with the glorious ripe fruit that was shared by the family and the family of birds that frequented that suburban Eden.

When Albie had slipped out of the entangled blankets and sheet, he had padded soundlessly across the slippery parquet floor in an effort to not wake his sleeping brother. Theo had always been the less sturdy of the two and Albie had made certain that he would watch over him no matter what. He was now, in his mind the father figure whom Theo had lost as an infant. Albie had been in pre-pubescent year of obsessive role-playing with the local girls of the neighbourhood. An obsession which had begun with his claim to fame amongst his peer group, that he had lost his virginity with the buxom young Charleen with whom all the boys had fretted over during their group sessions of sexual awakening. Calvinist or not, there were no secrets amongst those, testosterone piqued encounters.

Albie had looked after Theo throughout his teenage years, only too aware of his physical inadequacies and intent on ensuring he came to no harm amongst the brutal world of senior school antics, which recognised with animal instinct, the weak within the group, and isolated them for physical harassment. The stronger would drive the weak and defenceless from the faction and force them to retreat beyond that sanctuary, to be subjected to ultimate death. Albie had only served to prolong the agony. In nature, Theo would have been an outcaste before puberty, and the family would have moved on. This very animalistic behaviour was the only attribute that humans and their lesser mammals had in common. Nonetheless, the two would differ on a spiritual plane that only the more evolved of the human species was capable of. Albie was just such a human being. He had the ability to conjure the spirit world in his conscious mind, intent on protecting and nurturing. It was this sense of affinity with the spiritual guides that had ensured the family unit had remained together even after his father's untimely death. Albie had seen it as a five-year-old and it was still a source of his sub-conscious thoughts some twenty years later.

It had been that fateful morning during the significant period of his formative life that Albertus Wolfgang Tinnefeldt had sat with his family at the breakfast nook that served their early morning breakfast ritual, in that same kitchen which he now softly approached in the dark pre-dawn stillness of suburbia. He sat at that nook, on a kitchen stool with his mug of coffee and Ouma's Rusk, and watched yet another spectacular Johannesburg morning, with its iridescent cloudless skies and waning stars which dipped beyond the silhouette of the garden orchard. His Lever arch file open in front with his notes, Albie studiously scanned his notes. The pale grey hint of dawn had alerted him to his sense of foreboding for yet another time that morning, and whilst he sat in that kitchen he saw his father's shadow on the kitchen wall. He would have instinctively turned to gauge the source of that shadow, but he knew there was none. He had communed with his father this way before. Albie knew his father was here to tell him something, as he had done so on many occasions in the past twenty years. It was that awareness that prompted his recollection of the dream that had traumatised his fitful sleep earlier that morning.

His brother was screaming, turning with his contorted face towards the shattered window of his old hatchback VW. Theo was calling to him for help. The car was motionless at the stop street opposite the Graffstad graveyard. Albie watched as the dream recounted now in his conscious mind played itself out before him like a bioscope picture. In the vision he saw a hand reach into the car and remove the keys from the ignition. Theo sat motionless. Albie wanted to shout to him to move, do something! Jump from the shattered window, run for help, but suddenly Albie was aware of a hand which emerged from the right holding a gun and the appearance of a bright red hole between Theo's eyes. It appeared firstly like a dot, then grew with alarming size and began to seep a yellowish substance. Albie watched in horror. The wound seen to implode on itself as a great cavernous sink hole on Main Reef Road had done so all those years ago; like a voyeur he watched as the life had seeped out of Theo's eyes, the pupils dilating first from the horror, and then closing like a picture on the screen of their family cinefilm projector unit. The gaping hole had widened and then obscured Theo's face forever.

Albie shook himself out of the horror of that vision, and instinctively leapt to his feet and sprinted with stockinged feet to the door of their bedroom. He threw its brass lever open and shouldered the wooden panel door ajar. Wild eyed and breathless, Albie searched the dimly lit room for his brother's form, lying motionless and semi-comatose in the confines of his wrought iron bed. He was there and fast asleep. Albie breathed for the first time since his frenzied bolt to the door. He could feel his pulse in the temporal lobe of his forehead. A vein was pulsating in protest to the stress he had been subjected to. Theo stirred, the light from the hallway throwing a garish hue across his pale white features. He seemed so content, in such contrast to the vision Albie had just experienced in that flash-forward. The light from behind was throwing a shadow across the room, which seemed to elongate Albie's form in a grotesque apparition. The light was rousing Theo from his sleep. Albie slowly closed the door and silently eased the door handle back, before heading for the bathroom. His bladder was about to burst.

After relieving himself, he headed back to the kitchen and the long awaited tutorial. His mind was anxiously anticipating the vision he had seen. But all seemed to be at ease in that linoleum covered kitchen, with its steel coloured cupboard doors, a throwback to the seventies, when all kitchen cabinetry seemed to come in cold, sterile aluminium and grey handles, that evoked a post-modernism that today seemed old and lifeless. The kitchen had never been updated, as there was never time or money available for his step-father to revitalise that antiquated room. Albie did not mind, because this was the one place he knew he had a connection to his dead father. It was in this room nearly twenty years before, that Albie had dropped the bomb shell that would change his family's lives for ever.

Albie tried unsuccessfully to erase that thought, but it always came back to haunt him, especially when he was thinking in the paranoia filled state of mind that he was now subjected to. He would casually call his mother aside, once she had finished preparing the morning breakfast and his youngest sibling was safely off to school. His step-father would be gone by then, the work had been difficult to find and it meant having to commute fifty miles a day to Pretoria West. Ironically, only twenty minutes from where his father had worked all those years ago.

Yes! Albie would wait for the house to be quiet and then he would sit his mother down and try to explain his premonition. She alone would understand it. Maybe in some way this was an omen, but yet it may be possible to change the course of time and fate. The image had been so vivid that Albie could not have made a mistake. He was not on any amphetamine or neither had he been drinking too much coffee. Neither of these possibilities could explain the horror of that vision. Once, many years before, he had suffered a bout of yellow fever. Jaundice, caused from the dirty drinking water on a camp trip to Bufflesport! He had taken some aspirin to reduce the fever. Then some more, until eventually he had experienced the most intense delusions. He had been in bed sweating the fever and Mom was at work. The medical Aid had not been available so doctors were a dream they could only hanker for. No, he had stayed in bed and the fever was to pass, but not before he experienced the most obtusely intense overdose of the effects of aspirin. It literally sent him on a high; where the bed seemed to levitate, then spin around, with him firmly holding onto the caste iron bed frame. It was such a severe hallucinatory attack that he had got up and headed for the bathroom and the solace of that great white receptacle.

This had weaned him off any possibility of ever partaking of any stimulants again. In fact, it was so extreme that he had never partaken of any form of drug since then. So, it was inconceivable that his visions could be caused by anything other than his commune with the spirit world. His father had been appearing to him ever since his childhood, but it was only here in this kitchen that he seemed at leisure to do so. This made Albie all the more concerned. He had never experienced any vision quite so intensely before. His mind could not rest and his tutorial was a distant aspiration. It had been here on this kitchen stool that he had been the conduit to his father's world, and somehow he had always been at ease with the idea. But this was different!

As he sat there gazing unseeing through the lace curtains, ruffled for effect, Albie could not bring his mind to focus on anything. It was almost as though he were in a state of unconscious catatonia. His trance-like induced fixation held him fast. It was only the abrupt door slamming in the driveway that alerted him to the fact that someone else was up. It would be his step-father Bert heading for work. Strangely he normally came through to the kitchen for a coffee and a chat before heading to the construction site. This was unusual but at least meant he could get to talk to mom sooner, whilst the vision was still fresh in his conscious mind. A door closed somewhere down the passage and he heard the tell-tale signs of the shower. Mom was up.

Albie was still in a semi-conscious dwall when he heard his mom greet him from behind. He had still been staring through the curtains at nothing. He turned, pleased to hear her familiar greeting.

"Morning Mom!" He tried smiling, but those images were etched in his mind like an agonising kidney stone becomes lodged in the kidney track.

"Good morning pickle! What's up?" She still used all those terms of endearment which only a mother could, twenty-five years and so many greetings later.

He could not immediately answer, the images too severe a wake-up call. He should wait until she had the first cup of freshly brewed coffee. But to wait would only further his agony.

She looked over her shoulder when he had not immediately answered. This was not good. Mom had an innate sense of intuition and this morning she seemed only too aware of 'that look'.

"What is it?" She stopped. Not reaching as would necessarily be the case, into the freezer for the sealed coffee pack.

Albie looked all the more distressed. He was now beyond any semblance of rational logic. If he mentioned the dream now, it would only inflame the situation and force him to divulge his visions. But he was torn between his desire to protect her and his obligation to safeguard Theo from harm!

She was now staring at him intently. His eyes panicked and he could not escape her demanding look.

"Are you in trouble?" She could only imagine that his haunted eyes were shielding some dark secret that she knew innately was damning.

"No. Not me!" Albie spluttered. "I am worried for Theo."

"Why? What has happened?" She now countered on him. The breakfast nook between them, but a spiritual bridge somehow appeared.

"I had one of my dreams. But it was so intense that the images are still imprinted on the inside of my eyelids, every time I close my eyes." He could not begin to explain this image to her.

"What happens?" Somehow she could deal with the basics. But to give her more information would be counterproductive. Albie could at least prevent any harm to Theo if he kept him home safe today.

"When Theo gets up, I want you to ask him to stay home today with you."

Her eyes opened wider. She looked in shock, like she had seen that vision somehow telepathically.

He flinched in a moment of realisation. Walking towards him down the corridor, he could see over the left shoulder of his Mom, was Bert, his step-father!

In that moment of terror, Albie jumped to his feet. He sprinted down the passage nearly knocking Bert off his feet. Dismissing the shock and consternation of his mumbled greeting, he reached the front room in three long lunges and looking out into the driveway and his fears were metamorphosed into a gut wrenching agony. The pale yellow hatch back was no longer parked under the Jacaranda tree.

"No. No!" He screamed, running back down the parquet floor, twisting in one great leap for the door handle to his room and bursting through into his bedroom, he grabbed his denim jeans, a pair of loafers and a T-shirt.

When he turned to exit, his mother was standing in the doorway. Her ashen face pleading with him. Albie looked her in those glistening eyes on the verge of a breakdown and said.

"I have to get to the University and find Theo."

She nodded. He had not been wrong before. Those-terror filled eyes gave little comfort for error.

"I will come with you. Theo said he was picking up Natalie on the way. They were going into the Uni for an SRC meeting."

"Yes," Albie sat on his bed, he closed his eyes. He had not seen a third person in his dream. He tried desperately to recall the vivid images once more. As he sat silently, he tried to calm his breathing. "Was there someone else in the car?"

His breathing calmed as he held his right hand to his forehead, his index finger on his middle eye, his breath enhanced through his upraised head, straining for air as he drew the air in through his nostrils and calmed his pulsing frame.

The vision flickered in his peripheral vision on the verge of his conscious thoughts. He turned his emotions off, just as he had done as a five-year-old all those years before. In his mind's eye, the vision began to reappear, firstly as a red bludgeoned mess then slowly the image became more distinct. The lifeless eyes of Theo stared back at him through the shattered window, but somewhere in the distance he heard a crash. The window opposite him which had seemed to reflect Theo's image back in a contortion of sorts, suddenly erupted in a million tiny sparkles of diamond shaped pieces. It was odd. There was only the glass and a myriad of sparkling lights. But everywhere else it was dark and ominous. Suddenly and unrealistically a large dark object appeared through the air. Albie was watching this in minute moments of time. Slowed by his mind's eye for detail, Albie witnessed this black object appear in its grotesque form, then it hung suspended in mid-air before disappearing from sight. Albie concentrated. It was a large black stone, with sheer edges that was hurled through the blackened lifeless window. With this eruption of light and colour, Albie could see the shape of a form cowering in the passenger seat. It was Natalie!

Her cringing form seemed to shrink into the upholstery and her face mirrored the horror of that moment, but only for a second, before a hand appeared through the passenger window, holding another blunt form and which then crashed into her skull with a sickening thud. She slumped into the seat and in that instance Albie was jolted out of his own terror.

"Natalie is with him," he shouted, before jumping up again and racing to the doorway. He grabbed his mother's arms at the elbows.

"I will wait for you in the car." He held his clothes under his left arm and sprinted for the front door, whisking the keys from the sideboard, where the old Telkom phone unit should have sat. His mom had removed it to her bedroom. It would not make any difference. They had no contact number for Natalie, and Theo had not invested into one of those bulky new mobile phones, which were now all the rage. They were expensive and only a few students had taken to using them, much to the annoyance of lecturers who had been disrupted during class, once too often.

Albie made a dash for his car. It was parked a way down the side of the house, out of the way so as Bert could access the driveway for work. Albie sprinted down the gravel pathway his mind oblivious to the pain of bare feet on sharpened granite stones. He reached the sanctuary of his Toyota hatchback and leapt into the sterile worn plastic interior, still shivering from the fear and the cold that drove him. He threw his clothes onto the passenger seat, took his key and inserted it into the ignition, turning it once. The engine spluttered into life and he revved the motor to negate the coldness of that chilly morning. The windscreen was covered in a thin layer of ice, just thick enough to obscure clear vision, but not too thick so as to prevent the wipers from working. He turned on the heater full blast, the air that erupted from those vents stale and sour. His hand reached for the stalk on the left hand side of the steering column. Flipping the rudimentary switch on the side of the stalk, the wipers blazed into action, scuffing the ice from the glass, once, twice three times and the opaqueness seemed to clear. He left them to their own machinations and reaching for his faded denims, slipped his burgeoning waist line into those jeans, as best he could in the confines of that driver's seat.

His mother was at the window of the passenger side, before he could retrieve his T-shirt, so he scooted across, his flies still unsecured and popped the little plastic door lock on the sill. The passenger door clicked open and he slid his hand under the armrest and clipped the door hand open for his Mom.

She slid into the car her winter woollies enveloping her fairly stout frame, and she held her breath as her posterior hit the coldness of the fake leather seat. She winced once, drew her knees together so she could slip her frozen hands between them for warmth. The heater was starting to blow some warm air, and the trip to the University campus would at least be warmer.

As Albie backed out of the drive, he looked over his shoulder and caught his Mom's gaze. She was searching his face for a sign of his anxiety. He would tell her the whole story on the way. In Rietfontein Road, he broke the silence with a little trepidation.

"Mom. I had a premonition this morning. You know like had have had in the past?"

She just nodded. There was no need to comment.

"Well I had a dreadful flash forward to Theo and Natalie. They were in the Golf, and someone was attacking them." He let the explanation seep in. All his flash forwards until now had been spot on. He did not want them, but somehow he had become a conduit to the spirit world, and they needed him to tell their stories.

Theo would have picked up Natalie by now and they would be on their way to that sprawling University. He would be on the West Campus, where he was studying a Bachelor of Arts degree. He had always been the more artistic of the two, but Albie had been cursed with that 'gift' to see the future, for good or for bad. Although studying on the West Campus, Albie knew his way around the great old rambling buildings of the original East Campus, where the arts faculties resided and all the SRC activities took place amidst the pomp and history of its hundred years. The University had been located on top of the Braamfontein Ridge, with spectacular views over the Parktown Ridge and the excessive wealth of those early mining magnate's homes. They were perched above the Empire Road, a fitting tribute to the Colonial past. Theo, who had stood and was elected on the strength of his inability to countenance those vile excesses, had unwittingly strayed into an arena he had no control over and which prided itself in the rich history of those early mines. The Uni was funded by those large mining houses, whose names appeared all over the campus with tributes to their legendary exploits. The East Campus had been home to the children of many of the most influential in society and no amount of political interference from rabid socialist ideologies would ever change that. Albie knew exactly where to find Theo.

They raced along Heidelberg Road amongst the early morning commuters. The street lights would have still been on, if any of them had worked. It was symptomatic of a changing society, where the wealth of millions, was being expended on a few. Self-enrichment was soon to become the order of the day, and post Nationalist Politics was making way for redistribution of resources, which would never find its way into the hands of the proletariat. It was a very human condition called greed.

As Albie and his Mom hit the traffic on the M2 West, they were already among the large eighteen wheelers eager to disgorge their contents into the ordered cosmos of this very commercial society, where the Soweto riots were already a lost memory to the eager entrepreneurs of the fast approaching twenty-first century. The University once a breeding ground for liberation politics and liberal minded idealists, was up ahead and Albie would take the Smit Street off-ramp and head towards Senate House. It would be fairly difficult to locate Theo once they were in the cavernous halls of that great institution. Or so he thought.

When they entered the parking area on the East campus, Albie parked as close to the building as he could. There were already a large number of students gathering in the early morning sunshine, warming themselves despite the cool wind that blew in from south. The large columns towered above them and caught the best of those rays and caste bold shadows across the face of The Great Hall. Albie stood with his Mom at the top of those eight steps overlooking the gathering. They searched for Theo amongst the cosmopolitan congregation. No one seemed to know why they were assembled. There was a sense of anticipation nonetheless. Albie waited precious moments, before standing on top of the stone parapet, and shouting into the din of that melee, he called out Theo's name. There was a muted response, as a few hundred students interrupted from their earnest debate, looked up expectantly. They gave Albie a cursory moment of acknowledgement then descended back into their intensely confused discussions.

Albie could not see Theo among the students. Anyhow he would have seen him on the parapet, but there had been no reaction. Albie looked at his Mom, her over-sized cardigan double wrapped her torso and the bleached green sweat pants set her aside from students seemingly impervious to the winter chill. Albie thought for a second.

"These students had been called here for a meeting!" That would be SRC business. Perhaps the council was planning their strategy in Senate House, and then would arrive to address these waiting students. They would need to get to the cafeteria.

"Wait here for me Mom," he knew he could move quicker without her. "Keep your eyes peeled for Theo." He turned and was up the remaining stairs into the lobby, before she could ask where he was going. She dutifully waited, scanning the crowd.

Albie turned and rushed through the lobby of the hall, turning left and filtering down a series of corridors, down some stairs and along the bare floored walkway that connected the two buildings. The large vestibule that sufficed as the cafeteria for most students was already thronging with eager souls awaiting their first lecture. Ordinarily, this cavernous hall would echo the sound of laughter and the chatter of fervent intellects ready to soak up the knowledge of the God's. Those lecturers, stationed in their offices off the warren of passageways that served Senate House, would dictate pass marks, and release sentences upon their erstwhile scholars. This morning it seemed sombre and the conversations muted.

Albie sped past pockets of loitering students. He knew none of them, their faces a stark reminder that he had chosen a commercial degree. Among the seated gathering he looked for Theo. There was no sign of the SRC. They were known to Albie, because of the recent elections, but he could not see any of them here. By the time he rounded the large interior he was frantic. Albie had fully expected to see Theo with his council members, but they were nowhere in sight. Finally, he saw someone he vaguely recognised. He approached him.

"Hi. Have you seen Theo this morning?" Albie would dispense with niceties in his haste.

The student, who Albie vaguely recalled having been introduced to, remained nameless. He stared back at Albie, probably trying to recall who he was.

"Oh. Theo Tinnefeldt?" He acknowledged. Albie was hopeful.

"No. Sorry. Not today. He usually sits with the SRC in one of the meeting rooms." The student gestured upwards to one of the various mezzanine levels above. The open corridors with their balustrades surrounded the central atrium.

Albie thanked him and set off up the stairs at double pace, two stairs at a time, until he was on the first level. He caught his breath. Looking down the neatly carpeted passage, he could see only computer rooms, and closed doors. He had no idea which one sufficed as the meeting room. Perhaps there might be a sign on the door?

He rushed headlong towards the open glass doors to the east of Senate House. Nothing was obvious. A group of expectant students waited silently outside one room.

"Do any of you know where the SRC meeting is being held?" They returned his advance blankly. Then one of them hesitantly offered.

"The SRC are meeting outside the Great Hall." He had clearly got the message. No one else stirred from their solemn vigil outside that door.

"Yes. Thank you." Albie realised this was futile. He would need to get back to the quadrangle and check if Mom had seen Theo. These students seemed a lifetime and a world away from those he knew on West Campus. He dashed back down the corridor and descended the stairs in great leaps, impervious to disinterested stares.

As he galloped along the confusion of corridors, he had to contend with a growing mob, making their way to lectures. He skirted packs of three or four students, walking towards him, their conversations turning to pressing demands on time constraints; lectures beckoned. Albie, realising he would be swamped by the growing tide of students headed in his direction, found a side entrance and skipped out into the open paths that lead northwards around Senate House and the Great Hall. As he rounded the buildings, he saw the gathering mass of politically incentivised students had grown incredulously. It was now a seething mass of very vocal activists.

Albie's Mom still perched at the top of the great stairs was surveying the crowd. Albie leapt up the large stoned steps and was at his Mom's side in no time at all.

"Have you seen him?" Ever hopeful! That gathering was threatening to spill out into some violent mob hysteria. His Mom shook her head. The scanned the crowd looking for Theo.

Then just as it seemed hopeless, Theo appeared through the great doors behind them, and on seeing his Mom and Albie standing there broke into a huge smile. Natalie was by his side.

"Hey, what are you guys doing here?" Theo shouted above the rising drone of rapidly rousing rebellious students.

Albie smiled back; relieved!

"We thought we would come and give you some moral support. It looks like you don't need much more though?" Albie had never been an activist. His mission in life was to get his degree and make his fortune in the high stakes game of business. His best friends, Nkosi and Happy Khumalo, two brothers with great intellect and even greater aspirations for the emerging and lucrative B.E.E. market that awaited their final year results, were equally as uninspired by student politics.

"Yes. We've had a stunning response from the students." Below them the rainbow nation was represented in its entirety. There was no colour barrier here! Only the promise of democracy correctly motivated. Real issues that affect real people! Not crony politics which isolate and divide as would become the norm under the Zuma Administration.

"What are you protesting?" His Mom did not understand nor care for mob mentality. She was just relieved to see Theo.

"Student accommodation." He was assured and a metamorphosed, manifestation of his former self. University life agreed with Theo and meeting Natalie had transformed his awareness of himself. Albie was pleased for him.

"Where are you marching to?" The placards were raised and the crowd was beginning to filter out onto the terraces below.

"We are going to Toi toi outside the residences. There are too many black students who do not have accommodation."

Albie laughed. "Yes, but I don't think I would want to live in those rooms." He had heard the horror stories of conditions in the residences. Nkosi had spent an inordinate amount of time frequenting the female residence in the dead of night. Albie had warned him about using protection.

"Okay. Well we are going to go home now and let you get on with it." Albie signalled to his Mom. "See you later."

Theo flashed another smile. Natalie tugged at his arm. They waved goodbye and disappeared down the stairs and into the seething crowd.

Albie turned to his Mom. He looked her in the eye, as though to say. "Everything is going to be fine."

She smiled back. Grateful for this moment and content that they had seen Theo so empowered! They turned and he led her off to the car park, chatting animatedly. He knew he would never see Theo alive again. But strangely and in some peculiar motherly intuition; so did Mom.

On their way back home, Albie had asked his Mom in a matter of fact way, "When Dad died, was he still working out at Pelindaba?"

His Mom, staring like an autonome ahead into that uncertain future, had replied. "No, he had resigned almost six weeks before; but he was not employed at Pelindaba."

"He wasn't?" Albie was confused. "Why did I think he worked at the nuclear power plant?"

"He did not work at the plant; he worked at a very secretive site close to the plant, called Valindaba."

"Ohh!" Albie was intrigued. "What did they do at Valindaba then?"

"Dad was a Nuclear Physicist. He worked on the bomb." She grimaced at the memory of another cold soulless night so many years before.

"The bomb?" He was shocked. He never knew they had a bomb. Much less that his Dad had been involved.

"Like as in a nuclear bomb?" He turned and stared incredulously at his Mom. They were stationery at the set of traffic lights.

"Yes. We had six in all. Your Dad was one of the physicists who armed them. Valindaba was where they enriched the plutonium and constructed them."

This came as a bombshell to Albie. He had always thought his Dad was a scientist working in the power station. Well, that was what he had imagined. Strangely, his Mom had never spoken of his father's death before now. It was ironic.

Suddenly, there was a loud bang on the roof; Albie swivelled back in his seat. His pulse raced and he saw a pedestrian in his rear view mirror. He watched as the man disappeared back into the traffic on Heidelberg Road. Then there was a sharp horn that blared behind them. Albie looked up and saw the robot was green. He had no recollection of how long they had been stationery. It seemed like a dream.

"Oh shit!" He engaged first gear and pulled away, the car lurching as he applied too much force to the accelerator. The adrenalin coursed through his veins. Fight or flight came to mind. He had no idea why the street beggar had banged on his roof. Maybe Albie had not seen him standing at the driver's side door. Still, that was unnecessary.

By the time they were home, Albie had calmed down, but he needed to sit with his Mom and find out more. They boiled the kettle, and while his Mom made a hearty cooked breakfast of French toast, eggs and boerevors they spoke candidly for the first time.

"When did Dad die?" His vague recollection of his father's death had been piqued by their experience.

"April the first, 1980." Mom replied over her shoulder as the sausage sizzled in the pan.

"So I was five when he was killed." His choice of words forced his Mom to stop what she was doing. She turned around.

"Why do you say that?" Her face was ghostly pale.

"Why did I say what?" He was not aware that he had said anything untoward.

"You said, 'when he was killed'. It was an accident. He died in a motorcycle accident." She was watching him intently.

"Yes, but I meant he was killed in an accident." Albie was unsure what the difference was. He had meant it as a passing comment, but his question had stirred up an unwitting response.

"So Dad was working at Valindaba up to a month or so before he died?" He repeated the question as if to re-fresh his memory of that fateful night. "I remember being here in the kitchen that morning before he left. Where did he go that morning, if he was no longer working?"

"Do you know what you said to him that morning before he left home?" She stared intently. He shook his head.

"You said, 'Dad. When are you going to die?' And he replied, 'Oh, only a long time from now.'"

She turned back to the stove, throwing a tea towel over her shoulder as he had seen her do so often before. Her eyes glistening, gave away her emotions of that conversation so long ago. The thought was like a body punch to him. He had somehow seen that too. They were silent for a moment.

"Your Dad was out looking for work. He had been sending out his CV to quite a few places, and he had received a job offer from the faculty of Science at Wits." She smiled, the distant memory evoking her long forgotten fondness of that tall, willowy man, who had lived as he had died; unaware of the dangers of human ego. He had been riding his old Yamaha motorcycle, having left the family car for Martha to run the family errands. It had rained

286

that morning, an odd occurrence in April. It was the last of the autumn showers before winter took a grip on the Highveld.

"So Dad would have been a lecturer if he had not died?" He smiled at the thought of having been able to study at that great learning institution. It was the bedrock of academia in a society intent on self-destruction. 1980 was a year of many great seismic events in the history of that fragile nation. It had also snowed that winter.

"Wits was one of the first places to install a nuclear machine. They were doing research into something at their Science faculty. They were also the first University to install computers. Your Dad wanted to become a part of that great Institution."

"Is that why you wanted us to study there?" Mom had sacrificed a lot to get them there. She had remarried, when the life insurance policies had not paid out. Dad had resigned from Valindaba, and there was no cover there. Uncertain of who had paid his salary from there, the whole thing had been mired in subterfuge and shadowy characters which had followed his Dad after he resigned. The communists were a real threat to the Nationalist state of South Africa and with Cubans on their doorstep in Angola, they were not taking chances.

"Yes, your Dad would have been proud of you guys." She knew it would not have been possible if she had not had the help of Bert. He had adopted the boys and loved her unconditionally.

"So do you think Dad was killed by the South African government because he knew too much?" This question came out of left field like a bolt. She spun on the heels of her sneakers, making a screeching sound on the linoleum floor tiles.

"What? Do you honestly believe that?" Her face and her reaction told him she did!

"Well it all seems rather odd. Dad was a nuclear physicist with an awful lot of knowledge of the country's nuclear program and he was going to work for an Institution which quite frankly had somewhat left leanings." Albie was a hundred percent right on that score, despite the ironic founding principles of Wits. It had started life as a school for mining in the old diamond diggings of Kimberley, but had moved to Johannesburg when the gold fields had been unearthed. Its principle benefactors had been the big mining houses, intent on their very monopolistic form of capitalism, but keenly aware of the need to promote free thinking academia, so as to enhance the structure of their society. The problem would always be that between the Nationalists who were becoming increasingly paranoid, and the rabid hate speech of the Communistic ideology of the Liberation Struggle exponents, there was an ideology void.

"Your Dad never mentioned fearing for his life!" There was a 'but' somewhere in that statement.

"So Dad had told you he was being followed?" The State security apparatus had been all invasive.

"Well, yes. But he never imagined they would do anything to him. They were just watching him so that he did not make contact with the wrong people." Many liberal- minded South Africans across the colour barrier, had fallen victim to the political expediency of the day.

"From what I have studied, the French and Israeli's were involved in our nuclear research in the sixties." Albie had a passion for conspiracy theories. He had wanted to become an International hit-man as a child. He had no idea where that thinking had come from, but he was obsessed with that idea through his teenage years, to such an extent that he had researched it on the world-wide-web.

"Yes there have been some very salubrious characters in our history." Mom had not forgotten the passionless response she had received when she had gone to the Insurance Company to claim on her husband's life assurance.

"Did you ever tell anyone else?" Albie had never been party to any conversations about unusual circumstances around his father's death. He had intuitively known it all these years.

"No!" She turned deliberately to him. "Can you imagine me going to the police and saying, 'my husband has been killed and it has been made to look like an accident'?" She grimaced.

"I see your point." Albie knew that those days were filled with sinister forces intent on self-preservation. None more so than those involved in Armscor and related weapons manufacturing. It was an international business. After Independence and the ANC came to power those weapons were expeditiously removed from South Africa under an agreement with the IAEA. The idea that a bunch of ANC officials might be in charge of a nuclear arsenal, a little too much for even the most liberal minded.

"Your Dad told me that next to Valindaba and hidden in the hills surrounding Hartebeesport Dam was the headquarters of the Vlakplaas." He suspected it was them following him.

Albie knew enough that the Vlakplaas had been the training ground for the likes of Eugene de Kock and the notorious CCB.

"Ohh! That's it." Albie knew instinctively, that was where the connection was.

"Dad said that the leaks at Pelindaba had caused great concern during those days, and that we nearly had a Chernobyl style melt down. Some of the guys at the Nuclear power plant had been exposed to radiation. The leaks were so bad that they effectively leaked into the ground water. There was talk at the time that the temperature of Hartebeesport

Dam had risen by two degrees. Your Dad just wanted to get away before the whole thing became a disaster." She sat with the plates filled to the brim. They were both ravenous.

"Yes. There have been a number of incidents at Pelindaba. But I did not know about Valindaba until now." Albie realised that the Government had strategically kept this information out of the public domain. Imagine, he thought what would happen to property prices in the Hartebeesport area?

Albie cut through his French toast and forced a wedge into his mouth. They were both silent with their hunger to be satiated and their thoughts running amok.

His Mom broke the silence after a mouthful of coffee to wash down her breakfast.

"Your Dad was a hero, because he stood up against those bullies." He had never thought of it that way. 'Yes his Dad was his hero, but was he a hero to any other South Africans?'

Albie nodded. His father had been brave to stand up and allow his conscience to dictate his principles. He would become one of many unsung heroes' in the Liberation struggle, but to Albie it did not matter that others might not recognise his father's efforts. Albie resolved himself to become more politically aware. In the meantime, he would finish his degree and make his contribution to this society where it now mattered. In the growing of the economy and the unlocking of its future financial power! To do so, he, Nkosi and Happy, would need to wrestle some of that control away from big business.

Summary Author, Conservationist and Humanitarian, writing poetry about the plight of our homeless populations from Zimbabwe, created by the economic collapse of that economy, and political machinations. Working in the inner city of Johannesburg, and social issues of great importance.

Born and educated in Africa, Simon Paul is a post-colonial Whafrican, with a passion for the African Elephant and the plight of these magnificent creatures. Having been educated in a Catholic Jesuit environment, the ideals of fairness, equity for all, and the love of the wild African spaces, have informed Simon and his desire to see the African landscape preserved for future generations.

Simon completed his education in South Africa, and has spent the past twenty years researching and following the migratory elephants of the Chobe, and Whange National Game reserves, from their feeding grounds in Zimbabwe, across the borders with

Botswana and Zambia. These graceful and hugely family-centric creatures have informed and amazed the author, since he was a child. Growing up in Zimbabwe, the author has had a passion for the great African Elephant since witnessing his first Elephant on the banks of Lake Kariba, as a young and impressionable seven-year old.

With education, these magnificent beasts can be protected and preserved for the future generations of Africans, who have largely competed for territory and food, over millennia, in the vast African spaces. However, with land at a premium and competition now driven by large corporate appetites for land and food, these Elephants have become victims of man's greed. It is this greed, and the social dynamics that proliferate ivory poaching, which now spurs Simon to write.

When the Elephant herds, decimated once by colonial hunters, are left to their own ecology, they thrive on the land of their birth. Adapting to changing environments, Elephants have long and wonderful memories, and it is this critical factor that has brought them into conflict with man. Simon hopes to change the history of this fight for survival, by writing about the consequences of man's incursion into the wilds of Africa.

Simon-Paul Publications
'The Elephants Will Remember' Author: Simon Paul - "Here's a novel that seeks to bring back to life the Africa of old: the old, Dark Continent, full of its mysteries, dangers and wonders. But not just a look at the past: a blending of past and present as the novel moves seamlessly from Zimbabwe.....A perfect book for armchair travelers and those who dream of Africa." Jenny Crwys-Williams

'Moonlight, Monsters & Morality' Amazon - Authors: Simon Paul - African poetry elucidating the vast chasm that exists between the 'haves' and the 'have-nots' in African Society. Xenophobia is the main focus of the work, but the author delves deeply into the socio-economic issues that drive people to commit the oldest documented form of racism/ classism in the history of mankind. "Moonlight, Monsters & Morality" is a beautiful collection of

African poetry elucidating the vast chasm that exists between the 'haves', and the 'have-nots' in African Society. Xenophobia is the main focus of the work, but the author delves deeply into the socio-economic issues that drive people to commit the oldest documented form of racism/classism in the history of mankind. Most of these philosophical poems are set throughout the continent of Africa; they include famous landmarks that can be found in the historical books of the Old Testament such as the Mount of Sinai. There are numerous poems dedicated to animals (e.g., elephants, whales, vulture), flowers and deadly natural forces such as lightening. In this collection of poems, man is looked upon as a warring, sinful creature that can find hope and salvation in the beauty and grandeur of nature." ABNA Expert Reviewer - Tania French (In the Woods); Molly Stern, Editorial Director and Executive Editor of Viking Books; and Julie Barer, of Barer Literary, LLC.

Printed in Great Britain
by Amazon